HELL HATH NO FURY

GEOFF MAJOR

**Grosvenor House
Publishing Limited**

This book is published by
Grosvenor House Publishing Ltd
Link House
140 The Broadway, Tolworth, Surrey, KT6 7HT.
www.grosvenorhousepublishing.co.uk

This book is a work of fiction. Any resemblance to people
or events, past or present, is purely coincidental.

A CIP record for this book
is available from the British Library

Paperback ISBN 978-1-80381-349-3
Hardback ISBN 978-1-80381-350-9
eBook ISBN 978-1-80381-351-6

To Lucia, for supporting my dream (again).

To my girls, just for being 'you'.

To the noisy neighbours who'll never
know they inspired this story.

ALSO:

With heartfelt thanks to Jon T, Jon B, and Iain.
You did it, again.

Thanks to Naomi for diving right in.

To all who gave my first book – *DEADLINE* –
such positive and encouraging feedback. You fuelled
my desire to write another (aka that I wrote a second
book is your fault).

Cat Lane (@writercatlane) – your tweets of support
& kindness helped more than you'll ever know.

Catherine Knibbs MSc, PGDip, BSc Hons – because
you knew all I ever needed to know about 'her'.

Becky Banning, because you make
publishing such fun! Thank you.

PART 1: A CATALYST FOR MURDER

Chapter 1 – Christmas 2015

A man cried out as the woman fell to the floor. She was screaming and writhing; her hands pressed tightly against her face as blood poured through her fingers. Footsteps could be heard thundering towards the room. The host ran in and looked down at her. He clasped his head in his hands.

"Oh my god, what have you done?"

"It wasn't my fault. It was an accident," slurred a drunken guest. In his hand was a shattered wine glass, blood dripping from its jagged edges. She was shouting incoherently as she rolled from side to side. The pain was overwhelming and blood continued to seep through her fingers.

"SHIT! JAMES?" screamed the host, looking around, frantically. The man he was looking for, James Vickers, was a plastic surgeon. He ran into the room and sank to his knees next to the woman.

"Get me some warm water and clean towels," demanded Vickers. One of the guests ran into the kitchen while Vickers reached out and took hold of her forearms in an attempt to calm her.

"DON'T TOUCH ME. DON'T TOUCH MEEEEE," she screamed as she writhed and started to kick out. Vickers relaxed his grip on her arms a little but kept them firmly under his control.

"It's alright, I'm a doctor. I need to check your face. Please." Her breathing remained rapid, and he knew that the pain would soon be compounded by the effects of shock. He had to act quickly.

"I just need you to let me lift your hands. I know you're frightened and in a lot of pain, but I need to look at your injury and then stop the flow of blood." He felt the tension in her hands and arms ease slightly, so he slid his hands down to her wrists, but as he tried to gently pull her hands away from her face, her arms tensed and locked again.

"Where's that water and the towels? I need them NOW." The guest reappeared and placed the items on the floor next to Vickers, who soaked a towel and turned back to the woman.

"We need to clean the wound and stop the flow of blood. I'm going to pass you a warm, wet towel. You can hold it in place if you'd prefer that, but you MUST put pressure on it. It will feel very painful, but it's how we'll stop the bleeding. Do you understand?" There was no response, but she reached for the towel with one hand before hesitating, torn between wanting to feel in control but afraid of how much it would hurt. As blood continued to flow freely from the wound, she clenched her jaw and put the towel on her face, releasing a guttural howl as the pain tore through her nerve ends. When she moved her hands to put the towel on her wound, Vickers could briefly see the left side of her face. It looked like she had a four or five-inch laceration that ran from just above her eye all the way down towards the corner of her mouth.

"We need to get her to a hospital," Vickers mumbled to the others.

"How?" whispered the host. "If we call an ambulance, they'll want to know what happened. Then they'll call the police!" Vickers knew this was true, and he had no desire to have to deal with the police. The woman also heard.

"No police," she gasped. She too did not want to be questioned.

"We'll have to get her to the surgery at my private practice. There'll be no one there at this time of night. I'll do the work," said Vickers. What choice did he have? What choice did any of them have? If this incident became public, they would all be ruined. If she died, they would all be guilty.

Chapter 2 – February 2018

"We are legally obliged to leave a chair, a table, basic kitchen facilities, and a bed with bedding for everyone in the property, madam. Sorry, just doing our job," said the bailiffs as they gutted the property of its furniture.

Eight hours later and the bailiffs had finished. As their anonymous lorry trundled down the gravel driveway, full of her earthly possessions, Stella Kendrick could do nothing but stare. There was a gruff noise from its exhaust as it turned onto the road, and then it was gone, hidden from sight by the large cypress trees at the end of the long, expansive front lawn. It would soon be her turn to leave the house for the last time. The legal battle that she and her husband, Robert, had started just over a year ago had come to an end. She was left with a £6m debt, thanks to what was revealed as some disastrous investment advice that her husband had had from a now liquidated investment company in London. Her house was empty, and her husband was now dead.

"Suicide, apparently. He drove off a mountainside in Switzerland. Body was burned to ashes. They only managed to identify him because they found a couple of his severed fingers partway down the gorge," one gossipy neighbour had said.

"Wasn't he something to do with executive recruitment?" asked another.

"Recruitment? With that house? I was told it was human trafficking," added a third, just hours after the memorial ceremony for Robert. Now, two weeks later and on the eve of her 72nd birthday, she had lost the fight. She had no family and no money. In two weeks, she would also have no roof over her head. As she stood, looking out of the window, she saw two of her neighbours out walking their dogs. They had seen the lorry driving away, too.

"Oh perfect. Just what I need right now," Stella said. She turned away and closed her eyes, taking what was supposed to be a deep, calming breath. It didn't work, but it did mean she didn't see one of the women pull a mobile phone from her pocket. The gossip was about to start.

Stella and Robert Kendrick had been married for over 40 years. For the first 30 years, he had spent two or three months of the year overseas, hiring skilled people for a variety of clients. In the final decade, one of his clients asked him to work exclusively for them. With the very generous salary package that came with the position, they had invested in the house. They had no children, so their disposable income was high. When he was away, she would sometimes lunch with the wives of other busy millionaires, but Stella refused to let her own business acumen go to waste. She had a number of business hobbies, as she called them, and they all made a small profit. It wasn't that she didn't have the time to turn them into substantial enterprises, but she preferred to maintain a degree of free time for socialising. After all, when in Windsor, it was important to know what the gossip was rather than be the subject of it.

That, of course, had now changed, given the house she and Robert lived in had been virtually stripped bare.

On her single dining chair was a file containing the year-long correspondence between Stella, the investment company, and the solicitors that a group of creditors had jointly instructed. Resting on top of the file was the Writ of Control the bailiffs brought with them. Attached to it was a list, 17 pages long, of all the things they were empowered to take and try to sell at auction. She swept the paperwork onto the floor, slumping onto the chair as the sadness took her breath away. Tears began to stream down her face, and her quiet whimpering turned into heaving sobs. Her life was destroyed, and yet she knew the hardest day was to come: eviction. The financial nightmare had claimed the life of her husband, and the people she had once called friends had shunned her.

The doorbell rang, making her jump. She stood up and tentatively walked over to the window, from where she might be able to see who was on her doorstep.

"Oh, go away, Margaret," she hissed as she saw her neighbour stood at the door. Margaret scanned the front of the house for any signs of movement. That's when Margaret saw her peering from behind the curtain. She waved. Stella had little choice now. She made the best she could of her long unbrushed hair before trying to brush some of the creases out of her skirt and top. She dabbed her tear-filled eyes and, with her chin held high, she walked to the front door. She unchained the door and pulled it open. Her mood was a dangerous cocktail of stiff upper lip and indignation.

"Oh, hello Stella. I... Well, er... I thought I should pop round to make sure you are alright. I couldn't help notice that..."

Stella cut across her. "I'm fine, thank you, Margaret. It's been a traumatic year, but I recently decided that I'm moving abroad. I need to make a fresh start. My belongings have been taken to storage and, if you don't mind, I'm in rather a hurry; I have to prepare for my driver. He's collecting me later today, ready for my flight." Stella turned, slamming the door in Margaret's face. She started to walk down the hallway, but her steps turned into strides and then quickly into running as fast as she could. She had tried to retain her composure but had realised she couldn't. The nearest room was the kitchen. As she pushed the door open, the emptiness of the room struck her. The bailiffs were legally obliged to leave her with the oven, fridge and a table. Her washing machine was in the utility room. Everything else that wasn't screwed to the wall or floor had been taken. Her mobile buzzed; someone was trying to call her, but she was in no mood to talk. The emotional desolation she felt suddenly started to simmer into anger, and then the fury erupted. She stomped to the worktop, where the few remaining plates and bowls sat.

"Here, you forgot this. Take it. TAKE IT ALL," she screamed as she swept the crockery onto the stone floor. It smashed, sending slivers of fine china skimming across the room. She cried out a few more times and, eyes bulging with anger, she seethed as she looked around the room. Then she gave in. What good would smashing anything else do her, as she'd only have to clean it up before she moved out? The eviction notice stated she would be held responsible if she defaced or destroyed anything. Her mobile buzzed again to notify her she had a voicemail. Reluctantly, she pulled the phone from her pocket and checked the number that had called her.

"Withheld," she muttered to herself, but she was resigned to listening to the message from her mystery caller anyway. "What else is there to do?" she said with an ironic laugh.

"Hello, Mrs Kendrick. My name is Ralph Stubbs; from Stubbs, Gadsby and Pickford." It was the solicitors who had been handling her fight against eviction.

"I'm sorry to bother you on what is, I'm sure, a very emotional day, but your husband left a specific instruction with me a year ago to contact you should you eventually lose your property. He said to tell you, *'The keen hunter can find gold under a king's silver.'* I hope that means something to you, Mrs Kendrick? Again, my apologies for disturbing you today. If we can help with anything at all, please don't hesitate to call." Stella slowly placed the phone back in her pocket as she processed what the solicitor had just told her. Her maiden name was Hunter.

"Gold under a king's silver?" she mouthed several times as she tried to stop the cacophony of thoughts in her brain, to concentrate. As she finally focused on the riddle, she twirled around to look at the in-built kitchen drawers. Kings was the name of the sterling silver cutlery collection she had insisted on buying when they moved into this house: a design originally commissioned by King George III, hence named The Kings Cutlery. She walked over and opened the drawer. After looking under what was left of her cutlery collection, she pulled out the tray and looked underneath it, but there was nothing. She put the tray and the six pieces of cutlery back as she continued to think through the puzzle again.

"Under a king's silver? Under a king's silver? Under..." And then she stared at the drawer again. This time, she grabbed hold of the handle and tried to pull the drawer out, but it jolted against the safety bolts that were fitted. As her frustration grew, she pulled at it harder and harder until the drawer broke. The cutlery tray catapulted its belongings into the air, and the sunlight glinted off the sterling silver that flew in an arc, clattering onto the floor and sending a metallic ringing around the empty room. Stella stood with the empty drawer in her hand. She turned it over and saw a piece of folded paper taped to the underside. She peeled the paper off and rotated it in her hand, assessing it as an archaeologist might a mysterious artefact, before unfolding it. She recognised the handwriting immediately; it was Robert's. On it he'd written a series of numbers, three names, and the address of a solicitor in Maidenhead. Her expression morphed from confusion to relief as she recognised there was a pattern to the numbers.

"Robert, my darling, you are a clever boy," she said as she began to realise just what this information might give her. "Some people are going to pay heavily for what they have done to us."

Chapter 3 – February 2018

A desk lamp illuminated the pile of paper strewn across the mahogany desk. He screwed his eyes tight for a moment in an attempt to ease the burning sensation from the fatigue and eye strain. It was already deep into the night, but he still couldn't rest. He had reviewed the financial statements and recalculated the projections, but the answer remained the same: he was bankrupt, and his ego was the reason why.

"No, no, NO," he snarled as he thumped the desk before burying his head in his hands. How had it come to this? He knew the answer to the question, but he kept hoping to find a different one that would take the blame solely away from him. He had gambled himself into significant debt and then tried a bigger gamble in an attempt to get out of it, which had turned into crippling debt. He'd had millions in the bank, but it hadn't been enough for his ego. He wanted to be up there with his mega-rich friends: the ones with the luxury houses, expensive yachts, cars, and a seemingly endless queue of staggeringly beautiful women wherever they went.

An old-fashioned telephone on his desk rang, jolting him from his introspection.

"Hi, it's me. Any luck?" his friend asked.

There was a short pause which foretold the answer, but the man still replied, "I've lost it all. Even if I sell the house and the business, it barely covers my debts for a year. After that, I'm destitute."

"What about asking for a short-term loan from—"

Before his friend could finish the sentence, he cut across him, "No! It's his fault I'm in this situation. He suggested the investment and, when the assets were frozen, he just told me to '*Wait a few months, and it will all be over*'. What a bunch of crap that was."

His friend didn't reply. He truly felt sorry for the man, but they both knew the man had simply over-stretched his financial means. At any point, he could have declined to invest or triggered the withdrawal clause; that was the deal they had all signed up to, and everyone – except this man – had taken a calculated risk. "How much do you owe?" asked his friend.

The man closed his eyes again as he inhaled slowly. "£23m, at a compound interest rate of 12 per cent per annum."

"Shit," whispered his friend, "that compounds up to more than £40m in the five years you're locked in to the deal." They knew the likelihood of the investment funds being released early was extremely low. In fact, the more likely scenario was that his investment, along with that of all the others who had been lured by the chance of a speedy and sizeable return, would remain frozen by the authorities for months, if not years. "What are you going to do?"

"I'm not sure," the man replied. He broke out in a cold sweat just thinking of what his lenders would do to him next month. "I need to get some rest. Thanks for calling."

"If there's anything I can do…" offered his friend, but he knew there wasn't, which was why his words simply trailed off. Nothing else was said, and then his friend heard the phone gently click as the handset was replaced in the cradle. The recipient of the call slumped back into his chair, but not in defeat, in thought. He was reflecting on an idea his girlfriend had inferred a couple of months ago. Did he really have the stomach to go through with such a plan? But, then again, could he see any other way to avoid becoming destitute? His ego simply wouldn't allow the latter.

He needed to sleep, but his mind remained restless until he eventually decided to commit to the plan. He just needed to call someone to put everything in motion.

Chapter 4 – February 2018

The first rays of morning sunshine broke through the stone-grey clouds above East London. Bright light cascaded through the atrium roof of a small designer house and onto the black steel-and-oak staircase that led down from the rooftop terrace into a home office. Financial statements and a handful of printed emails lay sprawled across a large white desk that stood in the centre of the office space. Several pieces of paper also lay on the floor. There were two tall stools by the side of the desk, but both looked as if they had been carelessly cast aside. Several half-smoked cigarettes had been dropped into an empty wine glass that stood on the desk next to two empty bottles of wine. To the left of the desk was a large, dark grey Chesterfield settee.

Evie Perry was laid on the settee, fast asleep. It was 7am, and she slowly opened her eyes, grateful that the clouds had subdued the sunlight in the room, but it still made her head throb and, to add to her woes, her stomach churned.

"Jesus, never ever again," she muttered as she slowly forced herself to sit upright, the slower the better, or she might throw up. She sighed as she recalled how unrewarding last night had felt, and she groaned when she tried to stand. The problem was this scene had become all too familiar after her life-changing injury three years ago. Since the incident, she had seen several medical professionals; all of them confirmed there was nothing that could be done to resolve the physical scars, but all of them had advised Evie to seek counselling as the risk of psychological trauma was very high.

"From what you've described, Miss Perry, you seem to be suffering with what's known as cyclothymia," said one.

"What's that?"

"It's when a person goes through a series of mood swings, from feeling excited about the future through to a sluggishness, where they don't even want to get out of bed. It's not depression, but if it's left to develop, a person could sink into depression or perhaps even develop bipolar disorder."

"So, what do you recommend?"

"Thankfully, you've described having long periods of what sound like rational thoughts and calm moods, so I'd be happy to refer you to a trained therapist who can help you find ways to manage your symptoms by changing the way you think and respond. You've had a life-changing trauma, but the sooner we can help you adapt to your new circumstances, the happier you'll be."

"And what if I decide I can get through this without it?"

"Going to a therapist can help avoid the need for medication or even hospitalisation. I'd strongly recommend you go see someone, otherwise you could find yourself developing illogical thinking that might lead to delusions, overly aggressive behaviour, or even suicidal thoughts." Evie nodded, but she had no intention of seeing anyone. She had never needed anyone's help in the past and didn't want to start now. She would do some research and deal with this herself because that's what she needed; something to focus her energy and passion on.

Now, three years after that fateful night and two years after Evie had ignored the doctor's advice, she got up from the settee and staggered across the landing into her bedroom. She stood in front of the mirror and, as she stared at her reflection, one word entered her head: gruesome. The scar that ran down the left side of her face was still prominent, she was blind in her left eye, and the iris remained colourless and clouded. She had fallen into a pattern of drink and self-loathing, with both irrational thoughts and disastrous decisions becoming more frequent. Sometimes, the line between reality and imagination became blurred, but she had reached a point where she realised things had to be different. The money she had earned over many years had started to dwindle, which is why, a few months ago, she had sent a threatening letter to the man she held responsible for her injury – Niall Fitzgerald – to demand he pay her compensation or face public ruin. After all, if he hadn't invited her to that party, this never would have happened. She recalled her surprise when a reply arrived, confirming he was willing to pay her £10m if she promised to leave him alone, but that she would need to resolve any '*outstanding grievances*' with the others. At the time, the £10m quelled her anger, but it would never satisfy her underlying desire for revenge. Her entire life had been altered. Just a few weeks ago, she had been drowning her self-pity in cheap champagne as she assessed what was left of her savings. That was the moment she realised that to maintain a certain standard of living, she would need more money to pay for her silence.

"If you can give away £10m so easily, I'm sure there's more where that came from," she muttered to herself as she wrote the list of names she intended to target. It would be an expensive and possibly dangerous approach to wreak her revenge, but given the positions they held in business and society, if what they had done was ever exposed, they would be ruined. And, if they decided not to pay, then there would be consequences.

"Let the hunt begin."

PART 2: PICK A NUMBER

Chapter 5

The caller reviewed the figures they had compiled and nodded, content they were correct, before pressing the button on her Bluetooth headset, triggering the voice-filtering software on her phone and reconnecting to the man on hold.

"Deal," she said.

"That's £400k in total for four assignments, to be paid on completion, with a separate one-off non-refundable up-front fee of £500k to cover all future administrative activity," came the response from Matthew Berry, aka The Broker. He didn't have the time, the inclination, or the need to negotiate. He was an enforcer who had built a fearsome reputation among London gang leaders and illegal gambling syndicates, his usual clientele. A peripheral contact had introduced him to the woman, who had passed all the pre-qualification screening before she got anywhere near talking to The Broker himself. People hired him when they needed a debt recovering or a gangland judgement delivering.

"Yes," she replied, typing away on her keypad. "I've just sent the payment."

"Already?" he queried.

"It's called multi-tasking. You should try it sometime," she replied with a light jibe in her tone.

He smirked, appreciating the humour before responding with, "I have people to do the multi-tasking for me." He paused and then added, "You should try it sometime."

"That's why I'm paying you. You're MY hired help," she responded. This time her tone was flat and factual, almost dismissive. Apparently, she was already growing tired of the discussion. This didn't go down well, but he kept his irritation to himself. After all, why annoy his new client when he was apparently in line for a multi-million-pound pay-out just for asking some people he knew to do things they happened to be very good at? They too would be well-rewarded, of course.

"When should the first two packages be delivered?" he enquired.

"Surprise me. No rush. Just don't forget the paperwork and the photographs," she said curtly before ending the call without another word. He pondered for a moment. The person he had just spoken to was by far the most callous yet calculating client he had ever dealt with, but he did afford himself a smirk at the digitised masking of her voice. It was probably a cheap solution, like a Roland VT-4: something that could be easily decrypted, but he had no interest in finding out who his clients were. All that mattered was that they were discreet, paid in full and paid on time. He picked up his encrypted phone and sent a text message.

Usual channel. Delivery must take place within two days. A solid fifty. Email sent.

There was a pause as the man reading the text reflected on the fee: £50k. He assumed that the assignment must either be very complicated or high-profile to attract that sort of price. He turned on his secure email device and read the message that was already waiting for him. That's when he realised the hit was neither complicated nor apparently high-profile. In fact, it seemed quite straightforward, although it had two very specific requests as part of the deliverable. The first request was unusual, although not unheard of, whereas the second request was either for a very specific reason or was just perverse. For £50k, he didn't really care which. He clicked on the email's attachment and sent it to his printer. As soon as it was printed, he put a double pair of latex gloves on, cut the print-out down to size, and slid it into a small plastic sleeve. He then walked into his bedroom and opened the wardrobe, pulling the clothes apart and reaching behind them. He pressed a push-to-open door and it clicked open, revealing the tools of his trade. He chose three items and put them in bespoke pockets he'd had woven into the lining of his heavy overcoat. He also grabbed a fistful of £20 notes and stuffed them in his trouser pocket. Finally, he carefully placed the plastic sleeve inside his jacket pocket.

Chapter 6

The night sky was overcast and the late-March air was unseasonably chilly. The curtains were drawn in the lounge, and the faux log fire was burning as the Lowes settled down to watch television. Their 14-year-old daughter, Amy, was upstairs video-calling some of her friends. Music was blasting out of the speakers in her room at the same time.

"I've a good mind to send you up to talk to her, Derek. She won't listen to me, so there's no point me wasting my energy," said his wife, Celia, shuffling uncomfortably in her seat. Her husband shook his head ever so slightly at his wife's suggestion; the music was barely audible even when the television was turned off, but he didn't comment. He knew better than to say anything and trigger a barrage of unnecessary whining from his wife. She was a highly strung woman at the best of times. He poured some freshly made tea and passed a cup to her in an attempt to placate her.

"Let's not spoil our evening, darling. Our programme's just about to start and we've been looking forward to it. I'll talk to her when it's time to go to bed; give her something to sleep on," and with that, he sat down with his own cup of tea and a biscuit.

Derek Lowe and his wife, Celia, had lived in Harpenden for nearly 10 years. Both were in their late fifties and had a very comfortable lifestyle. While his accountancy business had provided them with a generous income, it was the occasional out-of-the-ordinary requests from his wealthier clients that had helped Derek purchase their five-bedroomed detached house on the highly desirable North Park Avenue. Understanding tax loopholes was a very lucrative business. As their programme started, there was a knock on the front door. It wasn't unusual for a wealthy client to call round this late.

"Oh, Derek! Why didn't you tell me you were expecting someone?" his wife asked, looking somewhat disgruntled at the interruption.

"I'm not, dear. I wouldn't have agreed to someone calling round as I knew we wanted to watch this. Let me see if it's an emergency, otherwise I'll tell them I'll contact them first thing tomorrow. Thank goodness for 'pause' on the BBC iPlayer, eh?" he replied, trying to placate her again. He rose from the settee and walked lazily to the front door. He flicked the switch for the outside light but sighed as, through the frosted glass of the door, he could see the light had not come on.

"Oh, for goodness' sake," he moaned, a little irritated that the bulb had blown again. This was the third time this year. He unlocked the door and turned the handle, but before the door was ajar, a bullet shattered the frosted glass and, with it, most of Derek Lowe's face. A second bullet was fired, sending splinters of wood and shards of glass across the entrance hall.

"Derek? What was that?" shrieked his wife. She raced out of the lounge and into the hallway. She stopped almost immediately and covered her mouth as soon as she saw her husband's mutilated and bloodied body lying in front of her. She looked up as she caught movement in her peripheral vision, just in time to see a handgun being levelled at her. She turned to run, but a bullet hit her square between the shoulders. Celia Lowe slammed into the wooden doorframe and slumped to the floor. The killer strode into the house, hoping the cries from the woman hadn't disturbed the neighbours, as he still had to find the third occupant of the house. He paused momentarily, listening for any variation in the noise coming from upstairs. He waited to see if the volume of the music dropped or if anyone shouted down to ask what was going on. Nothing changed. He leapt up the stairs, three steps at a time, with the minimum of noise. It was clear which room the girl was in as the light shone under her doorway, and the sound of squeals and giggles could be heard over the music. She was discussing the latest joke that she and her friends had played on one of the more unpopular girls at school – something they always revelled in.

"Oh, and she was like, Amy, what do you mean you've already kissed him?" Several young female voices could be heard giggling in response, although they didn't sound as if they were physically in the room with his target.

"I mean, come on, did she actually think she had a chance to date Gregory Oliver? Not even sure he knows who she is!" More bitchy giggles erupted from within the room. The killer placed the gun back in its holster and drew his knife. Slowly, he twisted the door handle and waited to hear if there was any change in the volume and nature of the noise from the girl's bedroom. There wasn't. He turned the door handle all the way and opened the door just enough to see in. The girl was lying across her bed, on her front, looking at the phone.

Her head was facing away from the door, and her feet were kicking playfully in the air.

"Listen, tomorrow, why don't we…" but Amy noticed that the other girls on the video chat seemed distracted. Their heads were tilted to one side, frowning quizzically as they watched a black-clad figure looming up behind their friend. The figure then lunged and grabbed Amy by the hair, dragging her backwards off her bed. She screamed in terror, and her phone fell from her grasp, landing on the floor. It bounced once and finally settled on its side. All the girls on the video chat could see now was a landscape shot of the bottom part of Amy's wardrobe and some of the carpet, but they could all clearly hear her. Thankfully, the screaming didn't last long, and then there seemed to be an eternal pause. It was so tense that none of her friends dare breathe until, suddenly, she fell to the floor. Her head bounced off the lush carpet and her body settled on its front, with her panic-filled eyes turned towards the phone's camera.

Her friends stared, open-mouthed, waiting for her to move. She was clearly still alive, as her nostrils were flaring as she breathed, so why didn't she get up and run? In truth, they were all hoping for the moment Amy could no longer hold her laughter in. Surely this was just a sick practical joke? The silence continued for several more seconds, though, until they all saw some flashes in the background. A gloved hand then reached down and pulled Amy's head up, just enough to be able to slit her throat. Teenage screams shattered the peace in four suburban homes across Hertfordshire as Amy began to choke, blood pumping onto the pale carpet as she lay helpless on the floor. Then she was still.

As police sirens could be heard in the distance, the killer went about completing the final request. He ran downstairs and, as he reached the body of Celia Lowe, he took the print-out from its clear plastic sleeve. Quickly but carefully, he rolled it up and placed it in her mouth.

"Careful you don't choke on it," he sneered as he took one final photo.

Chapter 7

The clock ticked past 10pm. Telephones were still ringing as the day shift began to place files back in cabinets, log-off computer screens, and gather their jackets from the backs of their chairs. As they wearily but cheerfully wished each other goodnight, Detective Sergeant Alan Armitage closed the latest file in a pile of cases he'd been reviewing. He had intended to head home as well, but a call had just come through to CID; the local boys in Harpenden had discovered what appeared to be a triple murder. He was at the scene in less than an hour.

"What do we know?" he asked a detective constable as they stood on the driveway.

"Family of three: Derek and Celia Lowe, and their teenage daughter, Amelia. Mr and Mrs Lowe died from gunshot wounds, and the girl had her spine severed and her throat cut," she replied. Even the hardened Armitage winced slightly at this description.

"Any obvious motive?" Armitage asked.

"Nothing yet. No looting of the house, and both Mr and Mrs Lowe's credit and bank cards appear untouched. Mr Lowe also had £300 in cash in his wallet, so it looks unlikely that this was a robbery gone wrong. There are a few items to check for trace, but we'll need to wait for forensics. SOCO says it seems a pretty clean scene, though." She paused as she looked at her notes. "Err, neighbours say they were a nice, quiet couple... always said hello, but pretty much kept themselves to themselves... daughter was one of those popular girls at school; well-known and polite. Nothing that would warrant this."

"Any initial assessment from SOCO?" enquired Armitage.

"Looks like Mr Lowe was shot through the door; glass and splinters of wood are embedded in his neck, chest, and what's left of his face. Mrs Lowe was shot in the back, presumably while trying to run away. Daughter was in her bedroom. Oh, and SOCO have taken a rolled-up piece of paper out of Mrs Lowe's mouth. They are planning to examine it at the scene to let you know if it's significant for the investigation."

Armitage paused to consider what he'd just been told. "A piece of paper?"

"Yeah, Sarge. SOCO told me it didn't look like something she was trying to swallow or hide, given the paper was rolled up very neatly."

"Thanks," muttered Armitage as he processed the information. "You head back and start typing up the incident report. I've got it from this end." She nodded and walked back to the car.

Armitage was in his late forties. He had a dark heavy moustache covering his top lip and mid-length hair already thinning at the front. Weary and war-torn from decades of looking at dead prostitutes, drug dealers and bodies that had been hacked, shot, slashed, overdosed, drowned or splattered all over the pavement, left him with a heavily lined face and an apparent inability to be shocked anymore. He wasn't fat, but his habit of eating mini-muffins and drinking sugary coffee throughout the day certainly put him firmly on the wrong side of healthy. As a result, he was often mistaken for a man in his late fifties, but he was a brilliant copper, and it was agreed he'd make a great detective inspector one day. He unconsciously grabbed a mini muffin from a protective napkin inside his overcoat pocket as he reflected on what he'd been told. Before he took a bite, he turned and called to the departing officer, "Do we know what the Lowes did for a living?"

She thought for a moment and recalled, "He was an accountant and she was a housewife, according to the neighbours. We're checking that out, Sarge."

"Okay, thanks," said Armitage before turning to look at the impressive family home of the late Lowe family. "Can't see an accountant being able to afford this unless there's something shady going on," he muttered to himself.

The lead SOCO emerged from the house. "Evening, Sergeant," he said warmly.

"Evening. Didn't realise you were on tonight's shift," said Armitage, putting the muffin back into his coat pocket. "What have we got?"

"We've extracted a piece of carefully rolled-up paper from Mrs Lowe's mouth. Thought you might be interested in it?"

"Let me guess, death threat? A message to tell us that they got what they deserved? A note left to taunt us, perhaps?" enquired Armitage.

The lead SOCO frowned and gently shook his head. "Nothing that straightforward, I'm afraid. It's a photocopy of a lottery ticket."

Chapter 8

Niall Fitzgerald had originally taken a career in banking. It wasn't long before his talent was noticed, and he was invited to join a private banking partnership. Sadly, that collapsed several years later when one of the partners was arrested for money laundering. He was sent for trial, leaving Niall to ponder his future. Eventually, and with the wealth of his new father-in-law to kick-start his own company, he set up Iliad Private Equity. He worked long hours and excelled and, despite 2017 being a difficult year for the economy with the sluggishness hitting most investors, he could still afford to draw a £64m bonus. Lean, tall, tanned, sporty, well connected and with a stellar reputation and a squeaky-clean image, he seemed to have achieved pretty much everything a man could wish for.

To add to all that, his beautiful and elegant wife, Yvonne, was always by his side at social events and business functions, smiling and listening attentively to his every word. While she always dressed in the latest fashion from Milan, London, and Paris, she ensured she remained carefully understated, as well as being adept at all the social protocols expected by such a high-powered circle of contacts.

Money was never an issue for them. During their 15-year marriage, Yvonne had never had to ask her husband if they could afford anything. Her American

Express Centurion Card provided for her every need and was paid for every month from a private account that held over £180m. Their custom-built house in the south-west of London was recently valued at over £20m, and their luxury villa on Turks and Caicos was frequently loaned to friends and celebrities when they were not there for their annual break. Everything in life seemed idyllic, except for one thing: Yvonne Fitzgerald despised her husband.

At home, they had not eaten a meal, relaxed, or slept together for nearly five years. They rarely had to see each other, though, given their 11-bedroomed mansion provided independent living space. It hadn't always been that way. They had been the model couple, but things had changed after Yvonne lost her ability to have children and then withdrew all affection for her husband. Initially, Niall made every effort to rebuild their relationship, but it was hard work with a wife who seemed determined to ignore his attempts at rekindling the romance. In turn, he became a very different person in his private life.

As she approached 40 years of age, Yvonne didn't want to give up her lifestyle. Niall also had no intention of watching his own lifestyle deteriorate as a consequence of an expensive divorce, but he was equally concerned about his social standing. Reputational damage in his line of business could be devastating. He would do almost anything to protect that. He had made mistakes in his life, yes, some of which he had subsequently compensated the people affected thrice over, but there were a handful of others where it was too late for financial redress. He had accepted that he had become a serial adulterer, but even that had gone too far. Eventually, that side of his life had culminated in the terrible events at a party three years ago, when a high-class escort called SILK was entertaining some of his friends, and one accidentally slashed her across the face. Niall had already paid her £10m as compensation, but the consequences of that night exploded back into his life when an envelope arrived at his London office a day ago.

"Maria, what's this?" he asked his PA when he saw a package that caught his attention. The address was handwritten, and it had a brightly coloured red logo crayoned in the bottom corner of the envelope.

"I'm not sure, Mr Fitzgerald. It was delivered by a courier earlier today. I was going to open it after my lunch with the other post, but I can open it now if you like?"

"Oh no, it's alright. You go have your lunch. I've got a few minutes spare, so I'll grab the post. Go on, off you go, before I tell your boss," Niall had teased, which made Maria laugh. He was a demanding boss, but she was rewarded well, and he would often surprise her with wonderful treats for both her and her husband. Last month, it was a weekend break away; all expenses paid.

"You work hard and I couldn't manage without you, Maria, but, on this occasion, I'm instructing you to take a long weekend," he had said as he handed her an envelope. In it was an itinerary that included an executive car to take them to the airport, first-class seats on a flight to the south of France, and a reservation for three nights, all-inclusive, in the best suite at the beachfront Hotel Plage Palace & Spa.

"Oh, Mr Fitzgerald!" she had squealed, but that was the type of boss he was. Work hard, play hard, enjoy the rewards. Today though, it was simply an instruction to take a lunch break. She picked up her handbag and jacket and smiled at him as she headed for the door. He pretended to look at his watch as if timing her, which made her smile even more. Niall took all the mail into his office. He was intrigued by the package and tore it open. When he took the contents out, his playful demeanour evaporated immediately. What was inside the envelope shook him to the core.

"Oh, I forgot to ask; do you want anything bringing back?" said Maria, who, on reaching the lift, had berated herself for not offering to get her boss some lunch. Niall looked up in horror, hoping that she couldn't see what was in the package.

"No! Er, I mean, no thank you, Maria. I, er, I'm not hungry." They stared awkwardly at each other for a few seconds before Niall forced a smile and added, "Actually, I'm feeling a little off-colour all of a sudden."

"Oh no. I hope it's not that thing that Trevor had?" she said, referring to a colleague who had spent the previous week vomiting. She narrowed her eyes as she looked at Niall's face. "Now you mention it, you are looking a little drained."

"Yes. Well, maybe I'll take the afternoon off, actually. Better safe than sorry, eh?" he replied rhetorically.

"I'll just grab something for myself and bring it back to my desk. That way it gives me a little more time to go through your appointments and rearrange them."

As soon as she had gone, Niall put the package in his briefcase and strode to the lift. He reached the basement car park and drove quicker than he had ever done before. When he got home, he went straight into his private study. He sat down and re-opened the package, laying its contents out on his desk. It contained a glass eye with a crack in it and a printed note: *The pitiful £10m wasn't enough. I want £100m for the pain, or you die. SILK.*

Niall felt an unfamiliar feeling: panic. Hadn't he already paid her to leave him alone, but now she wanted more? What if he paid her again, but then more envelopes arrived and, next time, what if Maria opened it in his absence? His mind danced from one unanswerable question to another until he forced himself to focus. That was when Niall realised they were not the questions he needed to answer; they were not the problems to solve. She was the problem. SILK was her online name, but he didn't know her real name because on the nights, weekends, and holidays when he had cheated on his wife, real names weren't important. He knew what he needed to do and, although it might be expensive, he didn't intend to pay SILK a penny more than she had already had.

He picked his phone up and sent a text to one of his friends: *Need information on a person. Has to remain confidential. What's the best way to get it?*

He knew this man would find a way and, sure enough, a couple of minutes later he received a response: *I'll put you in touch with an exclusive section of the old Friends Reunited website. It will take a couple of weeks though, as they are very wary of new member requests.*

Niall finally felt he could relax. He could wait. There was no immediate rush to meet SILK face-to-face again, and, in life as in business, sometimes the greater rewards came with waiting.

Chapter 9

The article stated there were an estimated two million safety deposit boxes in the Swiss banking system that held as much as $6.5 trillion of assets. That figure excluded the secretive vaults and underground bunkers in the foothills of the Alps, which were not subject to the same regulatory reporting as the mainstream banks. As the plane prepared to land at Zurich airport, Stella Kendrick placed the magazine she had been reading in the seat-back pocket. She was interested in just one of those boxes. As she stood in the queue waiting to clear Customs, she recalled that the folded paper she had found a few days ago, taped to the underside of the kitchen drawer, instructed her to go to a solicitor's office in Maidenhead. They told her that Robert had put some contingencies in place, which included £20k in cash he'd left with them, for her, but there was also another note: *I love Barbara's old book about a lone hiker so much that I've read it nine hundred and twenty-five times. It has everything anyone will ever need to know about taking their next steps on a journey.*

When she had arrived back home, she'd run upstairs to find a pile of tatty old books that stood in the corner of the old reading room. The bailiffs had declined to take a pile of particularly ragged books, given they probably had no resale value.

"Can't see anyone buying this lot unless they want to use them as kindling for a bonfire," they had joked.

Stella had overheard them and had almost shamed them into taking the damn books.

"Oh, what could have been," she sighed with relief.

With their mutual love of cryptic clues, she had deduced that Robert was talking about an author called Barbara Walker. She soon found their copy of *The Woman's Encyclopaedia of Myths and Secrets*. Its cover had a number of tears as well as stains, and the spine was fractured, but Stella could just make out the ISBN code which ended in 925X. She flicked through the book and came across several pages that seemed to be stuck together. As she gently peeled them apart, she found scores of pages had been hollowed out. Laid within the shallow hole was a small, thin notebook. Her mouth was dry with anticipation, and her pulse raced. With quivering fingers, she gently prised the little notebook out of its hiding place: holding it carefully as if it was a delicate manuscript. She drew a breath and slowly, carefully, opened the front cover. As she saw the inscription inside, she burst into tears.

To my darling Stella.
I knew you would find this. It is simply the start of your journey. Live life for the both of us, and make sure that the people who tore us apart know they will pay.
Forever, Robert xx

The entry was dated over a year ago. He had known what might happen, even then. It was odd; she felt both gratitude for his foresight and planning but also confused. If he had known this might happen, why didn't he do something earlier? They could still have been together! As she looked back at the inscription, though, her anger fell away. Deep down, she knew that if Robert could have done something to change the course of events, he would have.

"Reisepass bitte," asked the official at the border control, snapping Stella out of her continued pensive reflection. She gave an apologetic smile.

"Entschuldigung. Ich war in meinen Gedanken verloren," she said, apologising for being lost in her thoughts.

The emotionless man glanced up at her, reviewed her passport before inserting it into the scanner, and looked again at her face. After a couple of seconds, his machine beeped and he handed her the passport back with an assertive, "Vielen Dank. Nächster?" and he looked beyond her to the next person in his queue.

"Efficient, just as one would expect from a Germanic country," she mumbled under her breath. "At least it wasn't Schweizerdeutsch. Might not have understood a bloody word of it if it had been."

The taxi ride from the airport would take her to the Glaner Kantonalbank branch in Niederurnen, but on the way, she stopped at the hotel to drop off her bags. Given the trauma of the last few months, she felt she deserved some luxury. At £4,000 for the week, she was hoping the penthouse room that overlooked Lake Zurich would provide the brief respite she needed in preparation for the challenges ahead over the coming months. When she was sat in the back seat of the taxi again, heading to Niederurnen, she opened her handbag and took out the notebook, reviewing its contents. The notebook contained a number of cryptic clues, although they all made perfect sense to Stella. The last one was the final piece she needed.

"The Zulus say you must wait, until the dice read five and eight. The password will then come into sight, so you can put the injustice right," she mouthed as she read it. She knew this was a reference to one of their favourite films, *Jumanji*. The show's star, Robin Williams, had once claimed that 'Jumanji' was a Zulu word, meaning 'many effects'. Stella now knew she would find many of her dead husband's personal effects in the safety deposit box.

"So, for the PIN code, the fifth and eighth letters in the word 'Jumanji' are n and J," she said to herself, looping back to the start of the word and using the capital J for the eighth letter. "N is the fourteenth letter of the alphabet, and J is the tenth... so the six-digit code I need is 5-8-1-4-1-0." Although he was no longer with her, she felt a warm glow of affection for her husband flood her heart and mind.

Thirty minutes after leaving the hotel, the taxi turned off the main road and onto Lowenstrasseup, pulling up at the side of the Niederurnen branch. It was a modern yet indistinguishable one-storey building. Had it not been for the external signage, it could just as easily have been mistaken for a busy administration office or a real estate showroom. When she originally booked the appointment over the phone, they had said that for such an esteemed client, the branch offered appointments outside normal opening hours. She had wondered why they classed her as 'esteemed', but didn't bother to enquire at the time.

"And you will find suitable privacy in one of our VIP cubicles, Frau Kendrick," said the branch manager in almost impeccable English as he arranged for the deposit box to be brought up from the underground safe. Five minutes later, as she was drinking some cool alpine spring water, two men wearing jackets and pristine white gloves walked into the cubicle. Without saying a word or making eye contact, they placed the box on the table. One of them entered the branch's six-digit PIN, and then, just as silently, they left the room.

"This is it, Stella," she whispered to herself. "Salvation or ruin." She peered at the keypad and entered the PIN code she had decrypted: 5-8-1-4-1-0. With an almost imperceptible click, the box unlocked and the lid rose just high enough to allow her to lift it freely.

Chapter 10

Materia Prima Private Research & Investigations had excellent ratings, according to the research Evie had done. *As good as any, I suppose,* she had thought to herself, and she booked an appointment online. Three days later, she arrived for her appointment at their office: a small cluster of corner rooms on the second floor of a modern office block. All the windows had blinds to maintain privacy, but the office remained bright and airy. Modern yet subtle furniture ran throughout the reception area, with gentle piped music playing. For most people, first impressions were of a dentist's waiting room rather than a private investigations company.

"Good afternoon, Miss Perry," said the welcoming receptionist. It was a policy at Materia Prima, when booking first appointments, to ask for a brief description of the visitor. In describing herself, Evie emphasised she would be wearing a hat with a black blusher veil and large sunglasses; the latter being necessary to help combat light sensitivity, she lied. She assumed that with the veil, large dark sunglasses, and the specialist cover-up cosmetics she had started to use, anyone casually glancing at her might not immediately notice the scar. Within a matter of minutes, the founder of the company, David Homes, was ushering Evie into a corner office.

"Please, won't you sit down?" offered Homes, gesturing to a modern soft leather chair positioned at the side of his immaculate desk. "Thank you for your email. Very intriguing."

"Thank you," said Evie, as she sat down; "And thank you for responding so quickly."

He noticed her scanning the room. "Not exactly what you imagined a private investigator's office to be like? No battered pedestal desk covered with files. No grimy windows or old battered leather settee placed against the wall, perhaps?"

Evie smiled. She was a little embarrassed at having such a stereotyped expectation. After all, she too had chosen a career which led people to stereotype her. "I guess, as a private detective with the surname 'Homes', people often assume a lot about you."

The man gave a well-practised smile. It wasn't the first time someone had commented, and it wouldn't be the last. "So, how can we help you?" he asked. He walked over to a drinks tray that was laid out on a low cupboard and gestured towards the coffee and tea selection.

"No, thank you. Just some still water, please," she replied before continuing. "I have a number of men and a handful of women I need to find out some information on." Homes passed her some water in a tall slim glass. Evie gave a brief smile of gratitude as she took the glass and set it down on a coaster on the desk. He looked quizzically at her as he sat down.

"The internet holds a *lot* of information, Miss Perry. A lot more than people imagine if you know how and where to look. We offer some of our clients advanced search training..." He paused, assessing her facial expression. He quickly concluded that this elegant and expensively dressed young woman was unlikely to want such a service. "... But I'm guessing that won't be of interest to you." Evie tilted her head slightly to indicate he was correct.

"The information I want is perhaps... how can I put it... a little more personal in nature than one might readily find with a Google search." Her tone was light, but it carried more than just a hint of mischief. In fact, Homes thought he also detected some malice.

"Well, we offer a wide range of services here at Materia Prima. All within the law, of course," he replied. Evie couldn't decide whether he was warning her of their limits or inviting her to stretch them, perhaps even stray into the grey areas of what was legal. She gave a wry smile.

"Of course, within the law, Mr Homes. What on earth do you take me for?" she said, maintaining the smile. He took the hint and leant forwards in his chair. She followed suit, and Homes lowered his tone as he started to speak.

"I'm assuming we are straying to the edges here, Miss Perry? There is a very wide band of grey between being lawful and..." he pursed his lips and narrowed his eyes as he pretended to be searching for the precise words.

"And grey is an expensive colour, but expense is never a problem if you're getting confidentiality and quality," she replied. They stared at each other for a while; Homes weighing up whether to trust this prospective new client and Evie looking back without blinking. It worked. He stood up and gestured towards an internal door within his office.

"Let's talk about your specific requirements in my secure meeting room, Miss Perry. That way we can be sure there are no prying eyes, ears, cameras, or listening devices."

Evie rose slowly, keeping eye contact as she said, "Sounds perfect." She had prepared exactly what she was going to say, as well as what she wasn't prepared to share. The next step in her plan was hopefully about to reap rewards.

"I think you'll be surprised just how quickly we can provide some initial results," Homes promised.

"Oh, I'm counting on it," replied Evie.

Chapter 11

It was 4am and a spring mist hung in the air, making the early morning chilly. The alarm clock roused Malcolm Walsh from a deep and cosy sleep. He groaned as he fought the temptation to snuggle back under the duvet for just 10 more minutes. His flat was above the shop he had run for the last 15 years. Originally it had belonged to his father, who had "Proudly served the Skipton community" for 40 years before handing over the business to Malcolm. Those words, often spoken by his father when Malcolm had perhaps asked for a day off or claimed to be feeling under the weather, were now both the motivation that kept him working and the deadweight around his neck. It wasn't that Malcolm didn't enjoy his work, but occasionally he longed to say *'we're not open today'*. As the owner of the local convenience store and newsagents, it wasn't that he couldn't do that, but competition was rife in the market town, and customer loyalty was increasingly rare. His father's regular customers were sadly dying off, and the new citizens of Skipton were more used to a wider selection of products and the free parking at a number of local supermarkets, as opposed to the limited stock he held and the on-street parking fees the local council imposed.

He swung his legs out from under the duvet and headed for the shower. When he got out, he dried off, shaved, and cleaned his teeth before heading downstairs to the shop. He turned into the storage area, reaching for his jacket and fingerless gloves. He unlocked the external side door, which opened onto a private footpath at the side of the shop that led towards the street. As he opened the door, the crisp morning air felt refreshing.

"You must be going soft in your old age," Walsh muttered to himself. He pulled the keys from his jacket pocket as he walked to the bolted security gate, selecting the two keys he needed, one for the bolt at the top and another for a bolt at the bottom. At that time of the morning, he rarely saw joggers and none of his regulars would be walking past with their dogs. On the rare occasion he did see another person around at this ungodly hour, he'd nod at them and they'd raise a hand to signal 'hello' back. Opening the gate, he saw the stock piled outside and remembered it was Tuesday, which meant twice as much produce as the other weekdays. He sighed and started the task of lifting the items into the alley, after which he would lock the gate and then take the produce inside to re-stock the shelves. When all that was done, he always felt he had earned his cup of tea and some marmalade on toast. He looked forward to that indulgence. As he went to pick up another carton of produce, he overheard a man talking into a mobile phone as he walked across the street towards the shop.

"I know... yeah, I know. Look, it's not a big deal, don't worry. Look, love, I'm near a local shop, so I'll grab some from in there... Yeah, I know it's early, but it's one of those convenience stores... It's okay, I promise. Now go back to bed, sweetheart. Kiss the kids for me at breakfast." He put the phone away and tutted as he stopped outside the shop, shaking his head but smiling to himself.

"Morning," he said.

"Morning," replied Walsh as he lifted some milk through the gate.

"I know you're not open yet, but I'm new to the area, and my wife just called to say she forgot to put milk in my coffee." The man raised a flask from his side, so Walsh assumed the man was part of the crew building the new industrial complex down the road. "I wouldn't ask normally, but it's my first day at a new job and I can't afford to be late... but I really can't get through until the sandwich van arrives if I only have black coffee." The man screwed up his face slightly to show he knew he was being a little awkward but that he was also desperate. Walsh smiled. He too had to have milk in his tea before he started work.

"Sure, just let me open one of these packages and grab you one. The till's not open yet, but you can pay me later. I don't want to make you late for work." He assumed this could be the start of a regular account with this newcomer. The man relaxed his shoulders and smiled in gratitude.

"Oh, thank you. Look, I've got some change in my pocket, so please take it now and ring it into your till later. I don't like to owe money," said the man, as he placed the flask on the floor.

As Walsh turned and bent down to open a pack of 12 cartons of milk, the man furtively looked around the street. It was still empty, so he pushed Walsh through the gateway and onto the side path, letting the gate swing closed behind them. As Walsh recovered his balance and started to turn towards the stranger, his assailant pulled a cosh out of his overcoat pocket and struck him on the side of the head. Walsh crumpled to the floor, not quite unconscious but clearly incapacitated. The stranger continued his attack until he heard the sound of Walsh's skull crack and saw his body jerk one final time. The stranger then pulled a latex glove from his pocket, put it on, and removed a plastic wallet from inside his jacket. The wallet contained a piece of paper which he teased out, rolled up, and pushed partially into Walsh's bloodied mouth. All that was left to do was take a photo of the now lifeless shop owner and then make his escape. It was the easiest £50,000 he had ever earned.

Chapter 12

The usual 8:30am daily brief had started, and the next detective was ready to update the rest of the CID team on a new case. He stood and walked to the front of the room.

"Earlier today, we opened a new investigation into the murder of Mr Malcolm Walsh. He was a local shopkeeper in Skipton. The shop's external security camera shows that at 4:53am, a Caucasian male approached the shop. He appears to be over six feet tall, between 30 and 40 years old, and as best we can tell, of a muscular build. The security footage shows the man talking to Mr Walsh, and then we can see him push Mr Walsh through a gate at the side of the shop. After that, there was no coverage of what happened next, but SOCO say Mr Walsh was struck repeatedly on the side of the head with a blunt instrument. Their best guess right now is it was with a cosh. There's no obvious attempt at forced entry into the shop, and the cash register was untouched. Local CCTV shows the suspect walking away from the scene, towards the canal. After that, we lost track of him. None of the CCTV coverage got a view of the assailant's face." He looked up to see if DS Bob Williams had any immediate questions, but he had none and clearly assumed the briefing was over.

"Okay, thanks. Let's see if local uniform can find any early morning joggers or dog-walkers who might have seen something. Until then, follow-through on any leads regarding why Mr Walsh was a target." He stood to leave, but the detective had one more odd fact to share, so he loudly cleared his throat and Williams stopped. "Yes?"

"Er, one other thing to note, Sarge. SOCO reported they found a rolled-up photocopy of a lottery ticket in the victim's mouth."

"A lottery ticket?" Williams checked. "Okay; get me a copy of the file as soon as possible, please. Nothing quite like having a bizarre murder case to read with my morning coffee and toast." He turned to walk back to his desk.

He was on the phone when someone dropped the case file on his desk. Williams finished the call and flipped the file open, meticulously working through the details and absorbing the minutiae. He got to a photograph of the ticket.

"24, 29, 30, 36, 46, 48 and 7," he mumbled quietly to himself. One of the numbers caught his attention. He flicked back through the personal details on Malcolm Walsh, and there it was. At first, he shrugged his shoulders at the coincidence and was about to close the file, but something troubled him. He shouted across the room to the administration officer, gesturing him to come across.

"Yes, Sarge?"

"Have you entered this into the National Crime Database yet?"

"Not yet, Sarge; about a day behind on the paperwork," came the slightly embarrassed reply.

"Well, let me know when you do," Williams said. The team was swamped at the moment, so he wasn't surprised or disappointed that the paperwork was a day or two behind. He picked up his mug of coffee and the next file he had on his desk, but no matter how hard he tried, the question in his head simply wouldn't go away.

Chapter 13

There were five people sat around the conference table in the offices of the Iliad Private Equity Group. It was time for the team to prepare for the quarterly portfolio review.

"Mrs Pecha tells me she wants to sell at £12m," said one of the women in the room.

"Can we stop her?" asked one of the men, keen to retain the investment for another month.

"I doubt it. She's invested in Salacia for two years. That's a pretty good run."

Niall interjected, "Let her go. I think when she reviews her investment options, she'll be back next quarter, and we don't want to ruin the relationship." They all nodded because he had a knack of predicting investor behaviour that bordered on savant. He had established two cornerstone funds for the company: Salacia and Mercury. The former was for those who wanted long-term investments in volatile markets, biding their time before picking their moment to sell. Mercury was for investors who were prepared to invest in a number of start-ups, hoping for a speedy and sizeable return. In summary, Iliad wasn't of interest to the low-risk pension funds. The sort of people attracted to Iliad knew their investments could fly or sink. Niall had a reputation of being a specialist in the technology sector, with a comprehensive insight into what made a good gamble. His track record and impressive lifestyle was testament to that.

"Okay," said Niall. "That was the last transaction on this quarter's Salacia portfolio. Onto Mercury next, and I have some interesting information." They had all leaned forwards in anticipation of what insight he was about to share when there was a gentle knock on the door. It was Maria, Niall's PA, looking a little sheepish.

"I'm so sorry to interrupt, Mr Fitzgerald, but I have a call for you. It's your wife, and she sounds quite distraught." Niall exhaled forcefully through his nostrils.

"Thank you, Maria. I'll take it in my office," he said, more than a little irate at the interruption by his wife. After years of near silence between them, she had the temerity to interrupt his working day. "How about an early lunch break?" he suggested to the others. "Let's resume in 40 minutes." Everyone in the room nodded in agreement. As soon as they had left the room, Niall's smile dissolved as he walked towards his office. He gave a brief nod to Maria as he sped by her desk and slammed the door closed behind him.

Maria jumped. It was rare to see her boss this exasperated, so she fully expected him to be in an equally foul temper after the call. She glanced up just in time to see him silently enquire which line. She lifted three fingers, and he responded with a thumbs-up sign in acknowledgement.

"What is it, Yvonne? I'm in a bloody investment meeting." Niall hadn't spoken a word to his wife in the last six months, but now she decided she needed to talk?

"An envelope has arrived via courier, addressed to me. Inside was an unsigned Toy Town cheque for

£100m, wrapped in a piece of silk." Fear suddenly swept through Niall.

"It doesn't say who it's from. Is it one of your silly jokes, Niall? I know I've spent rather more than normal on clothes recently, but I blame Alix's influence." He covered the mouthpiece as he tried to control his emotions and gather his composure. After several seconds of silence, she asked, "Niall, are you still there?"

"What?" he barked unconsciously. He hadn't heard what Yvonne had said to him, as his mind was still distracted by the news.

"There's no need to be so angry. This is why I don't usually bother talking to you," she replied, and she ended the call.

"Yvonne? Yvonne?" His voice had a touch of desperation as he tried to stop her ending the call, but it was already too late, and he couldn't call her back, as that would be unusual behaviour and might arouse her suspicion. He unconsciously replaced the receiver as his mind continued to process the information. Still distracted, he slowly walked across his office, opened the door, and drifted past his assistant.

"Mr Fitzgerald?" she said quietly. He didn't react, let alone respond. "Mr Fitzgerald?"

"Hmm, yes?" he answered, still not really concentrating on her.

"Before you go back in, a courier just dropped this off for you. He said it was time-critical." Niall turned to look at her and then at the package in her hand. He saw the brightly coloured logo drawn in the bottom corner in crayon. He could do nothing but stare at the package, frozen to the spot.

"Do you want me to open it for you while you're..." she started to say, but he looked at her, wide-eyed, as he realised what she was offering to do. He snatched the package from her hand and pulled it to his chest.

"No... thank you. I, er, my wife was a little upset and, er, erm. No, that's fine, thank you, Maria. Why don't you go have an extra-long break? It's all a little stressful when it's quarterly reviews, and I'm sure I owe you some time for the extra hours you've been putting in." She slowly withdrew her empty, outstretched hand and gave him as best a reassuring smile as she could muster. He gestured his thanks and turned around, heading straight back into his office. He tossed the envelope to one side as if it wasn't important, but as soon as she had left her desk, he grabbed it and tore it open. Inside was an 'In Sympathy' card, with a handwritten message:

Now your wife is being drawn in, and I want my £100m. Oh, and I'll have another surprise for you soon, just to be sure you know I'm deadly serious

Chapter 14

The Alex Hotel stands on the western side of Lake Zurich. Its website offers guests five-star luxury as well as a quiet place for reflection. A gentle breeze blew off the lake and a few clouds scurried across the pale blue sky. Stella Kendrick sat on the balcony of the hotel's penthouse, curled up and wearing a large white wool cardigan and a matching bobble-hat. It wasn't particularly cold outside, but she had the urge to feel secure and snug. On the bed behind her lay the two-page letter she had found in the safety deposit box.

To my darling Stella

If you are reading this, it means you had found the note in the book at home and accessed the safety deposit box. I knew you'd solve the cryptic clues! Sadly, it also means I am no longer with you. I am so sorry, and I'll explain why it's come to this in this letter.

The most important thing though is that you are safe. I dread to think what you have had to go through, and I have taken the guilt of that with me to my grave. By now you will know we have a multi-million-pound debt, but you should not have to deal with the consequences of my decisions. I did see this coming, and while I could not do anything to stop it, I put together some contingencies for you, my darling.

Firstly, the plastic wallet in the box contains two different debit cards, which access two different bank accounts, each with £500,000 in them. The accounts have been set up under different names (none of them use Kendrick), so please ensure you only use them for contactless or ATM transactions, where you can walk away with items or cash. I realise this will be restrictive for a year or so, but after that perhaps you can establish a new bank account and slowly migrate the money? I'm so sorry this has to be so arduous and complicated, but I wanted to be sure this cannot be easily traced to you and offers you something of a future.

Secondly, we have a rented apartment near Southampton. The rent is paid until the end of 2018. I'm afraid it's not as beautiful as our home which, I assume, is no longer yours. Again, I am so sorry to turn your world upside down. If there was anything else that I could have done, I would have.

And thirdly, you will have found a sealed envelope. I beg you not to open this unless you literally have no other choice. Please do NOT underestimate the power and the risks that opening it will bring. Knowing the people that I worked for, this might be something you need to turn to. If you open it before you absolutely need to though, you risk losing everything I have put in place. I implore you, my dear sweet Stella, to trust my judgement and knowledge on this.

Before I finish this letter, I must remind you just how much I loved you and how much I will miss holding your hand, taking walks by the lake at Ullswater, and solving those fiendishly clever cryptic clues we loved so much. Sat in front of the roaring fire, with you looking so completely consumed until that beautiful smile would

spread across your face and you'd let out a small cheer.
Oh, you pretty little ladybug.

It was at that point Stella Kendrick had begun to cry. Robert had called her his little ladybug since they started dating over 40 years ago. It was his pet-name for her because she was so fragile yet beautiful and, like the hidden wings that suddenly appeared on a ladybug, he often told her that she had the power to surprise and delight. She ached for his warm, protective embrace. So much so that she cast the letter aside, intending to read the rest of it when she was a little less emotional. She had fallen asleep on the bed with tears still wet on her cheeks and slept for hours; the exhaustion and emotion of the last six months finally taking its toll.

When she eventually woke up, she felt better than she had in over a year. The tension and anxiety she had carried was finally released. There would be new challenges ahead, not least her enforced move from Windsor to Southampton. She didn't know what awaited her there, but she already knew it was going to be better than if she had stayed in their near-empty home until she was evicted. She ordered some room service and, as she nibbled at the food, she read the rest of the letter:

The investment company which I foolishly risked our livelihood and future with was called Thoresen, Fitzgerald & Holding. One of the men, Thoresen, is under arrest for fraud, aiding and abetting criminal activity, and money laundering. Even though the other two partners were cleared of any responsibility or involvement, I just can't believe both of them are innocent. Thoresen could not have managed that amount of illegal accounting without at least one of them knowing. With my passing, a package has already been delivered to the other two on your behalf. Holding is now retired and living in the South of France, whereas Fitzgerald continues to operate a new investment company. They know you might be in touch.

And so, my darling Stella Irina-Louisa, I will see you in your dreams and wait until we are once again reunited.

Yours eternally
Robert

Now, out on the balcony of the penthouse, her face was brushed by a cold northerly breeze that had swept down the lake, but it wasn't the breeze that sent a shiver running through her body, it was the question of what exactly had her husband gotten himself into that had led to his death?

Chapter 15

The CID team gathered in the incident room at their Harpenden headquarters. It was 7am. In front of them were scores of folders containing documentation that the forensics teams had tagged and bagged from the Lowe residence, as well as from the offices of his small accountancy firm. There were two desktop computers in the room, pre-loaded with copies of the electronic files that were recovered from Derek Lowe's hard drives and USBs.

"Right, listen up," called out DS Armitage to quieten the noise. He waited until he had the team's full attention. "We're joined today by two officers from the Met fraud squad. They will brief you and then lead the initial analysis of the data we have. We need to take in as much of their advice as possible because their secondment is only for two weeks." He glanced around the room to ensure everyone was paying attention before gesturing to the fraud squad lead that the meeting was now his.

"Morning all." His voice was deep and commanding, so he had no need to shout to grab their attention. "We're going to provide some instruction on the methods of accounting fraud, the most likely crime committed by people like Derek Lowe. If anyone needs to clarify anything, please ask. It's all too easy for us to assume that what we practise every day in the fraud squad easily translates to anyone not familiar with white-collar crime." He paused and looked round the room. "Any initial questions?" A hand went up at the back.

"What sort of things could we be looking for?"

"We'll go into more detail once the briefing is complete, but we'll explain a few simple tricks to identify suspicious financial practises. It should be easier to find irregularities with an accountant like Mr Lowe because they are rarely involved with anything other than tax evasion, low-level corporate fraud such as false accounting, or aiding and abetting simple money laundering schemes. The more complex frauds, your 'pump and dump' scams, the Ponzi schemes, and insider trading tend to sit within investment companies or large global organisations, rather than local accountants."

"Madoff; he was a Ponzi scheme guy in the States about 10 years ago, right?" called out another.

"That's right," responded the second fraud squad officer. "He was big league, though; tens of billions of dollars. It's highly unlikely an accountant like Derek Lowe would be operating at that level."

"And remember," interjected Armitage, "as far as we know, Derek Lowe and his family are innocent victims of a brutal crime until proven otherwise." No one in the room actually believed Lowe was wholly innocent, given the elaborate nature of the killings and the size and location of the house they owned, but the team knew they had a job to do.

"So, you five will work on the paper files and you two on the computers," said Armitage. He then glanced over to the lead fraud squad officer and gestured for him to step out of the room as the other member of the fraud squad began to organise the team.

"Thanks for your help on this. Not sure we're set up for fraud investigation, but this is such a bizarre murder. Did you get a chance to read the case files?" asked Armitage.

"I did. Any further clues on who did it, and what the lottery ticket is all about?"

Armitage shook his head. "No leads, but it has all the hallmarks of a professional hit. I'm not sure what Derek Lowe had got himself into to deserve that ending for him and his family? We're assuming the lottery ticket is possibly a message from a client of Lowe's: a warning, perhaps." The fraud officer nodded. In his 20 years on the force, he'd not come across anything like this and could only assume the same as Armitage.

"Well, best get on with it. We'll find you something to go on, if there's anything to find." As he turned, he patted Armitage on the shoulder. Armitage nodded unconvincingly, and then he gave his apologies because his mobile was ringing.

"Armitage," he said into the phone.

"Sergeant? I'm from the forensics team. Got a couple of minutes to talk about the Lowe case?"

"Sure. Take as long as you want. All I have is that, three arsons, and a hit-and-run murder attempt by a jealous husband to juggle."

"Ah, a quiet week then," said the forensics analyst, smirking.

"So, what have you got for me?"

"Not much, I'm afraid. Neither the bodies nor the scene itself provided any trace material, nor has the printed copy of the lottery ticket. Looking at the quality of the print, I'd suggest it was done on a standard scanner; the type you might buy from somewhere like Staples." Armitage's shoulders slumped further, and he massaged his forehead with his thumb and index finger. How could a crime scene give so little evidence?

"What about ballistics? What can you tell me about the firearm?"

"We know it wasn't a standard firearm. The casing we recovered from the scene was subsonic and, given no one nearby seemed to have heard much, we're assuming the killer used a specialist bolt-action pistol called the Welrod."

"What's that?" asked Armitage. He'd never heard of a gun manufacturer with such a name.

"It's actually a British weapon from World War Two special operations. The entire barrel acts as a suppressor, and it's incredibly quiet. It is used for close action kills."

"Is used? Don't you mean was used?"

"Oh no. Although it was invented and manufactured in the 1940s for special ops, both the British and the American Special Forces used it during Desert Storm in 1991. When discharged, the sound is almost imperceptible from just 15 feet away. This gun is a collector's item, and the user is possibly special ops trained."

"Wonder what the poor girl thought if she heard the shots or noise as her parents were murdered?"

"That's an interesting point," said the analyst. "While Mr and Mrs Lowe were clearly aware of the intruder, the evidence suggests their daughter wasn't. Interview notes from the girls on the video chat with her all say there was nothing in her actions or tone of voice to suggest increased anxiety or fear, and there was no physical evidence to suggest she had tried to escape or hide."

"You don't think she knew anything? Not even if there were screams or the heavy sound of a body falling to the floor?"

"It's amazing what the mind can disregard if the sound is partially drowned out. With her music playing loudly and all her attention presumably on the video conversation with her friends, her subconscious would, most likely, dismiss the noise as irrelevant," explained the analyst.

"So, if there's no indication that she heard anything or was running from anyone, why was she murdered too?" he asked rhetorically. Then he contemplated an alternative scenario. "What if the killer wasn't actually there to kill Derek or Celia Lowe? What if he or she was actually there to kill their daughter, and her parents just got in the way?"

Chapter 16

There was a dull thud as a brown manilla envelope was pushed through the letterbox, landing on Evie's kitchen floor. She glanced over as she made coffee.

"First things first," she said as she removed the cup from her espresso machine and took in some of the delicious aroma. Only then did she walk over to the front door. As she picked the envelope up, she noticed it was marked 'Client Confidential: Materia Prima'.

"Wow, that was quick." The envelope was thick and weighty, suggesting this was more than just a copy of the contract. She tucked the envelope under her arm and then carried the coffee cup and a bowl of muesli up the stairs to her office space. She put the coffee and bowl on the desk and then took the envelope from under her arm. She ripped the envelope open and tipped the contents out: paperwork, newspaper clippings, photos, and a letter cascaded onto the desk. Evie was surprised and delighted at the amount of documentation, but she reminded herself that she, too, had a lot of paperwork in her safe, which turned out to contain very little of value. She turned everything face up and spread it out on the table, so she could see it all. Before she started to analyse the individual documents, she read the accompanying letter.

Dear Miss Perry

Please find enclosed a series of documents and photographs that we have collated thus far.

Although we have not tried to assess their relative value to you, we hope you will find most of them of both interest and of use. As discussed, Materia Prima operates ethically and legally.

As stated in our terms and conditions, we want to remind you that our work can – occasionally – leave a digital fingerprint. It is possible that individuals or companies with sophisticated software could become aware that someone is analysing data about them. We do our utmost to avoid this, and it is extremely rare, but it has been known for an investigation to be curtailed in the interests of both our client and Materia Prima.

We will continue our work once we receive the agreed staged payment of £10,000. Our account details are listed at the bottom of this letter. We look forward to starting work on the second stage of our assignment.

With regards,

David Homes

D Homes, Managing Partner

Evie read the letter and then put it to one side. The statement about 'people or companies with sophisticated software' triggered a small nervous reaction and she clutched the side of the table, but after a few seconds, the irrational fear subsided. She re-read the final paragraph of the letter.

"Before I pay anything, I want to be satisfied the information is worth it." She started to skim-read the documents.

"Yes, I remember you," she said as she stared at a photograph of the first man, William Curtis. Attached was an array of articles and some additional photos of him, apparently taken without him knowing, given the locations and his activities, and copies of some confidential police files. In them were interview transcripts and supporting artefacts regarding several accusations of sexual harassment. Evie was no legal expert, but the submission by the three accusers was damning. The final page of the police paperwork revealed that all three accusers had suddenly withdrawn their testimony.

Threatened or paid off, more like, thought Evie. The anger inside her started to rise again, but then she realised the irony of her attitude. After all, wasn't she looking for money to keep quiet? Further information in the Materia Prima file revealed that, just six months later, he unexpectedly left an advisory position at one of the big banks. The newspaper clippings speculated that his abrupt departure was related to an unsavoury incident with a female intern, *'according to information from a reliable source'*. Evie's mood darkened again as she put the information about him into one of her own brown folders and placed it on the *'You are fucked'* pile. Then she picked up the remaining photo and summary document.

"Anthony Fairfax," she said, with an almost guttural uttering of his name. "I will remember you forever," and as she recalled that night, she began to tremble. Her breathing became laboured, and beads of sweat appeared on her hairline as the traumatic memory triggered a physical and mental reaction. She reached out with her right hand to lean against the table and steady herself. Slowly, her breathing started to ease, and she began to compose herself. As the trembling stopped, she raised her left hand to her left eye. Evie touched the scar as a sole tear trickled down her right cheek. "No, not again. No more," she said to herself. She clenched a fist and slammed it down on the desk. She could feel the immutable strength returning. Her resolve was back and, with it, the desire to punish those responsible for her disfigurement. Evie looked down at the documentation: home addresses, personal email addresses and phone numbers were listed.

"Perhaps now is the time to let these two know the price they'll pay for what they did to me."

Chapter 17

Her flight from Zurich to London had been delayed, so Stella had to wait for the evening London-to-Southampton flight. The twin-prop plane from London held no more than 12 passengers and was what she would mockingly describe as 'an experience', except everything in her life was likely to be 'an experience' now, such as standing at a taxi rank at the airport, rather than being collected by a driver.

"Welcome to your new life," she muttered to herself.

Twenty-five minutes later, the taxi pulled up at a small block of apartments. Outside was almost wholly concrete parking bays, with a thin band of grass and a handful of shrubs around the property boundary to add a little greenery. She took the key she had found in the safety deposit box and entered a communal hallway. In it, she found mail boxes for each apartment and the choice of stairs or a lift. She decided to use the lift, given she had the luggage from Switzerland with her. The lift buttons offered her the first floor or the penthouse. When the lift doors opened on the top floor, she saw the door to her apartment. She unlocked it and walked into her new home. It was tiny.

"A penthouse? Oh, my good god. When will estate agents start calling things what they truly are?"

She put the suitcases down and had a look around the apartment. The two bedrooms were smaller than her walk-in wardrobes at the house in Windsor, and the kitchen was more like a kitchenette. At least the apartment was furnished nicely, and the secluded sun terrace she had on the roof could probably be quite tranquil. She walked back into the tiny hallway and moved the suitcases into the open lounge area. Robert had turned the smaller bedroom into a hybrid wardrobe cum study. A laptop sat on a desk, and there was an ergonomic chair. On the desk sat an answering machine, with its 'Messages' light flashing. She walked over to the machine, found a pen and paper in the desk's drawer, then sat down on the chair and pressed 'Play'.

"You have five new messages" the automated voice announced. "First new message, received at 10:53am on Friday, the third of February."

There was a click, then a voice said, "Robert? Are you there? It's David. Pick up if you are, this call is costing me a ruddy fortune." There was a long pause, then Stella could hear some profanity being muttered before the line clicked to end the call.

"Second new message; received at 3:15pm on Thursday, the ninth of March."

"Robert, it's David again. Give me a call back; you have the Toulouse number, and I'm here every Thursday and Friday." The voice sounded a little impatient, but at least there was no profanity this time.

"Third new message; received at 7:47pm on Thursday, the twenty-seventh of March."

"Are you just pissing me about, Kendrick? Pick the bloody phone up before I get really angry. Last frickin' chance. This is getting beyond a joke!" Stella recognised the voice as that of David, whoever he was. He also sounded like he was losing his temper.

"Fourth new message; received at 10:43am on Thursday, the eleventh of April." This time, the familiar voice on the answering machine was subdued.

"Stella, this is David; David Holding. I was a friend of your husband. I've just received a package he sent, and I'm so very sorry for your loss. If you want or need to talk, I'll give you my private number over here in France. I am usually available on a Thursday or Friday. Please, if you need anything at all, just let me know."

Stella remembered the surname on the list she found in the kitchen. She finished writing the number down he had given her just as the machine clicked in again.

"Fifth new message; received today at 8:17am." When she heard it, she gasped in disbelief and covered her mouth with both hands. Wide-eyed, she could do nothing but stare at the machine. A hushed voice that sounded as if the person was wary of being found or overheard said:

"Stella, are you there? Pick up. It's Robert."

Chapter 18

The investigation into the murder of the Lowe family still hadn't produced any solid leads, but they had found Niall Fitzgerald's name in Derek Lowe's business records. Even though it was getting late when the news had come through, DS Armitage had driven across to talk to Niall.

"Did you know Mr Lowe well, sir?" Armitage asked a clearly shocked Niall.

"Derek was my very dear friend as well as my accountant, Detective Sergeant. We've known each other since university. I'm... I... I'm sorry; it's just this news is so shocking. Derek, Celia and Amy; murdered? Why?" Niall asked, clearly struggling to digest the news.

"I'm afraid I can't comment on an ongoing investigation, Mr Fitzgerald, but we wondered if you might be able to think of any possible motive? A business deal gone wrong, perhaps? What about you, Mrs Fitzgerald?"

Yvonne Fitzgerald looked up. "Me? I'd met Derek and Celia at a number of social functions and fundraisers. They help us with a lot of..." Then she paused before correcting herself. "They helped us with a lot of charity events that we organised. It really was... er..." but her voice trailed off as her mind drifted back to the dreadful news. She shook her head a little, as if in disbelief, and then reached for a tissue to dab her eyes.

She knew Celia Lowe, and although she disliked the blandness of the woman, she was so stunned at the news she instinctively reached for Niall's hand for reassurance. Armitage gave an understanding nod and a sympathetic smile and then turned his attention back to Niall.

"Mr Fitzgerald, did you notice anything unusual about Mr Lowe's behaviour recently?" Niall had been gazing at his wife's hand in his, almost smiling at the surprising moment of togetherness, but the question snapped his attention back to the cold reality of the murders.

"Erm, er Derek, yes. I mean no. I heard the question and just meant yes; I'd heard the question. I'm sorry; it's just such devastating news that I'm not quite myself yet. Neither of us are," he answered, unconsciously glancing down again at his wife's hand in his.

"I... I hadn't seen Derek for quite a while, although we talked a few months ago to discuss my quarterly tax assessment. He seemed perfectly alright." Niall struggled to concentrate, his mind still coming to terms with the horrific news.

"Would you know how long ago 'a few months' actually was, sir? It's probably not material, but it's always good to know precise information. Fills in all the gaps, that's all," asked Armitage softly. "If you're not sure right now, you can always..." but the rest of his question was cut off by Yvonne.

"You spoke to him over the phone six weeks ago, I think." She looked from Armitage back across to her husband, adding, "But, if you mean the last time that you actually saw Derek, well, that must have been three years ago at one of those silly 'Aeternum' parties?"

Armitage looked back at her husband. "Mr Fitzgerald, would that be correct?" he enquired.

"Yeeeees," came the slow, elongated reply from Niall as Yvonne gave his hand another soft, assuring squeeze. She smiled at her husband and pulled his hand onto her lap, so she could hold it with both of hers. Niall was distracted by her gesture. He paused momentarily and then continued with his answer, "It was the first time in a long time, actually. Christmas 2015, I think, when we dragged a friend down to Westminster for a bit of a celebration."

"We?" asked Armitage for clarification. "Is that the Aeternum your wife was referring to?"

"Yes. It's a bunch of old friends. Although we rarely do business together nowadays, we used to meet socially every few months. We've all known each other since university."

"And the Aeternum; is that a company or a club?"

"It's just the name of an agreement we have. We pledged we'd support each other financially if anyone ever needed it."

"I'd like to talk to the other friends you're referring to if that's possible? Perhaps, if one of them has been in touch with Mr Lowe recently, they might know something that could help us piece together why Mr Lowe and his family were attacked. Could you provide their details?" requested Armitage.

"Yes, of course. Just give me a moment." Niall walked away to write the names and numbers down. Yvonne and Armitage shared awkward smiles while they waited, but neither had anything to say. A few minutes later, Niall returned and handed a piece of paper to Armitage.

Armitage scanned the names on the piece of paper and said, "Okay, and are these the best contact numbers to reach them on?" he checked.

"Yes, although if it's alright with you, I'd like to call them all first. It's not the sort of news I want my friends to hear from the police if I could have told them; prepared them, so to speak?"

"Of course, Mr Fitzgerald, but please don't share any information; this is an ongoing investigation."

"I understand. I'll try to call them tonight, but if I can't, then I'll call them first thing in the morning if that's alright? I doubt they'll all have their phones switched on and, to be honest, I could do with some time to let this sink in. I'm just not sure I could talk to my friends right now."

"Totally understandable, sir, but as early as possible in the morning, please. It's critical we follow up on all possible leads as soon as we can." Armitage smiled, flipping closed his notebook. "Well, thank you both for your time, and I'm really sorry to be the bearer of such dreadful news. If you think of anything else, please don't hesitate to contact me." He passed Niall his card.

"Of course. If we think of anything at all, we'll let you know straight away," replied Niall as he gestured towards the hallway and the front door. Armitage left, and Niall stood behind the door, reflecting on the news of Derek's murder, but he also found himself a little relieved. Derek knew a lot about Niall's financial dealings, and he'd actually seen Derek two weeks prior to discuss a rather sensitive financial issue related to another member of the group. Weariness suddenly hit him, and he wanted to at least text the others in their group before he went to bed. He'd let them know he would be calling first them in the morning and that they had to answer the phone. He didn't want to say more, as the news about Derek and his family needed to be discussed, not read.

As he turned his phone off, Yvonne called from the top of the stairs, "Niall, I don't want to be alone tonight."

Chapter 19

It wasn't even 9am, but Detective Sergeant Steve Denton was already attending his third murder of the day. He was waiting for the lead SOCO to brief him on this latest scene when his mobile phone buzzed in his pocket. He wiped the perspiration from his forehead and then dabbed the back of his hand on his jacket. It was already a warm day, and it was forecast to get even warmer.

"Denton," he barked down the phone.

"Sarge, I'm down in Westminster; some bloke has been strangled," said the voice of Detective Constable Rachael Jones.

"Okay," said Denton, unsure what else to say. He had no context for the call and was already tired and irritable, so he waited for Jones to continue rather than ask the obvious question.

"I'm with the same SOCO team as the one in Dartford yesterday."

Denton closed his eyes as he tried to focus on which case that one was. After a couple of seconds, he opened them and screwed his face up. "Yesterday? The guy at the motor garage, with the hole drilled in the back of his head?" he asked, again wondering why she had called him.

"Yeah, that was the one," chirped Jones.

"What about it?" enquired Denton, starting to lose his patience. The heat definitely wasn't helping his mood.

"I think the deaths might be linked."

"Drugs?" guessed Denton.

"No, Sarge, and before we start playing Twenty Questions, just tell me what time you'll be free?"

Denton glanced at his watch. He was still going to be here for another hour but calculated that if he left around 10am, his journey back to HQ should take about 45 minutes. "If the A1203 isn't too heavy, I'll be at HQ for 10:45. That should easily give me chance to grab something hot and greasy on the way; bloody starving." Denton ended the call. He didn't want Jones mistaking his last comment as an offer to pick up some food for her as well.

At 11am, a hot and grumpy DS Denton arrived at a 3rd-floor briefing room, with some tiny ketchup splotches on his crumpled and sweaty shirt. DC Jones was already in the room. "This better be worth the trip," Denton began as he pulled out a chair and sat down.

Jones opened a manilla file and slid it across the table. "Peter Brown; aged 48. Lifelong motor mechanic who had worked in the Dartford area for the last 20 years. Well-known and well-liked by his customers and local businesses alike, apparently. He was found in his garage by one of the apprentices he'd taken on: an ex-offender who had been in and out of juvie for hot-wiring cars. Cause of death; a hole had been drilled into the back of Mr Brown's head. No forced entry to the workshop, no apparent struggle, and no trace material found on the initial sweep," she said, skimming through her own notes. Denton skim-read the report and glanced at the photos from the scene, while Jones opened a second file and slid that across.

"William Curtis; aged 62. Former diplomat-turned advisor for a number of FTSE 100 companies who operate primarily with Middle Eastern clients. Registered office is in the City of Westminster. Found this morning by his secretary, sat behind his desk. SOCO say he was asphyxiated." Denton glanced through that file, then closed them both and looked over to Jones.

"So?" he asked. Jones pulled two photographs out of a third file.

"We found a piece of paper in each of the men's mouths," she said as she passed both photos across the table. Denton quickly glanced at them and then looked back at Jones.

"Photocopies of lottery tickets?" asked Denton.

"Photocopies of the *same* lottery ticket," Jones pointed out. Denton picked up the photos again and had another look. In his tired and irritable state, he hadn't compared the numbers, but he did now.

"24, 29, 30, 36, 46, 48 and 7." He looked at Jones. "Date on the ticket is the 29th April, 2017."

Jones nodded and said, "A near £10 million jackpot prize; no winners."

"Why would someone kill two men but leave a copy of the same losing lottery ticket in their mouth?" Denton wondered out loud, now intrigued and a lot less irritable.

"Problem is it's not just two, guv," replied Jones. "I checked the National Crime Agency database, and both Hertfordshire CID and North Yorkshire CID have recently logged murders with a photocopy of the same lottery ticket in the victims' mouth."

Denton sat bolt upright; the heat and fatigue now forgotten. "Better get me the..." But before he could finish the sentence, Jones was passing him a piece of paper with the contact details for a Detective Sergeant Alan Armitage and his old friend, Detective Sergeant Bob Williams.

Chapter 20

The defendant, Dennis Ruiz, jumped up in the witness stand and launched himself at the prosecuting barrister. "Sergeant!" shouted the judge as spectators ran screaming from their seats.

Three policemen and two prison officers raced forwards as Ruiz screamed profanities in his native Spanish while trying to choke the barrister. "Tus palabras no significan nada, hijo de puta. ¿No sabes a quién estás juzgando? ¡SOY RUIZ!"

The officers pulled Ruiz off the frightened barrister and slammed him to the floor, face down. He kept writhing and cursing until his gaze fell on his own defence barrister, Daniella Maddox. As his hands were finally tied behind his back with plastic restraining straps, a sneer spread across his face. "Ha llegado tu hora. Saborea tu último aliento," he hissed. Ruiz was hoisted to his feet and marched out of the courtroom, keeping eye contact with Maddox until he was pushed through a door and taken down to the holding cells.

Thirty minutes later, Maddox was still sitting in the empty courtroom, calm on the outside but her heart continued to pound. She had been defending Ruiz, who was accused of cyber-fraud valued at over £1 billion. An expert had just revealed Ruiz's criminal strategy and his cyber-infrastructure, as well as detailing a number of digital footprints Ruiz's people had left as a result of a sting operation by Interpol. The prosecuting barrister was summarising the unequivocal and damning evidence to Ruiz, who had unexpectedly snapped. Maddox's problem, though, was not the damning actions of her client or the flawless evidence against him. Her problem was what Ruiz had hissed to her as he lay restrained on the floor. She drew a deep breath and slowly stood, absent-mindedly jamming her usually pristine legal files into her briefcase before walking out of the courtroom. Waiting for her was a throng of photographers and television camera crews. The trial was already a sensation, with argument and counterargument sounding like the script for a clichéd soap opera. This latest twist had just made the headlines on every social media channel across Europe. As Maddox was trying to make her through the newspaper and television reporters, standing five-deep in front of her, they all began to shout questions.

"Daniella, Daniella – is it true you knew about the crimes Ruiz was committing but kept them secret because you were his lover?" shouted a tabloid reporter.

"Where does this leave your already fragile defence, Miss Maddox?" asked another, perhaps trying to bait Maddox into a reaction.

Neither of these or any of the other comments worked, though, and she calmly eased her way through the crowd, repeating, "Excuse me, please. Excuse me, I need to get through. Please afford me some space. Thank you." She finally climbed into the back seat of a waiting executive car, which sped away quickly. She sank into the back seat and cursed loudly. It was more Anglo-Saxon than it was her native Italian.

While the media was paying attention to Maddox, the expert witness who had laid bare Ruiz's operation, strolled out of the courthouse and slipped down a side street to where his 1960s Jaguar XK-150 convertible was parked. In his waistcoat, flamboyant jacket and immaculately polished shoes, Professor Gary Hibberd was the epitome of a stylish and extrovert showman. Underneath it all, though, he was a man driven by a passion to find and dismantle the cybersecurity frameworks and cryptic coding used by the ever-increasing number of digital criminals. He had been an advisor to some of the top European companies and was a special advisor to one of the UK government's policy teams on cybercrime and cyber sexploitation. He climbed into the Jaguar and started the engine. Its gruff purr echoed momentarily before he pulled away from the kerb and eased his car into the late afternoon traffic.

Thirty minutes later, Maddox was in her office. Thankfully, everyone else had gone home. She sat behind her desk and buried her head in her hands before suddenly exploding in anger. She stood as she grabbed a stapler which, moments later, hit the wall on the far side of her office. It was followed by a pot of pens and a cry of frustration. She then slumped back into the chair, with tears trickling down her cheeks. She recalled how she had been left with little choice but to take this clearly indefensible case. Her client had been arrested after a two-year investigation into an international network of cyber criminals, all of whom were allegedly coordinated by Ruiz. She recalled how the managing partner at the firm had spoken to her:

"Mr Ruiz is one of our best clients, Miss Maddox. A successful businessman who has used our firm to represent him in all aspects of his commercial activities over the last 15 years. You will take this case," he said, closing his briefcase and with it any room for debate. As he was about to walk out of her office, he paused and turned back to her, adding, "And if you don't accept the case, not only will we reject the proposal to make you a senior partner, but we will consider it to be your resignation." With that, he forced a smile and headed for the door.

Maddox was the logical choice for this case. She was the best criminal defence barrister in the firm's worldwide team, and someone the managing partner had turned to many times. She was, however, also very experienced and knew the case was almost impossible to win. Only a technicality could save Ruiz. Originally that's what had kept her awake at night, but right now it was the threat he had made in court that played over and over in her head. She had never felt so frightened in her life.

"Your time has come. Savour your final breath."

Chapter 21

The funeral of the Lowe family was small, reverential, but mercifully short. Celia Lowe had wanted a dozen hymns sung as part of her planned ceremony, according to the funeral policy she and Derek had taken out several years ago.

"Can't be too prepared," was her usual rationale for anything she wanted Derek to succumb to. He wasn't a forceful man, so he usually agreed to anything for a relatively quiet home life. Thankfully for most of the people gathered, it had to be reduced to two hymns, a psalm, and three eulogies: one for each victim. Derek's university friends attended, of course, as did a handful of small-business clients and Amy's four school friends who were on the video call when she was murdered. They spent most of the time hugging each other and wiping tears from their cheeks. Niall looked across and, having heard who they were and what had happened, thought, *No one so young should have to go through what they went through.* As the second eulogy started, Niall's mind drifted back to a time when they actually could help Derek; it was late 2004.

"The doctor says I've got a less than 5 per cent chance of survival without the operation," Derek had blurted out in the middle of a conversation about future investments. The conversation stopped abruptly, and every single one of them had their mouths open in shock.

"What with Celia being pregnant, I'm really worried. I've hardly got any savings because I put everything into setting up my business. I don't have any health insurance to cover the cost of the operation, and no life insurance to cover the mortgage. We'll have to sell the house," he concluded, referring to a semi-detached family-sized property he and his wife had just bought.

"You don't have life insurance?" Charlie asked, surprised.

"I don't either; can't afford it on my civil service salary," replied Bill.

"Me neither. I'm using all my money to invest in property renovation," added Tony. "Besides, I feel as fit as a fiddle."

"So did I," replied Derek, which immediately killed Tony's misplaced confidence.

"And the NHS won't do the operation?" asked Peter.

"It will be classed as too expensive given the percentage chance of survival. They don't have an unlimited budget, and they'll view the £30,000 as money they can better spend elsewhere to help more people. I'm sorry, Derek," said James.

"Can't any of your Harley Street surgeon contacts help, James? Maybe they have someone who is willing to do the surgery?" asked Charlie.

"I doubt it. I don't really know any of them, and to them, I'm just an inquisitive medical intern at the local hospital who likes to ask them questions."

"No, I can't accept this," said Niall, who had been quiet throughout. "I've got some money I was saving for a rainy day, and we promised, back in university, we'd be here for each other."

"How much have you got?" asked Bill.

"£10,000. I know it's not as much as you need, but..." which is when James cut across him.

"I've got £5,000. I was saving it for a car, and I might be able to borrow a few thousand more."

"Don't borrow anything. I can add £5,000 too," said Charlie.

"Fuck it," said Tony. "I've got some money I was going to put into another property deal, but there'll be more houses. We've only got one Derek. I'll chuck in another £5,000."

"So that's £25,000 so far, but you'll need recuperation time after the operation, so I think we need to find £10,000 more so you don't feel under pressure to go back to work prematurely," Niall suggested.

"Celia has a little bit saved, ready for the baby. I'll talk to her," Derek said with cautious optimism.

"I'm sure William and I can find a few thousand," said Peter. The seven looked at each other and impulse led them into a group hug with Derek Lowe in the middle, crying with relief.

"Let's make a pledge to each other," announced a dewy-eyed Niall. "In life and in death, we'll always look out for each other, emotionally and financially."

"To the Aeternum group," said Charles, instinctively naming the bond they continued to form through adversity.

That seemed such a long time ago now. First, they had lost Alan Gerrard, and now the group had lost another friend. Niall felt an elbow nudge into him, which broke his moment of contemplation.

"It's you," whispered Charles.

"What?" asked Niall, trying to focus back on the present.

"It's your turn to give the eulogy," Charles hissed. Niall could now see people with expectant looks on their faces, waiting for him to say kind words without breaking down in tears. The previous speakers had all been unable to control their emotions, and Niall swallowed hard. He wasn't sure whether he had the strength to avoid doing the same, not because Derek and his family had been brutally murdered, but because he felt he was the root cause of their deaths.

Chapter 22

A very prim personal assistant pressed the intercom on her desk. "Who is it please?" she enquired.

"Evie Perry," came the reply. "Mr Wagstaff is expecting me."

"Ah yes, Miss Perry. Please push the door open when you hear the buzz."

Evie stood outside a Grade 2 listed building, next to the prestigious RAC Club on Pall Mall, in the heart of London. She had come to one of the biggest celebrity law firms in the country – Wagstaff, Earnshaw & Peters, who, in recent years, represented a Premiership footballer who was involved in a sex video and the son of Danish royalty who had been caught with a kilo of Class A drugs in their country house. It was that last case that caught Evie's attention. It had flashed-up several times as banner headlines on several of her favourite online pages. She had gone to discuss the opportunities and the risks of writing a tell-all book. The door buzzed, and Evie made her way up the wide marble staircase to their prestigious office. She had walked past several people in the building who didn't seem to glance at the large sunglasses and hat she was wearing to help mask her scar. Presumably, they were either too polite or simply had more important things to do than stare, because in a slim-fitting red dress with her plunging cleavage framed by her Loro Piana jacket, and the click-clack of her Roger Vivier satin high heels on the polished floor, Evie didn't exactly melt into the background.

She entered the reception area and saw the woman she assumed had just let her in through the electronic door lock. She was meticulously dressed in a white blouse with the slightest of frills on the collar, and a black jacket. Her hair was tied in a simple French roll style, without a single strand out of place. She was typing on a computer and only looked up as Evie stood at the reception desk.

"Miss Perry?" she enquired and, without waiting for confirmation, said, "Mr Wagstaff will just be a moment. Please, take a seat," and she gestured Evie towards a large leather chair. The reception area was eclectic, light and airy, decorated in delicate tones and included things you'd expect to see in a modern working environment. As a juxtaposition, it also had gilded frames for all the items that were hung on the wall, and the chair Evie sat in was the sort you might imagine would be in an old-fashioned gentleman's club. *But it works*, she thought. She felt comfortable in an environment she described as subtly elegant and even more subtly expensive.

Ten minutes later, the door to a room swung open, and a confident man with a beaming smile scanned the room briefly before spotting Evie.

"Ah, Miss Perry. Please, come in." Evie walked into a spacious office which, she estimated, was easily nine metres square. Marble-tiled flooring was partially covered by two large rugs that split the room in two: a working space with a stylish desk and chairs on one side and an informal space with a three-seater settee and a coffee table. Two free-standing Italian-styled lamps stood aside the settee, and behind it was a floor-to-ceiling window that extended across the entire wall. In her opinion, this was the perfect balance between powerful and welcoming.

"My apologies for keeping you waiting. I'm Charles Wagstaff," said the man. "Please, sit wherever you feel most comfortable. Would you like me to turn the lights off?"

Evie hesitated. "Thank you, but I'm fine," she replied, not yet wishing to remove her sunglasses. She took a seat opposite the desk, so Wagstaff walked round to the other side, easing himself into the high-backed swivel chair.

"I've read your email and understand a little, but please tell me more about how I can help you?"

"Please, call me Evie. Miss Perry sounds very formal and reminds me of being in the headmaster's office." She smiled momentarily but then realised she could feel the tautness of the scar on her face. Her smile quickly disappeared, and she looked down at her nervous, fidgety hands. Ever the professional, though, Wagstaff didn't react to the sudden change in expression and simply smiled back at his guest.

"And I'm not your headmaster, so please feel free to call me Charles," he said, smiling broadly.

"Thank you, Charles. Well, it's rather a sensitive subject." She started to feel vulnerable but knew she had to tell him everything, so she forced herself to sit up straight and slowly removed the sunglasses and her hat. Even with her scar revealed, Wagstaff did not react and did not break eye contact for a second. She smiled, grateful at his lack of reaction.

"I could dress it up, but I won't. I used to be an escort. I charged extra for sexual favours, and I was very good at what I did for a living." She paused, waiting to see if she noticed any raising of the eyebrows or look of disgust on his face. Not a twitch, just a nod of his head that told her, *Okay, please go on.* Evie puffed out her cheeks as she exhaled and then plunged into the story of the scar. Thirty minutes later, she had told him everything, from some of the details of the sexual acts she willingly undertook for her elite clientele to the life-changing incident with the broken glass. She also shared some of the documentation she had collected, although she had redacted the names on this copy. He studied the artefacts as he listened.

"And now, facing life alone and not wanting to show my face in public ever again, I'm wondering about writing a memoir. Not exactly an exposé, so to speak, but with enough information in there that the people responsible for my life-changing disfigurement know I have the evidence; you know, in case they want to try to encourage me to not publish."

Wagstaff was attentive, gently nodding his head to signal his understanding, as well as altering his facial expression appropriately throughout her story. After listening to her, he reviewed some of the photos and investigative reports, which were supported by emails, bank and credit card statements. They were nothing short of explosive. When he had finished, he placed the paperwork back in her file and sat, quiet and motionless. He could tell she was determined to scare the men she held accountable. Maybe she really didn't want to go to print, given her subtle reference to what basically amounted to blackmail? Evie stayed silent, giving him time to think. After a minute, Wagstaff summarised his position:

"I just don't know what to say, Evie. This is... well, let's just say we need to check we are on very solid legal ground before any of this sees the light of day." He was running his fingers through the manicured whiskers on his chin as he contemplated the enormity of what he had seen. "Are you sure you want to proceed with this? Finding a publisher who is prepared to even look at this information..." he started to say, when she politely but firmly corrected him.

"Evidence, Charles; not information."

"Yes, yes, of course, evidence. My apologies, but you do understand what this could do to all of these people?" he asked. She stared at him impassively, and he could tell how determined she was to proceed. "Well, I'm glad to say you've come to the right place and at the right time. Sadly, some of our clients look to sell their story first, and then we have to clean up the mess. Not ideal, as it means their book never gets off the ground. In fact, some are buried so deep in legal battles, the author usually regrets the decision to even discuss the idea in the first place. And legal battles are usually very expensive." This didn't frighten Evie; in fact, she felt relaxed. Knowing that he was happy to discuss her idea further was both a huge relief and a powerful motivation.

He continued, "The first thing we need to do is agree a commercially viable way forward for you. One that doesn't cost you the earth or tie you into an expensive legal agreement but recognises the value of the work we will be doing for you. If you and I think there's a mutually agreeable way forward after that, then I'm quite happy to discuss a possible risk and reward approach from our perspective, if you are?"

"Risk and reward?" She was unclear on how that could work.

"Yes. We don't know if anyone will dare commit to publishing this, although, as you said, perhaps the people you're featuring won't let it go to press. I do have an obligation to advise you, though, that while your story is compelling, these people sound powerful and will probably have deep pockets."

"I'm counting on it," sneered Evie.

"And what if they don't respond to your... offer... of paying to avoid it being published or serialised in one of the tabloids?"

"Their lives wouldn't be worth living if they don't respond to my request."

"Alright then, Evie," said Wagstaff. "Give me a couple of days and I'll be in touch with a proposal. Until then, if there's anything you need, please don't hesitate to call." He then stood and waited for Evie to do the same before he walked her to his office door. He opened the door, gesturing for her to walk ahead, and concluded with, "Alice will guide you through our standard exclusivity terms and conditions. It's important you understand those before we present you with our proposal." He gestured towards the receptionist and shook Evie's hand before walking back into his office and closing the door.

His warm smile fell away as he walked over to the large window. After reflecting on the meeting, he retrieved his mobile phone from his jacket pocket and clicked on a contact number. It rang for several seconds before the call was answered.

"She's been in, and she's thinking of going public. Let me know what you want me to do next," he said and then ended the call.

The recipient of the call paused, then sent a text in response: *Play along for now, and then leave her to me.*

Chapter 23

Two happily married people could hardly have come from more diverse backgrounds. At least that was the theme of Yvonne Fitzgerald's current therapy session. Niall had refused to entertain the concept of marriage counselling, but Yvonne found talking to someone helpful.

"Why do you think Niall is so reluctant?" asked the therapist.

"I think it's because trying to be self-reliant and strong is all he knows. When we were first dating, he told me his relationship with his father was one of tough love," replied Yvonne.

"How do you mean?" enquired the therapist.

"One example was when he was seven or eight years old, he went home crying. Some older boys from a nearby estate had teased him, and he had got angry. When he tried to punch one and called them 'dirty little Catholics', they turned on him and gave him a good beating. He ran home, blood dripping from his nose and his jacket ripped. Rather than show his son some protective tenderness and understanding, his father told him he shouldn't start fights and run away – that's not what a Fitzgerald does. Niall told me he didn't stop crying, so his father gave him the belt, telling him he needed to toughen up or he would have more, until he stopped crying."

"Ah yes; I see from my notes that he grew up in Belfast, near the Harland and Wolff shipyard. A tough neighbourhood. I suppose that would shape the way your husband responds to things. What about his mother? Was she the same?"

"Oh no," scoffed Yvonne. "She was firm, but she was also very protective of Niall. I remember him telling me that on more than one occasion, she took the blame for things Niall had done. I think she even took a bit of a beating for him once or twice when his father was drunk and angry. You know, instead of Niall getting the belt."

"And how would you describe Niall's relationship with his mother as he grew older?"

"Oh, he idolised her. I know, even after Niall's father died, he would still turn to her when faced with a difficult situation." Yvonne laughed lightly, but she couldn't hide the sad expression on her face, belying the lightness of the laugh. "He always knew if he had a problem that he couldn't fix, 'Mummy' was always there to help him sort things out." The therapist noted a slightly bitter tone in Yvonne's response and decided to probe further.

"I can't help but sense you disapprove? How is your relationship with her?"

"Mine? Alright, I suppose, but I know she struggled with the difference in status. When Niall brought her to meet my parents at their house, I couldn't tell if she was defensive because it reminded her of the gulf between what we had and... well, what they didn't have, or whether she felt uncomfortable in such a large, spectacular house."

"Were your parents wealthy?"

"They were," she said with a hint of melancholy. "My father believed he had a knack of seeing trends before they were trends, and investing in start-ups and new ideas. It was really difficult for quite a long time, with my parents arguing about how much money he was investing in his ideas rather than in his family. The simple things that we take for granted now, like fresh food and a hot bath, were…" and Yvonne teared up a little, "… were luxuries we simply couldn't afford. Thankfully, a few years after the winter of discontent, he negotiated a supply contract for the official commemorative merchandise for the upcoming Queen's Silver Jubilee celebrations. People were just so happy to be getting their lives back to some sort of normality, the celebrations and the commemorative market were huge. With the money he earned from that, he decided to invest in even more ideas including, in the early 1980s, the consumer market for the emerging mobile phone industry. By the time I'd met Niall, my father was well on his way to £50m and had started to invest in a few niche start-ups to build his portfolio, like digital marketing and quantum encryption, but I also persuaded him that he should invest a significant amount with Niall."

"I see," said the therapist. "I recall you mentioning…" and she turned to her notes, "… it was your father's money that, to use your own phrase, 'catapulted' your husband from being a good investment banker to a stellar investment broker?"

Yvonne nodded. "In 2010, my father provided £25m, which allowed Niall to get involved with some breakthrough tech companies. Niall used the money to support the creation of the distribution channels rather than high-risk tech itself. It proved to be a masterstroke, and my father's investment doubled in two years. After that, he trusted Niall with his money which, sadly, ended quite badly," she added, again, becoming reflective.

"What happened?"

"A few years ago, Niall was producing unbelievable returns. He and I had a prenuptial agreement. It was my father's idea, so he could protect my inheritance because, at that time, I was the one bringing the wealth into the marriage. Niall said he had felt belittled and subservient, but he loved me, so he agreed to it. I knew it bothered him, though. Anyway, during the ensuing years, my father had to spend a lot of his money on private healthcare for my mother and then some specialist care for himself. My inheritance was dwindling, so he put everything he owned into one last investment with Niall, which was when one of Niall's partners was arrested and admitted to being involved in a money laundering scheme. Niall had trusted his partner to invest what was to be the final gamble on my inheritance, but the funds were frozen, and my father died a broken man. He said his only request was that Niall forego any lingering animosity about the prenuptial, which he told my father he would, and did by unconditionally adding me to his will. My father then felt at peace, and he died the following day."

"I'm so sorry. And did things improve?"

"A little," replied Yvonne. "The problem was I started withholding any physical intimacy with Niall for quite a while, and even though the recent dreadful news about his friend seems to have brought us a little closer again, I know Niall had already revoked me from his will again. It felt like he was being spiteful and vengeful. That means if we got divorced, I'd now only take what would be a tiny piece of our overall wealth. I can't blame him. It was my actions and behaviour that drove us further apart and him into the arms of another woman."

The therapist was about to ask her another question when her watch bleeped. "Oh, I'm sorry. We're almost at the end of this session." She walked over to her desk and flicked through her appointment book. "We have two more sessions booked. Do you feel they are helping?"

"I don't know," said Yvonne hesitantly. "All I seem to be doing is talking about me. When do we talk about Niall and saving our marriage?"

The therapist smiled gently. "We are talking about Niall and about your marriage," she said softly. "I'm just not sure we understand what the real problem is yet, let alone what the solution might be."

Yvonne became agitated. "The problem? I know how hard my husband works to provide the quality of life I now have, but it would be nice if Niall would acknowledge everything that I did for him and what I've sacrificed." She paused to control her temper before continuing, "He used to. That's the problem. He just doesn't say thank you anymore. I felt useful; helpful. He'd ask for my thoughts on certain problems, and I'd go into the Iliad office to support him... you know, some admin work when he first started and then, as his company grew, when his PA was on holiday. His appointments and emails, and I'd even arrange his business travel. It wasn't exactly exciting or taxing work, but it made me feel part of that side of his life, and I liked that. I'm not as clever as Niall, but he always told me my opinions counted, and it felt like they used to, but he hasn't said it for years. It's not a lot to ask, is it?"

"Hmm. In our next session, let's talk a little bit more about that before we discuss his relationship with his mother, and then perhaps we can start to look at your changing relationship with Niall."

"I'd like that. We've been so cold towards each other over the last few years, but I've seen glimpses of the old Niall recently, the one I married. If only I could help him with whatever's bothering him, then perhaps..." but her voice faded as the reality of the current situation smothered the hope she held.

Chapter 24

He tossed the file onto his desk and slumped into his chair. DS Bob Williams was exasperated and tired. He screwed his eyes tight and pinched the bridge of his nose as he tried to fight the fatigue of another 14-hour shift. The forensics report on the murder of Malcolm Walsh hadn't helped his mood as it told him exactly what he feared; no trace material, no other physical items of evidence, and no clues as to why he was murdered.

"You alright, Sarge?" called one of the team from across the room. Williams opened his eyes and blinked in an exaggerated manner to clear his vision. "I'm not dead yet. What's up?"

"Got a call for you; a DS Denton from the Met." Williams gave a tired but genuine smile. He and DS Steve Denton had spoken many times since the Homicide and Major Enquiries Team they worked on a few years ago, and it was always nice when one of them called the other. He heard the team member mutter something into the phone and saw him smile before he transferred the call to Williams.

"Good to hear you're not dead yet, Bob," said Denton sarcastically.

"I do keep checking, Steve. Sometimes I'm not sure whether I'm dead or just in a nightmare," replied the equally sarcastic Williams. "How are you?"

"I'm overworked, underpaid, and under-appreciated. My bank account is running on fumes, my love life is dead, and I'm stuck in the office at 10pm on a Friday night, talking to you. You join the dots."

"So, what can I help you with?" asked Williams.

"I think we might have something that could be of interest to you," said Denton.

"Like what?"

"We're running a couple of murder cases, and one of my team, DC Jones, has found a case your team logged with NCA that seems to match ours."

"Which case?" asked Williams.

There was a short pause as Denton checked his notes before he replied, "Malcolm Walsh. The NCA report shows your victim had a lottery ticket in his mouth?"

"Yes, that's right. Just reading the SOCO report."

"Don't tell me; no trace and no other evidence that would help identify the killer?" Williams sat bolt upright as Denton continued, "We've had two murders, both with a photocopy of the same lottery ticket as yours, rolled up in their mouths."

"Shit," said Williams.

"And, according to the NCA database, there's a fourth case. Hertfordshire CID logged one: a triple murder with a copy of the same lottery ticket in the mouth of one of the victims. I'm talking to their DS, and I think we need to get together, soon. I've talked to my DCI, who's agreed to be the SIO, and she's looking to allocate a DI to lead a HMET. I'll be in touch when I know more."

The call ended and Williams rocked back in his chair. All feelings of fatigue were gone.

Chapter 25

The Broker pursed his lips and steepled his fingers in front of his mouth as he looked up from the piece of folded paper that was laid on the desk in front of him. One of his thugs sat on the other side of the desk, and he knew not to talk while his boss was contemplating. Eventually, The Broker had considered all the options.

"Do you trust him?" he asked. The thug knew this was as much a threat as it was a question. If he said yes and it went wrong, he would be held responsible for a failure of judgement. Say no, and if someone else took a payment that The Broker could have banked, you'd be held responsible for the loss. He drew a deep breath, swallowed hard, and then nodded.

"Yes, boss. His financials check out, and Bobby Messina tells me that he puts some of his income through him. If Bobby does, I'm happy to back the call." He then sat back and waited. He had done his research and, as far as you could trust anyone nowadays, the prospective client was a sensible bet.

"Have we got his deposit?" asked The Broker.

"Yes, boss," replied the man.

"And he knows it's non-refundable, even if I decide not to take your advice?"

"He does, boss, yes. He seems pretty determined to get things started."

The Broker pondered his options one more time before saying, "I get worried by anyone who is 'determined to get things started'. It's a sign of impatience and therefore a risk." He paused again before smiling and confirming his decision. "But it seems a good opportunity. Well done." The thug smiled and rose from his chair, about to leave. Without looking up, The Broker added, "Oh, and send Bobby something nice for his time and advice."

"Already popped a box of Cohiba Behike 52s across, boss," replied the man, smiling broadly. The Broker stopped what he was doing, looked up and frowned. A whole box of his favourite and most expensive cigars – for a reference? The thug kept smiling, though. "Bobby also gave us the tip-off about that professor you were looking for. I thought the cigars might be appropriate."

"And where is the professor now?" enquired The Broker, implicitly acknowledging that the gift was indeed appropriate.

"Tom and Jerry are bringing him in," said the man.

Tom and Jerry were the names given to a couple of The Broker's thugs who always liked to work together. They had been looking for the professor for several weeks without success. A lecturer at the local university, he owed £20,000 in gambling debts to some very unsavoury people but had gone missing mid-semester. The Broker had been offered £20,000 if he found and taught the errant professor a lesson, whether any of their original money was recovered or not. The people that the professor was in debt with felt a beating would send out the right message: there were severe consequences if you disrespected them. A message far more important than regaining the money itself.

"When they arrive, take him to the visitor's room. I'll be down to talk to him personally after I've made this call."

"Of course, boss." The man left the office, smiling wryly. No one should ever look forward to a personal chat with The Broker. Tom and Jerry would take the professor down to the cellar, known as the visitor's room because nobody stayed there very long. His time in there would be brutal. The Broker waited until the door had closed, then he leant forwards and picked up the piece of folded paper. A mobile phone number was scribbled on it.

"This better be a burner phone," he mumbled to himself as he flipped open his own secure mobile and punched the number in, his eyes flitting from his keypad to the number written on the paper and back. When it started ringing, he screwed the paper up and dropped it into an ashtray. He pulled a lighter from his desk and set fire to the paper. As he watched the flames dance, the call connected.

"I believe you've been waiting to hear about a Friends Reunited enquiry? It's been passed to me to deal with, so how can I help?" said The Broker.

"I need you to find me the current name and home address for my long-lost half-sister. I can tell you where she worked and that she used the pseudonym of SILK," replied Niall Fitzgerald.

"And why would I want to help you find her?"

"Because I'll be paying £25,000 for complete and accurate information."

There was a short pause before The Broker answered, "Give me 48 hours."

Chapter 26

The last few months had been both difficult and encouraging for Evie. Some days she would feel the despair, fear, and self-loathing rising to consume her, sparked perhaps by drunken voices as she scurried past a wine bar on a rare trip out. Then there were the good days when she felt she could conquer her fears and live her new life to the full. On those days, she would go for a long drive in her Lotus or perhaps do a little shopping. The discussion with Charles Wagstaff a couple of days ago had been a good day, and this morning, she had awoken feeling refreshed and confident. After a light breakfast and a shower, she intended to have a relaxing morning, sipping freshly made coffee and sitting in the sunshine, wearing just a lightweight waffle robe. Last night, she had spread out all the documents and photographs from the first package Materia Prima had sent, as well as her existing notes and evidence. As she walked past them, she paused. Glancing at the pile of documentation, she smiled triumphantly. There were individual profiles on several of the men compiled by the private investigators. Bank statements showed significant cash withdrawals or transfers around the date of her appointments and personal emails from what she assumed were hacked accounts.

"Hardly legal, but who cares. Fuck the lot of you," she said to herself in a grim tone. "Soon, you'll all understand the price you'll pay for what you've done to me." She raised her large mug of coffee as if saying 'cheers'. She was about to walk up the steps to the rooftop garden when the doorbell rang.

Evie sighed and placed her mug on the desk as she looked over the balcony towards the door. She started down towards the kitchen, but as she reached the bottom step, she unexpectedly froze. In the past, the doorbell was usually a welcome sound, announcing friends who had come to visit or a courier delivering the latest fashion releases from Milan. Today, however, it did not feel like a welcome sound. She wasn't expecting anything or anyone, and the paranoia began to rise inside her. The doorbell rang again, and her fear of the unknown swamped every nerve in her body. Her brain was screaming for her to hide, but it was as if her body was paralysed, unable or unwilling to take another step. Her heart began to race and her breathing became rapid. As she gripped the metal handrail, her knuckles turned white with exertion.

"Move," she said. Her rasping voice reprimanding herself for allowing the paranoia to resurface, but nothing happened. She clenched her jaws, tight. "I said move, damn it," she growled through gritted teeth. She could feel her determination starting to burn through her hesitation and slowly she forced herself to take a faltering step.

"That's it. Now, come on; another one." Her grip eased slightly, and she stepped down onto the kitchen floor. One step became two, and soon she was steadily making her way towards the front door. She could see the faint silhouette of someone's head and shoulders through the frosted glass portal in the door.

"Hi," she said tentatively, her voice trembling slightly. "Can you leave it outside? I'm not properly dressed yet." There was no reply. Evie bit her lip as she wondered why the person didn't respond.

"Hey, can you hear me? I'm not dressed, and I'm not going to open the door. If you can't leave it, then please just send it back," she said louder. Her tone now had a tinge of pleading, but there was still no response.

"Can you please just leave the parcel?" She was shaking but started to smile and whimper in relief as she watched the silhouette turn and fade out of sight. The tension in her body eased, but the silhouette suddenly loomed at the portal again and rapped on the door. Her heart leapt. Her eyes grew wide with fear, and she looked around the kitchen for a knife. She grabbed one from a block on the kitchen island, but her hands were shaking so much that the block and the rest of the knives toppled over and clattered to the floor. She snapped her head around just in time to see the silhouette raise a fist and knock on the door again, this time even harder. Had the person heard the knives clattering to the floor?

"He's not going away, so just open the door," she told herself as she tensed her body and held the knife behind her back. She slid back the bolts and unlocked the door but left the security chain on. She turned the handle, ready to jump back to give her time and space to use the blade if she needed to. As she opened the door, she ensured the scar on the left side of her face remained out of sight. Shaking with fear, she peered through the gap but then sighed in relief. A courier was standing on her doorstep, earphones in and quietly humming along to a tune, nodding his head gently in rhythm. He looked up, slightly startled.

"Oh hey, sorry. Didn't see you there. New Papercut track; it's awesome," he said, pulling his earphones out and pausing the music on his phone. "Miss Perry? I have a package that needs signing for." He reached into his courier's sack and pulled out a large manilla envelope like the one Evie had received before. As she reached round the door to take the envelope, her wrap parted, and her slender, tanned right leg was showing up to near the top of her thigh.

"Sorry; caught me as I was about to go into the shower. Not decent," she said as she noticed the man glance down. "Do you need me to sign something?" she enquired, breaking the man's concentration. As she spoke, she slid the carving knife into the belt at the back of her robe.

"Wh… er… oh, sure. Yeah. Sorry," replied the courier, his cheeks pinking slightly as he realised that he'd been caught staring.

"Thank you," said Evie as she took the device from the man's hand, signed her name, and handed it back to him.

"Sh… sure," said the courier, who took one more fleeting glance at her long, slender leg before turning and walking back down the steps. As she watched the courier climb back onto his bicycle, she glanced down the street. Did she just see a man in a car lower a camera's telescopic lens?

"Come on," she said to herself, "don't let the imagination demons back in," so she went up to her bathroom cupboard to get a couple of herbal anti-anxiety tablets. As she swallowed them, the man with the camera checked the photos he had taken of her.

"That'll do nicely," he said to himself as he picked up his phone and sent a text to his client.

Chapter 27

It had been 48 hours since Stella Kendrick had heard her husband's voice on the answering machine. She had played the short message over and over. The earlier messages on the answering machine had been from a David Holding, apparently an ex-business acquaintance of her husband's. Holding had left his contact details and been quite clear that he was only available on Thursdays and Fridays. The wait had been excruciating, but at exactly 9am on a Thursday, she picked up her new mobile phone and slowly dialled the number. It rang three times before she heard a gruff voice on the other end.

"Yes?" the voice enquired.

"Mr Holding? Mr David Holding?"

"Who is this?" came a hesitant reply.

"This is Stella Kendrick, Robert's wife." She had meant to say widow, but having heard Robert's voice just a couple of days ago, she absent-mindedly said 'wife'. Holding didn't pick up on it, though, or at least he didn't say anything if he had noticed.

He stayed quiet for a few seconds and then replied, "How do I know it's really you?"

"Well, you left four voice messages for Robert on 023..." she started to say, but he interrupted her.

"Don't!" he snapped. "You don't know who's listening. I know Robert made the number ex-directory and the CLI as secure as is technically possible, so let's not make it any easier than it needs to be."

"Make what easier?" Stella asked curiously.

"Finding where you are," he replied in a flat, ominous tone. The statement sent a sudden shiver down Stella's spine. She had never even considered that she might be in any sort of danger. Was someone really looking for her?

"So, what now?" she enquired.

"We meet, we talk, and then we never see each other again."

"Where and when?"

"Listen very carefully. You might want to write this down."

"Just let me get a pen and paper," she replied, reaching inside the desk drawer. "Ready."

"Where you live, there is a god-like head of the maths faculty. She uses her time to find people who are whacky-baccy-free, to help out in a historic location she studies in. The problem is it's been sold, and the next owner, Freya, likes Pu-erh an hour after a new day dawns." Then there was a click as Holding ended the call. Stella initially found it hard to concentrate, let alone comprehend the situation she found herself in, but as she gathered her thoughts and her composure, she started to analyse what Holding had told her. She was pleased she had written it down.

"The '*head of the maths faculty*' means I need to use the '*m*' from '*maths*' to start a word, and '*she also uses*' means I must add '*uses*' to the '*m*'; 'Muses'. If the person was god-like, maybe that's a reference to the Greek gods known as the Muses of Mount Parnassus? Okay; now we're getting somewhere," she said, happy to be able to unscramble the start of the clue. "The name Freya relates to one of the Germanic gods, which is what gives Friday its name. And if the *next* owner of the historic location is called Freya, he must want to meet me *next Friday*." Stella clenched her fist in self-encouragement. She couldn't help but smile because she was sure Robert had suggested Holding use a cryptic clue.

"The use of the word '*whacky*' means the next word or, in this case, the hyphenated words, are anagrams. So, '*baccy-free*'..." She started to scribble down the possible solutions. That was when she remembered an advert she had seen in a local paper. The paper itself seemed a waste of time, mainly adverts, which is how she assumed they paid for the printing and distribution, so she had thrown it in the pedal bin. She pushed her chair back and went into the kitchen. After throwing the paper away, she had subsequently tipped the leftovers from her lunch on top of it, so when she eased it out of the bin, there were some baked beans and leftover grilled tomatoes dripping off it. She gently laid the paper on the small Formica kitchen table and thumbed through it. Three pages in, she found it:

Under new management. Welcome to Clio's Bar. Open 8am until noon, and 6pm until midnight. By day, we sell coffee and cake (and offer free wi-fi to those who want to use it). By night, we are the bar you have been waiting for: sophistication, subtle music and ambience (with no wi-fi, because evenings are for talking, not typing).

Stella flopped onto a chair; she had cracked the puzzle and knew where to go, and when. "Clio; Greek goddess of history and one of the nine Muses of Mount Parnassus. The anagram of baccy-free? Cyber-café. I'll be there an hour after it opens."

Chapter 28

The visitor's room was a dank cellar with a single naked light bulb hanging from the concrete ceiling, and a very frightened man sat on one of two chairs. Tom and Jerry stared at him, emotionless but nevertheless menacing, given their stature. One of the thugs, Jerry, heard footsteps, and he opened the door so The Broker could step into the room.

"Well, well, Professor. It seems you've been leading some very important people I know on a merry dance," he said as he sat down on a chair opposite the man. "And these people don't have time to dance." The professor stared back, battling to hide his fear.

"I swear I was about to call them. You see, I have most of the money, and the rest will be easy to come by now." His voice was wavering, and when he looked into The Broker's eyes, he saw no reaction that suggested there would be any compassion. The Broker stood.

"My client is no longer concerned about the money, Professor. You've set a bad example, and should others be encouraged to follow your example; well, we'd just have chaos. They don't even want their money back now. They just want to send a message to anyone thinking of following the same path as you."

The professor began to tremble. His eyes skittered from side to side as his brain fought the rising panic. There must be something he could do or say? "Well, maybe... what if I gave you the money I have? You could tell them you taught me a lesson, and I barely survived the beating. I swear, I would leave the country and never go near another casino."

The Broker gave a single snort of derision as he turned to look at Tom and Jerry. They smirked back in unison. They had heard this appeal from many others before the professor, but the end result was always the same. This glance from their boss was the signal for them to slowly walk over and stand either side of the professor.

"No, Professor. I'm afraid that just wouldn't work. You see, my reputation is built on results and keeping my promises, and I've promised that I'll deliver the result they want." The Broker bent over to put his face inches from the professor's. "And this isn't the first time you've been warned, is it?" The man's eyeballs bulged and his mouth opened, ready to scream, but Tom wrapped a bulging forearm across the professor's mouth, and Jerry threw a sweeping left hook to his gut. The man crumpled and fell to the floor, still tied to the chair. This was the start of what Tom and Jerry did best. The Broker watched for a few seconds as the duo lifted the man back up and then took turns to beat his face into a bloody pulp, before walking out of the room and closing the door behind him.

Twenty minutes later, as he sat behind his desk, Tom knocked on the open door.

"Is it done?" asked The Broker.

"It is."

Despite the career he had chosen, The Broker still felt a twinge of sadness when a life had to be taken. The professor was probably a decent man, sharing his knowledge and insights with eager young minds at the university. Addiction was a cruel mistress, and no matter how much people tried to support addicts, sometimes it just kept eating them up from the inside.

"How much did he actually have?"

"Five grand. He kept telling us he had a sure-fire bet that would double it, but I guess they all say that, right, boss?" Without looking up, The Broker let out a long slow breath and gave a resigned nod.

"Oh, and he kept saying this could be worth millions in the right hands," added Tom as he placed a bound document on the desk. "It's all geek stuff to me, but you're a smart guy, boss. Maybe you'll understand it." The Broker looked up and reached out for the document.

"Split the five grand with Jerry. You boys deserve a little extra."

"Thank you, boss. We really appreciate it." Tom then almost ran out of the office. The Broker smiled at the response. They were thugs who, if he asked, would do anything out of loyalty, no matter how sickening the act might be. And yet these men, probably with more biceps than brain cells, had the biggest hearts and the simplest of needs. The Broker opened the document Tom had left and began reading.

"A Summary of my Doctoral Thesis, by..." but the name of the author had been covered in thick, black marker pen. "Fighting Data Security in A Digital World, Where Data is More Valuable Than Money," he said, reading the cover out loud. He pulled a face as this was surely the most boring subject he could think of. There were so many news articles nowadays on hacking and data breaches, with experts appearing in the media explaining how they knew something like this would happen. He shook his head but continued reading to see what the student had written.

"Probably got a good grade for this nonsense, too," he scoffed, but after five minutes he was mildly intrigued. After 15 minutes, he was enthralled.

The future threats from data hacking will not be from an attack on a company that holds a million records but from quietly hacking a billion personal devices without anyone realising that every financial transaction, every element of data they share, and their online identity itself is being harvested. The value of data is ten-fold that of actual money. Money can be spent once, whereas data can be sliced and used for multiple purposes. The military have the means to access all modern smartphones and any device connected to the internet but, to date, organised crime does not. This is because the digital industry is complying with government requests, which allow controlled access. But there is a way a personal digital device could be hijacked. I will now postulate how and what must be done to avoid it.

He breathlessly turned from page 25 and got to... page 28.

"What?"

He flicked back through the report and then on to the end. A 30-page report, but two pages were missing. He was about to curse in anger when the phone rang. It was the woman with the disguised voice again.

"Well done for delivering your commitments," she whispered.

"You had doubts?" he said, a seething tone still in his voice after the disappointment of the report.

"Not really, but it's always satisfying to see a job well done." She had no time for his emotion, or interest in why he sounded so irritated. "The police will be clueless, so I want to give them some more dots to try to join together."

"Same price?" checked The Broker.

"Same price and same deliverables," the caller said. "I've forwarded the information and payment." The phone line went dead. He turned to his secure laptop to read more about her request and to assess who best to call. He remained indifferent to the motive. This was a business transaction, that was all. He'd been dealing in illegal enforcement and death for over 20 years, although his wife and children didn't know anything about it. To them, he was just a busy import-expert specialist. He picked up his secure phone to call the people he trusted. The first call was answered by a woman.

"Yes?" she said before he heard her shout to someone, "Not now, sweetie. Mummy is just talking to a friend. Go put Disney on because it's nearly time for *Aladdin*." A tiny cheer could be heard, and a child's footsteps racing across a wooden floor. There was a pause, and then the woman mumbled, "I'm dying here with this shit. Tell me there's a present coming."

The Broker smiled. He knew the role the woman had to play during the day and how she yearned for the kind of work she was good at, which was a long way from watching animated movies with pre-schoolers. "Usual channel. Delivery this week. A solid fifty," he added, meaning £50,000.

"Yes!" came the excited but hushed reply. He could almost imagine her fist-pumping the air before she called out to the child again, but with a tinge of exasperation in her voice this time.

"I know. I *said* Mummy is coming..." followed by a whispered, "... for fuck's sake." She hung up and would now be watching the movie, while all the time wanting the child to fall asleep so she could log on to her secure device.

The rest of the calls were brief, so he could end the morning thinking about the £800k he had just agreed and the £600k profit that he'd made. Crime really did pay.

Chapter 29

"I'm really not that interested in knowing the details," Niall said, wriggling uncomfortably in his chair as they sat and ate breakfast.

"Well, if you want us to rebuild our relationship, we ought to talk about these things. They are, after all, important to me," Yvonne replied. "We used to talk about *everything*." Her emphasis on the word 'everything' caused Niall to pause, his fork halfway towards his mouth. He knew what she meant, and yes, they used to talk about every aspect of life, but that felt a long time ago. He shook his head ever so slightly, as he knew he was going to give in despite his instinct telling him he would regret it. He slowly lowered his fork, placing it back on his plate, and then dabbed the corners of his mouth with a napkin. He sat back and looked up at her. She was trying to look nonchalant as she ate another portion of the breakfast that she'd so carefully prepared.

"Okay, so tell me about the session with the therapist. What gems did she uncover?" There was a gentle sarcastic tone when he emphasised the word '*gems*'.

"If that's your attitude, I don't see the point of talking about it at all. I'm trying to rediscover what we had, Niall," retorted Yvonne. She looked back down at her plate, but he could see disappointment on her face. She was the one who had withdrawn all affection, even though he showered her with increasingly extravagant gifts. In fact, the bigger the gift, the more she seemed to suggest he was trying to buy her affection. Eventually he had given up trying, but he now missed what they had. The last week or so had been reminiscent of the old days; they had slept together every night since the police told them about the Lowe family murders, and had sex on most of them. And now here they were, eating breakfast and, despite the secret challenges he was facing, she was making a real effort to repair the damage.

"I'm sorry," Niall said. "You're right, and I reacted inappropriately. Please, tell me all about it." He watched as Yvonne pondered his response, but she then put her fork down and became very animated.

"Well," she started, brushing her hair away from the side of her face and gesticulating with her hands as she began to recount the meeting. "The other day was the second session I've had with her. She started to ask questions about my family, your family, and I told her about your upbringing, which, let's face it, was very different from mine. '*Opposites attract*' she said, which is possibly true."

"How much did you talk about my upbringing?"

"Not much. I mentioned how your father was tough and how, sometimes, you turned to your mother when you had a really difficult situation to resolve, like you used to turn to me."

"Hmm, not sure I'm entirely happy about how open you are about my personal life, but if you feel it's helping. What's her name? Maybe I should consider talking to her?"

"I have her card in my handbag; one minute." She reached down for the bag, enthused by his apparent interest.

"Unusual for you to have a handbag at the breakfast table. Are you going somewhere?" he asked.

"I am, yes; straight after breakfast," replied Yvonne. She passed the business card over to Niall and then reached back into her handbag, pulling out a small makeup bag. "I'm going to meet Alix. She promised me coffee, gossip, and a morning of shopping." Yvonne opened the makeup bag and took out some lip paint and a brush.

"Not seen that makeup bag before; looks very nice, very expensive," commented Niall, and he raised an eyebrow.

"Mm, it's new," mumbled Yvonne, and she dabbed her lips dry before getting ready to apply the lip paint. "It arrived yesterday in a gift box. No idea who sent it; there was no card or return address, but it's divine and had this lip paint in it as well," she explained as she lifted the lip paint up to her eyes to read the writing on the case. "It's bright red and called... *Blood & Silk*."

Niall coughed and spluttered into his napkin, apparently choking on his coffee.

Chapter 30

The court case started just two weeks ago, and already the trial seemed to be fast approaching its conclusion. As Daniella Maddox lay in bed with a large tequila in her hand and several already in her stomach, she reflected on what had happened and where it had gone wrong. The prosecution had called their expert witness, Professor Gary Hibberd, who for the last 18 months had been helping Interpol lay the foundations for the demise of Dennis Ruiz. Hibberd was asked to take the stand by the prosecution's barrister.

"Could you begin by telling the court who you are and the background to your investigation?"

"Certainly. My name is Professor Gary Hibberd, and I am CEO of Cyber Samurai Inc. I've worked in the cybersecurity industry for 20 years and have recommendations from the CEOs and the CIOs of 67 of the FTSE 100. I've worked with the police, and I'm currently advising Her Majesty's Government on a number of cyber-related working groups."

"And is it reasonable to say you are one of the top cybersecurity specialists in the United Kingdom?"

"Objection, Your Honour," said Maddox. "Counsel is asking the witness to speculate."

"I agree," said the judge. "Mr Savista, you know the rules."

"Yes, Your Honour. My apologies," said the prosecuting barrister. "Professor Hibberd, please explain to the court what you have found through your investigation into the defendant."

"On August 3rd 2017, I received a request from Interpol to research an online organisation known as 'BOrg'. They had been investigating the organisation for several years. It was alleged to be involved in ransomware activities. That's where software is maliciously installed onto a computer system, and the victim is blackmailed into paying a ransom. If they don't agree, the threat is all their data will either be published on the internet or their access to the data will be perpetually blocked. Some very sophisticated operators, like BOrg, prefer what is known as crypto viral extortion. It encrypts the victim's files until a decryption fee is paid via Bitcoin or other difficult-to-trace digital currencies. Interpol said they had information from credible sources that there might be a 'red thread' back to the person heading the operation. I was asked to complete some analysis, an initial summary, and provide a series of recommendations."

"For the benefit of the court, Professor, can you explain what a 'red thread' is, please?"

"The term 'red thread' is a link from each crime, back through the tiers of independent hackers, the mule manager; that's the person who ensures top class hackers are recruited, to the finance coordinator who ensures they are paid, all the way up to the head."

"Please explain to the court what red thread you found," asked the barrister, who turned to the judge. "If I may, we'd like to use exhibit 14A/3, Your Honour. The diagram will help explain the *red thread*."

"Would the clerk of the court please set up exhibit 14A/3," instructed the judge. A large easel was set up, and an A1-sized landscape graphic covered with a lightweight sheet was placed on it. The clerk set the display up to face the jury, with the judge and counsels having their own paper copy. Hibberd stepped down from the stand and addressed the court.

"Your Honour, this chart represents the 'red thread'; from when the accused resigned from his job as a systems and networks architect at Ram-Jam Technologies through to his arrest." He pulled the sheet off the diagram, revealing a colourful chart. Ruiz watched, slumped in his chair and apparently uninterested in the proceedings.

"This chart has been validated by Interpol and was shared with both counsels several weeks ago." Everyone glanced over towards Maddox, who responded with a dispassionate nod. She knew the chart offered little chance to challenge Hibberd or the prosecution's case. Hibberd picked up an extendable pointer and started his story.

"Dennis Ruiz worked in the antivirus team at Ram-Jam Technologies, until 2010. His role gave him an excellent insight into the inner workings of how such software operates and how best to circumnavigate the defences. Mr Ruiz was already a regular member of hacker group chat rooms, but he became a regular contributor on the 4Chan site: a site where, among other things, like-minded techies would discuss vulnerabilities. His views and insights began to garner respect, and some members gravitated towards his views on companies who refused to install even the most basic levels of security."

"How do the authorities keep track of such things, Professor Hibberd?" asked the judge inquisitively.

"The authorities set up fake accounts on various sites, Your Honour. These accounts are what's known as 'sock-puppets' and help them keep tabs on particular people, keywords, or topics." Hibberd paused for a sip of water and glanced over at Maddox, silently offering her the opportunity to challenge his opening statement. She didn't rise to the challenge, though, despite Ruiz whispering something into her ear. She didn't even turn to look at Ruiz as she dismissively shook her head. She knew she had to pick her fights in this case carefully.

The judge looked perplexed. "Mr Hibberd, this might be the first cybercrime case for some members of the jury. Please explain what you mean by 'the authorities' you referenced."

"My apologies, Your Honour. We geeks can get carried away sometimes," replied an apologetic Hibberd. It created a ripple of laughter across the jurors at his self-deprecation, removing a little of the barrier of formality between them. It was a tactic Hibberd was very adept at. He suppressed a smile and continued:

"The police, Interpol, and government agencies are the authorities I'm referring to. Sometimes they have to play the same game as the lawbreakers to catch them out. The 4Chan site spawned a loose collection of rules and aphorisms and, depending on whom you ask, they are either not meant to be taken seriously or are very serious indeed. Rule 29 states: '*On the internet, men are men and women are also men, and all kids are undercover FBI agents.*' That is to say, there is no trust on the internet and law enforcement are experts at exploiting that mistrust and suspicion. It's difficult, therefore, to get close and lay traps that tag certain people, so their activity can be monitored." Heads nodded at this explanation, and members of the jury were looking at each other as they quietly expressed their understanding. Maddox saw this and knew she needed to interrupt the flow of the presentation.

"Objection, Your Honour. Professor Hibberd has just described the use of entrapment and misrepresentation. I'd like to ask for a mistrial." It was a long shot, but Maddox had to try it.

"Denied, Miss Maddox. Professor Hibberd, please be careful in your explanations as there is a fine line to tread between informing the jury and guiding them," explained the judge.

"My apologies, Your Honour," replied Hibberd. Maddox knew that her objection was necessary, but it was clearly unpopular with a jury that was warming to Hibberd. She could tell by their disrespectful glances towards her. She knew she was in danger of creating a wall between her and them that didn't previously exist.

"You may proceed, Professor Hibberd."

"Thank you, Your Honour," said Hibberd before turning back to the jury. "Ladies and gentlemen, my apologies. Allow me to continue."

For the next hour, he walked the jury through the trail of evidence he and his team had uncovered. It demonstrated how Ruiz had garnered support for his actions by trying to emphasise that they were simply helping to show companies the error of their ways. He even played a video of Ruiz espousing his views from the dark web. On it he was saying, *"Companies make money out of data: data that belongs to the people. We are teaching them a valuable lesson. They are not the victims*." Hibberd then showed how Ruiz had started with 12 other like-minded hackers, but in just thirteen months, he had over 100 working for his organisation, which he had inexplicably named BOrg. Ruiz hired a finance specialist with experience in money laundering and a mule manager who recruited and looked after the team. Everyone who joined was given $1,000,000 immediately, even before they had delivered anything. That, and the promise of high-powered lawyers should any of them be arrested, drove immense loyalty among the hackers.

He concluded by detailing the end-to-end trail, the red thread from the attacks by hackers to the Bitcoin payments that companies and high-worth individuals made. He showed that payments were traced to a partner at 'Thoresen, Fitzgerald & Holding'. As part of a plea deal, Thoresen had already admitted he had been managing their finances. It was difficult for him to deny, given the police had recovered hundreds of emails he thought he had erased from his company computer. The email trail led to a security company operating out of India, which was solely owned by Dennis Ruiz.

"And how did you manage to turn people against my client?" challenged Maddox on cross-examination.

"We recommended Interpol programmers, who were inside the illegal hackers' chat room, start a rumour that Ruiz's group was, in fact, law enforcement, trying to infiltrate their network and get them arrested. With the levels of mistrust and jealousy among Mr Ruiz's competitors, they quickly spread the word. A bounty was announced across the dark web, payable to whoever could identify the man or woman behind BOrg."

"So, entrapment was used?" reiterated Maddox. "You created the situation where my client, a legitimate businessman, acted in self-defence by going onto the dark web to protect his reputation? You planted lies, bribed criminals, and fabricated a campaign to defame him?" Maddox was using rhetorical questions to push the boundaries, but she had to try to fight back.

"Miss Maddox, please refrain from badgering the witness," said the judge in a calm but authoritative tone. He looked over the top of his half-rim glasses to accentuate the point.

"Your Honour, I am simply trying to..." but she saw him tilt his head and raise an eyebrow in a 'are you challenging me?' gesture. She stopped abruptly, which made Ruiz glare at her.

"Understood, Your Honour." After the cross-examination of Hibberd concluded, it was time for the barristers to reflect on their case.

"Your Honour," started the prosecutor. "In summary, Dennis Ruiz ran an illegal operation that has blackmailed over $1.7 billion from legitimate companies and individuals of high net worth; simply because they misunderstood the value of, and the risk associated with, the data they held. Interpol had credible advice that he was about to move into a new area of fraud, where millions of people were to be his new target rather than companies. That's when—"

And that was the moment that Ruiz had launched himself at the prosecuting barrister. That was the moment Maddox knew she had lost the case and probably a lot more. He had warned her at the very start of the case that her life would be in danger if she failed. As the police led Ruiz away that day, he had told her to savour her final breath.

As her moment of reflection ended, she gulped the last of the tequila. "I'm missing something. Why can't I see it?" Then, for the first time in decades, she closed her eyes and prayed for help, and for her life.

Chapter 31

The mobile phone was laid on the bedside unit. It was 5:30am when it quietly buzzed and the screen lit up. Yvonne Fitzgerald lay fast asleep next to her husband, but the sound roused Niall from a restless slumber. He gazed at her with affection before slowly and gently turning over to pick up his phone. He didn't want to wake her. The message on the screen said:

This is Friends Reunited. We have sent the information you were looking for regarding your long-lost half-sister. Please arrange payment of your membership fee.

Niall glanced behind him. His guilty conscience imagined Yvonne looking over his shoulder, about to ask who was texting so early. Thankfully, she looked to be fast asleep. He eased himself out of bed and grabbed his dressing gown before tiptoeing over to the door.

"Niall, where are you going?" came a sleepy voice.

"Just need to check the Hang Seng and Nikkei markets now they're closing. You get some more sleep. You have a few more hours before your car arrives for the airport. Rest, my darling." He smiled at how naturally those last two words sounded. Trauma had driven them apart, but now could trauma be pulling them back together again? She mumbled something back to him as she rolled over to settle back into her slumber, but it was incomprehensible. As she turned over and pulled the cotton sheets back up to her chin, he opened the door from her room and made his way downstairs to his private study. Sat at his desk, he logged onto his email account, and there was an email, purportedly from Friends Reunited. The logo, font and branding were perfect, and there was a link to what looked like their website's landing page, except it wasn't their actual website.

"Impressive," he said to himself. On clicking the link, as instructed, he was prompted to log in to the mock site using the identity and password that had been previously agreed. He was then diverted to a white screen with just one line of black text on it: *Janet Evelyn Perry. The Garage, off Old Ford Road, Bow, LONDON E3*

The loving, gentle mood Niall had felt just a few minutes ago was gone. It was replaced by a desire to stare this woman in the face and demand to know what the hell she thought she was doing. He didn't have any desire to hurt her, but he needed to frighten her enough so she would stop. He picked his phone up and replied: *My half-sister found. Finders-fee paid once reunion complete.*

The immediate reply said: *You have 14 days to pay.*

In his currently assertive mood, Niall was about to text back to say he would be paying when he was satisfied the information was worth £25 000, but another text arrived before he had even started to type. It quickly killed his confidence as it contained a photo of the battered and bloodied face of a man and the words: ... *before penalty clauses are applied for late payment.*

Chapter 32

The bonnet of the Aston Martin glinted in the late evening sunshine, but the sales manager could see where the pre-sales team had left a small smudge of polish. He knew something so tiny could mean the difference between a sale and no sale. At in-excess of £120,000 for a new Aston Martin Vantage, it was the small things that made the difference, never the price.

As it was closing time, he knew everyone else would already have left work. In a few minutes, the regular night security would arrive, and that would signal the end of the day for him. An hour later, there was still no sign of the security man. The sales manager checked his watch again and then picked up the phone; he was going to be late for a date he had.

"Hello, is that Guardian Defence? This is the Aston Martin showroom in Sighthill. Our security man hasn't shown up this evening, and I'm keen to get away on time."

"Bob, Aston Martin place in Edinburgh; who's scheduled for there tonight?" shouted the man on the other end of the phone. A mumbled voice could be heard in the background, but the sales manager couldn't discern what was being said. The man on the phone shouted back to the other person, "I thought it was him... Well, he's not called in sick that I'm aware of... What?... Oh okay, will do." He turned back to the sales manager's call. "Hello?"

"Yes, I'm still here," sighed the sales manager.

"Harry is our usual guy. Not sure what's happened; he's never missed a day that I know of, and that's in five years."

"Well, I'm sure that's very impressive, but that doesn't really help me, does it. I want to lock up and go home."

"Our manager has just called one of our other guys in. He's supposed to be off tonight, but if you can hang on for 15 to 20 minutes, he should be there." The sales manager looked at his watch. That should give him just about enough time to shower and get ready for his date.

"Fine, but it can't be any longer than 20 minutes." He put the phone down.

The despatcher, meanwhile, tried Harry Weller's mobile. It rang but then went to voicemail. "Harry, it's Dean at the office. Just calling to check you're alright, mate? You've not got any leave booked tonight and we hope you're not poorly. Give us a bell when you can. Take care."

Harry Weller was a man in his sixties. He lived alone in a one-bedroomed flat in the Magdalene district of Edinburgh. His television was on, and a pan had boiled dry on the stove, but Harry wasn't bothered. When the light on his mobile phone lit up with a text, informing him that he had missed a call and a voicemail, he didn't pick it up. He lay perfectly still on his kitchen floor, where he had been for the last few days, with his hands tied behind his back and the handle of a butcher's knife sticking out of his throat. The killer had

had to rush his usual clean-up routine, as neighbours had heard noises and were knocking at the door. Even so, once Weller had stopped convulsing, the killer had enough time to place a rolled-up piece of paper in his mouth.

Chapter 33

The first meeting between the police forces was face-to-face. DS Bob Williams had travelled down on the train from York, and DS Alan Armitage had driven across London. Introductions were made, and then Denton led them to a conference room, where DC Jones had placed three thick files on the table, one for each of them. They contained the collective case notes and SOCO reports.

"Thanks for coming in," said Denton. "I know it takes you out for a whole day, and we've all got more than enough to do, but I thought this would be the best way to start. Okay, let's open the folders and we'll work through the information we have. DC Jones..." and he gestured towards her, almost as an introduction, "...will put any relevant points we raise up on the wipe-board. DS Armitage, can we start with your case?" They all opened their files.

"The Lowe family. Mr Lowe and Mrs Lowe were shot, and their 14-year-old daughter, Amelia, had her throat cut. No witnesses to the murders of Mr and Mrs Lowe, but we have four severely traumatised teenagers who witnessed the attack on Amelia Lowe. All four confirm the attacker appeared to be male, between six-two and six-four, dressed in black, muscular, but no facial features were visible as the attacker wore a ski mask." He paused for any initial questions before carrying on:

"Derek Lowe was an accountant specialising in taxation, with a number of corporate clients as well as some wealthy individuals. No criminal record, no debts other than a monthly credit card bill that he always paid off in full. There's no mortgage on the house. He has no known association with any criminals. Theft doesn't appear to be a motive, and the only clue we have so far is a photocopy of a lottery ticket, which forensics confirmed was placed in Mrs Lowe's mouth after she was dead. We've subsequently taken both the paper and digital files from Mr Lowe's home and business addresses for analysis but, thus far, we've found nothing that would indicate a motive for the attack."

"What about the wife and daughter; anything there?" asked Williams.

"Nothing. Mrs Lowe was a housewife, and even though the daughter had a reputation for being a bit of a bitch to the less popular girls at school, there's nothing that would warrant this."

"No clues as to who, from informants or any profiling?" enquired Denton.

Armitage shook his head. "Nothing from our networks, nothing to profile against, and no trace material at the scene but, given the specialised weapon used and the speed with which it all took place, it looks like a professional job."

"So, someone had a grudge perhaps? Maybe Lowe cost them a lot of money with some bad advice?"

"We're looking into it, but so far everyone has seemed legitimately shocked. We have a couple of guys from the Met fraud squad helping, but they've also found nothing so far. A friend of Mr Lowe has provided a list of some close friends, and we're contacting them as quickly as possible."

"Okay," said Denton. "Yours next, Bob."

"Malcolm Walsh. Owned and managed a local convenience store in Skipton. Minor public order offence, which led to a slap on the wrist from the judge and a community service order, but that was over 10 years ago. On the morning of the murder, CCTV shows him being approached by a man of similar build to the assailant described by the four girls, but we can't confirm it's the same person. The CCTV shows the assailant pushing Mr Walsh to the floor, and forensics say he died as a result of a fractured skull and brain lesion." Williams then looked across to Denton. "What about your two?"

"First victim was Peter Brown. Ran a motor repair shop and hired youths with juvie records to give them a second chance. Well-known by local officers and well-liked in the community. Seemingly regular guy with regular money worries, but nothing excessive. His body was found in the motor repair workshop. Someone had tied him to a drill press and put a hole in the back of his skull. No trace at the scene, but..." and he flicked over to a recent addition to the file, "... forensics found a high dosage of flunitrazepam in his bloodstream; a drug more commonly known as Rohypnol. It was also found in a partially drunk mug of coffee, and a large dose had been mixed into a newly opened jar of instant coffee they found in the small kitchen area at the garage. Apparently, Mr Brown never started work without at least two coffees every day."

"The date-rape drug?" asked Armitage.

"Yes. The samples suggest it could have been an 8mg dose, so he would have been disoriented within minutes and easily overcome physically. It's odourless and tasteless, so unless he looked inside the coffee jar and spotted the crushed powder, he would never have known."

"Was Brown heavy or slim? Tall or small?" asked Armitage.

"Oh, he was quite tall and thick-set, so if your question is, would it take a powerfully built man of six-two or six-four to handle him? Yes, but we have no evidence to suggest it was someone similar to the assailant described in the previous two murders or that there was just one person involved," replied Denton.

"But it's a thought," added Williams.

"It is," agreed Denton. The team paused for a few seconds, quietly reflecting on the facts they had shared. Denton broke the silence:

"And then there's William Curtis, a wealthy diplomat-turned-advisor. He had no debts; in fact, he had several million in the bank. He was highly respected and highly regarded in ministerial circles, with a lot of business contacts over in the Middle East. He was found at his office in Westminster. Forensics..." but Armitage interrupted him.

"William Curtis?"

"Yes," replied Denton. "Why?"

"Odd coincidence, but that's the name of a friend of Derek Lowe."

"I don't suppose you have Brown or Walsh on that list, do you?" asked Denton. Armitage shook his head. "Well, maybe there's another link. I'll get DC Jones to send you the information we have on Curtis."

"Thanks."

Denton resumed. "Forensics confirmed that while he had a head trauma, cause of death was actually asphyxiation. Apparently, wet rawhide was tied around his throat, and it constricted as it dried. If he was conscious, it would have been excruciating."

Based in London, Denton had investigated plenty of murders, but usually there was a clear motive: sometimes it would be a gangland turf war, a jealous spouse, or an armed robbery, but these all seemed different. Throughout these discussions and descriptions, Jones had been compiling a list of details on a wipe-board. Denton's moment of contemplation was broken as she subtly cleared her throat. He looked up and said, "Jones, what have we got on the board so far?" She stood aside and let them look.

- *4 of 6 victims are male: 2 knew each other*
- *3 different police jurisdictions*
- *Lottery ticket in mouth at every scene*
- *No trace at the scenes. Professional hit?*
- *Theft does not appear to be a motive*

"What can you tell us about the lottery ticket, DC Jones?" said Armitage.

"Ticket was for a draw made on 29th April 2017. £10m jackpot," she replied.

"Do we know if the date on the ticket has any relevance to the victims?" asked Williams.

"It doesn't seem to. We're still looking, but date of birth and national insurance numbers certainly don't." The room went quiet before Jones spoke again. "DS Williams, you made an interesting observation in his notes on the Walsh murder; page two?" They all looked over to Williams.

"It was only a theory, but Malcolm Walsh lived and worked at number 29 and..." He checked the notes he'd just made before adding, "... Brown's home address is number 36."

"What about the other two?" asked Denton, but Armitage shook his head.

"The Lowe house had no number. Properties on that street are just known by names. Maybe it had one originally, but all the properties around there have been redeveloped beyond recognition."

"And Curtis?" he asked, looking at Jones.

"William Curtis was found in his office at 52 Horseferry Road. He had an apartment nearby, but that's number 12a." The room fell silent as they all looked through the files once again. Denton began to flick from one file to another, scribbling on a notepad. He ripped the sheet out and passed it to Jones.

"Jones, write these up on the board and let's fill in the blanks; see if my logic is right. DS Armitage, what's the postcode for Harpenden?"

"Harpenden is St Albans, so AL5," Armitage responded.

"And Skipton is what, Bob?" Denton had an eagerness in his tone and dispensed with formality.

"It's classed as Bradford: BD23," replied Williams.

"My two murders were reported in Dartford and Westminster: that's DA and SW," said Denton. Jones added the information to the board and then stood back. She gazed at it for a while and then asked, "Is that just a coincidence?"

- *4 of 6 victims are male: 2 knew each other*
- *3 different police jurisdictions*

- *Lottery ticket in mouth at every scene*
- *No trace at the 3 scenes. Professional hit?*
- *Theft does not appear to be a motive*

Notes related to lottery ticket
| ?? | <u>29</u> | 12a | <u>36</u> |
| <u>AL</u> | <u>BD</u> | SW | <u>DA</u> |

"I see what you're thinking," said Williams, "but it's no more of a pattern than most of the victims are male."

Jones knew he was right but then narrowed her eyes as she tried to recall something. She started to thumb through one of the files as the three men watched, a little confused. She stopped at a particular page and ran her finger down the contents before jabbing the sheet. "There!"

"What is it?" asked Williams.

"William Curtis lived in apartment 12a, but..." she replied as she walked across to the board and rubbed something out. She picked up the marker and continued, "... the electoral roll still has his home address in Caterham, at 30 Pilgrims Lane." She stood back and let them all see what she had written. Everyone fell quiet as they stared at the board.

Armitage spoke first, "You have got to be kidding me?" He looked at the others in the room for confirmation. Their silence spoke volumes.

- *4 of 6 victims are male: 2 knew each other*
- *3 different police jurisdictions*
- *Lottery ticket in mouth at every scene*
- *Methods of murder*
- *No trace at the 3 scenes. Professional hit?*
- *Theft does not appear to be a motive*

Notes related to lottery ticket

??	<u>29</u>	<u>30</u>	<u>36</u>	46	48	7
<u>A</u>L	<u>B</u>D	<u>C</u>R	<u>D</u>A			

"Caterham has a Croydon postcode," said Denton slowly as he realised the significance of what Jones had found.

"Looks like we might have a pattern after all," said a stunned Williams.

"I'll check to see if the Lowe house has any link to the number 24," Armitage said, pulling his mobile phone from his pocket.

As Armitage began to dial, Denton said, "I'll chase the idea of the Homicide and Major Events Team with my DCI. It looks like we might have a serial killer."

Jones then interjected, "And we'd better start thinking about talking to our colleagues in postcodes beginning with E, F and G; with house numbers 46, 48 and 7. If we're right, we have three more murders to stop."

"That's a lot of houses! Where the hell do we start?" replied Williams rhetorically.

Chapter 34

Back in 2002, when Evie first read the terms of employment for a private members club called Luxe, she'd had some questions. Although she hadn't been formally trained in legal matters, she had a sharp mind and was surprisingly shrewd for someone so young.

"Okay?" the manager had asked.

"Seems to be, but what does the clause mean when it says you can accept ex-gratia payments, but only in relation to activities approved by the management of Luxe?"

"If a client wants to give you a thank-you payment for services rendered, that's fine. If they offer you goods or a holiday, you decline or you get fired."

"And, what's classed as unacceptable additional services?"

"It's everything and anything that's not in the official list of services we legally provide," the manager replied, knowing exactly where the conversation was going. "This isn't a brothel; it's a high-class and very exclusive members club which demands a £50,000-a-year membership fee before anyone can browse, let alone use, any of our very exclusive services."

The Luxe Club essentially offered three things for wealthy people: titillation without touching, as the staff they hired were all exceedingly handsome or stunningly beautiful; the hire of any of its private facilities, such as a secluded chateau in the Swiss mountains or their Italian villa at Lake Garde and, finally, they assured their members of absolute discretion and privacy, irrespective of what they did while at the club.

"Seems reasonable," she said. "Where do I sign and when do I start?"

"There, and how about tomorrow?" he suggested.

Miss Janet Evelyn Perry was stunningly beautiful. To those who knew her outside work, she was simply Evie, but at Luxe she was known by the name 'SILK'. For the next 10 years, she worked at the elite private club and took home a reasonable salary and lots of ex-gratia payments, but her real income came from providing the prohibited extras. These were charged separately, as they not only breached the club's rules but also the law. Evie didn't really care, though, as she was so popular that men and women formed a very long queue to hire her. They had the money and the desire to spend upwards of £20,000 to be with her for 24 hours, with sex included. A week with her would be £100,000 plus expenses, and she spent a lot of time travelling around the country as well going to some of the most exotic locations in the world.

When she first started providing extras, one of the more experienced women, Cheryl, had given her some advice. "Honey, they all appear to be respectable and polite, but when the wine goes down and the clothes come off, some of them are just downright primal. A few seem to forget you're a person. Before any appointment, make sure you write down all the details: who they are, plus the time and location. More importantly, make sure someone you trust knows where to find your records, just in case. Then, after the appointment, record the 'what' and the 'what not'. Not only will a repeat client be impressed you remember what they like and don't like, but it will help you remember clients you don't want to see again. There could come a time when that sort of information could save your life."

Evie had taken her advice and, just six weeks later, she was grateful she did. The third client of her career was a well-dressed gentleman with perfect manners. He opened doors for her and insisted she choose the venues where they'd meet so she felt safe. He'd listened intently to her sometimes surprisingly insightful views on world events, but just two hours later, he became a very different person. He nearly strangled Evie into unconsciousness and left her with a black eye. She knew she couldn't go to the police, but the notes she had kept meant she knew who he was and the position he held in industry. A photograph of her black eye and an email with some facts about their meeting had solicited an apparently genuine apology and a very handsome ex-gratia payment.

As she approached her twelfth anniversary of working at Luxe, she was about to become the favourite of a new client. She noticed he seemed apprehensive when he first frequented the club, but she also saw how his eyes followed some of her colleagues as they walked away after they had delivered his food or drink. There was both a clear sexual desire in his gaze, as well as a shyness that appealed to her opportunistic nature.

"Hi, want anything?" she said as she placed a menu in front of him, even though she had just seen a plate taken away from his table.

"Oh, I've just eaten," replied the man.

"What about dessert?"

"Erm, not sure. What is there?" he replied innocently. That made Evie laugh.

"You're so sweet. Hi, I'm SILK and..." and she lowered her voice as she continued, "...anything and everything is available if you ask nicely." She sensually swept the very tip of her tongue over the inside edge of her top lip. It was hardly visible unless you were looking directly at her face, but this man was transfixed by it.

"Erm," he started. His voice wavered and he dropped his gaze, so Evie sat down beside him and opened the menu, pretending to discuss the food on offer.

"Well, why don't you tell me your name and I'll give you my phone number. If you feel hungry later, for anything..." and she emphasised the word 'anything' "... I'm sure I can arrange a home delivery, if that's where you'd want it?"

"I'm... I'm Niall," he said as his confidence grew. Under the table, he tentatively put his hand on her thigh, and she neither flinched nor withdrew her leg.

"Pleased to meet you, Niall. Are you here just to relax or because you're looking for something in particular?" She dropped her hand under the table and pulled his hand closer to her crotch.

"I'm flying out to my villa in Turks next week, and I'd very much like a home delivery there, if that's possible?" he asked.

She pouted. "That's a long way away, so the delivery fee is pretty high."

"Money isn't a problem. Money will never be a problem for you and me."

Now, 16 years since that first day at Luxe, the sophisticated sensuality and self-confidence had all but disappeared. Sometimes she would find herself feeling assertive, like the visit to Materia Prima recently, but those days and that feeling were becoming increasingly rare. That's why she decided she had to turn to the one person she felt she could trust. She picked up her phone and made the call. The phone rang several times before it was answered.

"Yeah?" came the curt reply from a sleepy and irritated woman.

"Cheryl?" asked Evie. There was pause on the end of the line before the voice replied.

"Who's that?"

"It's me, Evie. You know, SILK." There was another pause before Cheryl realised who was calling.

"Hey! How ya doing?" came the weary attempt at sounding enthusiastic. "What time is it?" she asked, still laying in her bed and with her eyes struggling to open, let alone focus.

"It's a little after two," replied Evie. Cheryl slapped her own forehead.

"Already? Shit, I'm going to be late for work."

"You're working Sundays now?" a surprised Evie asked.

"It's Sunday?" Then another pause before, "Oh. In that case, I missed work yesterday." Evie let out a little giggle. She couldn't help it. She knew Cheryl regularly got stoned, but that statement was pure comedy gold. Cheryl snorted a laugh back down the line.

"So, how are you getting on?" The simple question threw Evie. Had Cheryl heard about her events of that night and now wanted to know how her plans were progressing? It was ridiculous to think so, but her growing paranoia put doubt in her mind. There was a long pause before Cheryl looked at her phone to make sure the call was still connected. She listened for another couple of seconds before saying, "You still there?"

"Yeah, I'm still here," said a suddenly subdued Evie.

Cheryl heard the change in tone and softened hers in response. "What's up? Are you in some sort of trouble?"

"I guess you could call it that and, well, I really don't have anyone else to talk to," replied Evie. She then explained to Cheryl a little of what had happened to her face and how, after the advice Cheryl had given her when Evie was starting her career in high-class escorting, she had looked at the notes she'd kept on the men involved. "I want them all to pay, but my notes don't give me any real leverage, and I'm running out of options and money. I've... started something, but I'm not sure if I can see it through." Evie knew she'd probably said too much, but she had to talk to someone.

"And what have you started?" asked Cheryl.

"I... I can't say. You'd be implicated if anything got to court. I just need them to know I'm serious."

Cheryl pondered and then probed a little further. "I remember some of the advice I gave you. If you want a working-class man's attention, you grab him by the balls. If you want a middle-class man's attention, you grab him by the wallet, but if you want a wealthy man's attention, you have to grab him by his ego. Which of those have you been doing?"

"Difficult to say," lied Evie.

Cheryl went quiet before replying, "Hmm, maybe this sort of discussion needs to be in person, not over a phone. You hear what I'm saying?"

Chapter 35

The taxi pulled up outside the towering office block. Denton and Jones climbed out and looked skywards at the summer sun shimmering across the forty-six floors of glazing on 110 Bishopgate, London.

"Can't decide who are the lucky ones," Jones said. "Those trapped inside and tied to their desks or those of us who are dealing with the murderers, never knowing the luxury of a regular job?"

"Oh, I'm sure there's plenty of back-stabbing goes on in there, and it won't just be between nine and five," replied Denton, smirking as they walked through the doors. The vast reception area of the building took up what appeared to be most of the ground floor, and it had an enormous aquarium behind the reception desks.

"Wow," exclaimed Denton.

"Impressive," said Jones, nodding.

"It's 39 feet long, 6 feet wide, and 11 feet deep: hosts 1200 fish in 15,500 gallons of water," said a man behind them. They turned to look at who was talking. "Or 12 metres by 2 metres by 3.6 metres, and 70,000 litres if you prefer the metric system. It takes two full-time attendants and three part-time divers to maintain it," he added and smiled broadly.

"Mr Fitzgerald?" asked Denton.

Niall's expression changed. "Yes. Do... we... have an appointment?" he asked them tentatively.

"No, we don't. Allow me to introduce myself; I'm Detective Sergeant Denton, and this is Detective Constable Jones. We're from the Metropolitan Police," he said, showing his warrant card.

"Is there a problem?" asked Niall.

"Perhaps we should take the conversation up to your office, Mr Fitzgerald?" suggested Denton.

The journey to the 35th floor was made in silence. People entering the lift noticed the formality of Denton and Jones, with Niall standing in the middle. He could feel their inquisitive glances without even looking at them, and as people exited the lift, he could hear hushed tones with the occasional look back at him and his police escort. When the lift arrived at the 35th floor, Niall led them to his office, mumbling something to Maria as they passed her. Her gaze followed them into Niall's office before she went to the small kitchen area to make the drinks he had just asked for.

"So, how may I help you?" he asked as Denton and Jones took their seats.

"I'm afraid we have some bad news. We're working with Detective Sergeant Armitage from Hertfordshire CID. I believe you've met DS Armitage?"

"I have, yes. He had some dreadful news about a friend."

"You provided DS Armitage with a list of names; is that correct? Men who were part of a group you called the Aeternum?" asked Jones.

"I did, yes," Niall replied with concern in his tone.

"I'm sorry to break this to you, but it appears another of your friends has been killed," explained Denton.

"Who?" gasped Niall before adding, "What happened?"

"I'm afraid I can't go into any detail as this is an active murder investigation, but I can tell you it's William Curtis." Niall closed his eyes slowly and rested his face in the palm of his hand. He let out a heavy breath as his shoulders sagged under the shock and grief.

"We were wondering if there was anything you could tell us that might help us piece together why Mr Curtis has been murdered?"

Internally, Niall's shock had turned to anger, and he wished he was face-to-face with SILK so he could vent his fury, but he continued to hold his face in his hands until he felt he was in control again. He slowly moved his hands away and pinched the bridge of his nose as if trying to stem a headache, before opening his eyes and replying.

"William and I talked intermittently, as I do with my other friends. I knew he'd been abroad for a few weeks, advising the Saudis on a trade deal. We were due to meet for lunch in a month or so; just the usual *'how are things'*-type of catch-up." He recalled a little of what Curtis had told him about the trade deal. "He did say the deal was quite controversial. Maybe there's a link between that and..." but Niall couldn't bring himself to finish the sentence.

"We'll look into it, thank you," Jones said as she wrote the information in her notebook.

"Was Mr Curtis regularly involved in controversial deals, Mr Fitzgerald?" asked Denton.

Niall thought about previous work he knew William had been involved in and replied, "Probably. He was never one to let politics or ethics get in the way of a profitable business deal." Niall then paused to reflect on how that might sound, and he felt the need to contextualise his comment. "That wasn't intended to sound how it probably did," he assured them. "William always acted with morals and ethics. Please don't think of him as unscrupulous or corrupt. That's absolutely not what I meant."

Maria appeared at the glass door and knocked. She had brought some coffee and water. Niall was grateful for the interruption and signalled her to come in just as Denton started another question about William Curtis. Drinks were poured, and she then excused herself and closed the door behind her, quickly leaning over her own desk to answer the phone.

"Iliad Investments. How may I help you?"

"Maria? It's Yvonne Fitzgerald. Is my husband available?"

"Hello, Mrs Fitzgerald. I'm afraid not." She could hear an irritated gasp from his wife, so she lowered her voice and added, "He's in his office with two police officers. He looks quite shaken to be honest, so I'm not sure it's a good time to interrupt."

"The police? Oh dear. I wonder what they want?" said a worried Yvonne.

"I think I heard them mention a Mr Curtis, but I'm not sure what the context was. I'll let your husband know you called and ask him to call you as soon as possible."

There was a short silence on the other end of the phone before Yvonne mumbled, "Thank you. Yes, that would be very helpful."

Back in Niall's office, Jones was asking about the last time Niall spoke to Curtis. Niall thought back and said, "No, he didn't sound concerned about anything. He was his usual thoughtful, considered self."

"This is a rather awkward question, and I'm afraid I can't qualify why I'm asking it, but did Mr Curtis have any business partnerships with Mr Derek Lowe, or do the names Malcolm Ireland or Peter Brown mean anything to you?" Denton asked. Niall realised the first question was to see if Derek and William's deaths could have been linked.

"Not that I'm aware of, but our group sometimes has business deals that only two or three of us are involved in or aware of, so it's possible Derek and William were mutually invested in something. It's very rare that we all collaborate. And as far as the other two names you mentioned, I'm not aware of any business deals they might have had with William or Derek, but then again, I don't really know that much about their other business relationships. I'm sorry."

"Not a problem. Er, did you have any current deals with Mr Curtis or Mr Lowe?" asked Jones.

Niall immediately shook his head. "No. I've never invested money for William. Derek was my friend and my personal accountant, and I like to keep that side of my life separate from any business dealings."

The final few procedural questions were asked and answered, and the meeting ended. Niall said he would let them know if anything came to mind that might help with their investigation and then led them back to the elevator.

As soon as the doors closed, Denton turned to Jones and said, "Something just doesn't feel quite right, Jonesy. When we get back, I want you to find out as much as you can about the murdered members of that Aeternum group, and about Niall Fitzgerald."

Chapter 36

It was a sunny Friday morning, and the local town centre was coming to life. The butcher was putting his pavement sign out, and the greengrocer had already topped up his fruit and veg display. Most of the other shops were turning their door signs from 'Closed' to 'Open' as the first customers of the day started to arrive. One of them was Stella Kendrick, who was on her way to Clio's Bar.

She had looked online the previous night to ensure she knew where she was going. She was proud of her newfound skills. In her earlier life, the thought of putting on some comfortable shoes to walk anywhere would have been completely alien. Less than a year ago, she would have paid someone to collect even the most trivial of items. Today, she was striding down the main thoroughfare and then turned down an alleyway, which led to a spacious courtyard. Around her stood eight whitewashed buildings, all of which had black doors and black window frames. Immediately to her right was Clio's Bar. As she walked in, she was surprised at how narrow the ground floor was. A serving counter took up most of the right side of the floor, with just a handful of vacant window seats off to her left.

I don't think I'll have any problem finding David Holding if he's actually coming. Stella had had a poor night's sleep, full of doubt. Had she solved the cryptic clue correctly? What if the people trying to find her also knew about the meeting?

"Can I help you, love?" said a voice. Stella turned to see a young woman smiling at her from behind the counter. The woman, around 23 or 24, had a round face and short hair that Stella thought could be best described as somewhere between 'bed hair' and 'angry hair'. A piercing on the side of the young woman's left nostril hosted a small gold loop.

"Oh, yes. I'm meeting a friend here this morning, but I'm unsure what time his train will arrive," she lied. "It's been so long since we last saw each other, I'm really not sure what he looks like anymore." She let out a short, nervous laugh.

"Well, let's get you started with a..." The woman paused as if assessing Stella. "... a Darjeeling? Or maybe a strong English Breakfast tea?" she guessed. Stella smiled back at her.

"I actually think I'll have a Pu-erh tea." The woman smiled and turned to the preparation area. Two minutes later, the tea was served, and Stella paid before turning towards one of the window seats. As she put the tray down on a tiny table, the woman behind the counter called after her.

"I think you'll find it more comfortable up on the top floor, near the bookcase. Perhaps you'll find a gentleman *holding* a travel book about France?" Stella stopped. She half-turned towards the woman to indicate she was listening, but she avoided direct eye contact.

"Thank you," Stella said before she picked up the tray and walked towards the stairs. The first floor was empty. There was plenty of seating, as well as barstools stood against a short counter. It was light and airy, with an unexpectedly high ceiling, and Stella assumed this was used primarily in the evening. As she walked further onto the floor, she looked around and saw a long balustrade on what she assumed was a mezzanine floor. She found the stairs and was about to walk up them when hesitation flooded her mind. There were butterflies dancing in her stomach. She had been through hell over the last year, and now here she was, about to take 20 or so steps to meet a man she didn't know, who might confirm where Robert was. Maybe Robert would be there, too?

She swallowed hard and, closing her eyes for a moment, mumbled to herself, "Please don't cry if Robert is here," followed by, "and don't cry if he's not." She opened her eyes, took in a deep breath, and began the short climb to the mezzanine.

Chapter 37

It had been years since the two of them had met face-to-face, but here they were, sitting in a small café just around the corner from Kings Cross Station. There were six small tables, all covered with red and white checked plastic table covers, and four chairs at each table. It didn't seem to be a popular location at that time of day, so they had the café all to themselves for now.

"Hey, how are you, lovely?" exclaimed Cheryl as she walked into the café. Evie, who had arrived early, stood and embraced her. "And what's with the super-size sunglasses and the hat?" she asked, given it was a cloudy day. Evie tried to smile back, but her face crumpled into tears, and she hung her head in embarrassment.

"Ruddy hell, what's wrong? I'm sorry; they're ace sunglasses, honest," Cheryl said apologetically.

"It's not that," mumbled Evie through her tears. "It's this," and as she raised her head, she removed her sunglasses and the hat. Cheryl couldn't help an involuntary intake of breath and a flinch. They were brief and barely audible or visible, but Evie noticed. She bit her lip to stop herself from crying again and dropped her gaze as she couldn't bring herself to look at Cheryl.

"Oh babe, I'm so sorry. It's just... oh, come here." Cheryl reached out and pulled her friend towards her giving her a long, warm embrace. She steered Evie to a corner table where she could sit with her back to everyone and everything. Cheryl took Evie's hands in her own and spoke gently.

"Listen, you have nothing to cry about. It was just my stupid reaction. Come on, how about one of those gorgeous smiles and we'll have a cuppa? Then, if you want to talk, we can talk. Otherwise, I'm happy to hold your hand and pretend I'm interested in being here when in fact I'm just staring at your boobs; you know, like a bloke would."

Evie glanced at her friend and gave a short laugh and a grateful smile, before wiping the tears from her cheek and the dampness from her nose. As she gathered her composure, she nodded to Cheryl, adding, "A cuppa would be lovely, thanks..." followed by "...you perv," and she playfully pretended to pull her coat over her chest.

Cheryl leant back and laughed, then looked over to the proprietor and signalled for two cups of tea. A couple of minutes later, he delivered two teas, sugar, and a small jug of milk. He furtively glanced at Evie's eye and scar before placing a small plate of biscuits on the table. Cheryl looked at the biscuits and then up at the man, slightly confused.

"Perhaps you and your friend could like biscuits, yes? They are on house," he said with a pronounced eastern European accent. Cheryl smiled warmly at the man and mouthed a 'thank you'.

"So, are we sitting in silence, or are we talking?" asked Cheryl once the biscuits had been eaten and the cups were empty. Evie's shoulders sagged in acceptance that she really did need to talk.

"I think I might have started something I wish I hadn't, but I don't know if I can stop it," Evie said, unable to look up from her near-empty cup.

"What is it?"

"I can't say or I'll be in legal trouble. I think I might be in way over my head, and I don't know how to get out of it. To be honest, I'm not sure if I actually want it to stop or not."

"If it's money you need, I've got some stashed away. You're welcome to it."

Evie's frown turned into a soft, warm smile. "No. Thanks, though, that's really sweet, but money isn't the problem. I've got money. It's disappearing fast, but I'm hoping to get it all back, ten-fold." Evie then puffed out her cheeks and ran a hand through her hair. She wanted to tell someone, but she was worried she'd be judged if she did, and Cheryl might walk away. Right now, she was Evie's only friend, but the need to unburden herself was consuming her.

"I can't tell you much other than a group of men are being offered the chance to pay me a lot of money. In effect, as recompense for this," and she indicated she meant the scar. "If they don't pay me, then there will be consequences. I've already put things in motion, so they'll understand I'm deadly serious." Evie sneered. It was the first time Cheryl had seen Evie's expression darken in all the years she had known her. She thought Evie actually looked vindictive. "Believe me, I want to tell you it all, but… it's complicated. I'd hate you to get involved if the police are called in."

"So, what happens next?" Cheryl asked. Evie stared at Cheryl but said nothing in response. She could see Cheryl was visibly anxious at her behaviour.

"Sorry," said Evie brightly, deliberately changing her tone and demeanour. She thrust out her hands to hold Cheryl's and hopefully reassure her. "It's just; well, if you had been through what I've been through and knew those bastards were out there, living their lives as if nothing has changed." She gave Cheryl a warm, reassuring smile. She could see Cheryl's uncomfortable demeanour easing slightly, but her friend still seemed guarded. Evie wondered if she had told her too much, so she doubled her efforts to take Cheryl's mind off the subject.

"Hey, remember when we used to go shopping and spend hours trying stuff on? Let's do that; I'm buying." Evie hurriedly put all the pots and plates back on the tray and carried them back to the counter before Cheryl could disagree. She pulled out a £10 note and said, "Keep the change. The biscuits were a lovely gesture, thank you." She smiled at the man in gratitude before turning to open the door.

"Right, where shall we go first?" asked Evie as they stood on the pavement outside the café.

"Oh babe, I can't. I'd love to, but I've got to get ready for a personal appointment if you know what I mean? Need to be home and have a bath, get ready, and then it's a bit of a journey. Maybe next time?" Evie was disappointed but knew Cheryl still worked on the sex circuit. Unlike her, Cheryl hadn't invested her money in bricks and diamonds. Back in the day, Cheryl preferred to spend her money on stuff to smoke, snort, or drink.

"Sure," Evie said dejectedly. "I get it. Thank you so much for this morning, though. Maybe catch up again at the weekend?" she proposed. Cheryl could see the look of desperation in Evie's eyes and knew she had to make time for her.

"Yeah, go on then," replied Cheryl. "In fact, come round to mine and I'll cook something. Bottle of wine or two, and then maybe watch a cheesy movie?"

Evie smiled. "Sounds great. Just like old times." They hugged one more time and then went their separate ways. Evie jumped into a taxi while Cheryl walked towards the Underground station at Kings Cross. Evie looked back and waved through the rear window of the taxi before it turned and Cheryl was out of sight. Cheryl slowed her walk as she contemplated the look on Evie's face when she spoke about consequences and the emphasis Evie seemed to unconsciously put on the phrase *'deadly serious'*. As an inexplicable wave of concern swept through her mind, Cheryl pulled her mobile phone out and dialled 101.

"Is that the police? Yeah, I'd like to talk to someone about a friend of mine. I don't know why, but I'm worried she might be getting involved in something she's gonna regret."

Chapter 38

Cutlery clinked and the air hummed with noisy chatter and laughter, but the four people around a table on the private dining mezzanine in this exclusive London restaurant sat stony-faced. The hurriedly arranged meeting was the result of a request by Niall that the Aeternum group members meet, although no one knew why he'd asked them all to drop everything and come to London. Every now and then, Mallory noticed the occasional furtive glance from one of his fellow diners to see if anyone else was feeling brave enough to break the silence, but none of the other three seemed to want to. Eventually, Mallory couldn't contain his intrigue.

"Well, this was worth travelling down from Manchester for," he said as he dabbed the corners of his mouth with his napkin. He was inviting a riposte, but no one seemed to want to bite. He looked at all the others, pausing on one before shifting his gaze to another, and then heaved a sigh of frustration. "Oh, come on. I know we're all curious as to why we're here."

"Yes, why did we have to race down here?" added an irritated Fairfax. "And if it's so important, where's Charles?"

"Charles said he was otherwise engaged," replied Niall.

"Shagging his new girlfriend, I expect," smirked Fairfax.

"New girlfriend? 'D' isn't new," said Mallory.

"He got dumped by her well over a year ago. Keep up, Peter." Fairfax replied mockingly.

"Well, excuse me for not keeping abreast of such earth-shattering news," Mallory snapped back sarcastically.

"I'll update Charles later, but I need to talk to you all about *that night*," interjected Niall firmly. The others stopped eating, and all eyes were focused on him.

"Why?" asked Vickers, concerned at the idea of old nightmares being revisited.

"Because a couple of things have happened that you need to be aware of. You all know about Derek's murder. Yesterday I had a visit from a couple of detectives from the Met…" He swallowed hard. The other three didn't know what was coming, but Niall took a moment to compose himself and then continued, "They told me that William had been found, murdered."

"WHAT?" exclaimed Vickers uncontrollably. "Wait; are they saying it's related to the accident at Christmas three years ago? Is that why we're here?"

Niall shook his head. "The police don't know anything about that night as far as I can tell, but she's been in touch."

"Why does it feel like you're linking the two?" Mallory asked.

"She's asked me for more money and said there would be consequences if I didn't pay."

"So, she told you that she'd kill William if you didn't pay her? How much was she asking for?"

"£100m, but she didn't say she'd kill William."

"Do you think she's threatening all of us or just those who were at the party?" asked Mallory, who, like Charles Wagstaff, hadn't been able to attend that night, but Niall had brought both he and Charles up to speed.

"As far as I know, she doesn't even know you exist, Peter, let alone that you are part of the group," Niall responded. Mallory puffed his cheeks out in relief and sat back.

"Oh sure, you're alright," snapped an irate Fairfax.

"Sorry," apologised Mallory, realising his selfishness and holding his hands up in genuine remorse. "That was insensitive, really, I'm sorry, Tony... and you, James," followed by an apologetic look to Niall.

"I know," said Niall, acknowledging that Mallory had silently included him.

"How did she contact you?" asked Vickers.

"I received another package. I think she's also sent something to Yvonne at our home address."

"You received *another* package?" asked Mallory. Niall blushed as soon as he realised he'd never told them about the first package. "Niall?" Mallory pressed.

"I received a package from her a couple of years ago. I didn't tell you because I'd paid her £10m to leave me alone, and the threat in the second package just said she had a surprise planned, so I knew she was deadly serious."

"Let me get this straight," interjected Fairfax. "She contacts you and demands £10m, which you pay. She then writes to you demanding £100m and threatens consequences if you don't pay that?"

"Yes," confirmed Niall.

"Poor William. He must have been the 'consequence'," said Vickers, who had remained very quiet after his outburst. "Do you think we're all in danger now?"

"I don't know... but... maybe," replied Niall. "I just think we ought to be extra careful." The table fell quiet as people contemplated the implications.

After a few minutes, it was Mallory who spoke first. "What protection is everyone thinking of putting in place?"

"I'll need to be careful I don't spook David," said Fairfax. David was his 13-year-old son.

"And Anna?" added Vickers, asking about Fairfax's estranged wife.

Fairfax scoffed. "Pfft, the way she's been acting, it would save me a pretty penny if she died. She's legally bleeding me dry through the divorce settlement."

"How's Yvonne?" Vickers asked. "Did I hear you've been getting on better recently?"

"We have, yes. It's almost as if Derek's death suddenly opened the door to us getting closer again." Niall sank into a moment of deep and sweet reflection after he said that. He remembered last night and Yvonne's smile when she woke up next to him.

"Niall?" said Fairfax insistently.

"Sorry, what?" replied Niall. He had been so engrossed in his momentary reflection that he hadn't heard a question that Fairfax had already asked twice.

"I said, what are we going to do about the little whore? This can't go on."

"I know where she lives, so I'll deal with her. The less you all know, the better."

"We need to know, Niall," insisted Vickers. "If there is a link between the blackmail letters and threats and people dying, I think we deserve to know, don't you?"

"What if we pay her off from the Aeternum Foundation?" suggested Mallory. "That way, at least the inheritance bequeathed from Derek's and William's estates will be used to protect us, their friends?"

"Are we allowed to use it in that way?" asked Fairfax, who was always keen to use other people's money for his benefit.

"We'll need to ask Charles," said Niall. "He's the treasurer."

While everyone had already put their private affairs in order, they maintained the promise from their university days to support each other should any of them fall on hard times. Recently, they'd formalised that promise into what was now called the Aeternum Foundation. Half their business wealth was pledged to the Foundation, and if any of them died, the others could decide what to do with the assets. The discussion also reminded Niall that he needed to talk to his personal solicitor to rewrite his existing will now there were signs his marriage was recovering. Four years ago, he had provided Charles with a written attestation to remove Yvonne from everything, but perhaps now was the time to discuss putting her back in? He had yet to discuss it with her but thought it would be a welcomed gesture, unlike his past attempts to buy her affection back. Once again, his reflective mood led him to miss the majority of what was being discussed.

"I agree, and in the meantime, I suggest we all review any security measures we have in place. Perhaps even changing our routines. It's too easy to keep doing what feels normal and therefore normally safe," said Mallory.

"Agreed," said Vickers. "I'm going to crash at a friend's place for a few weeks. It's out of town and he's away on holiday. I'll be travelling as well; up to Scotland to the new practice and across to Manchester to check a new site."

"A moving target is harder to hit, right?" Fairfax chuckled at his own grim humour.

"You're a cold-hearted bastard," said Vickers.

"Maybe you can fix it for me; you know, you being a surgeon and all. Oh, wait..." Fairfax snapped back in reference to the drinking issues Vickers had fought with in the past. Vickers was about to stand and face off with Fairfax, but Mallory placed a firm, reassuring hand on Vickers' shoulder and made sure he stayed seated.

"Let's all just calm the fuck down," Niall said, looking at Vickers and Fairfax. "Things are already tense enough without us infighting." Vickers glared at Fairfax, but Mallory could feel his friend's posture soften as his anger subsided. Both men then nodded in agreement, albeit tempers still simmered under the surface.

Mallory turned his attention back to Niall and asked, "So what are you going to do about her?"

"Frighten the life out of her," Niall replied. "Put her in the same position she thinks she's got me in."

"Look, I'm as worried and angry as any of you," said Vickers, "but maybe it's time to involve the police."

"The police?" Fairfax taunted, surprised at the ridiculous nature of the suggestion. "Are you clear on what that means? We'll have to admit to GBH and perverting the course of justice. We'll be finished. Everything you've fought for, James, everything I've built will disappear as soon as Anna's lawyers get a whiff of a scandal, and the dream Charles has of buying out his own company will be crushed. We'll be metaphorically hung, drawn and quartered in front of all our friends, family and everyone out there who envies our success. I vote with Niall; we teach this bitch a lesson that scares her off – for good."

Chapter 39

Detective Constable Rachael Jones enjoyed doing research. "You're like a pig in muck, Jonesy," her colleagues would joke. Today, the muck was knee deep, and she was loving it. She'd joined the Met as a graduate entrant and was often teased about her lack of experience on the beat. Thankfully, she had proven her value to the force several times over the last few years and was eagerly awaiting an interview for the Met's cybersecurity investigations team. Yesterday, she had been wading through various online sites to find out more about group members of the Aeternum, both those that were alive and the deceased. She walked into Denton's office and dropped a large folder of printed material on the desk, which landed with a dull 'thwump'.

"I see your digital research skills still aren't good enough to save the rainforest, Jonesy," teased Denton.

"I have to print things out, guv, for those unfamiliar with modern-day technology," she cheekily replied. Denton smirked at her humour and her bravery.

"What have you found?"

"Let's start with Derek Lowe. Accountant with no debts, which either means he had a remarkable inheritance from his parents or had additional undeclared income that paid for a very comfortable lifestyle. He used to work for a local firm until 2003, which is when he opened his own company, Lowe's Accountancy Services."

"Snappy and inventive title," Denton said, making them both smile.

"Public records are limited as it's privately owned. His wife became an employee in 2007. I assume that was for tax purposes, as she drew a minimal salary. Revenues grew steadily but then made a significant jump in 2013, from £500k to £3.2m. I asked one of the forensic accounting guys to look into it. He said Lowe had sent HMRC what's known as a Notification of Variance letter to explain the jump. When he shared the notes on their file on Lowe, three of the names caught my attention: Oleg Thoresen, David Holding, and Niall Fitzgerald!" Jones could hardly contain her excitement, but his expression was blank.

"Who are the other two?"

"The trial?" she said.

"What trial?" Jones was slightly taken aback. She'd been following the Ruiz trial for weeks and had incorrectly assumed everyone else had, too.

"Dennis Ruiz: biggest Interpol cybercrime bust in history?" Denton still didn't follow, and Jones could see it. "Derek Lowe had become the accountant for the three men whose financial services company was forced to close when one of its partners, Oleg Thoresen, admitted money laundering for a cybercrime group called BOrg. Interpol subsequently discovered it was run by Dennis Ruiz. The closure of Thoresen, Holding & Fitzgerald was mainstream news when hundreds of millions of pounds belonging to high-earning investors was frozen by the authorities. Two of the investors committed suicide."

"So, Lowe's revenues fell after that?" surmised Denton.

Jones smiled. "No. It's unclear why, but in 2016 his revenue jumped again, from £3.2m up to nearly £7m. I then looked into Niall Fitzgerald, who set up Iliad Private Equity Group in 2011. He drew a modest salary for a few years but then had remarkable returns on his investments in 2014 and 2015. So much so that he drew a £64m bonus in both 2016 and 2017."

"The same year Derek Lowe's revenue jumped, but if Fitzgerald draws £64m two years in a row and Lowe was doing his books, maybe Lowe earned his fee by saving him a lot of tax?"

"I agree, but I'm not buying that theory for now because I've also spoken to the National Crime Agency, who advised me not to start digging around on either of them, which can only mean..."

"They're subject to an active investigation," Denton concluded.

"I think it's tied in with the Ruiz trial," she said.

"Okay, so we need to tread carefully with Fitzgerald. Good work, Jonesy. What else do you have?"

"William Curtis. He'd been an advisor to the powerful and wealthy for much of the last 20 years, either in support of the British Government or helping foreign nationals trade with them. He deals with a lot of companies in the Middle East; most recently Enerflex, SABIC, Belschen Petroleum, and SIPCHEM, according to a quick Google search."

"What are they?"

"Energy and manufacturing companies in Saudi," Jones replied. "Prior to that, he had banking and diplomatic careers, but with two significant blotches on his record. In 2007 and 2013, he left high-paid roles after being accused of inappropriate behaviour and sexual harassment. Neither were proved, but both cases failed to get to court because the plaintiffs unexpectedly withdrew their allegations."

"Paid off?" hypothesised Denton.

"Yes, with all the plaintiffs signing non-disclosures as part of the out-of-court settlement. It was after the second event, in 2013, that he became an independent advisor."

"AKA unemployable by any organisation or person who cared about their reputation," concluded Denton. Jones nodded in agreement. Denton considered the information Jones had shared before summarising, "Not exactly boy scouts, although not exactly hardcore criminals, either."

"What do you want me to do next, guv?"

"At this precise moment, I don't have a bloody clue. The DCI will be asking me for an update, and all I can say is we have six bodies but nothing firm that ties any of these murders together other than the sequence on the lottery ticket."

Chapter 40

"Interesting. Very interesting."

The Broker had been intrigued about the recent Friends Reunited subscriber and had been reading about the tech-savvy Niall Fitzgerald, given the student's thesis the professor had unsuccessfully offered in exchange for his life. The Broker decided he would ask Niall to assess and offer any insight into if there was any real value in the document. He hit the intercom button on his desk phone.

"Yes, boss?"

"Our latest Friends Reunited subscriber; I want to talk to him at the club. Tell Alain to prepare the private room and tell our subscriber that we don't want any money for his membership, but I have something he might find interesting. Invite him for dinner at the club tomorrow night. Private entrance. Make sure he knows it's not optional."

"Yes, boss."

The following evening, Niall arrived at the Mansion Club, a grand country estate that had been turned into a private members club. His instructions were to follow the long, straight driveway and then turn left at the front of the house towards a private gateway. As he pulled up at the gate, it opened, and he swung his Bentley into one of the parking spaces. After a few seconds, a man in a crisp white shirt and a mid-grey pin-striped suit came out of the only door he could see that would lead into the building. Under one arm was what looked like a menu. He stopped short of the car and bowed his head slightly, acknowledging Niall. He then swept his arm out and gestured towards the door from which he had come. Niall unlocked the car door and stepped out.

"Mr Fitzgerald, I'm delighted to see you, sir. I hope you found your way here without concern or delay?"

"Yes, thank you," replied Niall hesitantly.

"Excellent! Your host is waiting for you inside. If you would?" The man again gestured towards the doorway. Niall followed him to the door, which led into a stunning hallway that exuded an air of understated sophistication and elegance. The man stopped and put down the menu, turning to Niall.

"Allow me to apologise, but the safety of our valued patrons is of the utmost importance to the Mansion Club. Would you mind if I undertook a sweep of your clothing?" He pulled a flat paddle out of a bureau. Niall had seen similar things in the VIP airport lounges whenever he and Yvonne had flown out to the villa. This was a most elegant and yet unusual establishment, with perhaps – he thought – some dubious clientele. It was a natural extension to think that guests of said clientele might be just as dubious. He held his arms out in implied agreement, and the man swept Niall, concluding he was not wearing any audio-transmitting devices or carrying a weapon.

"Thank you, sir. My apologies, but... well, I'm sure you understand?" Niall nodded. Strangely, he actually felt a small thrill at the idea that someone might think he was a danger to anyone. "If you will follow me, please?" The man turned sharply on his heels and led Niall down the remainder of the hallway to a large wooden door. The door opened into a private dining room. The wall facing the doorway hosted a large picture window that looked out onto a secluded floodlit lawn. The other walls had no windows but were adorned with paintings. Niall thought he recognised one of them.

"Yes, it is the original, Mr Fitzgerald. Thank you for coming," said The Broker as he walked across the room to greet Niall, although there was no handshake offered.

"But it's *The Weeping Woman* by Picasso. I don't understand; how can it be the original? Isn't it..." but before Niall could finish the sentence, The Broker spoke:

"Hanging in the National Gallery of Victoria, in Australia, after being supposedly recovered from a locker in a train station? Sadly, while the Australians eventually realised the original was stolen, they are yet to realise that they are now hanging a fake on the wall. A very good one, mind. A member of this club bought the original from the thieves who stole it." Niall smiled, even though he knew he shouldn't, but the painting was just magnificent, as was the sheer audacity of the theft. He turned his attention back to his host, who gestured to Niall to take a seat at the table.

"You clearly know my name, but I don't seem to know yours?" said Niall as he sat.

"Indeed," said The Broker, offering no information in return. The men settled, and waiters brought the finest wine and the most exquisite food. It was very enjoyable, and Niall found that his host was surprisingly well-informed about the private equity sector. After coffee had been served, the waiters disappeared and left Niall and his host to their privacy.

"So, why did you invite me here?" asked Niall, surprising himself at his self-confidence, given the situation and the nature of the man sitting opposite him.

"I would like you to read something and give me your opinion. It shouldn't take more than 30 minutes." Niall waited for the rest of the request. After all, surely that wasn't all this man wanted in exchange for Niall no longer having to pay the £25,000 for SILK's name and address? The Broker smiled gently. "Don't worry. There is no other 'ask' here. Read what I have and give me your opinion. After that, you are free to go, and your debt will be considered as paid."

"Alright," replied Niall. "But what if the document proves to be nonsense? Or what if it is pure gold? How do you know I won't simply act on it myself?"

"Because if it's the former, you will have provided a valuable service to me for which I'll be grateful. If it's pure gold, perhaps we will talk a little more? And if you do anything without my consent, you'll be dead within days." Even though his host was still smiling as he raised a wine glass to his lips, there was a look in his eyes that meant he was serious. This man would probably order Niall's death just as casually as he might order another bottle of wine.

"And I assume it would be unwise to refuse to read the document and just pay you the £25,000?"

"You catch on quickly, Mr Fitzgerald. I like you."

"When and how do I get the document?" The Broker gazed at Niall for a few seconds, then picked up a small bell from the table. He rang it once. A man walked into the room and passed Niall a folder before turning and walking toward a chair in the corner.

"You get to read it now. I assume it's not an inconvenience to read it here?"

Niall knew this wasn't really a question. "Not at all. No time like the present." Niall opened the folder. "A doctoral thesis?" He looked up at The Broker, questioning his request. The Broker raised an eyebrow and sighed in exasperation. He just wanted Niall to read it. Niall saw his reaction and decided the safest thing to do was to start reviewing the document. Ten minutes later, he turned over from page 25 and looked confused. He flicked through the remainder of the document and then looked up at his host. "Is this some sort of joke?" quizzed Niall.

"I wish it was," said The Broker. "I assume from your expression that you were looking forward to reading pages 26 and 27?" he asked. "But tell me, is it an intriguing concept?"

Niall paused to reflect on what he had read so far. "Yes, it's intriguing, but without pages 26 and 27; well, it's like reading about baking enough bread to feed the world's hungry, only to find you don't have the recipe." The Broker nodded, closing his eyes and taking in a few calming breaths before turning to look at the man on the chair in the corner. That was the signal that it was time. The man rose but stayed where he was as The Broker turned back to Niall.

"Thank you for your company and your expertise, Mr Fitzgerald. You are now free to leave, and your debt to me is cleared. Please leave the report on the table, and don't mention this meeting or this report to anyone." The Broker stared into Niall's eyes, emotionless, and the man in the corner cracked his knuckles. Message received.

As soon as Niall was out of the room, Tom and Jerry appeared from an adjoining room. The Broker picked up the report and held it in his hand for a moment before passing it back over his shoulder to one of the two thugs. "I want the two missing pages. I don't care if you have to pull the professor's apartment to pieces to find them. Do not return without them."

Chapter 41

"How did you expect me to defend him when he reacted to the prosecution's summation like that?" questioned an exasperated Maddox. The judge had decided that the prosecuting barrister needed some respite after the attack before the trial would restart. The managing partner and three of the senior partners in the law firm had requested an explanation of the situation.

"Perhaps his reaction was not so much about the prosecution's summation as it was to your ineptitude?" taunted one of the partners, Adrian Skelton, the last partner to glance through the legal binder. He slid the closed file back across towards Maddox.

"If you think you can do better, Adrian, I'm more than happy to be your co-counsel?" she challenged, barely managing her anger. The man blushed slightly and huffed at her in an attempt to deflect his embarrassment. "No, I didn't think so," she sneered.

She returned her gaze to the managing partner, Clive Jeavons, who said, "I don't think that sort of attitude towards a senior partner is either called for or constructive, do you?" Maddox wanted to respond; oh, how she wanted to respond. A competent, capable woman who was by far the best defence barrister in their firm, being scorned by a group of privileged white males in their fifties and sixties who hadn't seen a courtroom for a decade or more? It would have been laughable if it wasn't so real.

"With respect," she started, "the case against Mr Ruiz is as comprehensive as I have ever seen. The Interpol investigation is damning. Add to that, our client is clearly capable of pulling the pin out of his own hand grenade, and the only option I have is to find a technicality that puts the fairness of the investigation in doubt. I have my paralegals pulling together a digital dossier of the media coverage and if I..." She pointedly jabbed her hand into her own chest to ensure the message was loud and clear that this was her decision: "... if *I* am convinced that is a possibility, then I'll ask for a right of audience with the judge. If it's not, then I will continue to look for a technicality. That is our only hope with this case."

She looked at the men and prayed they wanted to argue about this. With their position of power and control being challenged, it was a fight she might lose, but she was ready and prepared for it. The managing partner knew Maddox would be well prepared, and he knew what she was capable of. He might not have fought a battle in a courtroom for years, but he had seen her in action and had the experience to know when to wait and when to pounce.

"Then we look forward to another update by the end of the week, Daniella. Keep up the good work," he announced, raising his hand as the aggrieved Skelton was about to take the fight to Maddox. He knew that she would eat Skelton alive, and that would weaken his own position as the managing partner. He stood and said, "Gentlemen. Time for coffee, I believe?" and he led the trio out of the room.

As soon as the door had closed, Maddox rested her fists on the table and bowed her head. She was exhausted.

"Damn it," she said as she thumped the legal binder that lay on the table. She took a moment to calm down and let the frustration subside before standing up and taking in a long calming breath. She opened the legal binder to tidy the papers that the partners had carelessly pushed back inside. As she did so, she noticed a post-it note in the inside cover. It said:

Talk later

She paused. Who could have put it there, and why? It wasn't her assistant's handwriting, nor did it look like any of her paralegals', although people rarely saw handwritten notes in the firm anymore, as almost everything was on email, group messages, or electronic notes on the firm's Access Legal software. As she continued to gather her paperwork, she glanced through the window. From her vantage point on the second floor, she saw the four men were already downstairs and walking into the small communal Georgian public garden in Park Square. After a few steps, they stopped and looked over to their right. A man rose from one of the park benches and walked towards them. As he reached the group, the managing partner shook the man's hand and then introduced him to everyone else. She could see most of the man's face as he turned to each of the senior partners to shake their hands. Then, the managing partner gestured for them all to follow him. As they started to walk away, one man in the group paused and turned, looking back up at the window. It was as if he knew Maddox would be there.

He glanced at the group to make sure none of them were looking before subtly raising his hand as if in mock salute. The gesture wasn't sarcastic, though; it was an acknowledgement.

"Adrian Skelton, you left me that note?"

Chapter 42

The officer kept rapping on the door, but there was still no answer. He could hear the television and, through a small gap in the net curtains, he could see a dog asleep on the floor.

"5-8-4-3 to Control."

"Come in 5-8-4-3."

"I need to forcibly enter the property at the address you sent me to. No one has seen or heard from the resident for a few days. I've checked the letterbox and there's no smell of gas. Can't see into the house, though, as there's a mail-catcher box on the inside of the door. I've called through the letterbox, but there's no response. Can you log a PACE Section 17 against the call? None of the neighbours have a key, and there's no other obvious way to get in."

"Roger that 5-8-4-3. Please keep the channel open and report if you need an ambulance or uniform support."

"Roger, will do." The constable called through the letterbox once more, "Mr Churchill? This is the police. I'm going to force entry into your house through a window. There's no need to feel anxious. I'll be in shortly to help you." He had no idea if the homeowner was actually in, let alone in any sort of distress, but it would be negligent to assume otherwise. He took his baton and smashed the small window into the front room, reaching in to unlatch the handle. After climbing in, he talked to the control room:

"5-8-4-3 to Control. I've entered the property. Can't see any obvious signs of a disturbance."

"Roger 5-8-4-3. Awaiting further instructions." The officer looked at the dog that lay on the floor at the side of the armchair. It didn't appear to be breathing. As he walked from the front room into the hallway, he saw a body lying on the carpet.

"5-8-4-3 to Control. I've found a man fitting Mr Churchill's description. He's lying on the floor in the hallway. I can already see that his lips are blue and there are no signs of respiratory movement. I'm going to check." The constable carefully walked to where Alfie Churchill lay and, after putting his protective gloves on, bent down to check his pulse.

"5-8-4-3 to Control. I can confirm we have a deceased male. No obvious external trauma, so no need for CID or SOCO." The policeman stood and looked down at Churchill. Only then did he notice what looked like a rolled-up piece of paper stuffed deep in the dead man's mouth; it was pushed so deep, he almost missed it. He looked back towards the dog and then glanced around the rest of the tiny house. That was when he saw the legs of a young child lying on the floor in the kitchen. She, too, lay motionless. He pressed his radio again:

"5-8-4-3 to Control. Change that last request, please. I think we might need CID and the forensic medical examiner as soon as possible."

"Roger that 5-8-4-3. Confirm address, please."

"Address confirmed as 48 Stark Avenue, Falkirk; foxtrot-kilo one, four papa-romeo."

Chapter 43

Over a week had passed since the voicemail from Stella's husband. The conversation with Holding did shed some light on her husband's previous job and made her want to know more about the third person at the investment company, a man called Niall Fitzgerald.

"There is no way Thoresen could have operated all by himself," Holding had explained. "With that level of money going in and out of the investment company, someone had to be signing off the transactions. I suspect Fitzgerald was involved, too. We operated using agreed authority levels, and the bank wouldn't accept transfers above £100,000 without two signatures." As he was retelling the story, she was beginning to tire, but she kept reminding herself of her primary reason for being there; she needed to find out where Robert was. Ten minutes into the meeting, she simply had to ask.

"Yes, he's alive. I can't tell you where he is because I don't know, but we do send each other signs to confirm they haven't found us yet."

"Who are '*they*' and why are they looking for you?" asked an increasingly worried Stella.

"*They* work for a man called Dennis Ruiz. Even though Ruiz is currently on trial, he's got the message out, and his men are looking for Robert and me."

"Why are they looking for Robert?"

"I can't tell you that; the less you know, the better," Holding said. "But now you know that Robert is alive, you need to be careful too." Stella's mind raced, but confirmation that her husband was alive pushed any fear about her own safety to the back of her mind.

"What are you going to do; stay hidden for the rest of your life?" she asked Holding, who looked away from her at that point. He knew he wanted to be the one to make the decision about when and how his life would end.

"I have made arrangements," he muttered quietly.

Stella understood what he was implying, and then her mind turned back to Robert. Perhaps that was why he had been reported as dead, to avoid a life of hiding? After that, the meeting soon came to a natural end. Holding had wished Stella well, and she had told him that there was always a safe and welcoming location for him to stay if he needed one. He thanked her, made a mental note of the address, but said he didn't think it would be wise for him to take up her offer. He then left the coffee shop.

As Stella walked back down to the ground floor, she was temporarily lost in her thoughts until the young woman behind the counter looked over.

"I hope the meeting went alright?" she said. "Your friend, he… well, he seemed deep in thought as he left."

"He had had some bad news, that's all," lied Stella. "But thank you for asking."

The next day, as Stella busied herself around the apartment, she kept replaying the meeting in her mind. She couldn't help thinking about '*them*'. Were they still looking for Robert, and were they now looking for her? Her introspection was interrupted when the phone rang, startling her. She picked the handset up tentatively but said nothing. A man with a cockney accent spoke:

"Morning. My name is Greg. Am I talking to the homeowner? Is that…" There was a pause as the man checked his notes. "… Mrs Kendrick?" Stella felt a shiver down her spine. How did anyone know she lived here and that this was her number? Could it be 'them'? Could they have found her already?

"Who… who is this?" she asked hesitantly. Stella felt the room close in on her. Then a seemingly different man started to talk to her, but this man didn't have a cockney accent.

"Oh, you are a fragile little ladybug first thing in the morning, aren't you?" Stella froze. Tears welled in her eyes, and she struggled to bring herself to speak. That voice. Her bottom lip began to tremble as she tried to grasp the reality of the situation. The voice spoke again, "Darjeeling for the burglar?" he said softly.

"A tea for the robber," she replied slowly as she tried to control her emotions. "Robert?"

The man remained silent on the other end of the phone for what seemed an eternity before he spoke again, "Yes, my darling, it's me."

Neither of them said anything for what seemed like a long time. Stella could barely hold in her desire to cry. She dared not utter the words she so desperately wanted to say for fear that this was a cruel hoax and her world would come crashing down around her again. All Robert could hear was the soft whimpering of his wife on the other end of the phone. He too was biting his lip, as the emotion and relief were overwhelming. When she did speak, though, it wasn't what either of them had expected.

"What the fuck are you playing at?" she demanded.

"What?" he asked, unwittingly giggling at her outburst.

"You bastard! You made me plan and go to your funeral. You put me through the trauma of losing our house, and now you're bloody giggling about it? What the hell is so fucking funny about ANY of that?" She was breathing heavily now and was about to explode.

He knew not to react angrily or submissively. Previous experience had taught him what to do and what not to do. He waited a short while and then said solemnly, "Because if I hadn't, we would both be dead."

For the next 10 minutes, Robert summarised what had happened. He had found out about Ruiz and the company's true purpose, which wasn't the one he had been sold, and how he had been planning to escape, realising the terrible ordeal he would be putting her through. As he talked, she knew he really had no other choice but to disappear.

"And what about the severed fingers they found? They said that's how they identified you?"

"Well, let's just say I can only count up to eight now. I knew the car was going to be destroyed and, as there was only a charred corpse of a homeless man in it, I realised I needed to provide some clues to the police so, a few days before the accident, I convinced myself that I had to sever two of my fingers. I threw one of them off the cliff after I'd pushed the car over and placed the other on the cliff edge. The plan was that the emergency services would find at least one of them before they became snacks for the local wildlife. Thankfully, I spotted headlights about a mile away just before I pushed the car over the edge. They saw the flaming wreckage and called the police. I know, because

I was hiding in some bushes up the mountainside. I had found a difficult route away from the scene through the hills several days before, where only very dedicated hikers might see me. Thankfully, at that time of the night, there were none."

"And so, as far as anyone else knew, you were dead?" said Stella.

"Almost everyone. David and I had met at work about two years ago. It was strange just how quickly we gained each other's trust, given we didn't really know each other or work together, but we had little choice. We both took a huge risk."

"And where are you now? Can I come and see you?" she asked eagerly.

Robert sighed. "Not yet. I can call you from a secure phone, but you cannot call me, and neither of us can risk being seen together. There could be people watching you."

"How long will this be for?"

"I don't know right now. There are plans already in motion, but there's something I need to ask you to do, to help. I want you to speak to Dennis Ruiz's lawyer, Daniella Maddox."

Chapter 44

Everyone felt tense. The funeral of William Curtis didn't feel like a moment for fond reflection or even camaraderie; it felt more like a siren that was sounding for the remaining five members of the Aeternum. They all felt mortal and vulnerable, which brought back memories of the man who would have been the eighth member of their group.

In May 1991, they'd sat next to each other on a row of chairs. When one went up to collect their degree certificate, the other six were the most enthusiastic, with their applause and cheers by far the loudest. How very different it now felt compared to the previous three years, which, at times, had been hellish as they tried to cope with life at a prestigious university. Even with the euphoria they'd felt, there was a tinge of sadness that the friend they'd lost wasn't there to share their success.

"Get down, Alan," Charlie had instructed their friend one night in their first year there. He was trying to remain calm but was running out of options. A group was gathering below to watch a student who stood precariously on a fourth-floor ledge. A handful were actually goading him to jump.

"No, Charlie. I can't stand this anymore. I can't sleep, I can't eat. I dread waking up every morning because I know what will happen," said his tearful friend, one hand holding onto the window frame and another onto the brickwork, with his back pressed against the window. Alan Gerrard had suffered beatings and had been pelted with everything from eggs to stones. Someone had even daubed the door to his student accommodation with dog excrement simply because he'd been accused of being gay. Life in the 1990s would have been hard enough had he actually been gay, given AIDS was still sweeping the globe, but Gerrard was just someone who empathised easily with others and wore his heart on his sleeve. Nowadays, he'd be described as simply being in touch with his emotions, but back in his university days, he'd been targeted for abuse. They all deserved to be at university: they were bright, eager, and had achieved the necessary grades in their A-levels that meant they qualified for entry, even though Gerrard's grades had crashed over the previous three months. What they didn't have was money, unlike over 90 per cent of the other students. These eight were all on scholarships, and while the vast majority of students rarely interacted with them, there were those who relished the opportunity to bully them.

"Oh look; apparently Oxfam is distributing clothing to students now," was a common insult, as none of the eight wore branded clothing, and they didn't have a lot of choice when deciding what to wear every morning. When Gerrard was struggling in lectures, the same handful of students sneered and mocked:

"Isn't this the degree class in Business Management, chaps? I think someone got off the bus at the wrong stop. Shouldn't you be at the local poly, taking a diploma in Public Services or something?" Once they knew their actions and words were having an effect, it simply accelerated their verbal, physical, and psychological abuse of him; abuse that finally led Alan Gerrard to step out onto the window ledge.

Bill and Derek burst into the room, breathless from racing up the four flights of stairs. Charlie didn't look round but held his arm straight out to silently tell them to stay where they were.

"Alan, we'll help you get through this if you'll just come back inside."

"Yeah, Al, we're here for you," Bill called out.

"It's Alan, not Al," Gerrard cried out in anguish. "Doesn't anyone hear me?" Both Charlie and Derek looked at Bill in exasperation; everybody knew Alan always wanted to be called by his full name.

"Sorry, sorry; William is an idiot," said Bill, using what he called his Sunday name.

No one knew how or why that short statement had affected Alan, but he suddenly giggled. "Yes, you're an idiot, but you're our idiot." Bill Curtis using his Sunday name had somehow broken through. It was the strangest thing, but Alan turned to look at his friends and, with tears of despair replaced by tears of hope, he actually smiled.

"Come on, Alan; take my hand," Charlie said softly. Alan felt a little ashamed, and he nodded in concession. He turned towards Charlie and, while keeping hold of the window frame, he let go of the brickwork. He swung his body around so that he could climb back in through the open window, but it was a cold night and he was exhausted, so he no longer had the strength to maintain his balance. As Niall and James got to the room, all they saw was their friend over-balance, arms cartwheeling in mid-air. His feet slipped from the ledge, and the gathered crowd below gasped and moved several steps backwards.

"Got you!" yelled Charlie as he grabbed Alan's wrist, but the shifting weight of his falling friend almost pulled him out of the window. Bill, Niall, Derek, and James all raced forwards to help, with Niall reaching out and grabbing a fistful of Alan's sleeve while the other three anchored him and Charlie.

"HELP. DON'T LET GO!" screamed Alan, but Charlie's grip was slipping, and he couldn't reach his friend with his other hand. Niall felt the polyester material burning his fingers as he, too, began to feel Alan being dragged down by gravity. He did manage to release his grip and grab another fistful of his friend's sleeve, but it was too late. As hard as they tried, Alan Gerrard now knew his fate, and his eyes stared blankly at his friends as he slowly slipped from their grasp.

An hour later, as the student support team continued their coordinated response to the incident, the five of them sat in silence. The cups of hot sugary tea they had been given to help ease the effects of shock were still in their hands but had long since gone cold. The door opened quickly as their other two friends, Tony and Peter, arrived.

"What happened?" asked Tony.

"Where's Alan?" Peter asked, in the hope that Alan was in hospital or the gossip racing round the university was a sick hoax. Niall looked up, but the others kept staring at the floor.

"Alan's dead," Niall said quietly. Tony stood, open-mouthed, while Peter started to weep. Apart from his quiet sobs, the rest of the room remained silent for several minutes before Niall spoke once more.

"This must never happen again," he said, his voice no longer wavering with emotion but assertive and determined. "We must always be there for one another from now on, agreed?" They all looked at each other and nodded. Something good had to come out of this night.

Chapter 45

Cheryl rushed into the galley kitchen in her apartment, dropping the shopping bags on the floor before heading upstairs to change. In just over an hour, Evie would arrive for dinner, and Cheryl was running late. Evie was not supposed to be coming so early, but she'd called yesterday to ask if they could meet up sooner. Evie said she had some important news and intended to move out of the city for a few months afterwards.

"Right; blue top and ripped jeans," Cheryl said to herself. Then she stopped. "No, not jeans. Come on, it's Evie; she'll look bloody amazing. I know, the black skirt!" She flung the jeans onto a pile of clothes that were already stacked on a chair in the corner. Fifteen minutes and four wardrobe changes later, Cheryl skipped down the stairs and back into the kitchen.

"Right; bottle in the fridge, dessert in the freezer," she said, mentally ticking off her list. She checked the slow cooker, carefully lifting the lid. The beautiful aroma wafted up and she inhaled deeply. "Cheryl, you're a bloody genius in the kitchen," she congratulated herself. She replaced the lid and went out to the enclosed yard. Twenty feet wide and ten feet deep, with eight-foot-high whitewashed walls on three sides, it was private and felt surprisingly spacious. After 3pm on a clear day, it was awash with sunlight. A small table and two chairs stood in the middle of the paving, and several citronella sticks protruded from some wooden planters standing against the rear wall of the yard. She nodded to herself with satisfaction.

"Nice," she said and then looked at her watch. "And with plenty of time to spare, too." She decided she had earned some white wine that was already chilled. After pouring it and drifting back out into the sunshine, her phone rang.

"This is Cheryl," she said jauntily.

"Miss Collins?" asked a formal voice.

"It is, yes. Who is this?"

"This is PC Jo Armstrong from Deptford Police Station. It's regarding your call to 101 a few days ago. Is it convenient to talk?" Cheryl closed her eyes. She had forgotten all about arranging a call back from 101 for today.

"Er, sure," she replied. "It's just that I have a guest coming in half an hour."

"I'm sure it won't take that long, but given the nature of your call, I'd rather not postpone." She didn't wait for Cheryl to reply before continuing, "First of all, could you please confirm your full name and date of birth, so I can validate I'm talking to the right person?" The original officer on the 101 service had forewarned her she should expect these questions when someone called her back.

"Cheryl Sophia Alexandra Collins; 27th September 1976."

"Thank you, Miss Collins. What's the nature of your concern?"

Ten minutes later, Cheryl had explained what Evie had told her. The officer thanked her for her time and said she would file a report in case Cheryl or anyone else called back about an incident. She assured her that most concerns about possible criminal activity never actually materialised, but she confirmed Cheryl had done the right thing. The call ended, and Cheryl walked slowly back into the kitchen, staring at her phone and deep in thought. Had she done the right thing reporting the conversation she and Evie had had? The police officer seemed satisfied that she had, but Cheryl still felt she had betrayed her friend's secret.

"Who was that?" said a voice. Cheryl looked up, startled to find Evie standing in front of her. She dropped her phone in shock but made no attempt to pick it up because her gaze was drawn to the sun glinting off the long-bladed kitchen knife Evie held in her fist.

"What?" blurted Cheryl nervously. Evie bent down and picked up Cheryl's phone, moving closer so she could hand it back to her. Cheryl was also conscious that the knife in Evie's hand was that much closer to her, as well.

"The person on the phone? All I could hear from in here was you saying you hoped you hadn't wasted their time, and you felt a little bit silly?"

"Oh... that... yeah. Well, it was about... er... an estate agent. I'm thinking of moving, right?" said Cheryl, taking the phone and nodding her thanks to Evie for picking it up. Cheryl checked her phone for scratches before she put it back in her pocket, which also gave her some valuable thinking time.

"Oh, how exciting! So why did you feel you'd wasted their time?" questioned Evie, gulping down some wine she had opened. Her demeanour was that of an inquisitive friend, which helped Cheryl relax a little, but not as much as when Evie turned and started to slice a crusty cob that she had brought with her. Evie looked up and smiled.

"I just thought this, dipped in some olive oil and vinaigrette I've made, would be nice to start with."

"Yeah, nice. Erm, how did you get in?" asked Cheryl, trying to be nonchalant.

Evie smiled, reached into her pocket and pulled out a key ring. "You gave me a key years ago in case I ever needed to crash after a local job, remember? Guess I forgot to give it back." She gave a girlie giggle.

Cheryl remembered. "Blimey, girl; that was a long time ago."

"So?"

"So what?" replied Cheryl.

"So, tell me more about the plan to move?"

"Oh yeah. Well, new neighbours are a bit noisy, and I'd had enough of it last weekend. Called their landlord and told him I'd report the problem to the police if necessary, but I wanted to check with him first. Dwight's a nice bloke, and I don't want to cause him any hassle. Anyway, he said he was moving them out soon as they were behind on their rent, but I'd already started looking. You know what it's like when you get proper excited about an idea and your mind starts to move on? Well, I'd seen a place over in Peckham; two-bed terrace with a proper garden." Cheryl sounded animated. She hadn't been looking to move but had clicked on an estate agent's site one evening when she was bored and was now talking confidently about a property they had featured. She didn't have the money, nor were her neighbours noisy, but she was grateful for the coincidence. Evie smiled at her friend.

"Sounds exciting and certainly puts my mind at ease. For a moment there, I thought you were talking to the police?" Evie's smile suddenly disappeared and her mood darkened, but only for a moment. The smile returned, wider than ever, and Evie turned to look at the crockpot. "Hmm, this smells delicious." Cheryl was shaken, though, and she knew she looked it. The ease with which Evie flipped from carefree and smiling friend into an accusatory glare and back again unnerved her. How much had Evie actually heard?

"Right, let's take our bread and dip outside. Looks gorgeous out there, and, oops, we won't be needing this, will we?" giggled Evie as she slowly and deliberately placed the knife back on the worktop.

"Hopefully not," replied a relieved Cheryl. They walked out and sat at the table, eating in silence for several minutes, with Cheryl picking at the food rather than eating it. Evie noticed and decided enough was enough.

"Why did you feel the need to talk to the police?"

Cheryl froze. How was she supposed to answer that? She turned to Evie and tried to put a confused smile on, ready to dismiss the very idea, but when she looked at Evie, she knew there was no point. The fake smile quickly disappeared as Cheryl prepared to tell Evie the truth.

"I'm sorry I lied to you. You didn't deserve that. It's just—"

Before she could complete the sentence, Evie interjected, indignation in her tone. "It's just what? I wanted to tell you what I was doing because I trusted you. What is so wrong about what I'm doing that meant you felt the need to talk to the police?"

"Because it's extortion, and…" Cheryl paused before completing her admission. She looked up and continued, "… and because although we earn money illegally, it's consensual. What you're doing isn't, and…" Cheryl paused again because while she hadn't finished saying everything she wanted to say, the rest of her message wasn't going to be easy.

"And what? Come on, Cheryl, spit it out!"

"Because I'd read that two of the men you talked about had been murdered; that's why. I just panicked."

Evie was stunned. "You thought I'd killed them?" she asked. Cheryl opened her mouth to reply, but she had nothing else to say and, having said it out loud, it did seem a ridiculous statement.

From Evie's perspective, though, the damage was done. "That's what you thought, was it?" repeated Evie, with growing disbelief, and then she screamed at her, "WAS IT?" Cheryl recoiled in fear. Evie sneered at Cheryl before standing quickly and sending her chair toppling backwards. Evie towered over her and glowered down at her increasingly fearful friend.

Evie's whole body was shaking, and her expression was one of disdain. "And I thought you understood. I thought you knew what it was like… what it *is* like, to be treated like meat. To feel disgusted at the way men abuse us and think that the money they pay means it's alright." Tears began to trickle down Evie's cheek as the intensity of her anger subsided.

"I'm so sorry," said Cheryl softly as she stood and took a step towards her friend. She held her hands out in readiness to hug Evie, but Evie took a step back.

"No," Evie said. "You've broken the trust that we had, and I can never forgive you for that."

Cheryl hung her head and interlocked her fingers, almost in prayer. "I'm sorry. It was wrong, and it's a mistake I'll regret for the rest of my life. I should have known," she muttered. She heard a few steps as Evie's heels clicked on the paving and then felt Evie's hand gently rest on her shoulder.

"It's alright. I suppose we don't really know what our friends are capable of until we're pushed to the very edge," Evie whispered, and Cheryl felt Evie's grip on her shoulder tighten.

Chapter 46

"I'm usually really careful. You know I don't make mistakes," he mumbled nervously. He sat in front of a laptop in his house; curtains closed and clearly agitated. On the other end of the video call was The Broker, who sat in his chair looking dispassionately at the man on his laptop screen. The Broker was stroking his jaw, with his thumb and forefinger slowly going back and forth, converging at his chin. He didn't speak straight away, which, if anything, made the man even more nervous.

"Stefan," said The Broker eventually. "You've been an effective and efficient associate for over seven years. I don't know why you've only mentioned this now, four days after the assignment, but I can only assume you were waiting to see if the police found any of your blood at the incident." He was referring to the Weller murder scene.

Stefan nodded almost imperceptibly, but it was an admission of guilt. The Broker had used him for several years, including many of the recent assignments, and there had never been a problem until now. Harry Weller had dragged his nails through Stefan's hair as he tried, in vain, to fend him off. When Stefan initially checked himself as part of his usually thorough assessment to ensure a clean crime scene, Weller didn't appear to have any of his hair or skin under his nails, but Stefan had felt pressured when people were knocking on Weller's door to see what the commotion was. Later that day, though, as he showered, he felt a sting when massaging shampoo onto his scalp. After a very careful examination, he realised that there was a minute cut and that it was possible some blood might have seeped out.

"Thank you for telling me. It's important that we can be honest with each other. Four days is a long time, though, Stefan." He paused again as if weighing up what to say next.

"If they'd found anything, I'd already be in custody, given my record. And, if they had arrested me, I would have protected you; you know that, right?" Stefan said. It was the first time The Broker had heard anything like pleading from the man. Stefan was strong and extremely capable, so The Broker viewed this as an indication of just how worried Stefan was that there might be some trace at the scene.

The Broker continued, "Okay, how about you get out of sight for a while; lay low until we're absolutely sure this has gone away?" he suggested.

"Sure, I can do that. Thank you," Stefan said, relieved. The Broker leant forwards and killed the video link. He sat back in his chair and puffed out his cheeks. He shook his head, saddened at the decision he was about to make. Across the other side of the room, out of sight of the camera but not out of earshot of the laptop speakers, a woman looked up.

"Clean-up?" she asked. With a heavy heart, The Broker nodded, resigned to what had to be done.

"Make it look amateurish." The Broker pulled open the bottom desk drawer and threw a plastic file onto his desk. "And plant this evidence. Don't make it too easy to find, but I do want the police to find it. I need them to think they've found the killer they're looking for." She stood, picked up the file and then turned and walked out of the office without saying another word. The Broker rubbed his tired face with his hands. He hated losing good people, but the message had to be loud and clear to the others – don't make a mistake because everyone is expendable. There was a knock on his office door, and one of his men pushed the door open.

"Just seen Sophia leave. Is this a bad time?"

The Broker leaned back in his chair and stretched. "Depends; do you have good news or bad?"

"Good news, I think," said the man. The Broker looked a little irritated at the response, so the man revised his answer. "It's good news, boss." The Broker nodded. No one wanted his mood to darken, and the man, confidence momentarily restored, added, "Tom and Jerry are back, with a guest."

The Broker narrowed his eyes as he tried to remember what he had them doing. He then raised his eyebrows in expectation. "The professor's house?"

The man nodded back. "Yes, boss. They didn't find the paperwork, but they did find someone else snooping around. Think we might have a bit of a problem."

"What makes you say that?" asked The Broker.

"The person they found snooping is an associate of that Ruiz guy; the one currently on trial. T and J tell me they *persuaded him* to share some information. It seems Ruiz is as interested in that report as you are."

The Broker sat upright, all thoughts about Stefan gone. "That means either it could keep Ruiz out of jail, or he thinks it's the key to billions." He looked up at the man and said, "Let's go down to the visitor's room. Bring refreshments; I think we might be there for a while."

Chapter 47

As he looked out over a dank, grey London skyline from his vantage point on the 35th floor, Niall found himself in an increasingly reflective mood. He'd told Maria, his PA, to hold all his calls and cancel all his appointments for the day. After Derek's and William's funerals, and SILK's renewed threats, he simply felt overcome by it all, although that's not what he'd told her. His mind wandered back to his university days when he and the others first became friends.

They'd all worked well as study buddies, and when they met socially. Even after they left university, they'd still meet weekly to discuss life, money, and girls.

'Mouse', or Peter Mallory to use his real name, was the quietest within the group. He never truly felt comfortable with all the extroverts around him. Quietly spoken and usually less interested in talking about girls, but always keen to talk about life. He'd since become the least successful of the group, with little more than £5m to his name, most of which had been inherited.

"Speak up, Mouse. All I could hear was 'squeak'," Anthony Fairfax would tease. He didn't mean to be cruel, but Niall was convinced that's where the tension between Mallory and Fairfax first surfaced. As Mallory became a little more confident, he would occasionally bite back at Fairfax, and if things escalated, they did so rapidly. Sometimes they had to be pulled apart, but it never actually became physical.

Anthony Fairfax was a brash Scotsman who would always be loud and could normally be relied upon to be insensitive. Since university, he had moved into property development and had a keen eye for a good deal. He had had a difficult time when the financial markets crashed in 2009, sending the value of his investments through the floor. Luckily, some of his friends actually flourished during the downturn and invested several millions of pounds to keep him afloat. Once he was back on his feet, it was he who had suggested they extend their support for each other even further than they had previously agreed, by setting up the Aeternum Foundation. As most of the group had had to lean heavily on the others at one time or another, he argued that this was the ultimate commitment.

William Curtis was the elder statesman of the group. When they were together, he rarely spoke, but when he did say something, people listened. He understood how big business and politics worked hand-in-hand and how real wealth was created and destroyed. Niall was one of his biggest fans, although allegations of him being a serial groper had tarnished his reputation, and Yvonne wanted him nowhere near her or their house. Still, Curtis was so well connected that Niall remained close enough to him to leverage both his knowledge and his contacts.

Niall's thoughts then turned to Charles Wagstaff. Always the optimist, but also usually the mediator of any debate, which served him well in the career he made. He always seemed to have a beautiful woman draped around his neck. He was suave, sophisticated, confident, and liked to 'splash the cash' as he put it. He was proud of his wealth, and if it meant he could pay for a week away in the Bahamas with an attractive twenty-something, why wouldn't he? The relationships rarely lasted, though, as either he wanted a new woman in his life or they got bored of his roving eyes when he should have been paying attention to them. Niall and Wagstaff had a mutual respect for each other, and he also had Yvonne's seal of approval. She liked it when her husband was around powerful men because she said it also made him shine. The group had decided Wagstaff should be the one to look after the Foundation agreement and any changes to it, given his legal training, and Peter Mallory was happy with that approach as, even though he too had taken law at university, he didn't want the responsibility.

As the members of the group got older and circumstances changed, the business-related meetings still happened, but the social events became less frequent and much less alcohol fuelled. Niall had stayed particularly close to Derek Lowe, who he felt like a big brother to ever since that day in the university library. He had also been close to James Vickers, the final member of the Aeternum. He was Niall's best man at his wedding to Yvonne, but their friendship was strained to breaking point when James botched a gynaecological procedure and accidentally destroyed Yvonne's ability to have children. Everyone knew the procedure was high risk whoever took it on, but everyone could smell alcohol on his breath after the surgery. It was never conclusively proven that drink had led to the error, but it was enough for his Harley Street partners to insist he leave the practice.

Yvonne then turned her anger on Niall, blaming his recommendation of Vickers and recoiled from any intimacy. From then on, their marriage crumbled. Two years later, Niall was happy to celebrate with Vickers when he declared his drinking problem was under control and that he was opening a practice to provide cosmetic enhancements. They drank so much orange juice that night, Niall felt sick. The new surgery had become successful and lucrative. It was such a shame that his most recent memory of Vickers was him trying to repair the damage to SILK's face. She had lost the sight in her left eye, which wasn't his fault: no one could have repaired the damage to her eyeball, but Vickers still felt he'd failed her. She had understandably been traumatised and, as a result, had now murdered two of their friends.

As the rain fell against the window, Niall's mood fell back to one of sadness. His marriage had hit the rocks, and he had exacerbated the gulf between him and Yvonne by turning to high-class escorts, and now that had led him to a darker place. The murder of Derek Lowe and his family had brought them back together, but SILK presented a problem and was a reminder of his wayward behaviour.

He was startled as his introspection was broken by a knock on his office door. It was his PA, Maria.

"Sorry; I didn't mean to make you jump," she said, "but it's 6pm, and I wondered if there was anything else you needed before I head home?"

"Is it that time already?" asked Niall, checking his watch. He had been lost in his thoughts for hours and hadn't realised how late it was, given the leaden sky had blocked out the slow, subtle change in the daylight.

"No, no, there's nothing. Thank you, Maria. Have a good evening." She backed out slowly, unsure whether to ask if her boss was really alright. He noticed her hesitancy and gave her a soft smile. "Just a long day, thinking about lots of things," he assured her. She smiled back, although she remained unconvinced. As she left the office, Niall turned to his desk to check his emails. His desk phone rang. It was Mallory.

"Evening, Peter."

"Evening, Niall. Just ringing around everyone to make sure they are alright after our discussion at the restaurant. Are you okay? And Yvonne?"

"We're fine, thanks, Peter."

"Had any more thoughts about how we might use the Foundation fund, with Derek's and William's money in it? I just keep thinking about the idea of investing some of it in our personal security. I'm sure it would be something they would want."

"I've not really given it much thought, sorry. It's been pretty full-on here at work," Niall admitted.

"Oh yes, of course. Sorry. I'll let you get back to it," said Mallory, knowing Niall would still be in the office despite the time. They said their farewells, but as Niall replaced the handset and tried to relook at his emails, his thoughts drifted onto the fund. Originally, they committed to invest several thousand pounds a year and, as there were seven people depositing into the fund and Niall ensured it was invested wisely, the fund had grown steadily to £10m. As they were all now wealthy in their own right, the payments into the fund were inconsequential, and it was likely that no one even noticed them going out of their accounts. What had brought it back to Niall's attention was William's death.

The fund agreement included a clause that when one of them died and had no beneficiaries to inherit their estate, it would be bequeathed to the fund, and the remaining members of the Aeternum could decide which good cause should receive it. Given two of them had now died and neither had any living relatives, the fund had suddenly ballooned.

No one had ever discussed the practicalities of deciding how to distribute it and to who until now, but suddenly some of his very wealthy friends seemed very interested in how the money might be allocated. Niall found himself speculating whether the devastating deaths of two of the group had turned into an opportunity for one of the Aeternum?

"I know one of you would very much like to get your hands on that money," he said out loud.

Chapter 48

"Morning all," said Denton to those attending the HMET early morning call. "Couple of things on the agenda this morning, with forensics hopefully confirming a lead a little later. First though, we have an update from Police Scotland and Gloucestershire CID on our latest victims; Alfred Churchill and his granddaughter, and a Trevor Hewland. I'll hand you over to DC Jones."

"Thanks, guv. Morning all. First up, a report from Police Scotland. A few days ago, local officers attended a property on Stark Avenue in Falkirk. A concerned neighbour had called to say they hadn't seen or heard from Mr Churchill for several days. The officer had to force entry into the property, and he found Mr Churchill, his granddaughter and his dog, all dead. There was a rolled-up copy of the usual lottery ticket in Mr Churchill's mouth. After the post mortems, the coroner and a vet confirmed there were lethal traces of thallium sulphate in all their bloodstreams."

"What's thallium sulphate?" asked DC Givens.

"It's a toxic heavy metal. In powder form, it's white, soluble, and odourless. It's normally used in very low concentrations; for example, they use it in fireworks and more commonly in rat poison, but the concentration in domestic products isn't high enough to kill a healthy human being. Unfortunately, the forensics report states all three of them had an excessive amount in their bloodstream."

"How did it get into their system?" asked Armitage.

Jones explained, "SOCO removed a number of items from Mr Churchill's property. In the kitchen bin, they found heavy traces of it, apparently mixed in with baking soda and with some flour. It seems that Mr Churchill and his granddaughter had been baking, and we assume that while preparing the raw ingredients, some was probably mixed with liquid, making it easily absorbed through the skin. As a poison, it affects almost every tissue in the body, especially the nervous system and the heart. In high enough doses, it's dangerous to handle even if you're wearing rubber gloves." She waited for any immediate questions before Denton asked her to move on to the second report.

"Yesterday, Gloucester CID was called in following the death of Mr Trevor Hewland, a retired director of a petrochemical company and now a successful local chocolatier. He was found dead, and after local officers retraced his steps, they interviewed a barman at the local pub. Apparently, Mr Hewland was in a physical altercation with an unknown man, and he too died from thallium sulphate poisoning. They found a small hypodermic puncture wound in his neck, just inside the hairline."

"The local CID teams have confirmed that a rolled-up copy of the lottery ticket was found in both Mr Churchill's and Mr Hewland's mouths. Mr Churchill lived at 48 Stark Avenue, which has an FK postcode, and Mr Hewland lived at 7 Charlotte Street, which has a GL postcode," added Denton, looking at the board.

- *7 of 10 victims are male: 2 knew each other*
- *5 different police jurisdictions*
- *Lottery ticket in mouth at every scene*
- *No trace at 5 of the 6 scenes. Professional hit?*
- *Theft does not appear to be a motive*

Notes related to lottery ticket

6 house numbers match the numbers on the first ticket.
Assumption is first house has #24 associated.

??	**29**	**30**	**36**	**46**	**48**	**7**
AL	**B**D	**C**R	**D**A	**E**N	**F**K	**G**L

"So, that's the ticket completed," Williams said.

Denton nodded and said, "Now we just need to find the sick bastard responsible. Here's hoping the forensics team has some good news about some trace analysis from the Weller murder."

It was over an hour later when Jones walked into Denton's office with the forensics report on the murder of Harry Weller.

"What have we got?" asked Denton.

"Trace and match," she replied.

"Who?"

"A career criminal; Stefan Popescu. Polish national who's been living in central London for 20 or so years. He's been in and out of jail over most of the last 15, although usually only on minor assault charges."

"How reliable is the forensics proof?" asked Denton nervously.

"The sample was small, but they're over 90 per cent sure it will stick in court."

"Thank you," said Denton, thumping the desk in triumph. A breakthrough, at last. "Now, go get him."

Chapter 49

His arms were bound behind him, and he was strapped to a chair that was bolted to the floor. His eyes were swollen and his face battered, bloodied and bruised, but he was clearly a powerful man because, despite Tom and Jerry's best efforts, he was still smirking when The Broker entered the basement.

"What have you found out so far?" asked The Broker.

"Not much, boss," replied Tom. "We know he works for Ruiz, but he said that as if it was a threat rather than a confession." The Broker noticed both his men had raw knuckles. He looked at the man in the chair, who spat some blood on the floor towards The Broker.

"Why were you at the professor's apartment? If you tell me, we'll make it painless, because you know this will only end one way, don't you? We have Nembutal, so you can fall asleep and never wake up, or we have a baseball bat. The end result is the same, either way. It's your choice." The man didn't blink or flinch; he just stared at The Broker with the same smirk on his face.

"As you wish," said The Broker, and he then nodded to his men. From a dimmed corner of the basement, Jerry retrieved the baseball bat. From a table in the other corner, Tom grabbed a handheld iron mallet. As Jerry produced swishing sounds from repeated practice swings, Tom brought the mallet down hard on the man's right shoulder. The man suppressed an anguished cry and then refocused his stare on The Broker, who impassively gazed back before nodding once. The mallet crashed into the man's shoulder again, breaking skin and bone in a bloody explosion. The man couldn't suppress his cry of pain this time, but he seemed to quickly control his emotions and stared at The Broker with gritted teeth and a glare. The Broker waited a couple of seconds before he signalled another blow, with another single nod of his head. This time, the man cried out in unadulterated pain.

"This can stop," he said to the man as he held his hand up to indicate Tom and Jerry should wait. "I just want you to answer a few simple questions, and all this pain and suffering will end." The man hung his head as if thinking about his options before he looked up with disdain in his eyes.

"You don't understand; if I tell you anything, Ruiz will kill my family. You think you are a sick fuck? You are nothing compared to him."

"But if you tell me what I need to know, how will he find out?"

"Because I am the only one that he has given the information to. He is clever as well as brutal. No matter what you do to me, my wife and children are my priority. I will never talk." He hung his head again as he awaited his fate. Although The Broker was a hardened criminal, the other side of his life meant he could relate to this man's predicament. He looked up at Tom and Jerry, who, for a moment, thought he was about to signal they should continue, but The Broker shook his head. He had an idea.

"What if there was an alternative?" he asked.

The man didn't look up but replied, "There is no alternative. You kill me, or he kills me AND my family," he muttered. "I am better dead to them than breaking my silence."

"What if none of you had to die?" The man said nothing for a few seconds but then slowly lifted his head. He wanted to know more. "What if we secured your family's safe passage, and you came to work for me?" The man narrowed his eyes as he assessed whether he thought the offer was genuine and viable. In an attempt to further placate him, The Broker indicated that Tom and Jerry should put their crude weapons down. The man's eyes flicked from one side to the other as he heard the clunking sounds of the weapons being dropped onto the floor. He then looked back at The Broker, appraising the situation a little longer.

"How do I know you are being truthful?" he asked.

"How do I know you've actually got anything of value to tell me?" responded The Broker. Another few seconds passed as the man considered the proposal, all the time watching the face of his torturer. The Broker remained impassive as he returned the gaze and then asked, "How old are your children?"

"Why do you care?"

"Mine are 5, 9 and 12; two boys and a girl. They are my world," replied The Broker with a warm and gentle empathetic smile. The man remained unconvinced, but he was softening.

"Sasha and Katarina," he eventually answered. "They are 9 and 6," he added. The Broker nodded at him again in encouragement.

"And what is your name?" asked The Broker.

"Luka."

"Thank you for trusting me, Luka. Before we continue, how about some pain relief for your damaged shoulder?" The Broker looked over to Tom, who pulled a small case out of his inside pocket and removed a syringe. Luka flinched. "Don't worry, Luka; it's only some low-dosage morphine, but it will ease the pain without dulling your cognitive senses." Luka relaxed a little, and Tom injected the drug into his upper arm. After a few minutes, the numbing agent started to work, and Luka nodded in appreciation.

"Can you undo the straps on the chair, so I can move a little easier?"

"No, not yet. The straps are holding your shoulder in place. If you move your body now, you probably won't feel the pain because of the morphine, but you could cause some irreparable damage. A bit like removing a splint too early." Luka was no medical expert, but while he was on morphine, he did feel a little unsteady. No point risking further injury by falling over.

"I don't know if that's bullshit, but as I can't move anyway, I'll assume it's good advice," he said, accepting his situation.

"Do you want to give my associates some information about your wife? I'd like to show my intent by at least putting some security around her," asked The Broker. Luka was torn. Could he really believe this man, or would providing him with some personal details actually give him even greater power and influence? Was this man just as sick and twisted as Ruiz?

"Why would you do this?" he questioned.

The Broker sighed, but he understood Luka's reluctance. He grabbed a nearby stool and pulled it towards him, so he could sit in front of Luka. "It's simple; you have information I want, and I have the ability to provide you with some peace of mind. It feels like a fair trade to me. If it was my family, I'd take the risk. After all, what's your other option, really? I kill you, but maybe Ruiz leaves your family alone? If I was Ruiz and I found out you'd been captured, I'm not sure I'd want to leave your family alone. That would show compassion on his part, and if he's anything like you say, I don't think he can afford others to see he has compassion, do you?" Luka listened, and although he tried not to, he swallowed hard as he thought about the scenarIo. What choice did he really have?

"What do you want to know?" he asked, submitting to the only option he felt he had left. The Broker gently laid his hand on Luka's undamaged shoulder as a sign of gratitude.

"What were you looking for at the professor's apartment?" he asked Luka softly. The man sighed in resignation as he prepared to tell his captors everything.

"Ruiz told me that the professor has something he needed, something which, in his hands, was of great value. He told me he would pay me £100,000 if I found them and delivered them to him."

"Them?"

"Yes; two sheets of paper. He needed them to complete something he already had. Without the two pieces of paper, the rest of it is worthless."

The broker leant in a little closer as he questioned Luka further. "Two sheets of paper, like from a report?" Luka slowly nodded his head a little, unsure how this man could possibly know they were from a report. "Were the pages numbered, like in a book?" Luka furrowed his brow, confused at how his captor seemed to know so much.

"Yes; pages..." and as he spoke, The Broker spoke as well, "26 and 27," they said in unison.

"And did you find them?"

Luka shook his head. "I looked in every possible place. I even hacked his computer and was searching the files on it before these turned up." He indicated he meant Tom and Jerry. The Broker reflected on the information for a moment and then looked back at Luka with one more question.

"And Ruiz didn't give any indication as to what was so valuable about the contents?" Luka shook his head, repeating that Ruiz had just said they were part of a report and, without them, the report was useless. "Like a list of ingredients, but without the recipe," whispered The Broker, remembering the metaphor Niall Fitzgerald had used when he had read the incomplete report. He stood and looked down at Luka, smiling. "Thank you, Luka," he said as he turned towards the door.

"Is that it?" asked Luka.

"Just one more thing," said The Broker as he fumbled for something underneath his jacket. He then turned back to look at Luka and shot him in the head. Tom and Jerry looked on, shocked. The Broker glanced at both of them, his eyes devoid of remorse. "You're too easily led. I don't believe he had a family. Besides, if he betrayed Ruiz that easily, he would just as easily betray us."

Tom and Jerry were not as convinced as their boss, but he didn't care. He now knew he wanted those two missing pages. "Clean this up; we have work to do."

Chapter 50

She is due here any minute. I'm not sure how much longer I can stall her.

His text initiated an immediate response:

Everything seems to be progressing according to plan. Do you really need to panic?

The reply both infuriated and chastened Charles Wagstaff. He was the one who had to manage a second meeting with Evie Perry. It was mid-afternoon and, ordinarily, he wouldn't touch alcohol while at work, but today felt different. Did the person asking if he needed to panic know what it's like to have close friends being brutally murdered, when the woman he was about to meet was responsible? He swigged a generous glass of scotch and then wiped his lips with the back of his hand, an uncouth behaviour he loathed but did unconsciously when he felt under extreme pressure. He straightened his tie, swept his hair to tidy it, and dabbed beads of sweat from his temples as he drummed his fingers nervously on his desk. His desk phone buzzed.

"Yes?"

"Miss Perry is here to see you, Mr Wagstaff." He stood, took a deep breath and walked over to open his office door.

"Ah, Evie; welcome. I was wondering if you'd had a change of heart?"

"Of course not," she responded. That was it, no polite conversation. He realised there was a change in her demeanour compared to the first time they'd met. She now appeared cold and confident.

"Well, you're here, and that's all that matters. Please, sit." Evie strode to the chair near his desk. "So, are you happy to continue or have you reflected on the proposal?" asked Wagstaff.

"Perhaps I was a little hesitant at our first meeting, but I assure you I'm very clear on what needs to happen next," Evie replied. She opened her oversized bag and reached inside for a thick folder she had prepared. As she put the folder on his desk, several sheets slid out onto the floor.

Wagstaff put his hand up. "I'll grab those, don't worry." He scooped up the papers and put them on his desk. "Now, I'd love to hear how things are going?"

"It's all starting to come together, although I'll have some more documents soon. Someone is helping me," she admitted.

"Oh good, that will help make things a little easier, I'm sure. Who is it? We need them to sign a confidentiality clause to protect your interests," Wagstaff said, hoping to find out some more information. Any potential loose ends would need to be dealt with.

"Don't worry; they're already legally required to keep everything confidential," Evie said with a sneer. "No one is going to screw me over ever again, or I'll have them begging for forgiveness… which now leads me to you," she said, staring Wagstaff in the eyes. He was unsure how to take her statement as she maintained the stare for a little longer than was comfortable. Just as he was feeling compelled to break the suffocating silence, she pulled out an envelope. "Here, the contract your PA sent me; all signed." Wagstaff dropped his shoulders as his anxiety eased.

"Ah yes, of course." He took the envelope from Evie's outstretched hand and pulled out the paperwork. After a cursory review, a warm smile spread across his face. "Right, well, if you let my research and design team review the material you have, I'll be able to draft a detailed proposal and plan. It will take a few weeks, though; there's a lot of material here."

"Is there any chance you could work on it a little quicker? I have a deadline to meet," she asked, not wanting to share that her finances were stretched.

"We'll do what we can. Maybe it will take a little less time, given some of the people you've been researching are, sadly, no longer with us." As soon as Wagstaff had finished the last sentence, he knew he'd made a mistake. Evie paused and looked up, scrutinising his face.

"What do you mean?" she asked. "You've not looked at the file, so how do you know who's in it?"

Wagstaff hesitated and then tried to buy a little time by shuffling the papers he had previously picked up from the floor. To his relief, he caught sight of a photo of William Curtis on one of them and, with a well-rehearsed smile, he said, "Because I noticed this sheet that fell on the floor. It has information about one of the men they've recently found dead." Externally, he was calm and in control, but inside he was silently saying thank you to whatever deity was listening.

Chapter 51

His mobile phone rang. Denton checked the CLI showing on the screen and grabbed the phone.

"What have you found, Jonesy?" he asked.

"Not much," she replied dejectedly. She had led the dawn raid on Stefan Popescu's house, but the news wasn't good.

"When the team entered the property, they found Popescu dead. There was a lot of blood, and SOCO has done an initial assessment. Bear with me while I get to my notes." Denton tapped the desk quietly but impatiently as he listened to her flick through her notepad.

"Right; SOCO says Popescu has over 15 puncture wounds, one of which probably penetrated the heart. They found a blood-stained carving knife on the kitchen floor, which appears to be part of a set he owned: the other four knives are still in the block on the worktop. He has patterns of sharp-force trauma on his hands and forearms, which suggests he had tried to defend himself, at least for a while. Couple of incised wounds on the legs are typical of someone kicking out while lying on the floor." Denton's shoulders drooped. He had hoped they could interrogate Popescu and understand more about the motive and the apparent coordination of the murders.

"Any signs of a break-in?" enquired Denton.

"Yes. A patio door in the lounge was broken, but SOCO say it's possible that it was smashed after the attack, as there appears to be blood underneath the broken glass, not just on it. They want to check, though, as the blood could belong to the person who broke the glass, or the broken glass could have been disturbed during the attack."

"So, are we saying there's a possibility that someone faked the break-in after killing Popescu?"

"It's possible. A few items appear to have been taken, though. For example, there's a monitor and a laptop docking station, but no laptop. His wallet was left on the floor; can't say if there was anything in it before, but it's empty now. They also found what looks like a charger lead for an 'encro' phone, but no actual phone. SOCO team has bagged and tagged some paperwork we found in a locked drawer, which included a list of all our current victims. We'll know more in 24-to-48 hours. If it's of any comfort, SOCO found a batch of the lottery tickets like the ones left with the victims, and he fits the physical profile we've been given."

"Okay; that's good news. Keep me posted," Denton replied, but he couldn't hide how disappointed he was. He assumed someone had got to Popescu first to stop him from talking.

"If that's your happy voice, guv, I'd hate to hear you when you're given bad news," joked Jones.

Denton smiled wryly. "Sorry, Jonesy; guess I just hoped we'd find the reason for the murders. Close the scene and let's get forensics working on the evidence. Maybe they'll find something that helps us understand why he chose those people. I need you back here as I think I know who to talk to about Popescu, and I know just where he'll be."

Chapter 52

For most people, it was quite an ordinary day. Some were headed to offices and jobs they either loved or loathed, while others took children to school. The postman commented to a passer-by that the weather was quite unremarkable. For Stella Kendrick, though, today might be an extraordinary day because Robert had said he was coming to see her at some point this week. For days, she had sat on the small roof terrace and would race to the balcony edge every time she heard a vehicle approaching, but it was usually someone picking up a work colleague or a delivery courier with a parcel for one of the residents. She had barely slept, too, wondering if he would arrive during the night and be unable to access the apartment if she was asleep.

As her tired eyes started to close, she heard another car pull up outside. Two car doors opened, and then there were two voices, followed by a 'clunk' as if someone was closing the boot of the car. Then she heard two car doors close, the engine start, and then the car drove off. She listened for any tell-tale sound, however faint. Was that the front door she heard clicking shut? Wearily she got out of her chair and went down into the apartment. A minute later she felt wide awake when she heard someone sliding a key into the lock of her apartment door. She didn't know whether to cry with joy or scream in fear.

The door opened, shut, and then a voice said, "Stella? Stella, are you home?"

She ran through the lounge and into the hallway but then stopped in her tracks. The person standing in front of her didn't look like Robert. This man was bald, tanned, had a beard and moustache, and was much slimmer than Robert had been, and yet the eyes and the cheeky crooked smile.

"Robert?" she asked tentatively.

His smile grew broader. "Hello my little ladybug."

For a second, Stella stood her ground as if still trying to process what was happening. The voice certainly sounded similar, although a little gruff compared to before. Then, in a sudden explosion of relief and belief, she threw her arms around him.

"Oh my god, is it really you?" she said, as tears began to roll down her cheeks.

"Yes, it's really me."

She looked into his eyes and at his face. "I see you've not been eating properly, and you seem to have run out of shaving cream," she scolded him playfully, tears of joy still rolling down her cheeks.

"It's the only reason I came back. Got tired of eating freshly caught seafood with my native island girlfriends. Well, that and I have laundry that needs doing," he replied. Stella exhaled and relaxed, so happy and content. "So, any chance I might actually get out of the hallway?" he asked.

"Oh sorry. Yes, of course, my darling. It's just…"

"I know," he said softly. "I seem to have been waiting forever to see you again. I'm sorry it took so long." His eyes began to glisten with joy and relief, as well.

"Come on. Leave your case there and I'll put the kettle on. Are you hungry?"

"Oh starving," he said, taking his coat and shoes off. Stella grabbed his hand and led him to the lounge.

"You sit there and make yourself comfortable. I'll make a pot of tea, and I'll see what choices we have for lunch." Robert plonked in the armchair as Stella rushed into the kitchen. As she prepared the drink and checked the cupboards, she called through, talking at a frantic pace, "I can't tell you how much I've been watching and waiting the last few days. I was so nervous; I've hardly slept a wink. I know, I know, that's silly of me but... Well, anyway, you're here now, and once you've had some hot tea, some homemade food, and a hot shower, I want to know everything. Well, perhaps not everything, but I'll let you tell me what you want to tell me and if I have questions, I'll just ask. Erm, we have tuna and some lovely fresh bread. Would that be nice? Robert?"

The sudden silence filled Stella with an irrational fear. "Robert?" she called out softly but with apprehension. There was still no reply. Stella gripped the bread knife she was about to use as she eased her way cautiously toward the lounge. She could see the top of his head just above the backrest of the chair, but there was no movement. The silence was suddenly shattered by the loudest snore she had ever heard. She tiptoed up to the chair and looked at him; he was fast asleep. She smiled at the peaceful expression on his face.

"Oh, you must be so tired, my darling," she whispered as she pulled a light blanket from the settee and gently laid it across her husband.

Two hours later, she heard him rouse, followed by him calling out, "Where's this cup of tea? The service in here is dreadful."

"Coming, your lordship," she called back. She made some fresh tea and uncovered the sandwiches she had made earlier. He drank and ate like a starving man at a banquet. Minutes later, he sighed with satisfaction.

"No one, but no one makes a tuna sandwich as well as you do, Stella."

"Not even one of your island-dwelling, bare-breasted, sun-kissed girlfriends?" she jibed. He feigned mulling the question over, but she just beamed. She was so happy, and life felt almost normal again. They laughed and joked about all sorts of things for a while until it was obvious that they were skirting around the big topic: what had happened to him? The laughter became a little forced and the smiling a little weary, so he stopped talking, looked her in the eyes and said, "Shall we answer all the questions you probably have?"

"Do I want to know the answers?" asked Stella, a little worried about what he might tell her.

"I don't know, do you?" he answered.

She paused, collected her thoughts and said, "What was your real job? I always wondered how recruitment could pay so much, but I suppose I was too frightened or simply too content with our luxury lifestyle that I didn't want to ask for fear I wouldn't like the answer."

He sat upright in the chair and his demeanour changed. He knew this was going to hurt his wife, but perhaps it was time to tell her everything she needed to know.

"As you know, I had a number of recruitment clients for several years, but one of them approached me with an offer which seemed out of this world. Too good to be true, some would say. His name was Dennis Ruiz, and he told me his company offered cybersecurity training and education to large corporations and high-worth individuals. I never questioned it, probably for the same reasons you didn't," he said, reaching out to take Stella's hand. "A few of years later, I began to suspect something wasn't quite right. I mean, these were really talented developers, but the incentives they got were just extraordinary. Usually, £1m as a golden hello; to help staff recruitment and retention because they were almost bleeding edge programmers, and there were lots of big corporates who would snap them up. Ruiz didn't want that; he demanded loyalty and got it. I can only think of one, maybe two people who left, and that was over a five-year period.

"Anyway, one day I accidentally walked into a meeting room and bumped into a man called David Holding. I thought he was there for the meeting I had been invited to, and I guess he mistook me for someone else who was due to attend a different meeting with him. We got talking about investments and returns and how the company he was part of moved the crypto-currency Ruiz's company demanded from clients. I thought he was talking about a licence-fee structure for the security software that Ruiz told me sat on clients' server estates. Ten minutes in and the real attendee for David's meeting turned up, apologised, and asked who I was. David said I'd offered to keep him company, as Ruiz didn't like unaccompanied visitors. That's when he said, '*Nice talking to you. Here's my card.*' I took it as a hint that he wanted to talk more."

"And did he?"

"Oh boy, did he! I called him 48 hours later. He asked for my mobile number and said he'd be in touch as he was busy for the next hour, but he sent me a text almost immediately from a private number because he thought his company phone might be mirrored. We agreed to meet up, but we had to wait several weeks before a story could be concocted to disguise our pre-planned rendezvous."

Stella, still holding her husband's hand, leaned in closer, fascinated as well as alarmed.

"When we finally met, he admitted he was frightened that he had unwittingly become involved and implicated in a cybercrime operation, and he wanted out. He knew he needed to find enough incriminating evidence to use as leverage against Ruiz. I think he also thought I'd be able to help because David said he sensed I didn't really understand what was going on in BOrg: 'naive' was how he described my behaviour. He suspected that his partners, Thoresen and Fitzgerald, were knee-deep in collusion with Ruiz, whose blackmail schemes were earning BILLIONS and, just for laundering the money, David believed his partners were banking millions for themselves."

"Blackmail; about what?"

"Oh, anything and everything but mainly ransomware against companies." Stella looked confused, so Robert explained what ransomware was.

"What did you do once you knew?" she then asked.

"David and I agreed to keep talking and, between us, we wanted to find out as much as we could."

"Why?"

"Because neither of us felt we could continue to work for criminals," he said.

"Why did you have to fake your own death?"

"One day, David stopped answering my calls and people around Ruiz started acting differently towards me. I assumed my cover was blown. I sent a text to David on his company phone, telling him I was heading to the coast for the weekend, but I actually went to a lodge in the mountains. I booked it under a pseudonym and paid cash on arrival. I planned my fake death, but it included cutting off two of my fingers." He looked down at his hand, examining the crude stumps where the two were missing. He began to get emotional as he described the pain of cutting them off, even though he had had some local anaesthetic courtesy of a doctor friend. "I just kept thinking of you. That's what got me through; the thought of being able to see you again," he said. "But it's not over yet. I'm still in danger, so I'm hoping you've done as I asked?" he said, trying not to sound as if he was questioning her reliability.

"Yes, of course. I've arranged a meeting with Ruiz's lawyer, but what will that do?"

"You must ask her to tell Ruiz that I've hidden the pages he's looking for, plus my solicitor has a file with enough information to destroy his empire. If he harms either of us, in any way, he'll never find the pages, and I'll bring his world crashing down."

Chapter 53

"Hello, Matthew," said Denton as he walked up to the table, with DC Jones at his side. "Fancy meeting you here?"

Matthew Berry, better known among the criminal fraternity as The Broker, was having his regular Wednesday afternoon family lunch at their local brasserie. His wife looked up but remained relaxed, as her husband explained he often helped the police with enquiries into drug and human trafficking, given his import-export expertise. She knew nothing about his real work. The children gave the two visitors to their table a cursory glance before returning to their Gameboys.

"Mr Denton, what an unexpected surprise. Congratulations are in order, I hear. Detective Inspector? Just a temporary promotion, though?" The news about Denton being temporarily promoted to lead the HMET hadn't been released beyond the HMET team and the Met's CID, but Denton wasn't the least bit surprised that Berry already knew. "I'm sure it's well-deserved. As you can see, I'm having a spot of lunch with my family. Could this wait?" he asked, trying not to let his irritation show. Denton pretended to wince in response.

"Afraid not, Matthew, but it won't take more than a few minutes of your valuable time. I'm sure Mrs Berry won't mind you helping us with an export query?" Denton nodded courteously to her. Berry dabbed his mouth with his napkin and gently pushed his chair back, ready to follow Denton and Jones, who led him to a corner booth where prying ears might find it difficult to overhear their conversation. As they sat down, Denton picked up a menu and whistled at the prices.

"Worth the price, Matthew? Might fancy staying a while and grabbing a soup."

"Let's cut the small talk, Mr Denton. I'd like to get back to my family as quickly as possible, so how can I help?" he said sarcastically.

"Stefan Popescu; what can you tell me about him?"

"Who?" lied The Broker.

"Stefan Popescu," he replied, and Jones pulled out a photo of him, laid out on a gurney at the morgue.

"Never seen him before, and thanks for ruining my appetite," The Broker replied.

"That's not what we've heard, Matthew. We're reliably informed that he's a long-standing associate of yours. He was recently murdered. It was made to look clumsy, but we think different."

"Sorry, but I can't help you. Wish I could. Perhaps your source isn't as reliable as you thought? Who was it? Maybe I can help them remember things properly?" Denton smirked at the offer. He and Jones knew exactly what Berry meant, and they didn't need another dead body on their hands.

Denton tried a different tack. "Not a nice man, Stefan. We think he murdered a family of three and at least two other people. The evidence we found suggests he planned to kill some more."

"Sounds like he got what he deserved, Mr Denton."

"Oh well, forensics tells us that they've lifted a partial print from his apartment, so maybe that will help us bring the murder investigation to a close."

"I'm sure we all hope you can solve a crime for once. You're so over-stretched at the Met. You'd think the government might provide more funding, given the rise in violent crime? Maybe you could apply for some lottery money?" said The Broker, taunting Denton. Now it was Denton's turn to hide his irritation and not react.

"Funny you should mention the lottery, Matthew. Bit like crime, really; it rarely pays, and most of those doing it end up losing."

"Is that all, Mr Denton? You promised my wife that you only needed me for a few minutes, and she's got a very expensive watch, so she'll know you are way over your allocated time."

"Just one more thing," said Denton as he stood. "Had any dealings with members of a group called the Aeternum?"

The Broker guffawed loudly. "The what?" He hadn't heard of the group and found the name slightly ridiculous. Mrs Berry looked over, relieved that her husband seemed to be enjoying his chat with the police.

"Two of the murder victims were part of a social group that went by that name. It's memorable, so I wanted to check if you'd heard of it, that's all."

Berry felt he had endured enough and wanted to get back to his meal. "Nice to see you, acting DI Denton. It was fun, but let's not rush to do it again, eh?" The Broker turned and walked back to his table. As he sat down, his wife began asking him questions, but he just smiled and tried to put her mind at ease.

Outside the brasserie, Jones said, "As expected, guv, although I think he was telling the truth about not knowing about the Aeternum. Pretty sure he asked

Stefan Popescu to murder those people, but I'm just not sure he knows why."

"A man like that rarely cares why; it's just a business transaction."

As they drove away, The Broker typed a text to Tom and Jerry:

The recent application we had to Friends Reunited. I want to know more about him and the woman he tagged as his long-lost half-sister

As soon as it was sent, The Broker smiled; he quite liked playing detective.

Chapter 54

It was nearly the end of a very long day. Daniella Maddox had worked tirelessly to try to find a technicality that would at least mean there might have to be a retrial of Dennis Ruiz. She had tried every angle and every trick a defence lawyer could call on, but there was still nothing. A knock on her office door interrupted her thinking. It was Helen, her assistant.

"Hi, Daniella. I'm heading off now," she said. "Anything you need before I go?"

Maddox shook her head and gave a weak smile. "No thanks, Helen. Have a good evening. I think I'll be here a while longer."

Her assistant knew a little about the case and how many hours Maddox had been in the office this week: 67 already, and it was only Thursday night. "Want me to grab you something from the restaurant downstairs? They do a mean Ziti alla Norma and have a to-go service."

Maddox smiled. Helen was so thoughtful, and the idea did appeal. "You know what, I'd love one, but can you let them know I'll collect it in about 15 minutes?"

"Sure. Oh, and some messages came in for you while you had the door closed." She had a number of sticky notes in her hand, which she put down on Maddox's desk. "See you tomorrow, and don't stay too late," Helen said and gently closed the door behind her.

Maddox turned her attention back to the file she had been looking at but, after several minutes, realised she hadn't taken in a word she'd read. Her phone pinged:

Food ordered. They also asked if you'd like a small glass of something to go with it. I said you wouldn't, but then I ordered you a taxi for 8pm and told them to add a small Pinot Nero to your order. You're welcome 😊 😊

Maddox laughed, and she realised that that wasn't something she'd done in what felt like an awfully long time. She thought for a moment and then replied:

Shank you awfullies for the likkle dwink – hic

She smiled at her own joke. A couple of minutes of frivolity and Maddox felt so much better. She put the file to one side and picked up the pile of written messages:

Please call Mrs Plaxo regarding her upcoming case.

"Jeepers, woman, it's not scheduled for another three months," she muttered, tired of the repeated calls from the nervous client. That message was put into the '*tomorrow*' pile.

Your landlord called regarding access to the balcony.

"I'll deal with that tonight." She popped the note into her handbag.

Ring Zoe at Weinstein & Deroche Solicitors regarding their request for advice for a client from a barrister. That also went in the '*tomorrow*' pile.

Let Andersen Direct know if you want to present at their Bournemouth convention.

Maddox screwed the note up. "We'll file that in my favourite pile of all," she said, throwing it in the bin.

Mrs Stella Kendrick called. Didn't leave a number, but she assumed you'd make space in your diary for her. She says she has something you might be interested in.

Sounded persistent, so I managed to squeeze 15 minutes in for tomorrow.

Maddox was tired and about to put the note in the bin when she realised the handwritten message continued on the back of the note:

She says it might be relevant for Ruiz case.

Maddox hadn't initially recognised the woman's surname, and in all the depositions, evidence, and cross-examinations, the name Stella Kendrick was never mentioned. Suddenly though, Maddox stood up.

"Oh my god!" she exclaimed. She pushed her chair back, raced around the side of her desk and towards the filing room. She punched in the access code and pulled the door open. As she got to the cabinet with the Ruiz documentation in it, she yanked it open. Maddox knew exactly which file she was looking for. She found the case notes on the Hibberd submission and began to flick through it like a woman possessed. After speed-reading 20 pages, she turned back a page, and there was the name she had suddenly remembered. It had only been mentioned once when the person had been confirmed as deceased. Maddox had scribbled a note on the case file purely out of habit:

"Robert Ian Kendrick. The mule manager," she gasped. Her phone pinged. It was Helen again.

Do not forget your food.

Maddox would have forgotten all about it, and the food would be most welcome, as she now had a long night ahead. She replied:

Going there now, thank you. Sorry to ask, but please can you cancel the taxi? I'll sort my own out when I'm ready. We now have a VERY big day tomorrow.

Chapter 55

The front door closed, and Yvonne's heels click-clacked across the polished floor of the hallway as she returned from yet another very long day of shopping and gossip with her friend Alix. She put her bags on the floor and saw the door to Niall's home office was ajar, and the light was on. She knocked gently before pushing it open and peering in.

"I'm expecting it in the morning, so I suggest..." he was saying to someone, clearly trying to remain calm. It wasn't unusual for Niall to be on the phone to an overseas investor at this time of night. He glanced up and gave Yvonne a warm smile but pointed to the phone and shrugged his shoulders. She nodded her understanding and backed out, closing the door behind her. Ten minutes later, Niall jogged up the stairs and walked towards their bedroom. He couldn't help but smile as he caught himself thinking 'our bedroom'. Less than two months earlier, that phrase would have been laughable, but things felt as if they were getting back to normal. As he entered, he saw lots of bags from exclusive London boutiques as well as the makeup bag Yvonne had shown him earlier that day. That's when it hit him; if SILK had sent Yvonne the lip paint, it meant SILK now also knew their home address. Everything that was making him feel good was vulnerable. His blood ran cold, and the fleeting joy he'd felt a moment ago was replaced by fear. He made a decision there and then; he had to protect Yvonne.

She walked out of the adjoining dressing room and smiled. "There you are. Everything alright, darling? That call didn't sound much fun."

"Oh that, that's fine. Just a chat with Charles Wagstaff about some investment news he's waiting for, that's all. He'll just have to wait a little longer," Niall lied. "You've been gone a while?" he asked as he glanced over to the bags of very expensive shopping.

"Oh, Alix and I were having such a lovely time that we decided to add dinner to our plans. Don't worry, it's just a few essentials," she said in response to seeing Niall glance at all the bags. "I do have my own money, Niall," she added, ensuring Niall remembered that she still had several million in her own bank account. It was a pointless gesture, but Yvonne liked to remind him she wasn't entirely dependent on him.

"Well, so long as you had a nice time. I'm sure the Centurion card will cope," he said as he put his arms around her waist. "Anyway, I've been thinking."

"Oh, have you now?" teased Yvonne. "That's usually a dangerous thing." She put her arms around his waist.

"It's been a little hectic recently, so I wondered what you thought about the idea of you and I going over to the villa for a couple of weeks? Get away from it all." Yvonne tilted her head, surprised by the offer and a little intrigued about why.

"What, you take time away from work, mid-year?"

"Well, I'd let you go over first. I'll finish off a couple of things and then fly over in a week or so?" he replied, trying to look as enthusiastic as possible.

"I won't say the idea doesn't appeal. After all, we have had a dreadful time recently with Derek's death, and you have seemed quite stressed," she said, pursing her lips in sympathy. She then paused and moved her arms from around his waist up to his shoulders. She leaned back slightly to look into his eyes. "But I'm not sure about being in the villa all by myself. Fenton won't be there, and there's been a number of break-ins in neighbouring villas recently."

"You'll be fine," Niall said reassuringly. "We have all those security cameras, and I'm sure that if we ask Fenton, he'll be able to arrange some extra hours from the security team so you feel safe. Then, by the time I come over, you'll be enjoying the peace and quiet so much that you'll probably want me to sleep in a hotel," he joked. Niall knew the security upgrade for the villa was excellent. After a spate of break-ins at nearby properties several years ago, he had given Yvonne free rein to have whatever security system installed and whatever security contract in place that made her feel safe.

"What are you smiling for?" asked Yvonne, seeing a faraway look in his eyes.

"Oh, just how lovely it is with you. I nearly lost you, and it's only now that I see and feel just how dreadful that would have been," he said, staring into her eyes lovingly. "And it was all my fault."

"Oh, let's not go there again, Niall. We agreed, no looking back. Just keep that loving look in your eyes and bring it with you to Turks. I'll repay it with interest," she said with a naughty twinkle in her eyes.

"Maybe you need to remind me just how much I should look forward to it?" replied Niall. He kissed Yvonne and embraced her once again.

Yvonne broke the embrace, though, and said, "No freebies here, Mr Fitzgerald. You need to earn your interest." She playfully put her hand on his face and pushed him back so he was lying on the bed. Niall laughed and stayed where he was, watching as Yvonne stepped back towards the dressing room.

"What are you doing?" he called after her.

"Why packing, of course! You're right. I think we've had our fair share of bad news with poor Derek, Celia and Amelia, don't you?" The comment dulled any amorous intent Niall might have had. He considered what to do next and then sat up.

"Actually, I'm afraid I have some bad news to tell you."

"Is everything alright?" Yvonne called back, distracted as she decided which shoes to pack.

"Not really. It's about William Curtis." After a few seconds of silence, Yvonne emerged slowly from the dressing room.

"What about William?" she asked, uneasiness etched onto her face.

"The call I had earlier; it wasn't just about an investment for Charles. I called to let him know William has been killed." Yvonne gasped as she put the palm of her hand to her mouth. She wanted to ask more but was fearful of the answer, given Niall wasn't looking her in the face. "The police came to see me a few days ago to tell me and ask about William's business interests."

Niall glanced up to check Yvonne's expression. She stood, mouth agape, before taking a few unsteady steps forwards, turning, and flopping onto the bed to sit beside him. He took her hand in his, as much a comforting gesture for himself as it was for her.

He looked sideways at her, waiting to see if she returned his gaze. She didn't at first but then snapped out of her reflection.

"Is it linked to Derek's death?"

Niall squeezed her hand gently and lied again, "No, I don't think so. I'm assuming it's just a horrible coincidence."

Yvonne searched his face, looking for assurance. "Are *you* in any sort of danger? Is this why you're sending me to Turks? Because you're worried?"

He squeezed her hand a little harder and assured her, "No, it's not. I promise it's fine. I just think we need a break. It's been a tough few years for us, and if we can't enjoy life, what's the point in having the villa? It feels like a good thing to do, that's all." He looked at her, and gradually her expression changed as a smile of relief grew. Her eyes brightened and she lightly squeezed his hands in response.

"I best go finish packing then," she said. As she rose from the bed and walked back towards the dressing room, she glanced at Niall to see if he had the same reassuring expression. He did, although it was only there because he knew she was going to look for it. As soon as she was out of sight, he dropped the façade. Everything was starting to weigh heavily on his shoulders. He wished he could share his greatest problems with his wife like he used to, but there were still too many unanswered questions.

"I assume we can get first-class tickets quickly?" she shouted back through. "Don't want to be doing all this packing if we can't."

Niall smiled weakly as he tried to sound positive. "There's one heading out from Heathrow on Tuesday.

I noticed you had an appointment in the diary for your therapist on Monday, so I thought I'd best not cancel that. I'll get Maria to confirm the seat first thing," he replied to her.

"Oh, I can confirm my seat. I'm sure you have lots of more important things to do, and I have a couple of appointments to sort out before I go. I'll book the seat and car to Heathrow." Although Niall was happy that Yvonne was taking things into her own hands, he wanted to be sure she was out of the country, and quickly. If SILK was now sending gifts to her at their home, just how long could he keep Yvonne safe and the truth buried?

Chapter 56

A return to heavy drinking had dulled Evie's senses but not her anxiety. She felt increasingly on edge about a threat she had no evidence of. What about the man she thought she saw in a car, taking photographs of her? Why would her best friend, Cheryl, have called the police; did she really think Evie was capable of murder? And her last meeting with Charles Wagstaff triggered an overpowering fear of a conspiracy against her, which wouldn't go away.

"What sort of things are worrying you?" her doctor had asked.

"Everything and nothing," Evie replied.

"Are you feeling depressed, agitated, or do you feel threatened by anything or anyone?"

Why did he ask about feeling threatened? Evie asked herself. *What does he know?*

"A little unsettled, that's all," she lied.

"But you're not sleeping, are you?"

"How do you know that?"

"Er, you told me... a couple of minutes ago. You said..."

"I know what I said," replied Evie brusquely as she cut across him. Her anxiety triggered another irrational thought. Could he be in collusion with the men from the party? Maybe he was actually at the party, and she just couldn't remember? Evie fiddled with her fingers and twitched a little as she argued with her demons. Underneath it all, she felt if she could just sleep, she would be able to sort everything out.

"I'm going to suggest a short course of medication, Evie. The drug is lorazepam; it's what's known as an anxiolytic. I'd also like to dispense it by injection; that way, you don't have to remind yourself when to take tablets or the liquid format. The injection provides a slow release over a number of weeks. After that, we can re-assess things and see what works best for you: is that alright?"

"I suppose so," she said unconvincingly. If she believed the doctor wasn't part of any conspiracy, not having to remember to take the medication would be really helpful.

"Good. Now, there are risks with all medication, so please let me know if you feel overly restless, your speech becomes a little slurred, or your muscles feel unusually weak or stiff. It's a low risk, but it's a risk, nevertheless. You also mustn't drive while you're on this medication."

Evie was disappointed about not being able to drive but acknowledged the risks. As she was about to leave, the doctor smiled and, in an attempt to reassure her, said, "Take care, Evie. Get some rest, and it will all be over soon, I'm sure." She smiled weakly at him, but the paranoia exploded. What did he mean it would all be over soon? She felt a growing urge to scream and run, but she fought it. If he was involved in the plot against her, she couldn't let him know that she knew. She walked out of the surgery, avoiding eye contact with anyone who was waiting and headed home.

It was only a 20-minute walk from the surgery to her house, but Evie felt exposed. Twice, she walked into shops and pretended to be browsing because she thought she had seen someone following her every move, and on both occasions, the person she suspected simply walked on without giving her a second look. The one person Evie hadn't noticed was the private detective Niall had hired on the premise of finding and assessing what his 'long-lost half-sister' was doing nowadays. When Niall received the information about her home address from The Broker, his initial instinct was to go there and threaten her, but he realised it probably wouldn't be wise to approach a woman capable of such depravity without at least understanding more about her; just as he wouldn't invest £50m without assessing the risk first.

"I'm hoping to reach out to her, to repair the rift between us before our terminally ill mother finally passes away. I know it would mean so much to our mother to know we were in touch again. I just don't know how she'll react as... well, she had a substance abuse problem in the past. I want to feel assured that her behaviour is rational and predictable before I go to see her," he had said to the investigator.

When the report arrived in Niall's inbox, he was surprised. The private detective's feedback was simple; he had witnessed a paranoid woman who appeared to be capable of anything and should be approached with caution. Having said that, he had observed a fragility that meant a sudden and unexpected reunion might lead to a flight rather than a fight response. It was over three years since Niall had last seen the very self-confident SILK, but the report suggested she might be suffering with psychosis, so Niall decided that a visit needed to wait. Then again, if he had gone to see her earlier, maybe his friends might still have been alive? Instead, he thought of a new plan.

"Time for the hunter to become the hunted."

Chapter 57

The session had been scheduled for noon, but Yvonne had made an urgent request to bring the start time forwards by several hours. She sounded a little fraught over the phone, so the therapist agreed to meet her at 7am. As she unlocked the door just before 7am, Yvonne was already standing outside.

"Goodness," said the therapist, and without any greeting in return, Yvonne pushed past her. It was clear she was very worried about something, and she walked straight into the private counselling room and sat in her usual chair. As soon as the therapist followed her in and closed the door, Yvonne started to talk.

"There's something going on; I can feel it. It's not the same feeling as I had before, years ago, but he is acting differently again. It's like he's suppressing something that he wants to talk about but can't... or won't," Yvonne tried to explain. "Does that make sense?"

"I think so," replied the therapist as she took her seat. "But let me ask you some questions. Firstly, is he less affectionate than he has been in recent weeks?"

Yvonne thought and then replied, "No. It's been wonderful, although sex has become a little less frequent and a little 'angrier'. Not aggressive or dominating; just more like sex than lovemaking." She looked up at the therapist with a perplexed expression, as she didn't feel she was explaining her emotions particularly well.

"I see. Could it be that your current worries might be being triggered by an unfounded fear of losing him again rather than anything he's said or done that's actually different?"

"Are you suggesting I'm imagining the change?"

"It's just a possibility, Yvonne. Sometimes in relationships, when we rediscover love after losing it, it's quite normal to worry about losing it again; perhaps even to unconsciously find oneself looking for things that aren't there. It's natural to prepare yourself for another disappointment, as it would ease the pain should it happen. It's usually nothing, but the behaviour can be quite damaging, to the extent that your husband could start to notice a change in *your* behaviour and react. It can become a vicious and destructive spiral," she explained.

Yvonne shook her head. What the therapist was saying made perfect sense, but Yvonne was sure that wasn't it. She considered sharing the information about the murder of William Curtis.

"I don't think so because... erm, this discussion is client-confidential, correct?" she asked the therapist before she finished her sentence.

"It is, although I must inform you that if a client told me they were about to hurt someone, or themselves, I have a responsibility to inform the police or the person under threat," she replied.

"No; it's nothing like that, or at least I don't think it is. Do you remember me telling you about a friend of my husband who was murdered?"

"Yes, I do," answered a slightly apprehensive therapist.

"Well, another of Niall's friends has been murdered." The therapist took a sharp intake of breath in shock.

Yvonne continued, "I overheard a call my husband had. At first, he told me it was a business call, but then he admitted that another friend was dead. That's when he told me there was nothing to worry about, but perhaps I should fly out to our villa, and he'll join me after he's concluded a business deal. I'm just not sure I believe him."

"Why don't you believe him?"

"I've been married to him for nearly 20 years. I know the difference between him lying, trying to hide a surprise, or about to tell me what he's done wrong. Underneath it all, he's still that frightened little boy from Belfast, talking to his mummy."

Chapter 58

"Okay, I'm ready to head off. Are you sure you'll be alright?" Stella called out nervously as she looked into the mirror and made final adjustments to the cashmere scarf draped around her neck.

"I'll be fine," replied Robert as he walked into the tiny hallway. He stopped and smiled, proud of his brave and clearly very stylish wife.

"Stop it, Robert. You've got that same goofy look you had when we started dating, for goodness' sake," she said, blushing.

"That's because you're just as beautiful as you were then." She shook her head at the silly yet romantic statement and took the few steps towards him, giving him a gentle hug.

"I promise, I'll be fine. Now go; the taxi is waiting downstairs to take you to the airport," Robert assured her again. They stepped apart, and she straightened her clothing in readiness for her early morning flight up to Leeds to meet Daniella Maddox.

The journey from their apartment to the offices in Leeds took a little over 6 hours. When she finally stepped out of the taxi in Park Square in Leeds, it was onto a quiet leafy street with rows of Georgian office buildings on all sides, bordering a small communal park. She turned and looked up at the row of buildings nearest to her and felt her anxiety levels rising.

"Come on, Stella, you've got to pull yourself together," she muttered. She opened her handbag and checked the contents for the twentieth time today, then checked her watch. She was a few minutes early, but she gathered her composure and walked purposefully up the steps. The building she had entered contained Jeavons & Chastain, a regulated firm of barristers. There was no formal reception area, but as she was instructed in last week's phone conversation, she knew she had to head up to the first floor and find the chambers of Daniella Maddox. The door was clearly marked, so she knocked and then opened the door. The room was a lot more spacious than the outside of the building suggested, with a large and very organised desk at one end. It provided a subtle barrier to an inner door that stood just behind it. Sat at the desk was a woman with a warm smile and gentle but firm voice, the woman Stella had spoken to last week.

"Good morning. Mrs Kendrick?" the woman enquired.

"Yes. I'm here for my meeting with Miss Daniella Maddox."

"Hello, I'm Helen, Miss Maddox's assistant. We spoke last week? Please, take a seat. Can I offer you a drink?"

"Oh no, thank you," replied Stella, who felt a growing trepidation about the meeting.

"Daniella won't be long. She's usually very punctual, but today is a bit of a manic Friday." The woman smiled apologetically. Moments later, the inner door opened, and a woman of what Stella thought might be Italian extraction appeared. Her English was near perfect, though, with just a hint of an accent, which

Stella thought only added to the woman's stunning good looks and fashion sense.

"Mrs Kendrick?" she enquired.

"Yes," Stella said, standing quickly. Maddox noticed her nervousness straight away.

"Please do come in. I'm so sorry if you've been waiting. I know coming to see a barrister can be a little stressful for some people." Stella smiled. She was grateful that Maddox had sensed her anxiety and taken the time to gently put her at ease. Maddox gestured for her to take a seat in one of two small leather chairs that sat in the corner next to a large window.

"Have you been offered a drink?" Maddox asked.

"Yes, your assistant did ask, although I would like a water now, actually. Tap water is fine." A couple of minutes later, Stella and Maddox were settled with a drink. Maddox took out a notepad but laid it on the table in readiness. While she was eager to ask Robert Kendrick's wife all sorts of questions, she felt it might take some patience to ensure Mrs Kendrick felt at ease.

"Miss Maddox, can I..." Stella paused, partway through her question. "... depend on you?"

"Mrs Kendrick, everything we say is considered privileged information that I cannot legally share with anyone unless you say I can."

"That wasn't my question," stated a nervous but surprisingly assertive Stella. "What you can do legally and what you might do could be two very different things." Maddox paused, assessing the statement. Clearly Stella Kendrick was shrewd, and her shy persona of earlier had vanished. Maddox nodded her head and gave a knowing smile.

"Yes, Mrs Kendrick, I appreciate the difference, but I can assure you I have morals and ethics, not just a knowledge of the law."

"You say that, but you are defending a callous criminal, a criminal who wants my husband dead, so how do I know you mean it?" Maddox narrowed her eyes as she replayed the phrase '*wants my husband dead*'.

"Mrs Kendrick, did you just refer to your husband in the present tense?"

Now it was Stella's turn to smile. "Yes, Miss Maddox, I did. Does that surprise you?"

Maddox deliberated for a moment. "Actually, no. Nothing about this case surprises me anymore." She stood and walked over to her office door, opened it, and asked Helen to rearrange her diary for the next hour, as she had the feeling this meeting was going to take longer than the 15 minutes that had been allocated. Stella's belief in Maddox grew a little more, so she decided to test her a little further. She reached down for her handbag, glancing at Maddox one more time before undoing the clip on the bag.

"Before I give you something and a message, I need you to confirm that you want me to continue and that whatever happens next, I'm doing this for the safety of my husband and me. I sincerely hope your client rots in hell. Do you understand?" Maddox nodded in acknowledgement. Stella reached inside the handbag and pulled out an envelope, passing it to Maddox as she recalled the words in Robert's letter:

I beg you <u>not</u> to open this unless you literally have no other choice. Please do NOT underestimate the power and the risks that opening that envelope will bring.

Maddox appeared almost hypnotised by the envelope and had to resist reaching out for it. What did it contain that meant this woman had flown from Southampton to give it to her? Stella stared at Maddox for a few more seconds and then extended her arm so Maddox could take the envelope.

"Miss Maddox, before you open it, I have to tell you the following. I don't know what the contents of the envelope are, nor do I know what doors they might open or nightmares they might trigger. All I do know is my husband tells me that you need to tell Mr Ruiz that Robert knows where page 27 is and, if Ruiz wants to know, he has to swear to leave Robert and me alone... and David Holding," she added, almost as an afterthought. Having met Holding a couple of weeks ago, she realised just how much trust there must be between him and Robert.

Having listened to Stella's statement, Maddox had a question, but she wanted to know what was in the envelope before she asked it. She calmly took the envelope from Stella and, hiding her own apprehension, slowly pulled the flap open. She pulled out what seemed to be a single piece of folded paper, so she could examine the contents. She was a little confused by the scientific diagrams and equations printed on it and saw that it had the number '26' printed on the bottom. Stella was intrigued as well and couldn't resist peering over to try to see the contents. Maddox noticed and passed the piece of paper to her. Stella looked at it with the same confusion as Maddox had.

"What does it mean?" asked Stella.

"I don't know, but I expect it might mean quite a lot to my client."

"When will you tell him?"

"I've not got a trip up to the jail planned, but I'll ask Helen to arrange one. I expect it will be the week after next unless..." Maddox stood and walked around her desk, leaning over and pressing a key on her keyboard to bring the device out of sleep mode. She didn't really want to visit Ruiz, given the threat he had made to her, but she knew she didn't have a choice.

She grabbed the mouse and scrolled, clicking several times, before saying, "Okay." She looked up at Stella and added, "I'll put a call in to my client early on Thursday to see what his reaction is. If he's either calm or disinterested in your message, I'll not bother to book time to visit him. If, on the other hand..." but she then paused, deep in thought.

"If, on the other hand, what?" asked Stella.

"Mrs Kendrick, my client is a very influential man with a lot of 'reach', even from inside a prison. I can't reveal any of my conversations with him, just as I can't talk to anyone about our conversation now, but I would suggest you consider keeping a very low profile for a few weeks. If this message means something to Mr Ruiz, things could escalate very quickly. If you can't get out of the country, might I suggest you stock up on food, close all the curtains, and do not answer the door to anyone." Stella now felt in danger and very aware that it would be several hours before she would be back at home with Robert.

"And I have another question for you. You do *not* have to answer it, but it will clear up something I'm confused about," Maddox requested.

Stella looked unsure, but she had trusted Maddox thus far. "Alright, what's your question?"

"Earlier, you mentioned that you hoped this conversation would keep you, your husband and David Holding safe; is that correct?"

"It is."

"How do you know Mr Holding, and why do you care about his safety?"

Stella paused, assessing whether she might be about to say something to Dennis Ruiz's barrister that she could regret. Her voice became hesitant as she replied to Maddox, "My husband told me he trusted David Holding, and when I met David a couple of weeks ago, we discussed everyone's safety. He seemed resigned to his fate and told me that he'd already made arrangements. I'm not sure what he meant, but it didn't seem very promising. Why?"

"Where did you meet him?" asked Maddox, intrigued.

"Robert had arranged for David and I to meet in a coffee shop not too far from where we live." Maddox now looked very confused. "Why do you ask?" said Stella.

"I'm surprised he's travelling, that's all."

"He did seem a little nervous throughout our talk, but I'm sure he must have thought through the risks. He seemed very aware of the danger he was in."

"I didn't mean that. I just meant it's not easy for wheelchair passengers at the best of times, so I was surprised he'd made the effort. You and Robert must mean a lot to him for him to have made the trip."

"A wheelchair?" asked a confused Stella. Maddox suddenly changed her expression from confused to concerned.

"Yes, a wheelchair. David Holding has been in a wheelchair since... Well, since he was attacked just before my client was arrested. The last I'd heard he was recovering well considering the beating he'd taken, but he still needs 24-hour care."

"The man I met wasn't in a..." Stella's face drained of all colour as she realised the implications of what she was about to say.

"Please describe the man you met, Mrs Kendrick," asked Maddox as she picked up her notepad and pen from the small table in front of them. Stella struggled to process her thoughts and speak at the same time, her mind racing.

"Well... he... erm... he... er, about six feet tall. Er... he was, was well built for a man of his age; more than athletic but not muscular, and he had short-cropped hair. I think perhaps... it was dark. No. No, maybe dark hair, but speckled with some grey. I'm... I'm not sure. He was well dressed in a suit but no tie. His eyes were... I'm sorry, but I'm not sure I can remember. I think they were brown," she mumbled as she continued to process the scenario. Then, it was Maddox who paled. Stella Kendrick had just described the mystery man she had seen shaking hands with the managing partner a few days ago.

"Mrs Kendrick, have you spoken to this man since you met him in the coffee shop?"

"No, but I offered him the chance to stay in our apartment if he needed to. He said no, although he seemed to commit the address to memory. I thought Robert would be happy to see him."

Maddox stood abruptly, her face grim. She picked up the handset from her desk and thrust it towards Stella. "Call your husband right now and tell him to pack some bags. He has to get the hell out of there," she urged.

Twenty minutes later, Stella was on her way back to the airport. There was only one flight back to Southampton, and that would be in four hours. She called the apartment and left a message. Robert hadn't answered, and she only hoped the mysterious man pretending to be Holding had not made a surprise visit. What would she do if she arrived home and Robert was dead?

As the taxi sped to Leeds Bradford Airport, Maddox paced around her office. She was processing the information Stella Kendrick had given her and deciding what best to do with it. She could keep it to herself for now, as sometimes waiting for the right time to share something like this is a sensible approach. Then again, she could book an emergency appointment at the jail and talk to Ruiz? No, that wouldn't help. If Ruiz had sent the fake Holding, tipping him off that they now knew about it would be dangerous as, even in jail, he could get a message out quickly about the Kendricks. As she pondered another option, she sat at her desk and opened up her file on Ruiz. That was when she saw the post-it note that one of the partners had secretly left for her. She stared at it, and a smile spread across her face; it was the obvious choice. She pressed a button on her desk phone and it buzzed her assistant. A few seconds later, Helen knocked on her door and came in.

"Helen, please arrange a meeting for me with Adrian Skelton."

"Okay, although you're pretty booked up until the end of next month."

"No, I mean first thing next week."

Her PA stopped and glanced at Maddox in surprise. "But he's booked into a…"

"I don't care what he's doing," interrupted Maddox. "Just tell him I want to talk to him about a post-it note and Ruiz. Tell him I won't take no for an answer." Two minutes later, Helen walked back into Maddox's office with a stunned look on her face.

"Adrian says he'll see you Monday at Mrs Atha's. 1pm and you're buying."

PART 3: IT'S A ROLLOVER

Chapter 59

James Vickers had opened a new surgery in Harrogate, such was the success of his London-based practice. He now used this as a part-time office, and the local clientele were very wealthy and very eager for his skills. His receptionist had had no lunch break, but he only had a pre-surgery check-up to see before the end of the day, so he told her she could go home early. When he went to greet his last patient in the reception area, he froze when he saw who it actually was. She had someone with her; a man who was built like an athlete and dressed like a private security guard.

"I'm a little surprised to see you up here. It's been a few years," he said, realising that she must have used a false name for the appointment.

The woman looked at him – a confident smile on her face – and replied, "I'm a little surprised too, truth be told. You're one of the last men on earth I'd want to see." She walked into his office, looking around at nothing in particular. It was intended to make him feel uncomfortable, and it worked. Her friend had walked in as well, but he just sat impassively.

"You seem well," he said, trying to work out why she hadn't arranged a meeting in London instead.

"Do I?" she replied in an exaggerated, questioning tone.

"I did everything I could; you know I did. I couldn't have done any more, and I'm not sure that anyone else could have either. I'm sorry for what happened. You are as…" He paused, trying to think of the right words.

She finished the sentence for him, "… as good as I can ever hope to be, James?" He looked at her with both guilt and sadness on his face before answering with a simple word: "Yes."

"Do you think having such a scar feels like an attractive feature?" she taunted as she ambled slowly around the office, staring at the certificates on the wall that confirmed his qualifications. "You are a remarkable surgeon, James, and I'm grateful, given what you tried to do, truly I am."

"So why are you here after all this time?"

"Because I've decided that the suffering I've endured since you tried to 'make me as good as you could' really isn't excusable. I no longer feel whole, whereas I used to feel beautiful."

"I know what happened to you was terrible." Vickers knew he was in danger of making the current situation worse, but what he said was true, and he had tried to do everything he medically could.

"Oh, James," she said, and she stopped walking. Vickers could hear his heart thumping and was convinced she must be able to as well. The friend who accompanied her put down the magazine he was flicking through and stared at Vickers with a mischievous smile on his face.

"What is it you want?" he asked. She smiled.

"I want revenge." She let the word hang in the air before she turned round quickly. He took an involuntary half-step back, which made her smile even more. "Don't worry, James, I'm not looking to destroy what you've built. Your reputation will remain intact for the rest of your life." She swished her dress playfully before she walked up behind Vickers and stood less than a foot away from him. He could feel her hot breath on his neck. "But let's keep this visit a secret, shall we?" She startled him by clicking her fingers as she said, "I've taken enough of your valuable time. Places to go, people to see." She gave a girlish grin and a wink as she left his office, but her friend didn't follow her. He closed the door behind her and pushed an increasingly nervous Vickers into a chair behind his desk.

Two hundred miles away, Niall was in deep thought as he looked out over the lawn and towards the outdoor pool. He had had a troubling week and needed to gather his thoughts in some peace and quiet now that Yvonne had left for the villa. His phone buzzed, and he recognised the caller ID on Zoom.

"Evening, James. I wasn't expec—" but he stopped mid-sentence as he took in the image on the screen. It seemed as if the phone was propped on the other side of James's desk because the whole of James Vickers' upper body was visible on the screen. He sat staring at the camera with a look of fear on his face. As he opened his mouth to talk, he unexpectedly snapped his head to his left and nodded frantically.

"James, are you alright? I think you're on mute."

Vickers swallowed hard but still didn't speak. Instead, he held up a piece of paper which read:

I am not allowed to speak.

Just as Niall was about to ask what was going on, he put that piece of paper down and lifted up another:

Hello Niall. Do I have your attention now?

"James, what's going on?" asked an increasingly worried Niall, but all Vickers did was cast that piece of paper aside and pick up another one:

The price has gone up, from £100m to £200m, because you don't seem to be listening.

Niall suddenly realised what was happening.

"Oh no," he gasped. "James, do whatever she asks. I'll help you; I promise." Vickers could hear the emotion in Niall's voice. With his own hands trembling and tears in his eyes, he held up a fourth message:

Lay waste to a woman's body and soul, and that pain will be returned thrice over. Hell hath no fury...

James stared into the camera, his bottom lip trembling as the barrel of a revolver appeared from the right of the screen and gently nuzzled against the side of his head. It had a suppressor attached. He dropped the piece of paper and picked up a fifth:

Pay me my money or this will only end one way, for all of you. SILK.

The person holding the revolver cocked the hammer. James Vickers must have realised that his life was about to end, so he tried to talk quickly and warn his friend:

"Niall, it's not..." but then the far side of his head exploded as the hollow-pointed bullet drove through his skull. James Vickers' body slumped out of sight, leaving Niall to just stare at an empty screen. He was stunned, speechless, horrified, and unable to move. There was a rustling sound, and then the screen went blank as the signal was cut, but Niall just kept staring at the blank screen.

Early next morning, James Vickers' receptionist found the corpse. Her terrified screams alerted other office tenants, and while most of them tried to comfort her, one of them called the police. Local CID arrived at the scene, and the lead SOCO compiled a field report. When DS Bob Williams arrived at the scene, he reviewed the report, found a photo of the lottery ticket that had been recovered from James Vickers' mouth, and immediately called Denton's phone. It went straight to voicemail.

"Steve, it's Bob. I'm at the offices of a Dr James Vickers. He has a practice in Harrogate. He's been murdered, and SOCO found a lottery ticket in his mouth... but it's got a different set of numbers on it." Williams unconsciously paused as if to let that bombshell sink in. He had just started talking again when the lead SOCO approached him.

"Thought you might like to see this, Detective," said the SOCO, and passed him a plastic evidence bag with a mobile phone in it. Williams looked at the phone as she explained where it had been found and how it was positioned. Williams thanked her and returned to leaving a message for Denton: "Sorry about the pause, Steve, but we might have some evidence. We've found the victim's phone, and I'm sending it to forensics straight away. I could ask SOCO to look at it here, but there's too much risk that we could compromise the evidence. I'll keep you updated. Call me back when you get this message." An hour later, Denton called Williams.

"Sorry, Bob, I was just catching up on some sleep. Tell me everything." When the call had finished, Denton called DS Armitage to ask him to come across to London as soon as possible.

Chapter 60

"Do you want to talk about the victim first or the new lottery ticket, guv?" asked Jones.

"Ticket," replied Denton; his tone and demeanour were cantankerous. It was bad enough that Bob Williams had woken him at 8am after an all-nighter, but he also had an update meeting with the DCI later that day, and, so far, he only had bad news to share.

"We know the ticket was a replica of a draw on 29th January 2016. The prize was a little over £100m and shared between seven people. I've added the details to the wipe-board," she said, and found she was avoiding eye contact with what was a clearly disgruntled Denton.

Commonalities	Differences
7 of 11 victims are male: 3 knew each other	5 different police jurisdictions
Lottery ticket in mouth at every scene	Methods of murder
No trace at 6 of the 7 scenes. Professional hit!	Age of victims
Theft does not appear to be a motive	5 sole murders; one triple and one double.

Notes related to lottery ticket
6 house numbers match the numbers on the first ticket.
Assumption is first house has #24 associated.

??	**29**	**30**	**36**	**46**	**48**	**7**
<u>A</u>L	<u>B</u>D	<u>C</u>R	<u>D</u>A	<u>E</u>N	<u>F</u>K	<u>G</u>L

Sequencing of numbers and letters following the same pattern on the second ticket.

1	5	23	29	32	41	7
<u>H</u>G	I	<u>J</u>E	K?	L?	M?	N?

"Why is the J already marked? Have we had a report of a murder in a J postcode?" asked Denton brusquely.

"There's only one postcode in the UK that starts with J, guv; Jersey."

Denton indicated he understood with just a terse lift of the chin in acknowledgement. There was a knock on the door, and one of the CID team poked his head round.

"Guv, there's a DS Armitage downstairs. Says he's got a meeting with you?" Denton looked at his watch and realised it was almost time for him and Armitage to leave. As they drove over to see Niall Fitzgerald, Denton took the opportunity to brief him on the way to Kingston-Upon-Thames.

"Bob Williams attended a murder scene early today at a private clinic in Harrogate. At 7:30am, a call was logged with 999 about a dead body. The victim was Dr James Vickers; he was a plastic surgeon."

"James Vickers?" queried Armitage.

"Yes, the same person that was on the list of the Aeternum members you got from Mr Fitzgerald," Denton replied. "They found him with a bullet wound to the temple. It wasn't suicide as there was no note or gun at the scene, and he had a copy of a lottery ticket in his mouth."

"What?" asked a shocked Armitage.

"I felt the same, and get this; it's a new set of seven numbers, and the office address in Harrogate matches the first number."

"Shit," replied Armitage.

"We're going to see Mr Fitzgerald because the last data on Vickers' phone showed there was a two-minute video call to his mobile number. We need to find out what was discussed on the call and if there were any clues as to what was about to happen."

"Do we know when Vickers was murdered?" asked Armitage.

"SOCO put the time of death anywhere in a four-hour window, so we don't know if the murder was just after the call or several hours later, but I'm hoping we'll find out more after the interview."

They pulled up in their unmarked car and gazed up at the Fitzgerald house. Although Armitage had been there before, Denton just shook his head. "What sort of money does it take to buy something like this?" he muttered.

Armitage had done some research, so had a good idea of the answer. "£15m," he exclaimed. "For that, you get 70 rooms spread over four floors, including 11 bedrooms, a cinema and a bowling alley, as well as live-in accommodation for staff. There are indoor and outdoor pools, a gym, and space for eight cars when you count the triple garage and the secure under-the-pool showroom."

Denton looked at the colonnade of four fluted Corinthian columns flanked by eight huge windows and shook his head. "We're in the wrong job, Alan." They knocked on the door and waited for someone to answer. Niall opened the door and was distressed to see the police standing there. He quickly tried to gather his composure.

"Sorry if we're a little early," said Armitage.

"I didn't realise you were coming over, Detective Sergeant. I've been a little busy this morning. Is there something I can help you with?"

"Ah," Armitage replied, feigning embarrassment. "I left a message on the house phone a couple of hours ago. Said I just wanted to pop over and, if you didn't mind, I'd be here about 11am." He glanced at his watch and then turned it towards Niall. "See, almost 11. Hope I didn't interrupt anything?"

"No, not at all," Niall replied.

"This is acting Detective Inspector Denton from the London Metropolitan Police. He's leading an enquiry into a number of incidents, and we'd like to talk to you about an acquaintance of yours: Dr James Vickers. Perhaps we could go inside?" Niall tried to look surprised at the mention of Vickers, but he was beginning to perspire.

Denton gave a nod of his head. "Yes, we've already met. Hello again, Mr Fitzgerald. Are you alright?" Denton asked, noticing Niall's discomfort.

"What? Yes, fine. Just a little under the weather, that's all. Been a tough week, what with this cold and without my wife around to look after me." He gave a feeble laugh and received a feeble smile in return.

"Mrs Fitzgerald is away?" asked Armitage.

"Yes. She flew out to our villa in the Caribbean a few days ago. She needed some rest and relaxation, given everything that's happened. I hope to join her once this ruddy cold has gone. Please, this way, gentlemen." He led them through the hallway and into the living room. Before they were even seated, the questions came thick and fast.

"Mr Fitzgerald, did you talk to James Vickers last night?" Niall felt the cold perspiration prickle on his neck.

"Err, yes. Can't remember the time exactly, but James rang me to discuss an upcoming party we were planning. Why?"

"I'm sorry to say that Mr Vickers was found dead this morning," explained Armitage. "The last contact with anyone before he died might have been with you." Niall's knees buckled, and Denton reached out to steady him. Simply hearing what he already knew still came as a shock, but thankfully for him, Denton and Armitage assumed it was genuine shock.

"Are you sure you're alright, Mr Fitzgerald?"

"Yes, yes; I just..." He slowly made his way to a nearby chair. He sat down and took a moment to gather his composure, buying himself time to try to control his nerves.

"We're sorry to break the news to you, but we need to ask you some questions. Firstly, did you notice anything unusual about Mr Vickers' demeanour or actions on the call?" Armitage asked.

Niall pretended to think back, slowly and then more rapidly, shaking his head as if he was more and more sure of what he was about to say. "Nooo... No, not that I noticed. He's always in a bit of a hurry, but... no, he seemed fine."

"Were you aware of any financial problems Mr Vickers might have had?" added Denton.

Again, Niall started to slowly shake his head and confirmed that he had only heard good things and that the business was booming. "He was even talking about opening a third office in Manchester."

"Do you know if Mr Vickers owned a gun?"

"A gun? James? Absolutely not. He abhorred firearms. A medical student of his once accidentally shot himself in front of James. It traumatised him, and he swore he'd never go near a gun again, although it drove him to drink, which almost destroyed his career and his life."

"What can you tell us about his relationship with William Curtis and Derek Lowe?" asked Denton.

"He rarely saw William or Derek. James was a quiet man, great integrity and an even greater friend over the years, but not the social type. To be frank, I think he was still re-finding his self-confidence within the group after his drinking problem."

"Do you think Mr Vickers could have been drinking again?"

"No, absolutely not. No, no, no. It's difficult to explain the renaissance James went through after he had hit rock bottom. I've rarely seen him with anything more potent than a root beer," explained Niall.

"Mr Fitzgerald, we think you should consider extra security precautions. Three of your friends have been murdered, and while I can't comment on an active investigation, I think it would be wise to be increasingly vigilant," suggested Armitage. Although Niall was already aware of the danger he was in, he acted as if he was worried by the implications of such a suggestion.

"Can you think of anyone who might benefit from the death of your friends?" asked Denton.

For a third time, Niall started to slowly shake his head as he thought about the question and the answer. "It would have been Derek's wife and daughter if they were still alive. William had no dependents, and I don't think he was in a relationship. James was probably the same as William."

The detectives asked a few more questions, but the answers didn't really help with the investigation, so they concluded the interview. "Thank you, Mr Fitzgerald, and I'm sorry we had to be the bearers of such bad news again. Please do take our request about your security seriously."

"I will, thank you, Detective. I'm hoping to fly out to see my wife as soon as I can. I'd feel a lot safer in Turks and Caicos than I do in England at the moment."

"I'm sure you will. Please let us know before you leave the country, just in case we have any more questions for you."

"I will."

"Hope you feel better soon," added Armitage as they headed for the door.

"I'm sorry?" queried Niall.

"I hope you feel better soon. Don't want you flying out with the cold you mentioned."

"Oh, yes, of course," Niall replied, remembering he'd told them he was suffering with a cold. Denton hesitated and glanced at Niall, who saw him look. He instantly felt under intense scrutiny, but Denton then smiled at him and thanked him for his time.

Niall closed the door as they walked out of the house and leaned against it, breathing heavily. He needed time to think, but as he stood there, he realised he couldn't hear footsteps walking away along the gravel driveway.

He turned to look through the peephole in the door and saw the back of Denton's and Armitage's heads. They stood just outside, presumably talking and comparing notes. Without warning and as if he could sense Niall's presence, Denton's head turned, and he looked at the door and smiled. Niall snatched his head away from the peephole and hoped Denton hadn't seen him. Although Denton had looked around, he was actually reflecting on a humorous comment Armitage had just made about some of the art in the hallway and was imagining where it hung, but he did notice a slight change in the light he could see through the peephole.

Under the weather, my arse, he thought to himself.

Chapter 61

It had been almost 9pm by the time Stella arrived home last night. She had unlocked the door to find the apartment empty. There was an envelope on the small table in the lounge, and she knew the handwriting on the front was Robert's. The very fact it was there meant Stella didn't have to open it to know that he had heeded the warning over the phone and gone. It was late, and she was so very tired after a long day, so she had gone to bed, leaving the envelope unopened. She'd read it in the morning because she instinctively knew what would be inside.

She got up at 7am but, despite a restless night's sleep, she was in no hurry to read Robert's letter because she wanted to avoid the reality of it. She got dressed, made herself some tea and toast while she listened to the radio and then meandered into the lounge, sitting down on the armchair, before finally giving in to her increasingly inquisitive mood. Thankfully, the note had positive news:

My darling little ladybug
Thank you for calling and warning me of the danger
I was in. I hope you will quickly pack your bags and
find somewhere safe to stay until you can join me. What
I can tell you is that the man you met is now no longer a
threat, but there could be others, so we must exercise
extreme caution.

I cannot tell you where I am – for your safety as well as mine – but I know, even if we have to take the longest roads and use our network of friends to help us stay in touch, we will see each other again. Perhaps, we can meet just like when you first said goodbye? I have already talked to my dear friend, the Commodore, and he says we can stay with him!

I know this will be hard for both of us, but it's for the best. As strange as this may seem, everything is going to plan; I promise.

All my love, Robert xx
P.S. Please burn this note.

Without a single tear or reaction, Stella calmly rose from the chair and walked to the kitchen. She turned the gas ring on and pressed the ignition button. As the flame burst into life, she rolled up the paper and placed the tip into the flames. She held it a moment longer and then dropped it into the sink, watching the burning paper flicker, curl, and crackle. As she watched, she mumbled the hidden message within it:

"The longest road network in England is in the county of Devon, as is The Commodore Hotel in Westward Ho! And we said goodbye in January, the month I supposedly buried you."

That funeral ceremony was only five months ago, and it would be another seven months until she would see Robert once more. Yet Stella didn't feel emotional about having to wait so long or the fact that he had left her alone again. She continued watching as the flames flickered and the final wisps of smoke melted away. Even though she was so tired, she knew she needed to plan her escape before she had any unexpected visitors.

Chapter 62

The phone rang for what seemed like an eternity before the call was answered.

"Hello?"

"For fuck's sake, when the phone rings, pick up straight away! Where the hell were you?" snarled Mallory.

"And good morning to you too, Peter," replied Tony Fairfax, already weary of Mallory and his dramatic and demanding demeanour. "What's got you so pissed off this morning?"

"James is dead. Murdered."

"James Vickers?" a shocked Fairfax asked instinctively.

"Of course, James Vickers. Know any other people called James?" snapped Mallory.

"I do, actually. I get out and meet people. You should try it sometime," came the spontaneous and sarcastic reply from Fairfax. He and Mallory had always had a feisty relationship, as he saw Mallory as the misfit of the group. In fact, he often regaled people with second-hand stories of Mallory in the Oxford University amateur dramatics club playing women, such was his ability to act and talk like a drama queen, literally. He knew Mallory saw him as a selfish man with no emotions or consideration for others, but Fairfax paused. His instinctive reaction was always to taunt Mallory, a trait that he sometimes wished he could manage, with now being a prime example.

"Sorry, Peter, that was a stupid reaction."

Mallory was pleased to hear the remorse from Fairfax. He, too, knew he could be dramatic and that Fairfax found that a sign of weakness.

"It's alright, Tony. I... I'm just a little bit scared, that's all. That's Derek, William, and now James; all murdered."

"How did you find out?"

"Niall called me. He said... he... he was on a video call with James when..." but Mallory couldn't keep his emotions in check any longer and started to cry. Fairfax remained quiet until the crying finally stopped. Mallory continued, "James was shot while he was on a video call with Niall."

Fairfax was stunned. For once, he had nothing to say. His mouth wanted to move, but no words would come out as the information sank in. Mallory became so unnerved at the silence that he checked if Fairfax was still on the other end of the phone.

"Yes, I'm still here." It was the first time he'd ever heard hesitancy in Fairfax's voice. "How is Niall?"

"Scared, angry, and traumatised, to be honest, but mainly angry. The police have already been to see him. I'm scared, Tony, really scared. I'm packing a bag and getting out of Manchester for a while. I'm not telling anyone where I'm going, but I have friends who own a very private and secure property overseas." Silence fell once again until Mallory added, "Please get out of Leeds. You have money and—"

Fairfax interrupted him. "No. I can't and I won't. My ex-wife's solicitor got an overseas travel ban placed on me because she's worried that I'll take our son abroad and we won't come back. Plus, I have a shotgun certificate, and I'll use the bloody thing if anyone threatens him or me."

"That's madness. What do you think is happening? Get out, for your son's sake if nothing else. Look what happened to Derek's family!" The exasperation in Mallory's tone was obvious.

"No. I stand and fight. I want this to end, once and for all. If that bitch tries to mess with me, there'll be bloody hell to pay."

Chapter 63

"I've already booked a flight home," said Yvonne.

"But you've only just got there? I really don't think it's a good idea, darling," replied Niall, trying his best to sound composed and not alarm her.

"Three of your dearest friends are dead, Niall. Do you really think I'd be happy staying here when you need me there?" reasoned Yvonne, calmly and convincingly.

"I just think you're safer out there. I don't want you leaving the security of the villa." Underneath that façade, though, he knew he really wanted her at home. Niall tried to discourage her for a few more seconds, but his fortitude quickly crumbled. "Okay, I'll pick you up from the airport. Just let me know where and when. I suppose I should bring the Range Rover, given the luggage you'll have?" he joked, barely able to hide his relief.

"Tuesday. I'm supposed to land at 11am; usual terminal." She paused, then added, "And yes, the usual luggage." He could hear the smile in her voice.

"Tuesday, 11am at Terminal 5?" checked Niall, but then there was a pause. A voice in the background was barely audible, but Niall responded to it. "What? Oh yes, damn it," he said.

"Everything alright, Niall? Who's there?"

"What? Oh, it's Peter. I'm over at his place. We're talking about security, and he reminded me that I have an interview booked with the police next Tuesday morning. I'll try to rearrange it."

"If it's a problem, I'm sure we can sort something out. I'm… I'm just keen to come home. I feel so helpless out here." The airline Yvonne flew on didn't provide a car and driver, not even for its first-class ticket holders.

Peter tapped Niall on the shoulder and whispered, "How about arranging a hire car?" Niall mentioned it to Yvonne, who thought it was a sensible option, and they ended their call.

"I'll organise one now," said a relieved Niall to Mallory. "Just let me call a company I've used before, and then we can carry on with our discussion." Mallory started to walk out of the room to give Niall some privacy, but Niall waved at him to stop, gesturing that Mallory could stay where he was. He dialled another number. "Hello, this is Niall Fitzgerald. I need to book a car." Five minutes later, Niall sent Yvonne a text:

Car rental arranged. The booking is under 'Fitzgerald'. Email on its way with the details

He then turned back to Mallory. "I think I need to rehearse my story. Would you mind being the aggressive, suspicious policeman?"

"Of course not," replied Mallory. "You know I love acting and a bit of drama." Niall smiled back at him as that response was typical of his friend. "What approach do you think they'll take?"

"I don't know. A couple of detectives came around to my house after they'd found James. They asked all sorts of questions and suggested I increase my security. Maybe they think I'm in some sort of danger but won't say why they think it's me rather than you, Charles, or Anthony."

"Perhaps whoever killed James is worried that when he was talking to you, he said something that might be a clue, or you saw something?"

"I don't think so. James only managed to say a few words, and I didn't see anything because…" but he paused as an elusive thought seemed to tease him.

"What is it?" asked Mallory, seeing that Niall was trying to recall something.

"I'm… I'm not sure. There's something in my mind, but it feels just out of reach. Do you know what I mean?"

"You mean like when there's something on the tip of your tongue? That type of feeling?"

"Exactly," replied Niall. "It's something… err… oh, for fuck's sake!" The harder he tried to remember what he had subconsciously registered, the further it seemed from his grasp.

Chapter 64

Mrs Atha's Coffee Shop was a popular spot with businessmen and women, as well as the casually dressed tea and coffee aficionados who wanted more than just a hot drink from a standard format outlet. The warm weather meant that only one of the handful of tables outside was free, but the two that were still available afforded some privacy and anonymity. Daniella Maddox was pouring her second cup of tea when Adrian Skelton finally appeared.

"I didn't think you were going to make it," said Maddox.

"Neither did I," said Skelton. "Jeavons was on the rampage about losing another client to Amber & Thomas, but I explained I had an important meeting to attend. This had better be worth me lying to him," he said as he sat opposite her at their corner table. Jeavons was the managing partner at the firm who'd taunted her at the Ruiz meeting the previous week.

"I hope it is too, given it was you who said you wanted to *'talk later'*," replied Maddox, air-quoting the words from his written post-it note.

Skelton surveyed the people on adjacent tables before leaning forwards and whispering, "I'm sorry it's taken this long, but Ruiz is as guilty as hell. We both know that, and so does Jeavons, so ask yourself, why does Jeavons keep asking you for updates?"

"Because he's trying to protect the revenue and reputation of the firm, and because he doesn't believe in me?" Maddox replied cynically.

He rocked back, shaking his head at her irrational viewpoint. "Come on, you're smarter than that. You're answering with your Italian passion, not your legal training. Jeavons knows you're the best we have."

"Oh, I don't know; he clearly has a stake in the outcome," she replied half-heartedly. Skelton gazed at her with an expression of encouragement on his face, silently egging her on. She noticed his non-verbal response, but before she responded to his encouragement, she wanted to understand a little more context.

"Before I say anything else, I have a question for you," she said.

"Admissible." He smirked.

"Who was the man you all met in the park outside work that day you saw me looking out of the window?" she asked. His smile grew broader.

"Good question, counsellor. That was an affiliate of Mr Dennis Ruiz, wanting to check on progress."

"What's his name? It isn't David Holding, I know that much, even though that's who he's been posing as recently."

Skelton narrowed his eyes, either as if that was new information or as if he was surprised that she knew that. He mulled over his options before responding. "I can't tell you his name because I don't know it, but I can tell you that he's possibly looking to run the... what shall we call it... business interests of Mr Ruiz, should the opportunity arise."

She took a few seconds to assess what he had told her before surmising, "So, if Ruiz goes to prison, Jeavons has revenue continuity; just with a new figurehead," she said, nodding to herself. "I can see why Jeavons would want to foster a relationship with the man, but presumably he needs to tread carefully in case Ruiz sees it as a betrayal?"

"Not really. Ruiz thinks Jeavons is just supporting the interim leader Ruiz elected to cover for him, someone Ruiz thinks he can trust, so Jeavons isn't the one Ruiz would feel betrayed by."

"That would be another shock for Ruiz. He's already struggling to comprehend the situation he's in."

Skelton shook his head. "Ruiz might be arrogant, but he's also smart. He will have calculated the likelihood of being arrested and convicted, so, if he's the person I think he is, he'll already have several highly influential people on his personal payroll: people who can make the four-to-five years either disappear or be a façade. He will still be able to oversee his operation from inside jail."

"He might be smart, but he's also a hothead; we all heard that in the courtroom," scoffed Maddox.

"Yes, he is, but that's just part of the act. By keeping people on edge, they work harder. After all, you're working harder to find a technicality, aren't you? His threat against you works in his favour."

She realised this was true and had to admit that Ruiz had manipulated her. "Do you... do you think Ruiz is capable of murdering me?" she asked.

"Let's face it, he'll protect his billion-pound business in whatever way he needs to. He's ruthless. His associate, the one you saw us talking to, told us Ruiz instructed his men to do whatever they felt necessary to ensure Holding stayed quiet. You'd just be…" Skelton paused as he saw the vulnerability and fear in her eyes. He immediately softened his tone. "Sorry; that must have sounded dreadful. I just don't know, Daniella; maybe Holding had a lot more information to threaten Ruiz with. Maybe he had tried to blackmail Ruiz? I'm sure Ruiz was just taunting you. In his own twisted way, he probably thought it would motivate you to work even harder. Even with all his connections, he probably needs you to find something; anything that will mean a retrial, at the very minimum. I know Jeavons is counting on it; he has a lot to lose if the verdict goes the wrong way."

"Reputation and revenue, it's all he cares about." But Skelton smiled and scoffed as she said that.

"Not quite, but you're getting warmer, Daniella. Do you know how much Ruiz pays as a retainer for our firm to protect him and his employees?"

"A couple of million a year, I believe?" she replied. Her PA had been gossiping with the other PA's as they discussed their tactics to collectively ask about a pay rise.

"And how much do you think Jeavons gets on top of that as a personal incentive?" he said, inviting speculation. Her bottom jaw dropped. She knew a lot of criminals used their wealth to gain influence and control but had never imagined Jeavons might be someone to take a bribe.

"Do you think Jeavons is in danger, too?"

Skelton shook his head. "Ruiz knows that Jeavons has so much information on the structure of BOrg that he could sink Ruiz and all of his operation, forever, so he won't do much more than threaten him if he feels Jeavons is stepping out of line."

"But if Jeavons shared client-confidential information, he'd lose his licence to run the practice," she said.

"And, compared to the risk of losing his life? Hardly a difficult decision," he responded.

Maddox sat back. She'd been so close to the case and under such pressure – from Jeavons as well as from the threat by Ruiz – that she'd temporarily lost her foresight. As she continued to reflect on the situation, she looked at Skelton. "Thanks for telling me, but what's in all of this for you?"

"What do you mean?" he asked.

"I mean, why did you risk telling me all this? I now know things that I might look to leverage."

"Let me ask a question before I answer," he said, diverting the conversation temporarily. "How did you know that man we were meeting had been presenting himself as David Holding?"

It was now Maddox who considered her options before answering. One scenario was that Skelton already knew the answer but was testing how open she would be in return. Another could be he was genuinely unaware that the man had been posing as Holding, and he wanted to know more. "Someone said they'd met him a week or so ago, and he had presented himself as David Holding."

"But the real Holding has been in a wheelchair for months, with round-the-clock care, hasn't he?"

"Yes, but this person didn't know that at the time," she explained.

"And why was this person discussing Holding with you?"

"They had a question they wanted me to ask Ruiz. They were acting as a proxy for someone else."

Skelton pondered the scenario before adding, "You've still not told me how you knew he'd been posing as Holding?"

"The description the person gave me of the man they'd met was a perfect match," she lied. Stella Kendrick's description of the man she met was fairly vague, but it was close enough for Maddox to believe it could be the same man, and now she felt she had confirmation from Skelton. He continued to ponder before seemingly concluding his thoughts. He then abruptly stood up; the meeting was apparently over.

"Mind answering my previous question before you go? What's in this for you?" she probed.

He leant forwards again and whispered, "When Ruiz goes to jail, perhaps he'll decide that he needs to invest the millions that he pays Jeavons elsewhere. If Ruiz is as brutal and calculating as I expect him to be, the outcome could be that there'll be a vacancy for a new managing partner at the practice?" he pretended to hypothesise.

"And you'd be the one to tell Ruiz that Jeavons had failed him?"

"It's a vicious game, and only the strongest survive," he replied, his sense of humour and warmth of voice gone. She was not surprised by the statement. Adrian Skelton was a cunning man and an ambitious one. Those two traits made him very dangerous.

"And you've still not explained why you're telling me this? Aren't you worried that I now know, and what I might do with the information?" she challenged.

He clearly expected the question and calmly shook his head. "No, I'm not worried. I'm happy that we share information, and I know we have very different ambitions, Daniella, but we both want to stay alive; to savour more than our final breath," he said, with a glint of malevolence in his eyes. The calm tone with which he said it sent a shiver through her entire body. He knew how Ruiz had threatened her that day in the courtroom; everyone did. If she was murdered, everyone would believe Ruiz had simply carried out his threat. Skelton stood, smiled at her and said cheerily, "Sorry, but places to go, people to talk to. I enjoyed our chat, Daniella. We should do it more often." He turned and strode away as if he hadn't a care in the world. She watched him go and decided to stay for another pot of tea. Had he really just threatened her?

Skelton walked for several minutes, checking behind him to ensure she wasn't following. As soon as he was sure she wasn't, he pulled his mobile phone out. After finding the number he needed, he called the man who had asked for an update.

"She's none the wiser," Skelton said.

"What *does* she know?" the man replied.

"Enough to know that she's in danger and that I hold the key to her safety."

"And did her information corroborate what we thought?"

"It seemed to. She mentioned the fake David Holding, but she didn't specifically mention the meeting she had with your wife."

"Good. Stella needs to keep thinking that the fake Holding and Niall Fitzgerald are the enemy, and I'm still her frightened husband, caught in the middle of a terrible situation."

"How are the plans going?" asked Skelton.

"We're still no closer to finding the real pages 26 and 27 of the thesis, but we have time, so I'm not worried."

"I'm worried about Maddox, though," Skelton admitted. "She's a smart lady, and now she's clearer about the bigger picture, she might try to turn it to her advantage if she realises that the page 26 you gave your wife wasn't the real deal."

Robert Kendrick replied confidently, "Don't worry. If we feel that's an issue, I'll get a message to Ruiz that she's trying to sell the rest of the report to the highest bidder, or she's sharing client-confidential information with the authorities. Either way, she'll be dead within days. Everyone heard his threat to her."

"More to the point, Robert, what happens if she talks to your wife and Stella starts piecing things together? She now knows the man she met wasn't Holding."

"In chess, it's the king that has to survive to keep the game going. If that means I have to sacrifice my queen, so be it. I've not come this far to lose it all."

Back at Mrs Atha's, Maddox felt in a daze, confused by what had just happened. All she really wanted to do right now was run; run to her family in Italy. They would certainly be able to protect her. What she didn't know was whether her returning home would be welcomed by all of them.

"Only one way to find out," she said to herself as she hailed a taxi to head back to her apartment.

Chapter 65

The door swung open, and Denton stomped into the incident room. "What have we got?"

"Two more," replied Jones. "Alison Montague, 64 years old, widow. Lived alone in a remote cottage in the village of Hintlesham, near Ipswich. Found this morning by her gardener. SOCO estimate time of death at between 2pm and 7pm yesterday."

"And the other?"

"Lisa Ruttle; 37. Lived on Jersey. Married, with three children. Found yesterday evening after she had failed to turn up to collect all three from school and wasn't answering her phone. The headteacher called the police. SOCO estimate a similar time of death. We'll need to wait for the post-mortem to get a more accurate window."

Denton's heart sank. "Do both murders fit the MO?"

"Both had a copy of the second lottery ticket in their mouth."

"IP and JE postcodes?" asked Denton to check his geography.

"Yes, and house numbers 5 and 23, just like the numbers on the ticket," offered Jones.

Denton hung his head in exasperation. He pulled a chair out and flopped onto it, deep in thought.

"Any connection between these two victims and the others?"

"Alison Montague had recently retired as Head of HR at Belschen Petroleum, but nothing yet on Lisa Ruttle." Denton stroked his temples repeatedly as he tried to clear his mind. This case was as frustrating as it was stressful. He knew the DCI would be calling him soon to demand an update on progress because the national press was starting to comment on the Met's ability to solve the crime, and hysteria was building. His problem was he had no news on progress. He looked up at Jones.

"Belschen Petroleum; haven't we mentioned them before?"

"Yes. William Curtis had them listed as a client, but that was just before the financial scandal. We've also got some information that the company Derek Lowe worked for previously managed their UK subsidiary accounts, but we're still looking into that."

"What financial scandal?"

"Price fixing and accounting fraud."

"Recently?"

"About 10 years ago. Don't you read any news, guv?"

"Nah; it's all too depressing. I feel safer and happier at work, solving murders," he joked. "Get the board out, will you? I feel the need to scribble and ponder." Jones uncapped a pen as she checked some information in the files. She turned to the board and added the new information:

Commonalities	*Differences*
7 of 12 victims are male: 3 knew each other	*7 different police jurisdictions*
Lottery ticket in mouth at every scene	*Methods of murder*
No trace at 8 of the 9 scenes. Professional hit!	*Age of victims*
Theft does not appear to be a motive	*7 sole murders; one triple and one double*
3 victims had links to Belschen Petro	

Notes related to lottery ticket

6 house numbers match numbers on first ticket. Assumption is first house has #24 associated.

??	29	30	36	46	48	7
AL	BD	CR	DA	EN	FK	GL

Sequencing of numbers and letters following the same pattern on the second ticket.

1	5	23	29	32	41	7
HG	IP	JE	K?	L?	M?	N?

Denton stared at it, but he couldn't clear his mind and began to feel increasingly helpless.

"It just doesn't make sense. Male and female; young and old; only three of the victims are linked, and yet the sequence is meticulous."

Jones was looking at the board as well, her head cocked to the side. Thinking out loud, she said, "Maybe it's not supposed to make sense?" Initially, Denton continued to look at the board, but as what Jones had said registered in his brain, he looked over at her.

"What did you say?" he asked.

She kept looking at the board as she shrugged her shoulders and repeated, "Maybe they're not supposed to make sense?" Then she turned to him and nonchalantly added, "Maybe it's supposed to confuse us?"

Denton shuffled in his seat and leaned forwards. His brain was trying to follow her thinking, and while hardly feeling enthused or enlightened by it, her statement intrigued him. "So, what you're saying is either it's all random..." he started.

"Or it's made to look random, on purpose," Jones said. Reflecting further, she added, "Perhaps the killer is forcing us to look too deep, so we can't see the wood for the trees?" She held her hands out as if to indicate '*don't know; just a thought*', but Denton was beginning to think she might be onto something.

"So, the meticulous sequencing is deliberate, but the reason for the sequencing is to distract us into thinking about the sequencing, hiding the true motive?" he said slowly as he followed the thread of thought. "Jonesy, get the team together. We need to talk," and he sprang from the chair.

Chapter 66

Both men sat in silence. There was no rush. In fact, any attempt to rush could prove disastrous as it might be seen as desperation, weakness, or like declaring one's hand too soon in a game of poker. One man was thinking as the other sat patiently, awaiting a reply. It was The Broker who spoke first.

"So, in summary, you're offering me a business proposition that you project could return ten-fold on my investment inside two years?"

The other man nodded slowly and calmly. He'd already explained the proposal, including financial projections and details of penalties should the investment fail to deliver. He had historical and audited documentation that confirmed the track record of the approach, as well as cash in reserve for the first wave of possible penalties, but he understood the hesitation from The Broker. It was a big decision.

"The £200m you're asking for represents a significant exposure for me," continued The Broker. "I'll need to call in several favours and probably owe a few more to raise that sort of cash." Again, the man nodded. He'd been operating in the criminal world long enough to know how risks were assessed and how outstanding debts were paid if money wasn't returned. He knew that the recent disappearance of a university professor was the work of this man and that the debt involved was minor. The Broker exhaled, long and slowly, evidencing his anxiety.

"What happens if your assumptions are wrong? Not only would my £200m be gone, but I'd be a marked man. People would want my blood... and your head." Once again, the man nodded. The deal was a financial no-brainer; the challenge was whether three critical assumptions he had made would come true.

"Talk me through the assumptions again," The Broker asked. He knew what they were, and he knew the probability was they were correct, but his reputation and his life depended on the right decision.

"Firstly, Ruiz will be found guilty. I have that guaranteed."

"How?" asked The Broker.

"Come on, you know I have all the inside information I need, and I've got more to share with Interpol, but it won't be needed. That expert witness, Hibberd, has laid everything bare. Ruiz is history, and there's a lot of people who were in his pocket who will be sighing in relief. They are in no rush to find a loophole that would get him released."

"The second assumption is that the core infrastructure is still viable?" challenged The Broker

"The team are still operating, albeit on a smaller, low-profile plan, and one of the money-men is free of suspicion; we made sure of that."

"And you think this Niall Fitzgerald will still want to play?"

"Oh, he has a big stake in the operation restarting. His investments and returns are heavily tied into BOrg, and right now, he's sweating on over £100m of client money that's been frozen by Interpol. So yes, he'll want to see things return to normal as soon as possible."

"How did you make him appear so squeaky clean in all this?" This was critical for The Broker to buy into the plan, as he too would need to appear 'squeaky clean'.

"I sacrificed Thoresen and framed Holding... who is now dead and can't tell anyone the truth."

"So that just leaves you; the third assumption. Are you sure you want to do this, including sacrificing your marriage?"

"I'm positive, and if things don't work or you simply don't trust me, you can shoot me," replied a confident Robert Kendrick.

"Oh, you can count on that," replied The Broker ominously.

Robert Kendrick had been the one to see an opportunity at BOrg, but Dennis Ruiz had too big an ego to think someone had a bigger, better idea than he had and refused to accept the plan. When he realised Ruiz would never agree to it, Robert worked out a plan to take control of the BOrg operation. To do that, he needed Ruiz out of the way, so he anonymously provided the authorities with enough information to identify Ruiz but not locate the people and locations the BOrg operation used. What he didn't have, though, was enough working capital, as most of BOrg's liquid assets were frozen. After several months of careful introductions and trust-building to even get to meet him, here he was, discussing a £200m deal. Was Robert's plan finally coming to a conclusion, or had he pushed too hard too soon?

"Alright; I've made my decision," announced The Broker, who reached into his desk drawer, pulled out a gun and aimed at Robert's head. "So now you know how I feel about your third assumption," and he smirked in satisfaction. Two of his thugs raced into the room when they heard the gunshot.

"Got a hole in my wall," said The Broker, as casually as ever.

Chapter 67

Yvonne prepared to disembark from the first-class cabin. As she thanked the onboard crew at the aircraft door, she glanced over at the queue of passengers getting ready to follow the first-class passengers off. Stood in the queue was Charles Wagstaff.

"Charles?" she queried.

"Yvonne?" he replied, in equal pleasure and surprise.

"I'll wait for you at the end of the bridge," she said, smiling. Shortly after, when they were both in the arrivals terminal, they gave each other a friendly embrace as passengers jostled past them.

"I didn't know you were on the flight, otherwise you should have come up to see me," said Yvonne.

"I didn't know you were out in the Caribbean," said Wagstaff. "Where's Niall?" and he looked around expectantly.

"He's not with me. With all this worrying stuff going on, Niall suggested I fly out, but when I heard about James, I just felt I had to come back."

"James?" questioned Wagstaff loudly; apprehension etched on his face. "What about James?"

"Oh, my goodness. You don't know, do you?"

"Know what?" asked Wagstaff, looking increasingly worried.

"Oh Charles, I'm so sorry to have to be the one to tell you, but James has been murdered."

"I... I didn't know. I've been away and... Oh my god!" His legs seemed to give way, but a couple of the disembarking passengers who overheard the shocking news quickly steadied him. They offered to help more, but Yvonne assured them they were alright, thanking them for their kindness.

"Charles, I'm so sorry. It never crossed my mind that you didn't know. Please, let me help you." She guided him across to some nearby seats. Wagstaff lowered himself into one of them, lost in his thoughts. Yvonne looked around the arrivals hall and could see people glancing over. A member of the crew had just disembarked, and she, too, saw the pair apparently in some distress.

"Hello. Are you two alright? Can I get you any help?" the air hostess asked as Wagstaff fumbled with his phone, accidentally dropping it on the floor.

"Thank you, that would be wonderful," said Yvonne, smiling weakly. "I'm afraid I've just given my friend some very distressing news about a death," she continued as she picked up his phone and put it in her handbag for safekeeping.

"Oh, my goodness. Let me get you some assistance. I'm sure we can VIP you both through," the woman said, and she walked over to a desk and grabbed the phone.

"You're coming back with me, Charles. Niall has arranged a car."

"I can grab a cab; it's alright," he offered feebly.

"Absolutely not. You're in no fit state to be alone. You're coming with me, and you can stay at our house tonight if you want to?"

Wagstaff didn't argue. He was grateful there was one less thing for him to think about. Ten minutes later, they were through passport control and their baggage had been recovered. They thanked the woman and the VIP team before collecting the car keys from the hire company desk and heading to the parking area.

"Where is it parked?" asked a still distracted Wagstaff.

"Row C, space 4; it's a blue Bentayga," she said as she pushed the trolley out of the lift and into the secure parking area. "Just let me get the security barrier code out before we get in; I wrote it on the hire agreement." Wagstaff nodded and took control of the luggage trolley. Yvonne pulled the paperwork from her handbag but clumsily pulled other items out with it, which scattered onto the concrete floor. "Oh, for goodness' sake," she exclaimed. Wagstaff had reached the SUV while she was picking up her belongings. He looked around for her, not having realised she had had to stop and was several metres behind him.

"Pop the boot open, will you?" he shouted. "I'll put the luggage in."

Yvonne grumbled to herself, "Just a bloody minute," as she put the final item back in her bag and stood straight. "Coming," she shouted across to Wagstaff as she pulled out the key fob. She pressed the small release button at the bottom of the fob, and the boot started to rise. He looked inside the boot and then at the pile of her suitcases.

"For such a big car, the luggage space is a little—" Before he could finish the sentence, the car exploded. Flames and smoke erupted from underneath the vehicle, and he was thrown backwards into the air. Yvonne, too, was knocked off her feet. Despite the sharp pain from the hard concrete and the buzzing in her ears from the sound of the explosion, she pulled herself into a sitting position. She stared in horror, her mouth open and her mind unable to comprehend what had just happened. As blood began to drip from her wounds, she screamed, "CHARLES!!"

Charles Wagstaff's mangled and bloodied body lay motionless.

Chapter 68

Niall burst into the private room that Yvonne had been transferred to. His eyes fell immediately on a group of medical professionals who were gathered around her bed. He froze mid-step, unsure whether to race forwards or stay back.

"Yvonne?" he called out hesitantly. The medical professionals parted, and there she was, heavily bandaged but clearly alive and awake.

"Niall!" she said, a weak smile starting to spread across her face, but then a wince of discomfort took it away just as quickly. There was a series of facial cuts, one of her legs was heavily strapped, and there was bruising on her arms, but other than that, she appeared far better than he had feared.

"Are you alright?" he asked as he strode towards her bed.

"Yes, yes, I'm fine." She looked at the medical staff who were clearing away some equipment. "They were just checking me before they unplugged everything," she added, once again trying to give a smile to allay her husband's fears.

Last out of the room was a doctor who smiled at Niall and, looking back at Yvonne, said, "Just for a short time, please. She needs her rest."

"Thank you, doctor," said a grateful and relieved Niall, tears welling in his eyes.

"We'll update you when you've seen your wife, Mr Fitzgerald. Nothing life-threatening, but we do need to have a quick talk," he said, trying to reassure Niall.

Once he had left the room, Niall walked quickly over to Yvonne as he wanted to embrace her, but he paused, unsure what was safe and what would actually cause her discomfort or pain. "The police called me. What the hell happened?" he asked.

Yvonne held her hand out and he took it gently. "The car exploded. Charles was... Oh, I can't..." She gently wept at the memory.

Niall squeezed her hand as tenderly as he could and ached to hold her close. He reached into his pocket and pulled out a clean handkerchief, dabbing the tears from her cheeks. "You saw Charles at the airport?"

"Yes. My flight from Turks was rerouted to pick up some stranded passengers in Jamaica. He told me he was on holiday there, getting some peace and quiet as he continued to work through how to buy the company he co-owns." She slowly composed herself and then continued, "At first, they told me he was in a critical condition, with 60 per cent of his body covered in burns. I... I just can't stop seeing him thrown into the air like a rag doll." More tears started to tumble down her face. "Niall, if I hadn't seen him on the plane..." She looked up as she finished the sentence, "... that could have been me." Yvonne's body gently heaved as the fear and sadness overwhelmed her.

He shook his head in disbelief and whispered caring words of assurance to her. As she became quieter and her sobs subsided, Niall became introspective. Yvonne assumed he was reflecting on the same horrifying thoughts, which he was momentarily before his mind turned to SILK. Could this be another piece of her twisted plan for revenge, to try to kill his wife now? She couldn't have known Charles would be on the flight, and he wasn't even at the party where she was injured.

"Ow! Niall, you're hurting my hand," Yvonne yelped.

"What? Oh, I'm so sorry, my darling," said a repentant Niall. As he thought about the possible link with SILK, he had unconsciously started to tighten his grip in anger. He released Yvonne's hand and began to gently stroke it before standing and letting her go.

"You need rest. Let me talk to the doctor and ask about Charles. I'll come back again later, but please get some rest." He leaned over and lightly kissed her bandaged forehead, placing his handkerchief in her hand. "In case you need it," he said softly. She smiled and nodded her head. She was physically and emotionally drained, and the medication that had been administered was finally starting to make her drowsy. Niall smiled at his injured wife as her eyelids began to close, and then he quietly made his way out of the room. The doctor was at the reception desk, completing some paperwork for the nurses. Niall politely cleared his throat, and the doctor looked up.

"Ah yes, Mr Fitzgerald." He looked around for something and then said, "Please, follow me. We can talk in the office," and led Niall across the corridor and into a room. "Please, won't you be seated?" he said solemnly. Niall pulled a chair as the doctor sat at the desk. He looked as if he was searching for the right way to open the conversation, but Niall talked first.

"Doctor, before we talk about my wife, what can you tell me about Charles?"

"Charles?" queried the doctor.

"Sorry, Charles Wagstaff. The man who was with my wife when the explosion happened. He's a very dear friend, and both my wife and I wondered whether he... well, whether he was..." but the doctor knew what Niall was trying to ask.

"I'm afraid I can't tell you much; that information is usually only discussed with members of the family, but I can say he is in a critical condition. We had to induce a coma to prevent his body from closing down due to the shock and trauma he's suffered." Niall hung his head and nodded in both acknowledgement and gratitude. He started to sniffle. The doctor reached over to a box of tissues and slid it across to Niall, who heard the noise and instinctively knew what it was. He looked up, grabbed a couple from the box, and muttered a thank you. He wiped his eyes and nose and took in a deep breath.

"I'm sorry. Charles is a very close friend, and we've lost a few good friends recently," he explained without going into any detail. "Charles has no family, so you'll not find anyone to talk to, I'm afraid."

"Well, let's hope he recovers in due course, Mr Fitzgerald, but I'd really like to talk to you about your wife if that's alright?" Niall, still wiping away the moist tears on his face, looked up, puzzled.

"What about my wife?" he asked, concern starting to creep into his voice. "She seemed fine just then?"

"She is," assured the doctor. "I'm sure she'll make a full and rapid recovery, but..." He paused.

"But what?" asked Niall, sitting up straight, unsure whether to be afraid or angry.

"We've not told her yet, but... I'm afraid she's lost the baby. I'm so sorry."

Niall's complexion paled. He was dumbstruck. He stared at the doctor for a few seconds and then gasped, "Yvonne was pregnant?"

The doctor was taken aback. "I'm so sorry. You didn't know?"

Niall just shook his head as he digested the news. "We thought..."

"Yes, I've examined your wife, Mr Fitzgerald. I'm aware of the damage to her uterus and the scar tissue, but it's not unknown for women to sometimes overcome incredible odds. I'm sorry to break such sad news to you, I really am." He explained to Niall that Yvonne had been 10 weeks pregnant.

"I don't understand," said Niall. "Why hadn't she told me?"

"At your wife's age, there is a higher risk of complications. Some women over 40 quite often wait for several months to be sure the pregnancy is developing before sharing the news with anyone, even their husbands."

After some more words of advice and sympathy, Niall finally stood. He shook the doctor's hand and thanked him. He walked out of the office and glanced up the corridor, towards Yvonne's room, before turning towards the stairs and heading out of the hospital. He hadn't wanted children, and it had been an enormous strain on their relationship when she had had the necessary termination a few years ago. Now, as he walked towards his car, he knew there was nothing he wanted more than to father a child, and his mood changed as the dark clouds of anger descended.

"You've murdered my unborn child and nearly took my wife's life," he growled under his breath as his mind turned back to SILK. He had read the report from the private investigator, which clearly highlighted the fragility and volatility of Evie Perry. Perhaps it was finally time to push her over the edge.

Chapter 69

"I want us to look through all the information we have again," growled a frustrated Denton. "We must be missing something."

"I'll get my team to review all the interview notes," said DS Alan Armitage.

"And I'll liaise with the NCA to see what else they can provide from the data they've got," said DS Bob Williams.

"Any news from your team about the Derek Lowe files, Alan?" asked Denton.

Armitage shook his head. "We've found nothing so far, and the two specialists from the fraud squad had to return to London. There's just that one file we can't crack, and they simply ran out of time." Denton flared his nostrils, even though he knew the fraud squad had pressures of their own. He tore a piece of paper from a pad and scribbled a name and number on it.

"Jonesy, give this guy a call and tell him I sent you. He's a geek in the fraud squad, and he owes me one. Tell him there's a file no one else can open, including two of his colleagues; he'll take the bait. Oh, and get me an update on how Mr Wagstaff and Mrs Fitzgerald are doing. And why have I got no ruddy coffee?"

"Yes, guv," she replied to the first two requests, but she just pointed to a coffee percolator that was dripping fresh coffee into the jug. She wasn't a waitress.

"I just need one break, one break," Denton muttered to himself. The last update with the DCI had not gone well, at all.

"Car was hired from a company called KOKENJIN; apparently, that's Japanese for 'guardian'. It was reserved in the name of Fitzgerald," called out Williams.

"Yes, reserved for Yvonne Fitzgerald; we know," said a distracted and frustrated Denton.

"No, just 'Fitzgerald'. Doesn't specify who. Invoice is addressed to Iliad Private Equity Group," confirmed Williams.

"What?" snapped Armitage. Everyone stopped.

"Car wasn't hired specifically in her name; just her surname," repeated Williams.

"Iliad is Niall Fitzgerald's company," said Armitage.

"If his company paid for it, and it just had his surname on it…" Jones started, but Denton finished her thought; "Then maybe someone thought the car was for Niall Fitzgerald?" They all stood and looked at each other for several seconds before they burst back into animated life.

"I'll check the details of the hire car booking," said Williams, grabbing a phone.

"And I'll chase forensics for any further information about the device, as well with the CID team about the CCTV coverage of the car park," said Jones, grabbing a second phone. Armitage and Denton, however, just looked at each other, thinking the same thing: Was this actually an attempt on Niall Fitzgerald's life? They walked over to the wipe-board.

"He lives in a KT postcode," said Denton.

"We don't know the house number, though," replied Armitage.

"You know it's got to fit in, though," Denton answered, and Armitage nodded in agreement. "We'd better get someone over to the Fitzgerald house."

Commonalities	*Differences*
6 of 12 victims are male: 3 knew each other	*7 different police jurisdictions*
Lottery ticket in mouth at every scene	*Methods of murder*
One attempted murder. Knew 4 others	*Age of victims*
No trace at 8 of the 9 scenes. Professional hit!	*7 sole murders; one triple and one double*
Theft does not appear to be a motive	
3 victims had links to Belschen Petro	

Notes related to lottery ticket
6 house numbers match the numbers on the first ticket. Assumption is first house has #24 associated.

??	*29*	*30*	*36*	*46*	*48*	*7*
AL	*BD*	*CR*	*DA*	*EN*	*FK*	*GL*

Sequencing of murders follow same pattern on the second ticket.

1	*5*	*23*	*29*	*32*	*41*	*7*
HG	*IP*	*JE*	*KT?*	*L?*	*M?*	*N?*

Denton shouted across the room, "Jonesy? Get a local team across to the Fitzgerald address. We need to make sure he's safe."

Even though she was already on two phones, Jones signalled she'd heard and grabbed a third phone.

Chapter 70

The postman left any letters and cards in a series of mailboxes affixed to the wall in the communal entrance hall. Depending on the tenant, some of the mail could be there for weeks and, ordinarily, Stella wouldn't check the mail for days at a time, but today she did.

She'd been food shopping and had to put her bags on the floor as she fumbled for the mailbox key that was on her key chain. She unlocked the mailbox and, after sifting through the usual junk mail that Royal Mail now regularly deposited, she found a plain manilla envelope. The address was handwritten, which suggested it wasn't a bill or a formal letter from a government agency. It wasn't Robert's handwriting either. A letter from him might contain a cryptic clue as to where he was or how she might be able to contact him, and she certainly had some questions she wanted to ask. Then again, he had simply vanished for both their safety's sake, so why should she expect a letter from him so soon?

She stuffed most of the mail back in the mailbox to be dealt with when she next went to the bins, but she put the manilla envelope into her skirt pocket. She picked up her shopping and walked to the lift. Once in the apartment, Stella unpacked the food and put it away before she made herself a cup of tea. Only when she sat down did she hear the crinkle of the envelope that she had put in her pocket earlier. She huffed a little as she placed the well-deserved cup of tea down on the small table, reached into her pocket and pulled out the envelope. She picked up her glasses and then opened the envelope. In it was a piece of A4 paper, carefully folded and with a short, handwritten message on it:

Dear Mrs Kendrick

You don't know me, but I am writing to inform you that your husband, Robert, is no longer with us. I cannot pretend to be sorry, but I do appreciate this news might be upsetting for you. For that, I can only apologise.

I do not wish to distress you further, but his final wish was that I write to you and say that you will always be his "sweet if angry little ladybug". He assured me that if I quoted those words, you would know that your husband had been talking to me. You are therefore safe to live your life without fear, and I hope that at least provides you with a small degree of comfort.

Robert did assure me that you were financially secure, and as the rest of the world already believed he was dead, I hope you will not need to go to the expense of paying for another funeral.

Please do not try to find out who I am or where I am. It would not be in your best interests.

With sympathies.

Stella stared at the unsigned letter, not knowing whether to cry in sorrow or scream in anger. It was so matter of fact, with the smallest element of respect towards her. So, was that it? The recollection of the memorial service they held for Robert came flooding back, but the emptiness she felt now was far greater.

Back then, she felt such sadness because her sweet hard-working husband, who had done everything to provide for her, had been tragically killed in a car accident. The promise of what could have been, lost so suddenly. Now though, she felt abandoned. He hadn't actually died in the car accident, and they could have had some sort of life together, perhaps a new country and a new identity? Not anymore.

Stella suddenly dropped the letter, recoiling from it. It was probably written by the person who had killed Robert, and it felt dirty. She rubbed her fingertips together as if to remove any residue it had left on her skin. She began to breathe rapidly and wanted to back further away from the letter, as far as she could. Her anxiety was turning into an anger that began to mushroom from her gut all the way up to her mouth.

"NOOOOOOOOOOOO!" she bellowed in fury before her face began to crumple into tears. She dropped to her knees, grabbed the letter and then clutched it to her chest as she rolled onto the carpet, weeping. "Why, Robert? Why couldn't what we had be enough?" she pleaded. "Why did you leave me again?" She cried and slapped the floor in frustration, once, twice, ten times.

Chapter 71

Evie was standing next to the open fridge, swaying unsteadily as she searched for more wine when there was a sharp rap on her front door. It startled her, and she tensed, her eyes blinking wildly with her hand instinctively reaching for a carving knife from the nearby kitchen island. Her knuckles began to turn white as she gripped its handle tighter and tighter.

"Who is it?" she called out, her voice trembling.

"Delivery," came back an irate-sounding voice. Evie's shoulders relaxed a little. David Homes had said there would be one more package of information. She needed its contents to be the missing pieces in her plan.

"One second," she shouted back, putting the knife down on the chopping board. She walked to the door and, in her desire to get the information and bring this saga to a close, she unlocked and opened it without checking who it was first. Then she gasped. Stood on her doorstep was the client who had hired her for that fateful night three years ago. Niall quickly pushed the door wide open, throwing Evie off her balance and sending her stumbling backwards into the kitchen island.

"Wh... what do you want?" she asked, her voice quivering in fear.

"WHAT THE FUCK DO YOU THINK YOU'RE PLAYING AT?" he raged as he slammed the door closed.

"What?" stammered Evie, looking confused.

"Don't try to act innocent. I know what you're doing! Do you know who I am and how easily I could crush you, you little whore?" Niall took a couple of steps towards her; his bulging eyes and the deep red flush to his cheeks adding to his menacing tone. "What the HELL are you doing murdering my friends? AND MY CHILD?" he snarled. He was so close to her that spittle from his mouth speckled her face.

"What do you mean? Who? What child? Please, leave me alone; don't you think you've hurt me enough?" she said, sobbing and in fear for her life. Words continued to cascade from her mouth as she fought to comprehend what the man was talking about, what she had allegedly done, and how had he found her? Niall wasn't listening, though. Rage coursed through his body. He wasn't here to listen to her pathetic excuses; he was here to put a stop to her actions, whatever it took.

"I swear, I'll KILL you if you don't leave my wife and I alone. You will not get a penny more from me, EVER! DO YOU UNDERSTAND?" Niall glared at her for a few seconds before turning, flinging the door open viciously and storming out of her house.

"How did you find me? STAY AWAY FROM ME!" she shrieked as she got to her feet, but either he didn't hear her or he just didn't care. She staggered to the door and watched as he strode to the end of the street and then turned, out of sight. She scrambled back into the kitchen and slammed the door closed, locking and chaining it before she started fumbling in her pocket for her mobile phone. She was breathing heavily, and her vision was blurred from the tears, so she wiped them until she was able to focus on the names in her contact list. She knew when she started her plan that it had risks, but she never thought she would have one of them in her house, screaming at her, threatening to kill her unless she stopped. She eventually found the name she was looking for and dialled his mobile. It rang out and then went to messaging, so she left him a voicemail:

"It's Evie Perry. Things are getting out of hand. The man I told you about... Fitzgerald... he's been here, to my HOUSE. He threatened to kill me. I don't understand what's happening. Maybe we should stop what we're doing? Please call me as soon as you get this message; I need to talk to someone. I need to know what to do. PLEASE." As soon as she ended the call, she collapsed onto the floor, pulling her knees up to her chest and burying her face as the tears and panic once again took hold of her. She even found herself contemplating whether ending her life was the only way out.

As soon as she had left the message, the man's phone lit up with a text informing him he had missed a call. A woman had the man's phone, and she tapped the link in the text; the phone dialled straight into his voicemail. She listened, smiled, and then deleted the voice message and any trace of the incoming call.

"At last; time to plan the final deliveries."

Chapter 72

A third fire engine pulled up at the burning building, but it was already obvious to the watch manager that the house couldn't be saved. He turned to the crew leader. "We have a fatality, but also another person reported as missing. Neighbours think there's a boy in there, the victim's son."

"We'll have a couple of wearers ready, but it looks too risky to send anyone in just yet," said the crew leader. The fragility of the structure concerned him, and the heat of the blaze could be dangerous for anyone wearing an oxygen tank on their back.

"Agreed, and although the roof has already collapsed, we don't know what accelerant there might be on site that could still ignite. The first team here reported a strong smell of paraffin."

"At least there's no proximity risk; the nearest building is over an acre away. I'll put the third crew on trying to douse a specific area."

"Okay, and once you've set that up, the fire investigation officer is here; let's see what she thinks of the situation," said the watch manager. The crew leader agreed and then ran over to the third team.

"You'll need to set up a water relay from the river, as the hydrant is at full capacity. We need to kill the fire in the left-hand sector," he said, pointing at the left-hand wing of what had been a large 6-bedroom house.

The first two crews had found a man, bloodied and blistered from the heat, still trying to get back into the house, presumably to try to rescue his son. As they pulled him to safety, he'd had a cardiac arrest.

The fire investigation officer walked over and gave her assessment of the blaze. "Sorry to say, I can't see anyone surviving that. I know the watch manager said there might be a boy in there, but..." and she just shook her head in resignation.

"Do you think the fire will continue to grow?" asked the recently arrived CID detective.

"I'd be very surprised if there's any accelerant left to ignite, given the intensity of the fire and with the house completely engulfed. I'd say the risk of further explosions is very low, but it's the watch manager's incident to call."

"And when do you think you'll have a view on the cause?"

"Tomorrow morning at the earliest. This fire will take some knocking down. I'll call you with any initial findings."

The detective thanked her and then pulled his mobile out of his pocket as he walked away from the noise and heat. He rang the West Yorkshire CID office and spoke to the officer in charge.

"Sir, it's DS Collins. You know the briefing this morning?" He listened to the reply, then continued, "I'm at a house fire just outside Shadwell. Paramedics have just taken a man's body to the LGI mortuary. Oh, and it's likely his son has died in the fire, as well... What?... No, the FIO doesn't think we'll know any more until the morning."

Chapter 73

The HMET meeting had a solemn air. The news that Anthony Fairfax and his son were dead felt like the team had failed again. Denton had asked both Williams and Armitage to travel to the incident room at Scotland Yard. Armitage was available, but Williams had another high-profile case that he had to attend court for.

"Wait a minute," said a puzzled Armitage, looking at DC Jones. "Are you telling me that the majority of murders are intended to distract us, to hide the real reason for some of the murders?" Jones nodded. Armitage looked over to Denton for confirmation, who also nodded.

"It's a possibility we hadn't considered," Denton admitted.

"How do we differentiate between the distraction and the pattern?" a perplexed Armitage asked.

"There's one theme emerging," replied Jones, and she moved aside to let Armitage see the board.

Commonalities	*Differences*
10 of 15 victims are male: 5 knew each other	*7 different police jurisdictions*
Lottery ticket in mouth at every scene	*Methods of murder*

One attempted murder, who knew 4 others	Age of victims
No trace at 9 of the 10 scenes. Professional hit!	7 sole murders; one triple and two doubles
Theft does not appear to be a motive	
3 victims had links to Belschen Petro	
5 of 9 adult male victims knew each other	No obvious ties with/ between the others

Notes related to lottery ticket
6 house numbers match the numbers on the first ticket (UK Lottery). Assume first house linked to #24.

??	29	**30**	36	46	48	7
AL	BD	**CR**	DA	EN	FK	GL
Lowe		**Curtis**				

Sequencing of numbers and letters following the same pattern on the second ticket (Euro Millions).

1	5	23	**29**	**32**	**41**	**7**
HG	IP	JE	**K**T?	**L**S	**M**?	**N**W?
Vickers			Fitzgerald	**Fairfax**	Mallory	**Wagstaff**

"Five of them knew each other?" checked Armitage.

"Yes, and they were all members of what's known as the Aeternum. If we assume the attempt on Yvonne Fitzgerald related to the letter K…" started Jones.

"And we now know that the Fitzgerald house was built on what the developer listed as lots 14 and 15," added Denton.

"14 + 15 equals 29, but how did the killer know that?" challenged Armitage.

"If I found that out, anyone else could have," replied Jones.

"Anthony Fairfax lived at number 32 The Avenue, which has a Leeds postcode," said Denton.

"And why is N marked as a death?"

Jones replied. "We've had a call to let us know that Charles Wagstaff died this morning. He lived in Belsize Park, house number 7. It's a NW3 postcode. That just leaves Peter Mallory, who lives at Salford Quays in Manchester in one of the new canal-side developments; apartment number 41."

Denton started to explain, "So, if the car bomb that injured Charles Wagstaff was actually intended for Niall Fitzgerald..."

"...because we know that the car was booked in the name of Fitzgerald; not specifically Yvonne Fitzgerald..." interjected Jones.

"... then I'm comfortable we have the real pattern," continued Denton.

"And the other murders were... random?"

"Random victims, but definitely not a random selection; quite the opposite," replied Jones. "Pick a sequential letter and the next number of the lottery ticket, and you have a ready-made target."

"So, we have a killer or killers murdering innocent people just to stop us seeing the real purpose, and we still don't know why the Aeternum are being murdered. And why the lottery ticket as the clue?"

"We don't know why those particular lottery tickets, but maybe they're just a twisted way to taunt us about the upcoming murders?" Denton said. Armitage sank back into his chair and just nodded to himself. It all made sense, and it was frightening. "And I still think Fitzgerald isn't telling us everything he knows, and Mallory is a new lead," added Denton.

"Do we interview them both under caution, guv? We've had Mr Fitzgerald in earlier, but shall I advise him we need him back and to bring legal counsel?" asked Jones.

"Yes," replied Denton.

"Perhaps the final unanswered question is who would benefit from the deaths?" Armitage suggested.

"What if the family members who died weren't just in the wrong place at the wrong time?" asked Denton. They all looked at each other because no one had the answer, and it was a painful reminder of just how far they were away from cracking the case. Denton was starting to feel under almost unbearable pressure, because if he couldn't find something soon to solve this case, he felt certain that his temporary promotion would be taken away and the case handed to someone else.

Chapter 74

Yvonne had returned home a couple of days after the attack, recovering from the after-effects of the explosion far quicker than the prognosis of her original injuries had suggested. Niall was returning from his interview with the police, and he slowed the car as he approached the house. Despite still being fuelled by anger and having driven over the speed limit on his way back from the police interview, he didn't want to disturb Yvonne's recuperation by screeching into the driveway. On the drive home, he had decided he needed to confide in her. The situation regarding SILK was beginning to overwhelm even his ability to rationalise and remain calm, but that would mean telling Yvonne everything, and who knew how she would respond to that.

Yvonne was walking through the hallway when Niall strode in. She was wrapped in a satin robe and was using a cane to help her maintain her balance. The explosion had flung her onto the concrete floor of the airport car park, badly bruising her hip. She hated the cane but had agreed to it as the alternative to staying any longer in hospital or temporarily having to use a wheelchair.

"I wondered where you'd gone?" she said as she tried to hobble towards him a little faster than usual, keen to welcome him home with a warm embrace.

"I just needed to pop out," he explained, joyfully accepting the hug from Yvonne.

"I'm going to make a cup of tea. I'm tired of lying on the bed and having Adrianna fetch everything for me. Would you like some?" she asked as she turned and headed towards the kitchen. Niall watched as she struggled to turn on the highly polished marble floor, but he smiled at the gradual return of her independent nature.

"You seem to be moving a little easier this morning. How are you feeling?" he enquired, hoping to find her in a good mood. The last thing he wanted to do was start to discuss SILK if she was in pain or irritable from a lack of sleep.

"Quite good, actually. I'm sure the painkillers the doctor gave me are helping, but..." She turned to look back over her shoulder at him. "... I'm down to just four a day now," she said proudly.

"Oh good," said a slightly distracted Niall. Now he knew Yvonne was in a positive mood, he started to doubt his previous decision to broach the subject of SILK. After all, if she was improving, perhaps it would be better to discuss it in a few days; by that time, she would be in even better health. As soon as that thought entered his head, though, he knew he was just looking for a reason to delay raising the subject at all. There would never be a good time, and this needed resolving now. He drew a deep breath and headed towards the kitchen.

"Fancy a tea, or do you want coffee?" asked Yvonne as she stood by the boiling water tap over the sink.

"Er, New York Breakfast Tea, please. I feel like having a change from my usual morning cwoffee, ma'am." He forced himself to laugh at his attempt to lighten the mood by using an affected New York accent, but it sounded false, and Yvonne noticed. She didn't say anything, though, as his nervous laugh usually preceded an admission of guilt or an awkward request or both. She didn't have long to wait.

As she filled the teapot from a tap that provided instant hot water, Niall said, "Yvonne, can I ask for your advice on something?"

"Of course, darling. You know I love it when my clever husband asks for my opinion. What is it?"

"It's a little... well, it's a little awkward. I know it will never be a good time to raise this, but I think we're in a positive place in our marriage again, and..." He took a short sharp intake of breath before continuing, "... and I need to share some information about the murder of our friends," he explained.

"Sorry, darling, but could you please lift the tray over to the table? I'm afraid I can't manage it just yet," she said, trying to hide the anxiety in her voice as she began to worry about what he might be going to tell her.

"Yes, yes, of course." Niall jumped up from the settee, walked over to the kitchen area and picked up the tray. He was conscious he had a few cold beads of sweat forming on his brow, and she noticed them too. Again, she thought it best not to say anything. They sat down next to each other on the settee. She felt it might be easier for him to talk if she focused on pouring the tea rather than looking into his eyes.

"What's wrong, Niall?" she asked, her voice suddenly trembling with concern. She had only ever seen him perspire like this twice in their time together. Once was just before they met her father for the first time, and the other was when he had to tell her that her parents' savings had been frozen as part of an Interpol investigation into Oleg Thoresen, one of his partners at his old investment company.

"This isn't going to be easy for me or you to talk about, Yvonne. It's about some information and some suspicions I have about the murders of our friends and... and the attempt on your life." He looked for a reaction from Yvonne. She appeared calm as she continued to pour the tea, but he then realised that the cup she was pouring into was filling up very quickly. Before he could stop her, it cascaded over the edge of the cup and filled the saucer. He reached out and steadied her hand, easing the teapot upright and then back onto the table. Niall could tell she was shaking. Perhaps this wasn't the right time to talk to her after all, but he had already opened Pandora's box. "Are you alright?" he asked her.

She slowly nodded and then added a quiet, "Yes, I think so," before her teary eyes peered up at him, searching for a comforting look in return. She couldn't see one, though. "What is it you need to tell me?" she asked, closing her eyes in fear of the scenarios that were racing through her mind.

"I think I know who is killing them, and I think I know why." Yvonne looked up at him but didn't ask him anything, so Niall continued. "A few months ago, I received a blackmail note from a woman I'd met some time ago. She and I had... spent some time together. I paid her and assumed it would all just go away." The subtext was enough for Yvonne to think she knew what he meant, and she didn't want or need to know the detail.

She closed her eyes again as she said, "Go on."

"When Derek and his family were murdered, I just thought it was a tragedy and didn't link it with an incident a few years ago. Even when William died, I assumed it was just a dreadful coincidence." He paused once more, not to see if Yvonne had any questions or words of assuring encouragement, but because he knew he was about to admit to the whole sordid saga with SILK.

He gave her a few more seconds of silence to process what he had just revealed and was about to continue when in a faint voice and with her eyes still closed, Yvonne asked, "Who was the woman you'd met, and what was she blackmailing you about?" Niall swallowed hard. His reply was slow, measured, and dripping with guilt.

"She was an escort. I met her a couple of months after we seemed to be falling apart. It started as a one-time fling, but..." He prepared himself for the anger and tears Yvonne would surely vent. "... but as you and I continued to drift apart, it became more regular."

Yvonne remained calm, at least on the outside, as she twisted a napkin in her hands and mumbled, "Is it over?"

"Yes," said Niall definitively.

There was another pause before she asked, "What does she want?"

"It started out as £10m, but now she's asking for £100m."

Yvonne continued to twist the napkin into an ever-tighter coil as she reflected on the information. Again, calmly and almost whispering, she asked, "Why haven't you told the police about this? About her?"

"It's gone on for far too long for me to tell them now. I'd probably be prosecuted for perverting the course of justice."

"And what happens if you pay her? It's not a lot of money if it means she goes away and we're safe," she asked in a hopeful tone.

"I paid her once, and that stopped her for a few years, but what happens if she keeps coming back?"

Yvonne raised her gaze and shrugged her shoulders before replying, "What happens if she keeps killing our friends?" Then she concluded her question with something that Niall simply had no answer to, "Including me and any chance we might have of another child?" She looked back down again as she started to weep at the loss of her pregnancy. The doctor had told her about the loss before she left the hospital, and both she and Niall had cried together when they returned home.

"Don't worry, I'm dealing with it," he said in a determined voice, intended to ease the pain and uncertainty that Yvonne must be feeling. She stopped crying straight away and slowly raised her head. This time, though, there was a look of determination in her eyes. She took hold of Niall's hands.

"No, don't do anything yet. We're in this together, and I need time to think. Tell me everything you know."

Chapter 75

Despite the sun streaming through the large windows in the conference room at Wagstaff, Earnshaw and Peters, an air of gloom weighed heavily on those gathered. Brian Earnshaw had already broken the news that Charles Wagstaff had died. Some of the employees stared out of the window in quiet reflection, while others comforted those who were crying. The rear door to the conference room opened, and one of the reception team ushered two plain-clothes police officers into the room. He looked over and gestured the police duo towards him.

"Mr Earnshaw?"

"Yes."

"Acting Detective Inspector Denton; CID. This is Detective Constable Jones." Earnshaw looked over at Jones and nodded in acknowledgement.

"We realise this is a difficult time, and I'd like to thank you for gathering everyone together at such short notice," said Denton.

"Anything to help," replied a subdued Earnshaw.

"If you could get everyone's attention, please; we'd like to start the meeting."

"Of course," Earnshaw said, turning to the gathered employees.

"Good morning… er, good morning, everyone," he said in a raised voice. "If I might have your attention, please?" The whispers and murmurs around the room quickly died as people looked up at Earnshaw and then at the two people who had just arrived. Earnshaw waited for complete silence before saying, "Thank you for coming in today, especially as I know some of you had the day off. I'd like to introduce you to Detective Inspector Denton and Detective Constable Jones from the Metropolitan Police CID. Detective Inspector?" he said, gesturing to Denton that he now had the floor. Denton walked forwards and cleared his throat.

"Good morning. As you are probably aware, Charles Wagstaff died yesterday. His death is part of an active investigation, so while I'm unable to share any information with you, we..." He turned to gesture towards Jones. "... will be here all day, taking statements. We have no reason to suspect anyone in this room of being involved, but you might have some information that ultimately could be helpful with our investigation." Denton then scanned the room to see if anyone had a question, but no one did. "Thank you for listening." He looked at Earnshaw to hand back control of the meeting.

"Right, one more thing... please, a little quiet," said Earnshaw, raising his voice again so he could be heard over the conversations that had re-started. He reminded everyone they had work to do and that they would be called for an interview.

As people left the room, Denton pulled Jones to one side. "I'll take the senior managers; you talk to Wagstaff's PA first. I think she'll feel more at ease with you rather than me. I'll ask Earnshaw to gather names and job titles, and we'll compare notes in an hour or so."

"Okay, guv." Jones then headed out to one of the interview rooms, where Alice Perkins was waiting; she had been Charles Wagstaff's PA.

"Miss Perkins, thank you for waiting."

"Please, call me Alice. Miss Perkins makes me feel I'm under suspicion." She laughed nervously.

"Thank you, Alice. What can you tell me about Mr Wagstaff?"

"Charles is... was... a very generous, hard-working partner in the firm. He expected dedication but rewarded people for their efforts. He could be a little full of himself, always wanting to be centre stage. Sorry, I didn't expect that to sound so mean; it wasn't intended to be."

"I didn't take it that way, so don't worry. Can you give a few examples of what you meant? That would help," offered Jones.

"He was a little bit like a peacock; effusive and confident in front of clients, but not so much as he'd ever come across as arrogant or rude. He was never rude to any of us."

"Okay," Jones said. "Any other examples?"

"In private, he would sometimes talk about how much he'd spent at lunch, or on a car, or a holiday with one of his girlfriends. You know, bragging a little but not showing off. I suppose he was proud of what he had achieved and could afford."

"Has he had many girlfriends?" enquired Jones.

"A few. Not at the same time, he wasn't like that, but he liked having beautiful women in his life. It was strange; he never talked about any of them by name, at least not while he was dating them. He was a very private man with his personal life. I think it started when the press almost got a photo when he was dating Amy Westhuizen, the lingerie model. That's when he stopped telling people where he was going and with who. You see, most of his girlfriends were standard fare for the paparazzi, so Charles would keep his whereabouts secret from just about everyone and only referred to them by their initial. She would have just been 'A' if he was dating her now." Alice then snorted a little with laughter. As she dabbed her moist eyes, she smiled as she thought about her ex-boss.

"What's so funny?" Jones enquired in a light tone, intrigued.

"I was just thinking; after Amy, he dated Dee Phillips, who was known as '*D*'; then there was an 'S'... Sarah Delevan, the actress with the big boobs and long legs. Oh yes, and 'C' was for Christy James, the reality television personality. She was so not his type."

"Was he dating anyone recently? Perhaps someone we could talk to?"

"He got quite serious with a woman a couple of years ago. I think she was a client, but he only met her outside work. She was different to the previous ones." Alice smiled softly, caringly.

"Different in what way?"

"Well, she certainly captured his heart. He rarely stayed in a relationship for longer than six months, but as I said, he started to date this woman a couple of years ago. I don't think she's famous, like the others, and he implied she was probably a good 10 years older than most of his previous ones, but no doubt still very beautiful."

"How do you know?"

"Charles told me a little about her one day. He was definitely smitten. He said she was his E, F and G, because he said the relationship had lasted so long. He really was quite taken with her."

"E, F and G? Does that mean you still don't know who she is?"

"Sorry, but no I don't. If Charles had lived, he'd still be dating her, so she'd still be just a letter to all of us."

"Charles liked his alphabet, didn't he," said Jones, immediately intrigued. "Alice, did Charles date any of these women in alphabetical order?" Alice looked confused by the apparently random nature of the question.

"Er…" she replied, as she thought through the sequence as best as she could recall it. Jones had to bite her lip to stop her from asking the woman to damn well hurry up. "No. No, I don't think so. Why do you ask?"

Jones relaxed a little and smiled, replying, "Just wondering, that's all. What can you tell me about the days and weeks before Mr Wagstaff was killed? Was there anything unusual in the post; any unusual phone calls?"

"No, I don't think so. I know Charles was preoccupied with the proposed takeover. He was desperate to buy out the company and keep it private, but he kept saying he was just waiting for his money to be released, and then it would be his."

"Was that something he talked to you about, money?"

"Oh no," Alice said, looking a little sheepish. "I was here later than usual one night; Charles had asked me to stay behind to help. I heard him talking to someone. I didn't hear much, but he hadn't completely closed his office door. He said something about all his money being currently tied up and inaccessible. His tone made me think it wasn't like an investment account that you or I might have, where you can get access to your money with three months' notice. No, he sounded... helpless. I'd never heard him sound that way before. He told the person he was flying out for a last-minute break with his girlfriend to get away from it all for a while. With the pressures of the takeover and the death of a couple of his friends, I imagine he needed the break."

"What did he tell you about his friends?"

"Just that they had unexpectedly died. It clearly worried him, but I suppose it made him think about his own mortality. I would if any of my friends died."

"Yes, me too," said Jones sympathetically. "But I'm lost; sorry. If all his money was inaccessible, how did he manage to pay for a holiday?"

"He didn't; his girlfriend did. I know because he was supposed to be away for 10 days, but he had to come back early for a funeral; another friend had unexpectedly died. I offered to rearrange his flight, but Charles said she had already done it as she'd paid for everything."

"Do you know the name of the friend that died?"

"I do. He mentioned the name 'James'."

Chapter 76

The woman reflected on how long she had waited for this moment. She looked through her list and drew a line through the name 'Charles Wagstaff':

~~Derek Lowe (wife Celia and daughter Amelia; all three are only children: no other dependents).~~
~~William Curtis (single, no dependents in his will).~~
~~James Vickers (single, no dependents in his will).~~
Niall Fitzgerald (married, no dependents. Wife Yvonne).
~~Anthony Fairfax (divorced, with one son)~~
Peter Mallory (single, no dependents in his will).
~~Charles Wagstaff (single, no dependents in his will).~~

After that, she called The Broker. When he answered, all she said was, "We are almost ready," and then ended the call. Their agreement was that the call would trigger five tasks. First, a package was to be delivered to Evie Perry's house, which was intended to add to her growing paranoia. Secondly, incriminating evidence was to be placed in the apartment of a member of the Aeternum. Thirdly, she needed one person to be shot dead and another to be badly wounded but not killed. Two days after that, the fourth task was for another new lottery ticket to be sent to the police, with a final murder one week after that final ticket was delivered.

"It will be an expensive job," he told her when she had originally explained her final plan, but she agreed to the final fee of £2m in advance for the five deliverables. That would take the total she had paid him to over £4m for the contracts, with a further £2m bonus she promised him once it was all over.

"Does it matter that the new ticket has the same final digit as the first ticket, '7'?" he asked her.

She scoffed in derision. "Of course not. I plan these things meticulously." The Broker didn't respond, despite a growing desire to do so. As soon as the call ended, he used his encrypted phone to send a text to one of his contract killers. In the next two hours, the package would be delivered, people would be despatched with the evidence to plant, and plans would be put in place for the final death.

After her call had finished, she congratulated herself on the success of her plan. She looked at her watch; it was just after 12 noon. The courier company estimated it would take about two hours to deliver the package. She returned to her list, drew a line through Niall Fitzgerald's name and his wife's, and circled Peter Mallory's.

"And I have a special end planned for you."

Chapter 77

It was a little after 2pm when Evie Perry awoke. The injection she had received from her doctor had provided some temporary easing of her symptoms. He had told her the drugs wouldn't stop the anxiety, but they would at least allow her some much-needed sleep. Now she was awake, and as her mind raced, wrestling once again with her fears and imagination, a motorcyclist climbed off his bike outside her house. He had already turned the bike to face up the street in case the recipient of the package he was delivering looked out the window when he had pushed it through the letterbox. Although he had clothed himself in unremarkable leathers, a plain black helmet, and temporarily covered the registration plate on the back of the bike, he wanted to minimise the risk that she saw him or his bike at all.

She heard the thud of the envelope and then a motorcycle starting and racing away. She began to twitch as her brain raced through a series of implausible scenarios: *Who was that? Who would come here and then race away? What if it was an explosive device?* She lay in bed for almost an hour, unable to move. If she stayed where she was, she would remain safe and not have to face the reality of whatever awaited her downstairs. Eventually, though, she mustered enough courage to slide her legs out from under the sheets and put on some slippers. She reached for her robe and, after pausing to check if she could hear any unexpected noises, she tiptoed to the top of the stairs. From there, she could see a large brown envelope lying on the mat.

"Of course," she sighed, laughing nervously, "it's the final package from Materia Prima." She raced down the stairs, glancing warily at the door as she stooped to pick up the package and then ran back up into her home office. She ripped the package open, and items cascaded onto the desk. As she scanned the contents, she reeled in shock. As usual, there was a photo in the envelope, but it wasn't of any of the men she was investigating; it was of her. It was taken the day she had teased the courier with her bare skin; the same day she thought she had seen a man in a car taking photos. Stapled to the photo was a small noose and a note that said, *We all have secrets we want to keep. Judge not, that ye be not judged,* written in red crayon. She snatched up the outer packaging to check it, which was when she realised there was no delivery address on the front of the package and no Materia Prima logo stamped on it, either. Her name was written on the front in the same red crayon. Evie dropped onto the settee behind her, closed her eyes and grabbed fistfuls of her hair before she let out a choked scream. A powerful fear was in danger of overwhelming her, and the idea of the noose was suddenly a very compelling one. If she took her own life on her own terms, she would be free of this torment. When she opened her eyes, her gaze fell on her mobile phone, which lay on the desk.

An alternative idea came to mind. She picked up the phone and, with trembling fingers, dialled the number. When the call was answered, Evie said, "It's me. I'm sorry, and I know this is a lot to ask, but I need you. I need you so much right now."

At the other end of the phone, Cheryl didn't know what to do. Her friend had threatened her the last time they had met. Now she needed her help?

Chapter 78

Packing her belongings into boxes, ready for the removals company, Stella was ready to move one final time. She knew she couldn't stay in the apartment; it didn't feel safe to be there. She grabbed the few papers she needed with her into a large handbag. As she did so, a folded piece of paper fell onto the floor; the piece of paper Robert had taped to the underside of the kitchen drawer. She had forgotten all about it. She bent to pick it up and unfold it to remind herself what he had written. On the paper was the pattern of numbers which had been the clue to the bank accounts and the names of three men.

"Oleg Thoresen, David Holding, and Niall Fitzgerald," she mumbled. She knew Thoresen was in prison and had no idea where the real David Holding was. She stared at the final name. "Niall Fitzgerald," she mouthed. Robert had said that he had sent Holding and Fitzgerald packages and told them that she would be contacting them. She'd forgotten all about Fitzgerald. Next to his name was a sequence of letters and numbers, as well as a code phrase:

z 2 a s c s 1 z c 4 4 – John loses to Bjorn

Stella recognised the simple number-letter encryption and went to get a pen from her bag to write the decoded message down. As she put her hand into the bag, she paused. *Why am I doing this? Putting myself through torture? It doesn't matter what he knows. Move on!* She thought, but the temptation was strong. Her hand hovered inside the bag as the instinct to know more grew. She grabbed a pen and wrote the message down. The doorbell suddenly rang and made her jump. She wasn't expecting anyone yet and had had more than enough surprises in the last few days, so she cautiously tiptoed towards the door and called out, "Who is it?"

"Peterson's Removals, Mrs Kendrick. Sorry we're a bit early, but thought better early than late."

Stella opened the door steadily in case she needed to try to slam it shut, but it was the two men who had come to assess her apartment for the removals quote.

"Oh, good morning. Well, I'm ready, so please feel free to start loading things," she said. The men placed some protective sheeting down on the carpet and then went about their business. Two hours later and the apartment was empty. Stella had been given the option to sub-let, but she had decided she needed a clean break from everything and everyone. Looking at the bare apartment she was voluntarily leaving wasn't comparable to her forced exit from the empty house in Windsor, but both were as a result of her husband's death. The painful memory of the eviction was surprisingly raw, and when one of the removal men came back upstairs to check they had everything, he saw tears in her eyes and asked if she was alright.

"Can be painful moving from a home full of memories," he offered in sympathy.

She smiled a sad smile and said, "You have no idea, but thank you for asking. That was very kind."

The man gave a short, bashful smile before replying, "Well, Mrs Kendrick, that's it. You're fully packed, and we'll be heading off to the storage unit. Going anywhere nice?" Stella had already booked a villa on the Algarve for three months and intended to read, rest, and look forward to having someone else cook for her every day, but she was wary of telling anyone her plans. She didn't want to spend her time in Portugal looking over her shoulder.

"Er, I don't know yet. I might go and visit my sister in Bournemouth for a few weeks," she lied. She had no sister, let alone any intention of going to Bournemouth. Her flight from Southampton to Gatwick was in four hours, with an onward flight to Faro just a couple of hours after that. He didn't need to know that. No one did. Once the removals van had left, she called a local taxi company and asked to go to the airport. She made sure she had a book to read and would watch the planes take-off and land at the airport for a few hours while enjoying a glass of chilled wine. The taxi arrived within minutes, and soon she was sat on the back seat, watching Southampton race by.

"Drummer, are you?" asked the driver after they'd been travelling for a few minutes.

"I'm sorry, what?" she asked.

"You a drummer? You seem to be drumming that handbag pretty steadily."

Stella had been unconsciously tapping her handbag with her fingers since the taxi set off. She now realised just how much the piece of paper was on her mind. Instinctively, she opened her mouth to apologise and explain why she was tapping, but she caught herself.

"Sorry. I suppose I'm more nervous than I realised. I'm going to see my brother. He lives up in Glasgow. Not seen him for years, so I'm finally flying up there," she lied again. She had no brother. "Sorry if it was annoying you."

"No problem," said the driver. "Hardly noticed it." This time it was his turn to lie.

At the airport, Stella checked in for her flight and then went straight to the airport lounge she had paid for. It was quiet, which suited her, and the lady on reception explained about the free buffet and drinks. Stella thanked her and made her way to an armchair near the window. She put her bag and coat on the chair before going to pour a coffee and choose a pastry. Once she had sat back down, she opened her bag and took her book out, catching sight of the slip of paper from earlier. She clenched her jaw a little and closed the bag, pretending not to be drawn by the paper, but within minutes, she placed her bookmark on the page she had re-read three times and got the piece of paper out. After looking around for prying eyes, she unfolded it and gazed at the decoded message. Temptation was growing. She put the paper back inside before picking up the bag and walking over to the receptionist.

"Excuse me, but I need to make a rather personal phone call. Is there somewhere I could use?"

"Normally our business suites are chargeable, but…" The woman looked around. "You can use room 3." Stella hesitated, as the woman hadn't explicitly said there was no fee, but the receptionist saw her hesitation and gave her a wink and an assuring nod.

When she got to the room, she closed the door and locked it. She pulled the paper and a new pay-as-you-go mobile phone from her bag. She checked the decoding and then dialled the number it revealed. It rang three times before she heard a click, and a voice said, "This is

Niall." Stella froze. She didn't know what to say. After a few seconds, he said, "Hello? Who is it? I can hear you breathing. I know someone is there." Stella panicked. She was about to end the call when she heard his voice become quiet but raspy. "If that's you, SILK, you can go to hell. I've told Yvonne all about your games." Stella slowly edged the phone back towards her ear.

"H... hello? My name is Stella Kendrick. My husband, Robert, said I should call you."

There was a short pause before the man replied, "I don't know anyone called Robert. You must have the wrong number. I'm sorry."

"No, don't go," she blurted out.

"I'm sorry, Mrs... Kendrick, did you say? I'm afraid I—"

Stella cut across him and hurriedly blurted out the code-phrase from the piece of paper. "John loses to Bjorn."

There was an extended period of silence, but eventually Niall replied. "What do you want?"

"I don't know," said Stella. "Robert told me he had sent you a package on my behalf and that you'd know I was going to contact you. Your name was on a list he left me."

Niall blinked rapidly. The only package he had received had been the blackmail package, and now he had a woman calling him about it? He was confused. He had been sure it was SILK that had been blackmailing him, so who was this woman calling him? And how did she know about 'John' and 'Bjorn'? Stella remained quiet, knowing from years of living with Robert that there were times when you had to let the conclusion surface at its own speed. Niall gathered his thoughts; he didn't know what to do, but he knew what not to do. He said, "We can't talk over the phone. We need to meet."

"Meet? When? Where?" asked a surprised Stella.

"Later, in London. Are you in the city?"

"Not exactly, but I can get there." All thoughts of her flight from Gatwick to Faro were gone.

"I'll text you the location of where to meet me," said Niall, and then he ended the call. Stella was deep in thought as she slowly put the phone and the paper back into the bag. She unlocked the door and drifted back past the receptionist while still reflecting on the call.

"Are you alright, madam?" asked the concerned receptionist.

Stella looked up and realised what she needed to do. "How do I book a return ticket for the Gatwick Express, please?" she asked.

Chapter 79

"Oh, my goodness! Are you alright?" exclaimed the therapist. Although she was feeling significantly better, Yvonne Fitzgerald was still using a cane for longer walks, and her face still had a few tell-tale signs from her injuries. The fact she was wearing minimal makeup accentuated the image.

"Thank you; I could certainly do with a moment. It's my first real journey outside of our house, and it's rather taken my breath away," she replied as she eased herself into the usual chair. She closed her eyes as she took several slow, deep breaths. The therapist prepared a cup of tea for them both while keeping a watchful eye on her client. She placed the cup and saucer on the small table next to Yvonne, who slowly opened her eyes and gave a grateful smile. "Ah, that's better. I suppose you never know how much something has affected you until you try to live life as normal."

"What on earth happened?"

"Did you read about a car bomb at the airport a few weeks ago?"

"Yes. Did I read that the man caught in the explosion has died?"

Yvonne's eyes welled up as she nodded and sniffed back a few tears. "Yes. I was with him when it happened. Luckily, I was several metres away, but poor Charles…" She stopped talking as she tried to retain her composure.

"How awful," replied the therapist. They sat for a moment, giving Yvonne a little more time. She sipped her tea and nodded her gratitude for the therapist's patience.

When she was ready to restart, Yvonne said, "The police think it was actually an attempt on my life or my husband's. Charles just needed a lift back from the airport, that's all. I'd just given him the news that one of his friends, our friends, had been murdered."

"Another one?" enquired the therapist.

"Yes, that's five of our friends now, and I know it's more than just a terrible coincidence."

The therapist stared at Yvonne, unsure what to make of the revelation. "Wh… what do you mean?" she asked Yvonne hesitantly.

"My husband explained what was happening and said he was dealing with it, but the police keep talking to him and… and I don't know what to do."

"Mrs Fitzgerald, I have to remind you that we are now discussing something that I might need to share with the police under my legal obligation and code of ethics."

"I understand. I think perhaps I want to talk to them myself, but Niall will be so angry if I do, and our marriage seems to be getting stronger and stronger."

"Have you considered talking to the police anonymously? You are welcome to use a private room here if that would help?"

Yvonne was unsure whether she felt guilt that she was about to betray Niall's trust or relief because he would never know. She swallowed hard and said, "Yes, this madness has to stop. I have to tell them everything I know."

Chapter 80

Niall arrived at the police station with his solicitor. They were met by Denton, who introduced them to Jones.

"Thank you for coming here today, and I'm sorry about your wife. How is Mrs Fitzgerald?"

"Thank you; she's recovering as well as can be expected. Poor Charles," replied Niall reflecting on the news that Wagstaff had died from his injuries. "I feel terrible. I'm happy that Yvonne wasn't by herself, otherwise she would have been the one who was killed, but..." He bit his lip in an attempt to control his emotions.

"How did Mr Wagstaff come to be travelling with your wife?" asked Jones.

"They bumped into each other as they exited a plane from the Caribbean. Apparently, the flight from Turks was diverted to pick up a handful of stranded passengers from Jamaica. Yvonne somewhat clumsily broke the news about James's death. Poor Charles hadn't heard and was distraught. She told him he could stay with us for a few days as he really wasn't in a fit state to be at home by himself." As the ensuing silent reflection became a little awkward, Denton offered to lead them into an interview room. After following due process, Denton and Jones started the interview.

"Mr Lowe was your accountant, wasn't he?" asked Jones.

"He managed my personal finances, yes, but I used someone else for my business finances. I've always found it wise to have separation between business and family matters."

"Did any of the other members of your informal Aeternum group use Mr Lowe?"

"I don't know. Some of them were very guarded about their financial situation, like Derek and Peter, whereas others wanted to shout it from the rooftops, like Anthony. Most of us took independent financial advice, although I know some sought Derek's informal advice from time to time."

"I'd like to ask a few questions about the others in the group, if I may?"

"If we're talking about other people, Detective Inspector, my client cannot be held responsible for the accuracy or completeness of any of his answers," interjected the solicitor.

Denton nodded to show he understood before he continued. Niall had remained calm and confident but had already planned that when the subject of James Vickers came up, he would ask for a moment to gather his thoughts, using his genuine concern about Yvonne's health to make him look sad. It was a trick that one of his investment clients had taught him, an actor of great repute. '*I think I'm fine, but thank you for asking. It all still feels a little overwhelming,*' he would say, to give himself some thinking time.

"Given the death of Mr Lowe, Mr Curtis, Mr Vickers, Mr Fairfax, and Mr Wagstaff, as well as the possibility that there was actually an attempt on your wife's life, can you think of any reason someone would want to kill your friends and your family?"

"What? I don't think so. Why? Do you think there might be?" Niall asked in a well-rehearsed and perfectly timed response.

"I'm afraid we can't comment on an active investigation, Mr Fitzgerald. It was just a question," said Denton.

"Sorry. My brain just isn't functioning at the moment." He pretended to search his memory for any further insights but pursed his lips and shook his head. "No, still nothing, I'm afraid."

"Can you think of anyone who would benefit from these deaths?" Jones asked.

"Derek's wife and daughter were the beneficiaries listed in Derek's will. William had no family, nor did James. Anthony had his son. If Yvonne had been killed, I would have been the theoretical beneficiary, but to be frank, Yvonne doesn't really have a great deal of individual wealth, and we don't have life insurance."

"Who arranged the car hire for her?"

"I did; why?"

"Just confirming a few details," replied Jones calmly. "And what about Mr Wagstaff?" she continued.

"Charles? Unless he bequeathed everything to one of his girlfriends, then…" Niall stopped mid-sentence. As he thought through the scenarios, two things unexpectedly struck him. Firstly, if SILK wanted revenge on everyone who was at that fateful party three years ago, Charles Wagstaff should have been safe because he wasn't there. Yes, he knew what had happened to SILK because Niall had told him afterwards, but SILK didn't know that. Secondly, with Charles dead and if SILK then killed everyone else from the party, including himself, Peter Mallory would be the sole survivor and

358

would inherit the Aeternum Foundation. Why hadn't he thought about this before? If that scenario played out, then Peter Mallory would inherit over £800m.

"Mr Fitzgerald?" probed Jones. "Are you alright?"

Niall hesitated before he stuttered a reply, "Er, yes. I'm sorry, but I need a comfort break."

"Of course," said Denton. "You'll find the bathroom is straight across the corridor, and when you're back in the interview room and ready to resume, just open this door and call us back. We'll be right outside." He recorded that the interview had been temporarily suspended and then paused the recorder before he and Jones left the room. Once they had left, Niall turned to his solicitor.

"I need to go home. Get me out of here."

Chapter 81

For the first time in a long time, waking up was a joy rather than a moment of dread. Summer had arrived, and the birds were awake and in full song. Evie's arm was wrapped around her only friend in the world, but at that precise moment, it was the only friend she needed. Cheryl had responded to Evie's frantic call, realising her almost suicidal tone. On arriving at Evie's, they had said a tentative hello, touched on topics that neither of them particularly wanted to, and then had a huge argument that raged for nearly 20 minutes. At the end of it, everything that needed to be said had been. Both had then fallen into bed, exhausted, emotionally and mentally. Eager for the warmth of another human being, without the expectation or need for sex, they had held each other like young children would have. It was 10am when Evie quietly squeezed her friend in genuine affection.

"Hey, careful; some of us ain't so young anymore. Squeeze too tight and I might just pee myself," mumbled a sleepy Cheryl. Evie laughed, something she realised she hadn't done for months.

"You stay there and I'll go make breakfast, although at this time of morning, it's probably more like brunch. Eggy-bread and black coffee okay for you?" she asked. "If you want anything else, I'll just need to nip to the cash machine."

Cheryl mumbled something and then, seconds later, sat bolt upright. "What do you mean, brunch? What time is it?" There was panic in her voice.

"Er, just after 10am. Maybe calling it brunch was a bit dramatic, but—"

Cheryl cut across her. "Oh fuck; I'm supposed to be at an appointment in Woodford Green in 45 minutes." She rubbed her eyes and leapt out of bed.

"Hey, the client will understand. Maybe offer them a discount to rearrange?" offered Evie.

Cheryl looked up at her. "It's not a client. I'm looking to go straight; you know, earn an honest living? I can't keep doing what I'm doing." She hung her head in her hands. "Doesn't matter. I need to shower and dress. Then I've got to wait for a taxi, and it's a good 20-minute drive to get there." Cheryl flopped back on the bed, but Evie had other plans.

"Take my car," she said.

"What?"

"Take my car. I don't need it today, and I'm not really supposed to be using it anyway, so why not jump in the shower, and I'll make some toast and a flask of coffee for you? You'll fit into some of my clothes, easy. Take whatever you need."

"Your car? Really?"

Evie threw her head back and laughed out loud. "Of course." They stared at each other for a moment before Evie clapped her hands and said, "Come on then, lazy bones, or you'll be late." She pulled Cheryl up from the bed, playfully smacked her on her bottom, and pushed her towards the bathroom. Twenty minutes later, Cheryl ran down the stairs, washed, dressed and smiling.

Evie mouthed 'wow' and smiled broadly. "You look great."

"Thanks," said Cheryl. "Saw some stuff in your wardrobe and it just 'spoke' to me." She did a twirl. Evie smiled, although she screwed her face up when she saw the coat Cheryl had chosen.

"Hun, it's started to rain. Take the coat by the door instead; it's got a big hood," suggested Evie.

"Will do, thanks." Evie then passed Cheryl a slice of plain toast, a small flask of coffee, and the keys to her Lotus; the one remaining luxury Evie had yet to sell.

"Go get 'em."

Cheryl beamed and then turned and strode towards the door. As she swapped the coats, she turned back to Evie with a quizzical expression. She had no idea where Evie's car was.

"Green garage door, third down on the left."

Cheryl pulled the hood up over her head, opened the door, and was gone. She ran to the garage door, undid the padlock, and climbed into the Lotus, relieved not to have got too wet. She put her hood down and pulled the car keys from the coat pocket. Five seconds later, Evie heard the explosion, and everything in her kitchen rattled. The man on the motorcycle who had been watching Evie all week was parked at the end of her street. He saw the explosion and sent a text to confirm her death.

Job done

As he sped away into the busy London streets, Evie ran outside and saw flames licking around the green garage doors, with a pillar of black smoke rising into the sky.

"CHERYL!" she screamed as she ran towards the fire.

The Broker was briefing Tom and Jerry about their next assignment when the text arrived. He immediately sent a text to his mystery client:

Boom

She read the text, which told her everything she needed to know. She put the phone away and returned to her coffee, sipping it as if it was celebratory champagne.

"And now the truth will be buried forever," she muttered to herself.

Chapter 82

As part of the agreed final deliverables in the multi-million-pound deal with his mystery client, it was important that the police find some incriminating evidence in Peter Mallory's apartment, so Tom and Jerry had been sent up to Manchester. While 'she' had asked for photos of victims and to have the lottery ticket placed in their mouths, she also wanted his team to collect additional personal items. As The Broker briefed Tom and Jerry, he explained:

"In this vacuum-sealed bag, we have a credit card from Alison Montague's purse; a Thallium-coated latex glove and some fibres from Mr Churchill's house; the gun used on James Vickers, and a copy of the emailed car hire confirmation that Niall Fitzgerald made. The glove and fibres are sealed inside another plastic bag because one moment of carelessness with just a speck of that powder and you could be dead within hours. I want these in Mallory's apartment, and somewhere he won't easily find them."

They'd made their separate ways to Manchester; one via train, and the other one flew. They'd taken it in turns to monitor the apartment block at Salford Quays, a task made all the more enjoyable by the warm weather and cool alcohol-free drinks. They made two quick reconnaissance trips to map the security camera coverage and, when they were sure Mallory wasn't home, one to assess the apartment itself before they planted the incriminating evidence. The kickboards in the kitchen came off easily, and they agreed on two other places to conceal some of the items. They continued to monitor the apartment complex before taking the items up early the following morning. Once the evidence was in place and they were on the return trip to London, Jerry sent a text:

Secret Santa in June

The Broker read the text and smiled. He was about to turn his attention back to another piece of client work when an idea popped into his head. It made him so happy thinking about it he began to laugh. Thirty minutes later, the phone rang on Denton's desk.

"DI Denton."

"Detective Inspector Denton? George Malachiah from the *Express*. Do you have a minute to talk about the lottery murders? We might have some information that would be of interest to your investigation, and perhaps you could give the British public an update on your progress?"

"I'm sorry, Mr Malachiah, but I can't discuss an active investigation."

"A source of mine tells me you have a particular line of enquiry that involves a group of men?"

"That's speculation, and you know I can't comment," Denton replied, hiding his shock and annoyance that a member of the press might know about that, but he knew Malachiah wasn't just fishing with that question; he knew something. "Why do you ask? For all I know, you're picking motives out of a hat and have decided to go fishing."

"My source is usually very reliable, and I never waste police time. Does the name Mallory mean anything to you, Detective Inspector?" Denton unconsciously hesitated at the mention of what he assumed was a reference to Peter Mallory. Malachiah heard the silence, and it confirmed he was on to something. "So, my source is correct? Interesting."

"No comment," was the only thing Denton could say.

"You might want to search Mr Mallory's apartment in Manchester. I'm told you might find some interesting artefacts hidden there. I assume our North of England team will see members of the Manchester CID team there early tomorrow morning?"

Denton put the phone on mute and considered his options. If this turned out to be a waste of time, he'd have no hesitation rebuking the reporter. If, on the other hand, it was actually a valid tip-off, and he did nothing...

"Shit," he mumbled to himself, surrendering to logic. "We'll look into it, but if it proves to be a waste of police time, I'll personally be in touch with your editor."

"Hopefully, you'll also be just as keen to thank the *Express* for our work in helping bring a serial killer to justice? Perhaps we can ask for an exclusive interview or at least be the first to discuss the case with the Met?"

Denton simply put the phone down and then dialled through to Manchester CID. As he spoke to them, he could see Jones standing outside his office door, tapping her toes impatiently. As soon as he had finished on the call to Manchester, she almost ran over to his desk.

"Guv; we've got a lead," said an animated Jones. "Crimestoppers have had an anonymous tip-off about some of the murders."

"How much of a lead?" asked Denton.

"We have a link between some of the victims, a possible motive, and a named suspect. The call was from a woman who mentioned the names of Lowe, Curtis, Fairfax, and Vickers. She also explained they were related to a blackmail campaign that Charles Wagstaff was involved with. The suspect's name is Miss Janet Evelyn Perry; The Garage, off Old Ford Road, Bow, LONDON E3."

"Sounds like the best lead we've had in weeks."

"The caller also suggested Wagstaff was having an affair with Miss Perry," added Jones, reading through the notes she'd scribbled down from her call.

"Maybe she's the 'E' that Wagstaff's PA mentioned to you? Right, I'm going to see the DCI for approval to bring Miss Perry in for questioning." Denton made his way up to the DCI's office.

"Ma'am," he said, waiting for her to complete the paperwork she was reviewing. She looked up.

"Sit down, DI Denton. What can I help you with?"

"The HMET I'm running; we have some new and promising information, and I wanted to run my proposals by you before we proceed." Half an hour later, the DCI approved Denton's proposals and congratulated him on the team's perseverance. He marched out of the office with a renewed sense of purpose.

Chapter 83

"HOW COULD YOU HAVE BEEN SO INCOMPETENT?" she shouted. Her voice was difficult to understand when she shouted, with the digitised filtering system reacting like a distortion pedal on an electric guitar.

"What do you mean?" replied a softly spoken but irate Broker. No-one talked to him that way except perhaps his wife from time to time.

"I paid you to kill Evie Perry, but you killed someone else!" The Broker hesitated; this was news and unconfirmed news, at that. If this was true, though, it could have serious repercussions on his reputation.

"Let me come back to you. I need to talk to someone first," he said, simmering as he turned his laptop on.

"You don't need to talk to anyone first. You need to honour your commitment. I paid three times the usual amount for this assignment and you fucked it up, you amateur!"

If he was simmering before, that comment took him to boiling point. He gritted his teeth and hissed, "I will contact you again very soon," and jabbed the 'end call' button. He then pressed a button on his internal desk phone and, in a low voice, said, "Get in here." The door to his office opened, and one of his thugs tentatively walked in. It was never a good sign when The Broker sounded annoyed, and the quieter his voice got, the more people were worried.

"Yes, boss?" asked the man.

The Broker just stared at him as he tried to compose himself. It wasn't this man's fault things had gone wrong, although The Broker would have been quite happy to pull the gun out of his desk drawer and put a bullet in someone's head there and then. "Get me Tom and Jerry."

"Yes, boss."

Five minutes later, The Broker was explaining the situation to them. He recited the key information from a small article in a local online news site:

"Friend killed in car bomb. Cheryl Collins, 39 and from Deptford, was killed in a car explosion yesterday at a garage in Bow. She was borrowing the car from a friend to go to a job interview. Police are investigating." He looked up at them both. "You know how I despise failure." They understood the message. Within the hour, they returned and confirmed the contractor in question was dead. While they were out dealing with that problem, The Broker was reflecting on how the client had made him feel. He wasn't used to anyone talking to him that way, and he didn't like it. He rarely took things personally, but this time felt different.

"Our client. Find out who she is."

At the same time, his client was rethinking her next steps. She had planned to frame Evie Perry for the murders, and if the car bomb had killed her instead of her friend, then the truth would have been buried with her. Instead, the police would now be interviewing Evie. Her plan was unravelling fast. She couldn't turn to her husband for help, and the man she had been having an affair with was now dead. At least she had a backup plan and that was running smoothly, as far as she knew.

Chapter 84

"Did you know my husband well?" Stella asked tentatively.

Niall hesitated and appeared unsure of how best to answer the question. He looked around the coffee shop, trying to reduce the tension and discomfort he felt and then, without looking at Stella, replied quietly, "We'd met... once or twice."

"Was it about his work, or was it at a social event?" she asked.

Niall remained uncomfortable, and he hoped she would continue to skirt around what she probably wanted and needed to ask. "Erm... work, mainly."

Stella took a sip of herbal tea, and Niall took the opportunity to drink some of his now lukewarm espresso. She knew the conversation was in danger of petering out, and she couldn't accept the idea of walking away from this meeting without some clarity, so she decided to move on to a potentially more volatile subject.

"I found your name and number on a list that my husband had hidden," she said. "He'd taped it to the underside of a kitchen drawer. Not somewhere you expect to find a list, let alone a list of just three names." She glanced up at Niall and saw a slight tensing of his posture, as well as a flicker of concern. It emboldened her, so she continued, "You, David Holding, and Oleg

Thoresen." Again, a flicker of recognition at the mention of the names. This time, Stella decided to wait and see if he would break the silence. It worked.

"What is it you want, Mrs Kendrick?"

"I don't know. My husband is dead, and I suppose I want answers."

"Yes, I'd heard. I hope the passing of time has helped y—"

Stella interrupted him. "He died last week."

Niall turned slowly to face her. The news confused him. "I thought he..."

"No. That was a diversion he created to make Dennis Ruiz think he was dead. The body belonged to a homeless man, but Robert cut off two of his own fingers and left them as evidence."

Niall was impressed with the cunning nature of the plan and the sheer guts it must have taken to cut off two of his own fingers, but then Ruiz wasn't someone you wanted hunting you, let alone finding you. "Answers about what?" he asked.

"What he really did as a job, why someone impersonated David Holding, and why a piece of paper with all sorts of technical calculations and the number 26 printed at the bottom is of such interest to Mr Ruiz?"

"Page 26?" Niall unintentionally queried.

"So that means something to you, does it?" she proposed.

Niall realised his error, but of greater concern was whether Dennis Ruiz and the man he knew from the fake Friends Reunited were now both looking for the paper? If they were, Stella Kendrick would be in extreme danger.

"Mrs Kendrick, my advice to you is to destroy page 26 as soon as possible and never mention it again; to anyone."

"Why? What is it?"

Niall now leant forwards and, in a caring way, said, "It's either a billion pounds, or it's your death warrant. I don't know you, but there are some very serious criminals looking for it, and you don't want it in your possession when they find you... because if anyone realises you have it, they will find you." Stella took the warning as it was intended, and her heart began to race.

"I showed it to Dennis Ruiz's barrister," she muttered, assuming it would sound nothing short of stupid to Niall. She was right. His face went from concerned to stupefied.

"You did WHAT?"

"My husband told me to," she blurted out, panicking a little.

Niall was about to explode, but he stopped himself and contemplated why Robert Kendrick would have asked her to do such a thing. It felt akin to a bullfighter sending in his aged mother to fight for him, but without the skills or a sword or the agility to run away.

"What exactly did your husband say you should do with the page?"

Stella tried to remember the precise words. "He said *'to tell Ruiz I have the pages he wants, and information that can destroy him, so that Ruiz won't hurt us in any way'*. Oh, and that *'his plan'*... Robert's... *'was coming together'*, so I did as he asked."

"The pages? Plural?"

"I think so," said Stella.

"Did your husband tell you what his plan was before he..." but Niall didn't finish the sentence. They both knew he was going to say 'died'.

"No, he didn't. When I explained to Miss Maddox... that's Dennis Ruiz's barrister... that I'd met David Holding, she explained to me it wasn't actually Holding. She urged me to ring Robert immediately, to tell him to get out of the apartment."

Niall mulled over the situation, and Stella watched, hoping for something to make her feel safe and allay her fears. Instead, he abruptly stood up and looked her straight in the eye.

"Burn the page or pages you have, get on a plane and head anywhere. Don't stop in one place for any longer than three days... no, make it two days; then climb on a train, a bus, a boat, or another plane to somewhere else. Pay with cash whenever you can. You're in danger, Mrs Kendrick, and no matter how much you think it might be over after your husband's death, it's not." He picked up his overcoat and was about to stride out of the coffee shop, but he stopped and said, "And never contact me again; ever." With that, he pushed the door open and disappeared into the busy London streets.

Stella just sat, contemplating what to do next. She looked down and saw that her hands were shaking. She dared not move from the apparent safety of her seat, and yet she knew she had to.

"Oh, Robert, what am I going to do?" She began to cry. Strangers at nearby tables went over to a frightened and frail-looking Stella Kendrick in an attempt to comfort her.

As she sat weeping, Niall walked quickly to his car. As soon as he climbed in and locked the door, he pulled out his mobile phone. "Darling, it's me. I'll be home in a couple of hours, but how about you pack a suitcase for both of us. I think we should fly to Turks tonight and get away from it all for a while."

Yvonne Fitzgerald smiled; she couldn't have wished for better news. For Niall, it was a chance to temporarily escape from everything and everyone.

Chapter 85

"How's it going?" asked Denton.

"Slowly. We're in danger of running out of time at this pace. She's got a smug legal advisor with her who keeps interrupting; asking if the questions are absolutely necessary," replied DC Jones.

"What do we have so far?"

"Janet Evelyn Perry: known to most simply as Evie but also goes by the name 'SILK'. Ex-employee of a high-price membership club called Luxe, which offers its very exclusive clientele a wide range of very exclusive services. She stopped working there just after Christmas 2015; no reason given. The site is legal and legitimate, and the rules for employees and clients are very specific according to its owner. He also explained how much Miss Perry earned, including likely tips, but it doesn't sound high enough to pay for her lifestyle. I'd guess that she perhaps offered additional off-the-menu services, very much against club rules, but with access to people that are very rich and with the looks she had... Well, even now with the scar, she's still a very attractive woman."

"A scar?" Denton asked.

"Yes; it runs down the left side of her face and cuts through the eye. It doesn't look like a kitchen accident; perhaps she was attacked or something, but she refuses to talk about it," answered Jones.

"What is she talking about?"

"The car bomb a couple of days ago. Woman who died was called Cheryl Collins; known hooker and addict but, according to Miss Perry, her one and only true friend. Miss Perry said she had let Miss Collins borrow her car to get to an interview. We've checked that out and it's legit; looks like Miss Collins was trying to earn a legal living. Other than that, she was really skittish at first, but she took some prescribed medication and seems to have calmed down now."

"How do you know it was prescribed?"

"She showed me the bottle when she asked for some water. The pharmacy label was genuine," replied Jones.

"Lab report on that car bomb came back today. Sophisticated stuff, just like the car bomb that killed Charles Wagstaff. Whoever put it there wanted to be damn sure there was no chance of survival," said Denton.

"Any leads on who might have wanted Perry or Collins killed, as well as Wagstaff or Mrs Fitzgerald?"

"Not yet, but we've got the word out, and the NCA is doing some more analysis. What have you said to Miss Perry about the lottery murders?"

"I haven't mentioned anything about the murders specifically, but I did read out most of the names of the people that have been found with the tickets in their mouths. I've got one of the behavioural guys in with me, and I saw him scribbling some notes. Apparently, when I mentioned Vickers, Curtis and Fairfax, there was a slight grimace, rubbing her hands together, biting her bottom lip... nothing hugely visible, but enough, according to the behavioural specialist. No reaction whatsoever to any of the other names. Oh, other than he said she appeared to show genuine shock and sorrow when I mentioned Derek Lowe and his family."

"Have you mentioned Charles Wagstaff yet?"

"Not got round to him or Mrs Fitzgerald," Jones said.

"Okay, let's go back in." Denton and Jones entered the interview room.

"Good afternoon, Miss Perry. I'm acting Detective Inspector Denton. I'll be running the interview from now on." He nodded to the behavioural expert, who stood and left the room. "Do either of you need anything to drink or a comfort break?" he asked Evie and her legal advisor.

He responded before Evie did. "Zachary Barlow; Miss Perry's legal advisor. I'd like to know why…"

Denton held up his index finger to indicate he wanted a moment. "Let me start the recording again before I comment." First, he turned back to Evie and asked again, "Do you require a drink or a comfort break, Miss Perry?"

"No. I just want to go home."

Denton smiled sympathetically, but they all knew that wasn't going to happen. Denton sat down and pressed the record button.

"This is acting Detective Inspector Denton. It's 14:23 hours, and this is a continuation of the interview with Miss Janet Evelyn Perry. Detective Constable Hardwicke has now left the room. Also, still in the interview room is Detective Constable Jones and Miss Perry's solicitor, Mr Zachary Barlow." Denton opened his case file.

"Miss Perry, you are being interviewed under caution, and all the same requirements and rules remain as they were after you were first briefed earlier today. Do you understand?"

"Yes," replied Evie, who was already fidgeting in her chair.

"Miss Perry, I believe that DS Jones read you some names earlier in the interview. I'd like to revisit that list, if I may, and explain a little more about why they are relevant to the interview. Before I do, please let me pass on my condolences for your loss. I know the recent death of Miss Collins must have been a terrible shock, but I will need to ask you some questions about her death." Denton looked at Evie and then at her legal advisor to ensure they understood.

"Ask whatever you want. If it helps catch the bastard that murdered Cheryl, it will be worth it."

"What job did you do at Luxe, Miss Perry?" Denton asked, changing tack.

"What?"

"You worked at Luxe until a few years ago, didn't you? What did you do there?"

Evie glanced at her legal advisor, who replied, "Miss Perry has already provided answers to that question. It's on the tape."

Denton stared at the man but kept a gentle smile on his face. "I wasn't in the interview at that time, Mr Barlow, so rather than waste time rewinding the tape, I'd like my question answered."

"Hostess. It was all perfectly legal," said Evie.

"Good pay?"

"It was alright."

"Alright?" queried Denton. "What? £50,000 or £100,000, or quarter of a million alright?"

"Probably closer to £100,000, excluding personal gestures of gratitude," Evie replied.

"Miss Perry, do you currently have a source of income?" enquired Denton.

"Don't answer that, Evie. My client doesn't work any more, Detective, and her savings are irrelevant to this conversation," rasped her advisor, who knew exactly where the questioning was leading, but he had to register a protest. Denton was already beginning to tire of the man.

"The source of Miss Perry's current income is very relevant. She owns a property in London that's been extensively renovated since the purchase, but she has no mortgage. Her wardrobe contains what I'm told is a very expensive taste in clothes, including lines from this year's Milan collection. She has an extensive collection of bespoke jewellery, some of which I'm told she has had valued recently, and she had a Lotus. She's had no obvious income for a number of years since she left Luxe, so unless the personal gestures of gratitude were regularly more than twice her annual salary or she's inherited a small fortune, I want to understand the source of Miss Perry's wealth." He turned to look at Evie.

"We are investigating a series of murders and blackmail. Miss Perry, you've been implicated in both, but we'd like to hear your side of the story." Denton saw her flinch. Jones was right; she did know something.

Evie pressed her lips together, tried to compose herself, and then reached into her handbag. "I'd like some water, please. I need to take one of my pills." Jones reached over to a table behind Denton and took a small plastic bottle of water from it, and passed it to Evie, who tried to unscrew the lid, but her hands were beginning to shake. Denton reached for the bottle and took it from her, unscrewed the lid and passed it back to her. She sipped some water to help her swallow her tablet and then composed herself for a few seconds before exhaling and putting the lid back on the bottle.

"Thank you," she finally said to Denton, glancing up at his face.

"You're welcome. Are you alright if we continue?"

Her legal advisor started to talk, but Evie held her hand up to indicate he should stop. She turned to look at him and said, "It's alright. Let's get this over with, so I can get out of here." Evie looked back at Denton and said, "Yes."

"Miss Perry, Detective Constable Jones read you a list of names earlier in the interview. Do you know any of those names?" Again, her legal advisor was about to talk, but Evie held her hand up to indicate he should not speak. "We have reason to believe you knew James Vickers, Anthony Fairfax, Derek Lowe, and William Curtis. And did you know a Charles Wagstaff?" continued Denton.

"What about Charles Wagstaff?" Evie blurted out.

"So, you did know Mr Wagstaff?" clarified Jones.

"Why are you talking about him in the past tense?"

Jones looked at Denton, who nodded back at her. Jones explained. "Sadly, Charles Wagstaff died a few days ago from injuries sustained in a car bomb incident at Heathrow. I'm sorry. I know that must be quite frightening, given the recent death of Miss Collins. I assume from your reaction that you knew Charles Wagstaff?" Denton watched as Evie tried not to crumble. The reference to another death by a car bomb was clearly upsetting.

"Miss Perry, do you know a group of men who refer to themselves as the Aeternum?"

Evie raised her gaze and stared at Denton. "Why?"

"Mr Lowe, Mr Vickers, Mr Fairfax, Mr Curtis, and Mr Wagstaff were all members."

Evie's shoulders suddenly sagged as the reality of the situation hit her. "Charles was a member?" she blurted uncontrollably. She recalled Niall Fitzgerald had said, at the start of that fateful party, that not all the members could make it that day. Her jaw dropped. She realised that whatever she had told Wagstaff in supposed confidence had probably been shared with the rest of his sick, arrogant friends. They knew all along what she was planning to do, so now she understood why Niall Fitzgerald had been in such a rage when he burst into her house the other week, but he had accused her of killing them!

"Miss Perry, how do you know about the Aeternum?" Denton pressed her for an answer.

Evie's eyes bulged with fear. She snapped her head around to look at her advisor, silently pleading for him to do something to help her. He said, "I think now would be a good time to take a short break, so I can talk with my client."

Denton announced the break on the recording machine and then pressed 'pause'. "We'll be outside when you're ready to resume," he said.

Outside the room, Jones asked, "We don't have enough to charge her, but is it worth pressuring her, suggesting obstruction of justice if she doesn't share what she knows?"

"It might be a good idea, but let's see what happens after this break. If she decides to go back to being defensive, then yes, let's pressure her."

In the room, Evie was telling her legal advisor everything about Niall Fitzgerald and that party. "I'd met him at Luxe. I wasn't the only girl he hired, but I became a regular. He even took me to his luxury villa on Turks and Caicos, showering me with gifts, and the sex was okay."

"What else do you know about him?"

"Nothing, other than he's married and rich."

"After the incident at the party, have you been in touch with him or he with you?"

"Twice. Once to ask him for £10m or I'd reveal his dirty little secrets and that of his friends, who were at the party. Then when he burst into my house a week ago, accusing me of killing his baby and his friends. I was confused and frightened, and he said if I ever contacted him again or hurt any of his friends or family, he'd kill me. A couple of days ago, I also got a package that had a photo of me in it, with a small noose attached to the photo."

"Do you think maybe he arranged the car bomb that accidentally killed Miss Collins?"

Evie paused, recalling the explosion and her friend. "Oh god, what is happening to my life? I didn't do anything wrong!" and she began to hyperventilate. Her legal advisor called out for help. Denton, Jones, and a qualified first aid officer raced into the room.

"I think we need to re-convene in a day or two, Detective Inspector. My client has suffered a trauma and needs rest."

"No," gasped Evie. "This ends today. I'll tell you everything," she said as she looked at Denton, who nodded back.

PART 4: WINNERS & LOSERS

Chapter 86

The Broker was gazing out of the window, watching the raindrops trickle down the glass when one of his thugs knocked on his open door. He turned and waved the man in.

"Sorry to interrupt, boss. Thought you might want to see this?" He handed a photograph to The Broker, who quickly glanced at it and then looked back at the man, questioning what it was for.

"There's some information on the back. Bobby Messina said it would mean something to you."

The Broker turned the photo over and started reading what Messina had written. He'd not read far when his head jerked in surprise. He turned the photo back over and looked at the image before returning to the remaining information on the other side. As he continued to read, he began to smile.

"So that's who you are. Interesting." He reached over to a box on his desk, took out a large cigar, clipped it and then rolled it in his fingers for a moment. The thug reached into his own pocket and pulled out a lighter, offering the flame to his boss. The Broker puffed on the cigar, nodding in appreciation of its taste and to the man as a thank you for the light, before sinking back into his chair and staring at the photo with a contented smile. He took a deep draw and let the smoke swirl in his mouth before slowly and theatrically blowing it out in a long, slim plume.

"This is the client who called me a *'fucking amateur'*," he said to the man, who reacted with a shake of his head. It was not a wise thing for anyone to accuse his boss of. The Broker narrowed his eyes as he stared at the photo and wondered what to do about the situation.

The thug broke the silence. "Loose ends job, boss?" he suggested.

The idea made The Broker smile. "Yes, a loose ends approach feels good," he replied. "Do we know where she is?"

"We'll find her."

"Find someone local and tell them it's a solid fifty." The man nodded to confirm he understood the instruction and turned to walk out of the room, but The Broker suddenly called out, "Actually, let's make it a double. Fifty each." He scribbled something on the back of the photo before handing it back to the man. "This person too. Let's make sure this problem goes away – completely."

"Yes, boss." The man grinned as he walked out of the room.

The Broker swivelled his chair back around so he could look out of the office window again, and he took another long draw on his cigar.

"Ahh, some days warm the soul even when it's raining," he said to himself, satisfied that his reputation would be restored. "Let's see who's a fucking amateur now."

Chapter 87

Denton looked up wearily as a file landed on his desk. He and Jones had spent three more hours with Evie Perry, listening to her story. They had learnt about the injury, the link to Niall Fitzgerald and her demand for £10m, which he had paid.

"But I've never killed anyone; I've never sent any threatening emails or packages. Yes, I intended to ask them for as much as I could get by drafting a tell-all book. I assumed they and a few others I'd feature would pay handsomely for me not to publish it. Wagstaff was my legal representative, but I didn't realise he was part of their group."

"How did you come to choose Charles Wagstaff in the first place? It seems an almost unbelievable coincidence, given London literally has thousands of legal firms and PR agencies."

"Adverts about him kept appearing on my banner feeds, or articles would appear on my news page about people he'd represented. It was almost as if fate had brought him to me."

"And what about the murders, Miss Perry?"

"I swear I know nothing about them. Why would I kill them if I wanted money from them?"

"Perhaps you needed to show them that you were serious?" suggested Jones, referring to an extract from the call to Crimestoppers about the demand for £100m and the associated threat.

"I don't need or want anyone to die. My draft publication would have shown them I was serious."

"Then why do you think Mr Fitzgerald came looking for you; came to your home and threatened you?" questioned Jones.

"And what about the other deaths?" Denton asked accusatorily. Yes, Evie Perry had offered to tell them everything, but he'd heard that so many times from people who were eventually far more involved in a crime than their supposed confession suggested.

"I don't know about any murders. I don't know anything about the lottery tickets that you keep mentioning, and I just want to go home." Evie Perry finally broke down and sobbed. What had happened to her life, and how had she got into such a dark, dark place?

"What's your gut telling you, Jonesy?" Denton asked after Evie had been charged and arrested for blackmail.

"She's not a murderer, and I don't think she knows anything other than what she's told us. There's something else going on, guv."

"I agree. Question is, what?" That was how they had left things an hour ago, but now, as he reached for the file and looked up, he saw Jones smiling back at him.

"Your friend at the fraud squad; he cracked the encryption code on the computer files Derek Lowe kept," she said. Denton snatched the file up from his desk and flicked it open, but Jones gave him a verbal summary anyway.

"A folder entitled 'Wimbledon' contained seven files; six of which – Connors, McEnroe, Nastase, Newcombe,

Sampras, and Ashe – were completely empty, but the seventh file, named Borg, contained details of a £20m investment made for Charles Wagstaff, by the Iliad Private Equity Group. Lowe was keeping a record, but we don't know why."

"Iliad? That's Fitzgerald's company, isn't it?" checked Denton. Jones confirmed that it is. "That's a lot of money. Didn't his PA tell you he needed money because he was trying to buy out the company he co-owned?"

"She did. According to bank documents that were drawn up to assess his request for a loan, he needed £30m to buy it. They refused to support the purchase beyond providing a loan of £500,000, and the bank confirmed he's never had more than £5m in his account. His assets didn't come anywhere near £30m, and his available credit didn't help either," explained Jones, pointing to a spreadsheet she'd compiled and put in the file. "I did a little more digging into Wagstaff's finances. A credit reference agency has confirmed he'd already missed multiple repayments on his credit cards, and he'd defaulted on the bank loan."

Denton nodded. "If Wagstaff needed £30m, and it sounds like he needed it quickly, why did he only make a £20m investment if his existing assets only amounted to £5m? Why didn't he borrow £25m, and who was he borrowing from? Where would he get such a high and quick return on £20m?"

"The current Dennis Ruiz court case is about cybercrime, and one of Fitzgerald's previous business partners is now in jail for money laundering for Ruiz, whose cybercrime organisation is called BOrg," Jones said in an increasingly excited tone, as she joined the dots. "Fitzgerald was cleared of any involvement in the scheme, and the third business partner was implicated, David Holding, who has been found dead. What if Fitzgerald decided to fill the money laundering void?"

Denton nodded in agreement. "The Iliad link intrigues me. He knows far more than he's telling us. Let's get him back in."

Chapter 88

"I'm telling you I don't know how they got there! I've been away for the last two weeks."

The detective in Manchester CID sighed in exasperation. The interview with Peter Mallory had already taken several hours, and an acting DI from the Met kept calling for an update.

"Detective," interjected Mallory's solicitor, equally wearily, "my client has confirmed, several times, he knows nothing about the credit card or the latex glove and fibres that you found in his kitchen. The gun isn't his; he doesn't know where it came from or how it got into his sock drawer, and yes, he is familiar with the car hire that the email print-out refers to, but he was no idea how or why a copy of it was in his bookcase." He looked at the detective and his antagonistic colleague, adding, "And he doesn't know and has never met anyone called Alison Montague or Alfie Churchill."

"You do know James Vickers though, don't you, Mr Mallory? And you're aware that the hire car exploded, eventually taking the life of Charles Wagstaff?"

"Yes, of course I know!" cried Mallory in frustration. "They were my friends!" He started to become emotional, and the policeman sat back, waiting for him to regain his composure. This wasn't the first time Peter Mallory had broken down in tears.

"Mr Mallory, look at it from our perspective. We have a number of unsolved murders, and we find four items in your apartment linked to four of the victims. All you're telling us is you know nothing about them, but that's what both an innocent and a guilty man would say. Do you see my problem?" said the lead detective, trying to build some empathy with him.

"But I really don't know what else I can tell you? What else is there to tell you?" pleaded Mallory.

"Alright, let's take a different approach. Let's assume you're innocent—"

"Which he is," interrupted the solicitor.

The detective worked hard to hide his impatience with the legal advisor, but he nevertheless reworded his opening statement. "Let's assume you're helping us understand who else could have done this, yes?"

Mallory looked at his solicitor, who nodded to him. "Okay," replied Mallory.

"Firstly, are you aware of anything that links Ms Montague, Mr Churchill, Mr Vickers, and Mr Wagstaff together?"

"No, other than James and Charles knew each other."

"Our colleagues in London tell us you and they were part of a group?"

"Yes, we were."

"And they tell us that several other members of the group have been killed. Is that right?"

"Yes. Five of them have died. There's just Niall and me left."

"Niall Fitzgerald?"

"Yes."

"You also said that Mr Fitzgerald arranged the hire car that's detailed in the copy of the email we found. How do you know that?"

"He was at my house when his wife called him from their villa in Turks. We'd been advised by the police to be vigilant, so rather than Niall having to drive to Heathrow to pick her up, he arranged a hire car for her. I was in the room when he spoke to his wife and then to the hire car company," Mallory replied nervously. He glanced at his solicitor again and got an assuring nod.

"Can you tell us whether you or anyone else would benefit from the death of your friends? Maybe giving someone rights to a property, a business idea, or any other financial benefit?"

Mallory thought about it but shook his head. "No, we try to keep separate business relationships. I suppose some of them might have had joint interests; it wasn't something we ever discussed."

"You don't have any joint ventures that involve you all or sit together as advisors on boards or VCs? Maybe there's a common good cause you all support? Perhaps you all bet on the Grand National in a private high-stakes sweepstake?"

"No." But Mallory smiled at what he assumed was an attempt to lighten the mood.

"What about if one of you dies? There are no shares to dispose of or an investment programme to divest from?"

"Well, there's the Foundation fund, but…" Mallory hesitated. He'd momentarily forgotten about the fund, but now he couldn't think of anything else.

"A fund?" asked the detective, sitting forward.

Mallory's solicitor placed his hand on Mallory's shoulder. "Perhaps now would be a good time for a short break, Detective? I'd like to speak with my client." At no point in their previous meetings had Peter Mallory mentioned a fund, and the solicitor's instinct told him that Mallory had just realised something and that the police smelt blood.

Ten minutes later, the interview continued, and Peter Mallory explained everything about the Aeternum Foundation fund. His solicitor had warned him, "It won't look good, Peter. With the incriminating evidence they've found and this information, it looks like one heck of a motive."

Chapter 89

DS Bob Williams shuffled along a corridor in the North Yorkshire Police HQ; his head bowed. Denton had updated him on the interview with Janet Evelyn Perry, but it hadn't satisfactorily answered any of their questions about the murders. His mood wasn't helped by a lack of sleep; he had stayed up until the early hours of the morning, sifting through all the paperwork one more time. *There must be something I'm missing; why can't I bloody well see it?* He thought, chastising his inability to find a link or clue that would stop the seemingly endless dead ends. He reached the incident room door and flung it open. DC Ahmed Akbar was in the room with another member of the team.

"I'm telling you, there's no way you'll be able to list 100," Akbar said to the other man.

"You make the coffee for a week if I do?" replied the other detective.

"You are on!" Akbar said, clapping his hands together and pointing at the man, taunting him. On hearing the door bang open, he looked round. Akbar saw the expression on William's face, and his silent demeanour meant Williams was tired and grumpy, so Akbar silently indicated that the other detective should leave.

"Sarge," said the detective, acknowledging Williams as he made his way out of the room. Williams glanced up and gave the briefest of nods in response before tossing the thick file he was carrying onto his desk. He pulled the chair out and thought about sitting but then pushed it back in and headed over to the coffee percolator. He saw that the coffee jug was almost empty and exhaled loudly to express his disappointment.

Akbar walked over, grabbed the jug and said, "Was just about to make a fresh one, Sarge. Want one bringing over?"

Williams took a steadying breath and then looked at Akbar. "That would be good; thank you, Akbar," and he gave Akbar a 'sorry – bit grumpy' look of apology.

"No problem, Sarge," said a relieved Akbar. He opened the large tin of ground coffee and started to spoon it into the top of the machine. As he poured fresh water into the reservoir, he didn't look up but enquired, "No new leads, Sarge?"

Williams smiled, knowing Akbar had recognised his mood and was handling the situation well. He was grateful. "You're a good copper, Akbar. How about you grab yourself a cup and maybe run through this file with me one more time?"

"Sure, Sarge, but maybe you ought to let the coffee work its magic first? You look like shit, if you don't mind me saying?"

Williams laughed out loud and replied, "That obvious, huh?"

"Just call me observant, Sarge," Akbar responded, pleased at his ability to defuse the tension. He waited for the coffee to percolate and the jug to fill before pouring two mugs of steaming-hot fresh coffee and taking them over to Williams' desk.

The men sat and blew on the hot liquid, enjoying a moment of silence before Williams asked, "So what were you and the other detective betting on?"

"Oh, he thinks he's such an expert in the English language, so I set him a challenge: come up with 100 words that don't sound like they are spelt." Williams furrowed his brow as he was confused and far too tired to try to understand. Akbar explained, "You know, like the word 'pneumatic' sounds like it starts with an 'n', not a 'p'; or 'phrase' sounds like it should start with an 'f'." Williams signalled he now understood, but he was clearly unimpressed and uninterested in such trivial games. Akbar said, "I bet you could think of a few straight off the top of your head."

Williams shuffled uncomfortably but decided a little distraction might be a nice break from the frustration of the investigation. "Alright, let me think." He paused and pondered, "Er, one would be 'phantom'; another would be 'knee'. Like that, you mean?"

"Exactly, Sarge."

Williams licked his lips and found himself surprisingly eager to continue. "What about 'whole'?"

"Now you're buzzing, Sarge," encouraged Akbar.

"Er, 'giant' sounds like a 'j'? 'Wreck' sounds like it should start with an 'r', or the name..." Williams abruptly stopped talking. The relaxed smile on his face faded, and his jaw dropped. "Could that be it?" he muttered.

Now it was Akbar's turn to look confused. "Could what be it, Sarge?"

Williams held up his hand to indicate he needed Akbar to be quiet. He picked up the file from his desk and began flicking through it. He stopped at a page and ran his finger across some notes as he read them. "Interesting." He looked up at Akbar, who didn't know what had triggered the response, but the smile on Williams' face suggested it was probably good news. Williams started to explain his train of thought.

"When we interviewed Niall Fitzgerald after his wife was injured by the car bomb, he said his wife had bumped into Wagstaff as they got off a British Airways flight, and that she'd broken the news to Wagstaff about the murder of James Vickers."

"Okay," said Akbar, not knowing what he was really agreeing to.

"And yet, when we interviewed Wagstaff's PA, she said Wagstaff told her that he had to arrange an earlier flight; to come home for the funeral of a friend called James. That means either Mr Fitzgerald was mistaken in his recollection of what his wife said, or the death of James Vickers actually wasn't news to Charles Wagstaff when Mrs Fitzgerald told him at Heathrow; it was something he already knew."

"Okay," said Akbar, a little more enthusiastically but no less confused.

Williams' eyes danced as his brain replayed the facts, his lips moving as he silently mouthed what he was thinking. "Could it be?" he whispered as his own smile grew wider and wider. "Akbar, you're a genius! Not only can I add another word in the game, but we might have a breakthrough in the lottery ticket murders." He picked up the phone on his desk and dialled. After a few seconds, he said, "Steve, it's Bob. I think we might have a new angle on the lottery ticket murder case. I just need to contact British Airways to confirm something... Yes, that's what I said; British Airways."

"Well, hurry up, Bob. We're about to drag Niall Fitzgerald back from his holiday villa for questioning."

Chapter 90

The HMET meeting was called for first thing the following morning, with Williams and Armitage travelling to London, along with selected members of their teams. DC Jones was present, and the wipe-board was ready in front of the meeting table.

"Bob, over to you," said Denton. Williams had briefed Denton on his suspicions and the subsequent conversation with British Airways. Denton asked Williams to run the key points past the HMET team and, if they thought it a solid case, then they could be close to making an arrest.

"Here are the facts as we currently know them: we have 17 murders, all with the common calling card of lottery tickets. There are three groups of victims; those involved in the petrochemical company, Belschen; those who were part of the so-called Aeternum group; and the rest. Apart from the alphabetical sequencing of postcodes and the numbers on the tickets, what else do we know? Not a lot, or perhaps far too much? DC Jones suggested a theory about how the killer or killers might be deliberately trying to confuse us, so we couldn't see the real reason for some of the murders. If we analyse just some of the information, we might have a much clearer picture. Let me explain..." He passed each member of the team a brand-new file.

"Let's currently discount those not involved with Belschen or the Aeternum, and I think we are all agreed that this isn't the work of some random psychopath, given Stefan Popescu was linked to at least one of the murders. That leaves us with two possible common threads. Yes, there was the financial scandal a few years ago at Belschen, but there are thousands of people and hundreds of companies who suffered as a result, so, for now, I want to ignore that too. That leaves us with the Aeternum."

The file Williams had handed out contained a profile of all seven members, with a handful of additional pages that supported what he was about to say.

"Why were these people murdered? Who would benefit from their death? As we all know, three typical reasons for murder are a crime of passion, revenge, or money. Derek Lowe and his family were murdered. There's no evidence to suggest anyone had a vendetta against him, and both he and his wife were only children. With their only child also murdered, they had no living relatives who would benefit from their deaths. From the interview with Janet Evelyn Perry, we know she met Derek Lowe at least once, at the party she was injured at. That raises the possibility of revenge, although he wasn't cited by her as being responsible.

"Next; William Curtis. He had a long-standing business relationship with Belschen Petroleum, but there was no evidence linking him to the financial scandal. He was also a member of the Aeternum. No dependents, and Miss Perry clearly identified him as partially responsible for her injury, along with Anthony Fairfax. We'll come back to Fairfax."

"James Vickers, a successful plastic surgeon, shot in his practice office in Harrogate. No dependents and again identified by Miss Perry as a person who tried to help. Although he appears to have used his surgical skills to try to save Miss Perry's sight and face, it could be considered a failure.

"Anthony Fairfax and his son both died in a house fire which, according to the fire investigation officer, was a very sophisticated arson attack. His ex-wife had already signed a divorce agreement, so she wasn't going to benefit financially from his death, and why would she want her only son murdered? Miss Perry said he was the other main culprit in her injury.

"Charles Wagstaff died as a result of his injuries after a car bomb. No known dependents, just an anonymous girlfriend, according to his PA. He wasn't at the party where Miss Perry was injured, but unbeknownst to her, he was a member of the group and may have broken client confidentiality by sharing information about her planned tell-all book, which would have featured some of his friends. That leaves Niall Fitzgerald and Peter Mallory as the surviving members of the group. Mr Mallory also wasn't at the party when Miss Perry was injured."

The HMET attendees were listening intently. There were no questions, and no one was doing anything other than reading the files and looking at Williams.

"We know Miss Perry denies all knowledge of the murders, claiming she was only looking to extort money from the group. We also know Niall Fitzgerald had already paid her £10m to maintain her silence, so where does this lead us?" he continued.

"And the behavioural specialist confirmed there were several triggers in her behaviour in the interview that suggests either the news of the murders was a shock, or she should be teaching kinesics," added Jones. There was a ripple of laughter around the room at her attempt at a joke.

Denton jumped in. "And, if she was looking to extort money from people, why would she want them dead? DS Williams and I both believe Miss Perry's story, so we'll assume she's not involved in the murders," he confirmed. Williams nodded to him and asked everyone to turn to page 8 of the file, which was a copy of a car hire agreement.

"Charles Wagstaff was killed by a car bomb that might have been intended for Mrs Fitzgerald. According to the interview with his PA, he was flying home early from a holiday paid for by his anonymous girlfriend to attend the funeral of a friend called James. We assume it was James Vickers, as the timing coincided with Mr Vickers' murder but, according to Mr Fitzgerald's account, his wife said she'd bumped into Wagstaff on the aircraft and broke the news of Mr Vickers' murder *after* they had disembarked. According to eyewitnesses and airport records, Wagstaff was in a very emotional state in the terminal and needed fast-tracking through security. Mrs Fitzgerald reportedly offered him a lift in the car her husband had organised because Wagstaff wasn't in a fit state to be by himself."

"The only people who knew about the hire car were Mr and Mrs Fitzgerald and Peter Mallory. Mr Fitzgerald confirmed the two men were in the same room when the booking was made, which Mallory corroborated in his interview with Manchester CID. If someone was planning to kill Mrs Fitzgerald, then, apart from the car hire company, they were the only two who knew enough of the details," said Jones.

"You think Wagstaff was faking it at the airport?" asked one of the team.

Williams shrugged his shoulder. "I don't know, and unfortunately we can't ask him, but after playing a word game in the office yesterday, I did a little more digging. The name Yvonne sounds like it should start with an E, yes?" Everyone looked either amused or bemused at the comment, but Williams didn't notice; he was too invested in his theory.

"We know Wagstaff kept his personal life very private. He only referred to current girlfriends by using their first initial, A for Amy Westhuizen or C for Cathy Delevan, as examples. We know who they were because once the usually short relationships were over, his PA said he told her who he'd been dating." He saw some more nodding around the table.

"In the interview with his PA, she said he had referred to his most recent girlfriend as his E, F and G; because it had lasted a couple of years, and he felt it had a long-term future. What if the E stood for Yvonne, the F for Fitzgerald, and the G was for girlfriend?"

"Feels a bit tenuous, Sarge," said one of the team.

"It does, until you look at the British Airways records. I checked the Caribbean seat bookings for both Yvonne Fitzgerald and Charles Wagstaff. Separate flights out to Turks & Caicos, but the same flight back, and all the seats were booked with the same credit card: Mrs Fitzgerald's."

"So, it wasn't a coincidence they were on the same flight?"

"That's right," confirmed Williams. "And the flight was never diverted to Jamaica to pick up some other passengers."

"Okay, so he and Mrs Fitzgerald were possibly having an affair. So what?"

"I asked myself that and came up with the following questions. First, did Wagstaff lie about when he heard of James Vickers' murder? If so, why? If he didn't, did Mr Fitzgerald get mixed up when telling us what his wife had told him, or did he contradict Wagstaff on purpose? Second, we all know that passion and revenge are common reasons for murder. What if Niall Fitzgerald had found out his wife was having an affair, and he arranged the car bomb to kill her? He had the motive, and he knew when and where the car would be?"

"And if he was targeting his wife, but Wagstaff was killed; presumably it still destroyed their affair?"

"Possibly so, and from the encrypted file Derek Lowe kept, we now know that Wagstaff had invested £20m in a scheme that Niall Fitzgerald was managing, which might have been frozen by Interpol as part of the Dennis Ruiz cybercrime investigation."

"Which would mean Wagstaff wasn't just in debt; he was destitute," explained Jones.

"His dream of buying out the company he co-owned was gone, and he now had several defaults on his credit score, so he had nowhere to turn. Him dying meant any guilt that Mr Fitzgerald felt about the investment disappeared."

"Hang on, we're talking about Wagstaff and Fitzgerald. What about the evidence Manchester Police found in Peter Mallory's apartment?"

"If Peter Mallory had been clever enough to plan this and presumably hire someone to murder so many people, it's a schoolboy error to keep trophies from some of his victims in his apartment," said Williams.

"And why just trophies from some of his victims? No; we think the evidence might have been planted to deceive us, in the same way we believe the evidence at Stefan Popescu's was planted," acknowledged Denton, as Jones had originally suggested.

"Even though we know Popescu was hired for at least one of the murders; Harry Weller."

"That leads to an interesting possibility," Armitage concluded. "Mallory and Niall Fitzgerald are the last two surviving members of the Aeternum group. From the interview notes with Mallory, we know they all signed an agreement that, if any of them died and had no living benefactors, they would bequeath their wealth to the fund they'd set up years ago."

"What would that mean now, for Fitzgerald and Mallory?"

Williams answered, "Depends on the conditions in the agreement, but, in theory, they'd have access to hundreds of millions of pounds. If you take Derek Lowe as an example, his wife and daughter were murdered, so his inheritance went into the fund. If Mrs Fitzgerald had been killed by the car bomb and if Peter Mallory is excluded from the Foundation fund inheritance because he goes to jail..."

"Or maybe if he's about to be murdered as well," suggested one of the team.

"... then Niall Fitzgerald would be 'Richie Rich' rich if he was the sole heir to the fund," gasped Jones.

"So, here's where I think we are," Denton began. "The real reasons for the murders are passion and greed. Niall Fitzgerald was under pressure from Charles Wagstaff over his £20m investment that Interpol has seized. He also either suspected or knew Wagstaff was having an affair with his wife: Wagstaff's 'E, F & G' girlfriend. Derek Lowe held information in an encrypted file that showed the investment and the likely link to a cybercrime organisation called BOrg. We don't know whether Derek Lowe was using that as leverage against Fitzgerald. Once Lowe and Curtis had been murdered, Evie Perry seemed an easy target to blame. Fitzgerald cited the incident at a party just over three years ago as her reason and told people he'd deal with it. It was fortuitous for Fitzgerald that Miss Perry had approached Charles Wagstaff about her book, and, we assume, Wagstaff told Fitzgerald what she intended to do to get them to pay her not to publish it. Remember, she's already admitted to demanding and receiving £10m from Fitzgerald."

"Would a man with all the money he already has really want to risk jail to get more?" asked one of the team.

"There's only one way to find out," said Denton. "Turks & Caicos police will be putting Mr and Mrs Fitzgerald on a flight tomorrow. We need to find out more about the Foundation fund contract, and I've been in touch with Interpol; it seems that Niall Fitzgerald might actually be the missing link in the cybercrime organisation, BOrg."

"I thought Fitzgerald was cleared of all involvement by Oleg Thoresen?" interjected one of the team.

"Maybe Thoresen was pressured into blaming David Holding, who, inconveniently for us, is also dead?" Armitage responded.

Denton concluded his summary. "Fitzgerald covered up the real reason for murdering his friends by having other people killed, including a number of people who had Belschen Petroleum as a common denominator. The lottery ticket was just to distract us, and we readily fell into his trap, analysing the alphabetical pattern of the postcodes and the numbering sequence on the tickets."

"Fucking brilliant," murmured Jones, begrudgingly acknowledging how clever Niall Fitzgerald was at planning it all.

Chapter 91

The azure sky seemed to go on forever, with the sun rising high above the surface of the turquoise Caribbean Sea. Even from their hillside property, gentle waves could be heard rolling onto the beach below. Niall sat on the large sweeping balcony outside their bedroom. Fenton, their butler, placed some fresh toast, orange juice, and a pot of hot coffee on the table. Niall had arrived late the night before and had slept in this morning.

"Is Mrs Fitzgerald downstairs?" he asked Fenton.

"No, sir; Mrs Fitzgerald went to the Provo Golf Club a few hours ago. She asked me to tell you she'd be back quite late this evening."

"Thank you, Fenton," said Niall, and the man bowed his head slightly before turning sharply and walking away. Niall sipped the coffee and took a bite out of his toast. "Oh, this really is the life," he said to himself. He continued to gaze out to sea, watching a catamaran ease its way towards North Caicos. As much as he was enjoying the tranquillity and mid-morning heat from the sun, with Yvonne out for most of the day, he had the opportunity to complete a simple but significant task. He wasn't at the villa when the security cameras were installed, but he had some additional ones added: secret ones. It had been agreed that bedrooms and bathrooms were off-limits, but Niall had broken that rule and had two cameras installed in the main bedroom.

He knew it was violating the agreement with Yvonne about the sanctity of their bedroom, but his desire to film and then review the videos of him and SILK having sex was almost as compelling as the sex itself. The cameras were triggered when someone entered the room between the hours of 6pm and 10am, when the cleaners weren't in the property. Whenever he was at the villa, he often took time to replay some of the videos, and if he didn't want any of them, he would simply delete the files. He had set the software up to automatically file the bedroom videos in a hidden, security-protected folder so that even if Yvonne stumbled across the folders, she would be unable to access the content. He kept lots of confidential folders as a matter of routine for his private equity business, so she would probably assume it was just one of those, anyway. On this trip, though, and given the renewal of their affection for each other, Niall had decided the time was right to delete the files forever, even if the symbolic gesture was only ever known to himself. As soon as he had finished the coffee, showered and dressed, he would go to the locked security room and delete all trace of his past betrayals.

An hour had passed by the time Niall entered the security room. He sat opposite the monitor and keyed in his security code to access his files. The screen sprang to life, and a series of folders were listed on-screen.

"Hard deletion software is applied," he muttered to himself. He knew, from painful experience as part of the BOrg investigation into his partners at Thoresen, Fitzgerald and Holding, that software that claimed to delete all files simply didn't. The authorities had recovery protocols agreed with the larger, more reputable software and hardware providers that undermined the activity of most criminals, as Thoresen had discovered. Thankfully, Niall had had the foresight to request some specialist software that meant he had avoided all charges, despite Holding telling the authorities about his suspicions of what Thoresen and Niall were doing. He was about to delete the entire folder when he decided to have one last look through a couple of favourites.

"For old times' sake. No harm in that," he assured himself. After browsing the list for a couple of minutes, he stopped and stared at one file listing on the screen.

"44.2mb, at 19:30 hours on 2nd March 2018?" He realised he wasn't in Turks then, although Yvonne was. He thought about deleting the file without reviewing it, but he was drawn to it like a moth to a flame. He opened the file, pressed play, and saw Yvonne enter their bedroom. She seemed in good spirits and was either singing or talking to herself; without audio capability, it was difficult to tell. She danced while occasionally sipping champagne and seemed quite playful as she began to unbutton her blouse. Niall began to feel titillated watching his wife undress, so rather than delete the file straight away, he decided to watch a little more. Yvonne theatrically removed her blouse and then made a show of unclipping her bra before turning back towards their bedroom door. She continued to dance, but that was when Niall's mood changed; from aroused to inquisitive as he saw her extend her arm and hold out her hand. Was she still dancing, or was she beckoning someone to join her? Niall then saw an arm reach hesitantly into the room, and Yvonne grabbed the person's hand, a man's hand. She slowly pulled the reluctant man into the camera shot. Niall gasped as he saw Charles Wagstaff being pulled into the bedroom. He paused the video just as she started to unbutton Wagstaff's shirt, and stared at the screen, speechless. He felt as if the air had been sucked from his lungs as he contemplated what the video was showing. Had Yvonne really been having sex with Charles Wagstaff? Niall knew any feeling of betrayal was laughable, given his infidelity over the previous five years, but the fact it was his friend hurt him.

"Let it go," he told himself. "She was only doing exactly what you have done for years, so stop being so bloody self-righteous," which he might have been able to do if it was a stranger in the video, but it was Charles! Suddenly, he felt overcome with emotion. He cried out in anger as he jumped up, sending his chair toppling backwards. He needed some fresh air, and he needed time to think. He lunged for the door and wrenched it open, striding out as the anti-slam mechanism gently pulled the door shut.

As he strode back towards the terrace, he didn't see Yvonne lurking in a nearby bedroom. She had returned home to change after a waiter had accidentally spilled a cranberry cocktail on her white dress. On arrival, Fenton had told her that her husband was in the video security room, where he'd been for several hours. She was about to knock on the video security room door when she heard his angry outburst and the sound of a chair falling onto the floor. Instinctively, she knew something was wrong and quickly stepped back into the nearby bedroom. As she watched him quickly walk away, something about his demeanour unnerved her. She waited until he was out of sight and then tiptoed into the video security room. She noticed the video screen was dark, but the power LEDs were pulsing, which indicated that the video system was just in sleep mode. She picked up the chair, sat on it, and then pressed the spacebar on the keyboard. The screen lit up, and she let out a muffled shriek of horror when she saw the paused image of herself topless with Charles Wagstaff. That was when she understood why Niall had cried out. She also realised he had secretly had a camera put in their bedroom.

"You bastard. We agreed there would be no security cameras in there," she hissed. She felt a sudden sickening tug in her gut, as she knew the rest of the video clip would show her and Wagstaff having sex. As she deleted the file she had just watched, she heard footsteps in the hallway outside the room. If Niall had spoken to Fenton, he would have told Niall she was back at the villa. Thankfully, it was unlikely Niall would come looking for her as he was not one for impetuous, emotion-filled confrontations; he much preferred to plan a strategy and be prepared. She assumed she had time to get away, and when she heard the footsteps fading into the distance, she waited a few seconds before opening the door. After checking the hallway, Yvonne made her way out of the villa. She had no time to change her dress and certainly didn't want to bump into Niall.

Niall hadn't seen Fenton, so he was unaware that she had even been back. When he heard a car engine starting nearby, it never occurred to him that it might be her. As he sat by the pool, he began to do what he did best; assess a situation, think through the possible scenarios and decide on an approach to the problem. First thing he had to do was download the file to a USB for safekeeping. He stomped back to the room and sat down on the chair. He found a fresh pack of USBs and unconsciously unpacked one as he reflected on the revelation that his wife was an adulterer too. He slid the USB into the computer but couldn't file the file he was looking for.

"What the..." he sighed in exasperation. After 10 minutes, he gave up. In his state of distraction, had he accidentally transferred the file to a different folder? He changed the access code on the system before walking back out to the terrace. Fenton was there.

"Did Mrs Fitzgerald mention she wouldn't be home in time for dinner, sir?

"I haven't spoken to her today, Fenton, so I don't know. You mentioned earlier that she would be late home from the golf club?"

"No, I meant in case she had mentioned anything just now before she went back to the golf club?"

Niall furrowed his brow. "Back to the golf club? Was she here?"

"Yes, sir. I saw her leave about five minutes ago."

Niall thought about that for a moment, and then he glanced back towards the video security room and remembered the chair. He asked Fenton if he had been in the security room recently, but he shook his head. Niall hadn't picked the chair up before he stormed out after seeing the clip of Yvonne and Charles, and if Fenton hadn't been in the room recently, that could only mean one thing: Yvonne had been in and might have seen the paused video. That's why it wasn't still on freeze-frame on the screen when he went back in, and maybe she had deleted the evidence?

At an upmarket clothes boutique in the Ports of Call shopping plaza, Yvonne was preoccupied with the revelation of the bedroom camera as she paid for a dress to replace the cranberry-stained one she was still wearing. She had walked back into the changing room to reapply her makeup and tidy her hair, but she couldn't find the lipstick she always carried with her. She retraced her steps in her mind, from picking up the bag in the restaurant to putting it in its usual place in her car to getting home. That's when she remembered that the bag had fallen over in the video security room. What if it had fallen out, and Niall found it? If he did, how should she explain its presence, and would he know she'd been in there today and seen the video clip? She grabbed her mobile phone and saw there were five missed calls from Niall. That's when she realised that she would have to face him, but it would definitely now be on her terms. She sent a text in readiness.

Third, at 10am

Chapter 92

"Where are you, Yvonne? We need to talk," insisted Niall. Fenton told him that she wanted to see her husband in the villa's library at 9:50am, just before she sent him home for the day. He'd not seen her the previous evening and assumed she had stayed at her friend's villa, given she probably knew that Niall had seen the incriminating video.

"Yes, we do," came a voice as the door was pushed closed. Niall turned to see his wife, who had been standing behind the door.

"I know what you and Charles did," he said indignantly.

She scoffed at him; it was such an ironic statement from a serial adulterer. "I know you do. I've seen the footage from the secret camera you installed in our bedroom, you bastard," she replied as she pulled a revolver from her handbag. Niall instinctively took a step back.

"Put the gun down, Yvonne, before you accidentally shoot someone." He paused, but when the gun wasn't lowered, he called out, "Fenton? FENTON?"

"It's no use, Niall; I sent him home. There's just you and me here now. Oh, and if I shoot you, it won't be an accident; but don't worry, I have no intention of shooting you."

"Look, we have clearly got things to sort out between us, but maybe who we should both be angry at is the woman who's been blackmailing me and killing our friends? Her name is SILK, the woman we discussed."

Yvonne threw her head back and laughed scornfully. "You still don't get it, do you? The great Niall Fitzgerald, the man who makes billions for other people through complicated manipulation and analysis of worldwide markets, can't see the obvious truth. That little slut had nothing to do with your friends' deaths; it was me."

"You?" asked Niall, stunned.

"Yes. I paid for them to be killed, along with some others." Niall stood opened-mouthed, unable to comprehend what his wife had just admitted to. Yvonne revelled in the moment.

"But why?" he asked, still struggling to comprehend the truth.

"Let me talk you through it. First of all, I despise you. You cheated on me for years, possibly even paying women to stay silent about terminations or perhaps you have an illegitimate child somewhere, while all the time you refused to have a child with me. I also already knew you'd paid that slut £10m, and why. How? Because when you started Iliad, I acted as your PA; remember? You gave me access to your emails and your diary, and I still have access to them today because you're a creature of habit. You never changed your password, even after all these years. I saw all the dirty, disgusting messages you sent each other, and I saw the demands she made; for the £10m and then about the tell-all book!"

Niall had always considered his password so strong that he never thought he'd need to change it, and, over time, he'd simply forgotten he'd given it to her.

"I know you were going to leave me virtually penniless. How? Because Charles told me. You see, he and I started seeing each other because I wanted revenge sex, but when he said he was falling in love with me and he'd do anything to prove just how much I meant to him, that's when it became more than just sex; that's when he became useful."

Niall closed his eyes as a thought occurred to him. "But Charles would never willingly see his friends murdered."

"You're right; he wouldn't, but all I had to do was convince him that her book idea was just a pretence to hide her murderous scheme, and once I had planned what I wanted to do about you, I pretended to want to build a future with him."

"What about all the threats from her? The packages I received?"

"I sent them, including the cracked glass eye to you and the Toy Town cheque for £100m to me. I also sent myself the lipstick that made you choke on your coffee that morning: 'Blood and Silk', remember? I'm wearing it today. Suits me, don't you think?" She pouted her lips sarcastically. "Charles was angry with you, though, so I was pushing at an open door."

"With me?"

"Yes. You advised him to invest in the money laundering scheme you and Derek had taken over and were running with Ruiz, to raise the £30m he needed to buy his company. Because of your advice, he borrowed money from everyone he knew and a few unsavoury people he didn't know. He trusted you, the great Niall Fitzgerald, and because of that, he not only lost the chance to buy out his beloved company, but he was going to be destitute. Charles had become so desperate he agreed to be the person that stupid little whore turned to, to get her exposé written. That's what gave me the idea to pretend to be her and send you the packages."

"So, none of the threats were actually from her?"

"None. Charles didn't know the truth, either. He was so needy in the relationship, all I had to do was offer him some affection and he was like a love-sick puppy. Shame I had to have him killed."

"You arranged the car bomb?"

Yvonne smiled. She loved to see how surprised Niall was as he uncovered yet another part of her meticulous, murderous scheme. "Yes. Once I got a copy of the confirmation email, I arranged to have the car 'fixed' and told Charles we had to fly home early because James had been murdered."

Niall replayed the video call with James Vickers in his head. Yvonne could see he was close to tears, and she revelled in it. "Oh yes, you poor thing; you saw James die, didn't you?"

Niall gritted his teeth and glared up at her. "How do you know that?" he growled.

"That day was emotionally and physically exhausting, wasn't it?" she sighed, mocking him. "Do you remember offering to arrange my flight to Turks, but I said I'd be able to sort it myself? That gave me the chance to arrange a later flight to Turks, so I could jump on a flight up to Leeds, just in time to talk to James before he was shot. Then I jumped back on a plane to Heathrow, so I could catch the flight to Turks the next day."

Niall erupted. "WHAT? You were there when James was murdered?"

"After what he did to me? Telling us he had probably destroyed my ability to have children? Yes, I was there.

Hell, I wrote the cards he held up in front of the camera for you. I'm surprised you didn't recognise the handwriting."

Niall's 'tip of the tongue' experience when he was with Peter Mallory suddenly came into focus.

"It was your handwriting. That's what I'd subconsciously noticed."

"Then, after you told me James had been murdered, I arranged for Charles and I to fly back from Turks. We put on quite a show for the witnesses walking through Terminal 5 at Heathrow; him crying like that, but he'd stopped being useful, so I pretended to drop my purse on the way to the car. It was just too good an opportunity to miss. What with him dying, you thinking I was the target, and the police thinking maybe you were? Perfect."

Niall was still livid. "How did Evie find Charles's company? There are hundreds around London she could have chosen."

"Oh, it's Evie now, is it? The power of internet banner-ad marketing, Niall. Do you remember that my father left me a number of disparate start-ups to run? Well, as it turned out, one of them was fantastic at finding out what websites a person visits and using that data to target adverts straight to their desktop or mobile. Genius really, and way ahead of its time when he invested in it."

Niall's head was spinning. "But I thought you and I were rekindling our marriage… and you were pregnant until the car bomb…" A sneer on his wife's face stopped him mid-sentence.

"The baby wasn't yours, Niall," she scoffed.

He looked at her and then realised. "Charles's?"

"Apparently so, yes," she replied. "It wasn't part of my plan, so it came as quite a surprise. I was a little sad at not finally becoming someone's mummy, especially as you and I had given up hope after your friend told us he had accidentally butchered my ovaries, but I decided it really would have been quite an inconvenience really, so…" She shrugged her shoulders. Niall did notice a tear in her eye, so he wondered if there was an opportunity to play on her emotions.

"Maybe we still can?" he suggested, but if he hoped it would lead to Yvonne smiling warmly at the idea, throwing the gun down and running into his arms, he didn't have to wait long for that concept to be shattered.

"Pathetic. You really think I want anything to do with you? I'm going to be rich beyond even your wildest dreams, Niall. Why would I want anything other than pure, indulgent luxury for the rest of my life?"

"But I wrote you out of the Aeternum Foundation fund, so killing me really won't give you access to my money."

"Did you just call it 'your' money?" Yvonne's face went red with anger.

"I… I… I just meant…" he started to reply, but she exploded in rage.

"Do you not see what I've put up with for all these years? The endless meetings you wanted me to go to, feeling like your trophy wife? The boring, drunken oafs who propositioned me because they thought I was there to help you seal a deal? And your adultery which, by the way, all our friends seemed to know about. Do you know what it's like to pretend everything is alright between us when I can hear our friends whispering behind our backs?" She cocked the hammer on the gun, and Niall dropped to his knees, holding his hands up in a futile attempt to block any bullet she fired.

"Don't, Yvonne. I'll give you the £100m, and you can have the house and the villa." The gun shook in her hand as she clenched the grip, but slowly she brought her fury under control and lowered the gun. Niall looked up in hope, and when he saw the gun wasn't pointing at him anymore, he stood up.

"Oh, I'll not need your £100m when I inherit the Aeternum Foundation fund."

Niall looked confused. How could she inherit that money when he had given Wagstaff specific written instructions a few years ago to have her removed? Then he realised and, as Yvonne saw the dawning of realisation on his face, it filled her with almost overpowering satisfaction.

"Charles didn't remove you from the Foundation fund agreement, did he?"

Yvonne could hardly contain her pleasure. "No, he didn't. The attestation you sent him went into the shredder. We had already started our affair, and I suggested there was a way we could be together and he could buy his company." She smiled. "If the figures Charles shared with me just before his death are correct, the fund has a little over £850m in it right now."

Niall felt hollow. "You're going to kill me and Peter Mallory, aren't you?"

"Yes and no. Peter will die soon enough, I'll make sure of that, but I'm not going to shoot you," she replied softly. Niall wondered if the softness of her tone was a tinge of remorse, but it wasn't. It was simply relief that her three-year plan had entered its final seconds.

"And Evie never had anything to do with any of the murders or the demands, did she?"

"No, and if the bomb under her car had killed her instead of her friend, all her secrets would have gone to the grave, including the details of her proposed agreement with Charles."

"What about her? Are you still going to kill her?"

"No need. The police are probably already talking to her after I made a tip-off call. Even if she only admits to blackmail, the doubts about her innocence will remain."

"And what about all those other people the police say were murdered?"

"A necessary sacrifice. I'll anonymously pay for a memorial bench in some local park or something, so they'll be remembered," she said as she rolled her eyes. She was getting tired of all the questions and the need to spell everything out for him. She then recalled the lottery tickets and told Niall about them.

"You wanted pictures of the victims with the tickets in their mouths? You're sick, Yvonne. You need professional help."

Yvonne laughed. "Yes, I do, and that's why I've been seeing a therapist for a while, darling, dropping little clues into the conversation so that if she ever has to share any information with the police, she'll be telling the right story: my story."

"The police will realise that you have inherited all that money."

"Maybe, but they'll be preoccupied with other things. Peter Mallory will be dead soon; suicide, after incriminating evidence was found in his apartment. I'll be grieving over my dead husband who, according to everyone, had rekindled the love in his marriage.

So sad, and I have a little surprise waiting to go to the police, which will only confuse matters. I'll be in the clear."

Niall was disgusted by the woman he saw in front of him. "You…" he started to say, but Yvonne had run out of patience and time. She pointed the gun at his head as she looked at her watch. It was 10am.

"Three, two, one…" she said. Niall looked on, confused, but it wasn't for long. The glass window nearest him shattered, and a bullet ripped through the side of his chest.

"Sorry, Niall," she said as he gasped for air and sank to his knees. She watched as he fell forwards into the gathering pool of blood. "Right, can't stand here watching you die; I need to get myself ready."

The final step in her plan was for The Broker's contractor to now shoot and injure her, making her a victim of an attempted double homicide. She was smiling as she put her gun back into a cupboard and locked it away and then took up her position, standing next to her dead husband. She waited for the pain in her shoulder, the agreed impact point of the bullet. It was going to hurt, but it was going to £850m-hurt. Five seconds later, another window shattered and a bullet struck her in the temple. She was dead before her skull cracked on the tiled floor. The assassin quickly and silently disassembled the rifle and, having checked the immediate surrounding area, walked back to the waiting car. As he climbed in, the driver looked at him. The assassin nodded and held up two fingers. The driver smiled and pulled out his secure mobile. He typed a text and pressed send. It said:

100

As he read it, The Broker muttered, "That's the most satisfying £100,000 I think I've ever spent," and he transferred the kill fee. "Now who's a fucking amateur, Mrs Fitzgerald?" he said as he shredded the photo Bobby Messina had sent him of Niall and Yvonne Fitzgerald at a society wedding.

Chapter 93

The journalists rushed forward as newly promoted DI Steve Denton walked down the stone steps towards them. News had come through that both Niall and Yvonne Fitzgerald were dead. Evie Perry was going to stand trial for blackmail, and Peter Mallory was currently awaiting the outcome of the investigation into the artefacts found in his apartment.

"Can you confirm who the Lottery Murderer is?" shouted one of the waiting journalists.

"DI Denton, can you assure the victim's families that the way the police handled the investigation didn't mean lives were lost unnecessarily?" shouted another.

"Do you think Evie Perry and Peter Mallory might be jointly charged for murder?" speculated yet another.

"We are working with the Turks & Caicos Police to establish the circumstances of the deaths of Niall and Yvonne Fitzgerald. We have enough evidence to believe that Niall Fitzgerald was guilty of what you've labelled the Lottery Ticket Murders. I'll not be answering any further questions at this time, but I do want to say the following: The Metropolitan Police wants to express its sympathies to the families of all Mr Fitzgerald's victims, both those who suffered as a result of the criminal money laundering activities he oversaw, and especially those who have lost loved ones. We ask that you give those families privacy to grieve now the case is closed. Thank you."

The journalists still tried to ask questions, despite Denton telling them he wouldn't be answering any. Denton just turned and headed back up the stairs and into the building, where DS Armitage was waiting for him.

"Your DCI agreed to blaming Fitzgerald then?" he asked rhetorically as he pulled a small bar of chocolate from his pocket. Denton glanced at the bar and then back at Armitage.

"It's healthier, and it's less messy than having mini-muffins crumbing in my pockets," Armitage mumbled in an attempt to justify his new habit. Denton shook his head wryly and carried on with the update for Armitage.

"It's the neatest solution until we find out anything more. The DCI has agreed we can keep looking into it, but it's low priority."

"Sorry to interrupt DI Denton..." said the press officer, who had made her way back into the building, "... but there's an urgent call for you from a Detective Constable Jones," and she held out her mobile phone. Denton had turned his phone to silent for the duration of the press conference, but as he was juggling several cases, the call wasn't a surprise. He excused himself from the discussion with Armitage, took the phone and thanked the press officer; his polite way of saying 'go away'. As she turned to walk back towards the handful of remaining journalists, Denton put the phone to his ear.

"Jonesy?" he said.

"Sir, we have a problem."

"What do you mean?"

She took a deep, calming breath before breaking the news. "A new lottery ticket has arrived. With a fresh set of seven numbers."

As the news sank in for Denton, The Broker sat in his office just a few miles away, watching the end of the press conference. He was grateful that Niall Fitzgerald had been accused of the murders, and there appeared to be no link back to himself through the money he had received from his client, Yvonne Fitzgerald. He muted the television and turned his attention back to the men across the desk from him. "My apologies, but I needed to watch that. So, tell me, what happens next now that Fitzgerald is dead?"

"There's plenty more where he, Derek Lowe and Oleg Thoresen came from. In fact, I'm meeting someone tomorrow to discuss their possible employment," replied Robert Kendrick.

"Don't make me regret not killing you," said The Broker.

"I won't," Robert replied, glancing back at the bullet hole in the wall next to where he had sat just a few days ago. The Broker had originally planned to kill him, but at the last second, greed had gotten the better of his judgement, and he decided he needed Robert if he was going to step into the world of cybercrime. They had discussed how to deal with Stella, and because The Broker had a sliver of compassion, it was he who suggested the letter to her, not Robert. He also decided that the bullet hole would stay in the wall to remind Robert that there was no room for complacency.

"I also thought you might like to know that I've traced the author of the thesis. Perhaps he still has a copy of missing pages 26 and 27?" Robert added.

"Good work. What's his name?" asked The Broker. Robert smiled. Did the man really think he was so stupid that he'd tell him? He just raised his glass of scotch to toast their future joint venture as they looked across at the other man in the room.

"And what about Ruiz?" Robert asked.

"He's going away for a long time, and Adrian Skelton will soon be implicated, or dead. With Daniella Maddox now out of the way, we're good to go," he said.

"And no one suspects you're involved?" challenged The Broker.

"Absolutely no one," replied the man.

AUTHOR'S NOTE

Writer's block (noun)
DEFINITION: *a psychological inhibition preventing a writer from proceeding with a piece.*

This wasn't going to be my second book, but as the seed of an idea exploded one afternoon into the first three chapters and a handful of characters, I knew the idea had captured my imagination. What I didn't know was just how different and difficult my journey – from idea to printed book – would be compared to that of my first book.

Whereas the idea for my first book had developed over 20 years, the inspiration for this story was sudden and overwhelming. I was stood at the kitchen sink, cleaning a dishwasher-unfriendly pan, when I heard a young child nearby having a screaming tantrum because it couldn't get what it wanted. The more the parents said no, the more it screamed. My peaceful afternoon, with the sun shining and the birds twittering in the garden, morphed into me wondering what lengths a person would go to, to get their own way? That's when I grabbed some paper and a pen and started to scribble things down. For the next three months, I'd offer my wife the chance of a lay-in at the weekend, and I'd sit in front of my computer at 6:30am, and the words simply poured out. What a difference when, in late 2021,

I took a three-week break from work to try to power through the final 20 chapters – but actually went backwards. It was such a negative experience that I scrapped 10 existing chapters and decided to re-draft 10 more (on top of the 20 I was originally hoping to finish). The effect of it all was I walked away from anything to do with writing for almost eight weeks, because every time I sat down at the keyboard, I froze. I was worried that if I tried to write, I might add even more chapters to my list of rewrites. What if the whole story unravelled rather than converging on a great ending?

That was my first experience of writer's block, and I'm sure it won't be the last. Thankfully, I allowed myself the time and space to let the story come to me. I accepted that the draft would be well over a year later than I had hoped for, and whenever I re-read some of the draft, it really did still feel like there was a great story. In the summer of 2022, I decided to completely re-draft the remaining block of 15 chapters. As soon as I allowed myself more time and stopped trying to tweak them to make them fit, everything seemed to fall into place.

It's at this point I want to thank Elizabeth Webb, the Head of Wills & Probate at Emsleys Solicitors, who helped me understand some of the legal aspects of private wills and business trusts. If I've misinterpreted anything, or where I have added some 'poetic licence' to the facts, that's down to me, not her.

And so, dear reader, hopefully you've enjoyed this twisty, complex, multi-character story. I'm always grateful for ratings, reviews and constructive critique on Amazon or Goodreads, as well as loving it when a reader sends me a selfie of them holding my book.

I hope you might be willing to do the same (please send selfies to @ GradusPrimus on Twitter or, if you know me personally, you'll know various ways to get the image to me).

Until next time…

Lightning Source UK Ltd.
Milton Keynes UK
UKHW011152171222
414082UK00005B/651